The Art Forger's Daughter

Anita Belli

Published in 2014.

All rights reserved

Copyright© Anita Belli, 2014

The author asserts the moral right to be identified as the author of this work in accordance with the Copyright, Designs and Patents Act 1988

No part of this book may be reproduced, stored in a retrieval system, or transmitted by any means without the written permission of the author

This novel is entirely a work of fiction and incidents and characters portrayed in it are the work of the author's imagination. Any resemblance to actual persons living or dead, or events portrayed, is entirely coincidental.

Cover image© from a painting by David Skynner
Cover design©: Charlie Peacock

For my Peacocks:

Charlie and Charlotte,

Eddie, Emily and Matilda Rose

with love

Part One

Memories and Madness

Colchester 1956

Prologue

One of my earliest memories is of my mother killing my father and getting away with it and Jellicoe taking the blame; at least, that's what I remember in the feeling memories of my bones which I can no longer trust. I don't remember much more of the early years in my native Holland during the Nazi occupation, just glimpses; the smell of linseed, oil paint and turpentine and the sticky feel of carmine red between my fingers, like blood; like the red in the Nazi flag which flew outside my father's studio. I remember the stacks of canvases of Mother and Jellicoe painted in various styles and stages of undress; his muses he called them. Mother called Jellicoe *'that whore'*, a word which I didn't understand then.

I remember the smell of the cigars my father smoked when he could get them, usually after a man in uniform visited the studio in which we lived and my father worked, and I would hide and my mother would spit another word I didn't understand - *'collaborator'*. I practiced the word and skipped around saying it until Mother heard and slapped me. Jellicoe didn't understand the word. She was Dutch.

Jellicoe never really liked me, ever since that first day when I took my father's attention away from her. Lots of people came to my father's house and wanted to be painted and some came in daylight and some at night and some wore uniforms. But the day Jellicoe came was different. She brought a smell with her which I have never liked and never got used to as a child. It smelt strange, and challenging, like she was from somewhere dangerous and I sensed trouble with a part of me I took for granted then; the basic instinct of a sensitive child which I lost in the growing up years.

I remember this episode because it is in the same collage as the death of my father and the turmoil which followed. I have no idea of the sequence of events or the number of days, weeks or months which passed between them. It is all a patchwork of fragmented memories, the feeling memories in my bones, so different from the later memories; stories my mother told me in the little house in Stockwell Street when we moved to Colchester and I became properly English; the second hand memories filtered through the damaged mind of my mother. Now, alone in the world, anything could be true, even the lies.

Chapter One

The day I met T'Ash changed my life. I was sitting against the old stones of The Castle in the park and the memories crowded in on the spring breeze. I watched the long shadows of the bare branches cast by the low sun as they moved across the wet grass. It was early spring so the day was short but it seemed like the longest day of my life. I sat there oblivious until I felt someone next to me and turned to look. A young man, tall, even when sitting, fair where I was dark, his eyes like slate. He held out a bag of sweets.

'Pear drop?' he said. I shook my head and got up to walk away but he followed me and I was annoyed. Any other time may have been fun but not today.

'It's just that I saw yous earlier today at that dreadful place out there. I saw yous walking amongst the cherry blossom of that beautiful garden they've got at the Asylum. You wouldn't believe a place like that would have such a lovely garden would you now? It's enough to make the Angels weep having to go there but the garden makes up for it.' I was taken aback until I realised that he looked sympathetic.

'Are you following me?' I asked, although he looked so unthreatening with his unruly hair and pear drops that it was almost comical.

'No, Gods honest truth I just happened to see you there and then I was walking home just now and sees you looking sad and thought you might like a pear drop. Who is it? Who'd they take in there? Me, it's my gran. Been there two years and I goes to see her but she's no idea who I am. She thinks I'm Bert! Still no idea who Bert is,' and he laughed a tinkling, Irish laugh. 'I still go though. She might come to her senses one day but I doubt it now. She's so old.' He was looking at me and I let the tinkling laugh whisper a little longer on the spring air. The moon was rising, full and fierce. A statement moon.

'My mamma,' I said and felt the tears prickle and he put his hand very gently on my shoulder.

'How'd she end up in there then?'

'Long story,' I said and he shrugged and we sat together on a fragment of wall which was two thousand years old at least with the wisdom of the ages ingrained. Right now however, I had no words left and I didn't want to talk. So we sat and watched the moon rise over the oaks which framed the edge of the park and ran down to the river. A bat flew overhead as we sat in silence side by side.

Where would I start to unravel a story I hardly understood myself? How do you begin to tell a stranger that you lived with your mum and her sister, until Aunt Maude killed herself in March - a month ago - and Mum didn't get over it?. She fell apart and I was suddenly the grown up, thrown into the world of funeral directors and decisions and autopsies and Mum wringing her hands and wailing in the corner of the parlour.

'Why? Why didn't she speak to me? Why didn't she talk to me about it?' and I never thought to ask, *'Talk about what?'* because there were things to do and funerals don't arrange themselves and neither does the paperwork and ownership of the house and the roof over our heads.

Then they took her there. To Severalls Asylum.

'I'm not sure when she'll be home,' was all I said, so quietly into the twilight that it sounded like a whisper on the breeze.

'Is there anyone else at home? Your dad? Any brothers and sisters?' he asked, as quietly into the growing stillness. Traffic noise from the road rumbled in the distance and blended with the sound of the weir as the river was in full flood. I shook my head. I had already lied to 'the authorities' about my age so that I wouldn't be taken into care but the truth was, I was now alone. I was concerned that they may think I was too young at sixteen, so whilst they were doing the paperwork for Mother's admittance, I let it slip that my Aunt Jellicoe – *yes it is a funny name, she's Dutch, my father was Dutch, it is his sister; Jellicoe is coming to stay. She is coming to look after Mamma anyway and will be arriving on the ferry from Holland tomorrow so I am getting the train up to Harwich to meet her....*'

I wove a story which they accepted although the truth was that Jellicoe, whom I remember from my early years, was no friend to my mother and had caused her great pain. She was my father's 'model' and Mum implied, his mistress as well. I didn't want to go into the tangle of my parents past, so I simply said to the young man beside me,

'I'll be fine tonight and Mrs Walker next door always looks in on Mamma and me at tea time.' The street had formed a guard of honour at their front doors and windows when the ambulance arrived, so I had no doubt that Mrs. Walker, 'Lil', would tap on the back door and ask for a cup of sugar and check that everything was all right.

I felt calmer now and it was getting dark, but I had the courage to face the house on my own and tomorrow I would make a plan. I stood up to go and he held my hand.

'Can I see you tomorrow? Here maybe? After work?' I nodded and as I turned to flee for home, he shouted after me,

'I'm Tarron. Tarron Ash. My friends call me Tash. What's your name?'

I awoke after a sleep of jumbled dreams and 'What's your name?' was echoing in my head.

Betty Quinn. No, that was never my name. That was the name I was given when I returned to England with my mother after the war, returning to live in Grandpa Quinn's house with Aunt Maude. My own first name, *'Beatrix'* changed to *'Betty'* to sound more English. Aunt Maude had insisted that Mum revert to her maiden name as she didn't want 'foreigners' in the house, not after the war when people might think we were German. Sometimes in the small hours I remember that flight from Holland in the dark, with the rubble of war still warm underfoot.

The Allied Soldiers were said to be on their way and there was shouting and joy and then Papa lying in a pool of blood, and a baby crying and Mother and another man – Felix? Jellicoe being taken away and Mum and me hurried by the man –Felix - into a car and the long nightmare journey beginning with a car and a boat and wanting my papa to be with us and crying until I cried myself to sleep and into a silence which lasted many years. Aunt Maude meeting us in a strange place on a wet grey day in England and the images shift into slow motion.

'Home now,' says Mother.

'No never, I want Papa and my tower and the smell of the studio,' I wanted to say, but my voice has been left behind in the studio, before the nightmare journey and I didn't know how to find my way back to Papa.

I didn't speak for years and they said I was traumatized by the war, *shrug,* many children are, *shrug,* she'll get over it or we'll send her to a psychiatrist. They might have said, *'we'll sell her to the white slave trade'* for my mother's reaction would have been the same. I learned that to see a psychiatrist was worse than being a foreigner, which was also partly to blame for my condition; maybe I was confused by speaking Dutch as a small child and not English, and so I should only speak English now. As there was nothing wrong with my hearing I was either being wilful or I would speak when I wanted to.

I did, eventually. I was 10 years old and taken on a coach trip by the Round Table charity to see a Pantomime with other 'deprived' children and joined in the shouts and forgot completely that I couldn't speak, just shouted *'it's behind you,'* and sang the songs and afterwards we were given presents out of a big Santa sack by a Radio Star whom I didn't know and pictures were taken for the newspaper of all of us poor children with our gifts. When I got home I told Mum and Aunt Maude all about it and they both had tears in their eyes and hey presto I was cured by a Pantomime and a doll with sleeping eyes and a patchwork dress presented by a star I didn't know. I still have the doll and secretly, I call her Jellicoe.

Beatrix Prins. That's my real name and there was no-one left to tell me that I couldn't use it again. But....

I sat in Grandpa's armchair in the corner of the kitchen and heard the clock ticking my life away and with a great certainty, which is not the product of hindsight, I knew that this moment was a milestone and I had reached the crossroads and in each direction there were possibilities beyond the quiet life I had lived. I could go anywhere, do anything, be anyone I wanted to be. I could write the story of my own life and direct it, like a film, and have a happy ending if I wanted to, and not be defined by my parents and the central drama of the war and my father's death around which life had danced so precariously forever. His death or murder – he was killed – I saw it. Did I, or was that a dream too?

'Hi, I'm Beatrix....' I was talking out loud as I made tea and opened the back door to let in a bit of the pale sun which was losing its battle for supremacy of the sky, and a dirty blanket of cloud wrapped the earth in its folds and fogged my mind.

'Hi I'm Scarlett...' that sounded better.

'Scarlett O'Hara...' Obviously not – he'd know that was wrong.

'Tara, I'm Tara....' Didn't feel right.

'What's your name?'

'Scarlett Quinn,' no that wasn't right and he was Irish and I wasn't, except I think my grandfather was but I knew very little about him and he died before I was born.

'Hi, I'm Scarlett Prins.' That's better. More exotic and if I said it enough, I might just believe it myself. *Scarlett Prins*. Why not? I could call myself whatever I wanted now. I was alone. I could take my father's name again. Mum would never know and there was no-one else who cared and anyway, it was only for him – for Tarron Ash, *'my friends call me Tash.'*

'Tarron.' It rolled in the air and evaporated. Tash, or maybe T'Ash would be more accurate. T'Ash. That's what I would call him although it sounded the same as Tash, and then we would both have made up names. Would he be there? Did I dream him? Was he real?

I made breakfast and washed up. There was only one cup and saucer. One bowl and spoon. Once upon a time, there had been three and then two and now, just one. The loneliness pressed in and I stuffed my hand in my mouth to stifle the sob which rose like a wave from the ground up and shook me until I could no longer stand, and so I sat instead in Grandpa's chair until the sobbing stopped and I forced myself to be strong. Mum was still alive. I would visit the hospital and they would make her better and she would come home, strong and well again....Oh God, Oh God oh God! Would I ever get away? And then I thought of T'Ash; a small pinprick of light in an ocean of black and I had to focus only on that light and move on.

'Hello,' I said shyly, approaching the bench and I held out my hand formally, as I had practiced in the kitchen.

'Hello, I'm Scarlett. Scarlett Prins.' He looked astonished and didn't move like he had never seen me before. I flushed the colour of my made up name and let my hand drop and wanted to turn and run away but I was rooted to the spot. He recovered himself and picked up my hand and kissed it and with a gallant laugh said,

'Pleased to meet you Miss Scarlett,' and then I laughed too.

'Scarlett. I like it. Prince, not Princess?' he asked as we sat on the wall together; the grass was wet from the earlier rain and smelt fresh.

'No P-R-I-N-S. It's Dutch. My father was Dutch. He .. died .. in the war.'

'Dutch? Were they on our side?'

'Occupied by Nazis. I was very young.

'How young?'

'I was 5 when we left. I was born there.'

'5? So when was you born?'

'Start of the occupation. We left when we were liberated.'

'By the good old British Army.' He said it as a statement not a question.

'Allied Forces,' I corrected him.

'Ah, that's fine then. The British Empire comes to the rescue....' I was confused. Why did he sound so cross about it?

'It was an awful time. I don't remember it and I'd rather not talk about it. My mother and Aunt Maude.... It hurt them both a lot.'

'It hurt a lot of people. All of us. No-one got out unscathed and the long shadows cast longer shadows. Do you like that? *The long shadows cast longer shadows...*' and he pulled out a notebook and scribbled it down and then remembered I was there. 'D'ya like poetry?'

'Erm, yes. A bit. We did some at school…' I was mesmerized by his Irishness.

'You still at school?' he asked

'No, I left a while ago, just after I turned 16. Mum needed me at home and I managed to get a job in a bakery and the money helped.

'Yes. I know what you mean,' he said and we lapsed into silence.

'Scarlett. Is that your real name?' I flushed but he was looking out across the park and may not have noticed.

'Yes,' I said defiantly.

'Gone With the Wind?' I nodded.

'Your ma loved the film?' he asked. I nodded again.

'Did they show it in Holland then during the war?' I was caught out. I knew Mum had seen it before we all went for my 16th birthday which now seemed like decades ago but was only a month – with Aunt Maude still alive and Mum in her right mind and all so happy and we ate fish and chips on the way home…..but in Amsterdam? In 1939? When did it come out?

'Not sure,' I said vaguely. Was he testing me? 'I know she'd read the book though.' This was true. She had a copy in the house and I was planning to read it myself.

'Scarlett Prins,' and he whistled.

'What?' I said.

'Oh, nothing. Tarron isn't my real name.'

'It's not?' I felt cheated.

'No. It's my mother's maiden name. I hate my real name so I never use it.'

'What is it? Your real name? Go on, tell me. I've told you loads about me.'

'Everything and nothing,' he said.

'What do you mean?'

'Just that. I could have found those things out for meself once I know your name. I can trace people and find things out about them.'

'Why would you want to do that?' I asked.

'Because I can,' he said and laughed at my innocence, enjoying himself immensely.

'So what's your real name?' I asked again.

'Find out!' he said and laughed.

'How?'

'I'll teach you. I'll teach you how to be a spy.'

'Is that what you do? You're a spy?'

He laughed again. 'I love that you're so gullible. Course I'm not a spy. I'm not 12 years old and making it up. And besides, if I was, I would hardly be blurting it out in the park now would I? But then again, if I was, I would be denying it as well…..'

He was complicated and obviously much older than me. 'How old are you?' I asked.

'What do you think?'

'20?' I guessed.

'Spot on,' he said but I wasn't sure if I believed him. I didn't know what to believe. I was way out of my depth and had never spoken to a boy at any length and certainly not one as old as him and as worldly. I felt insecure again and gauche and naïve. I had nothing else to talk about. I had done nothing, been nowhere.

'So,' he said, leading a new strand of conversation. He was really good at this. 'So what do you do with your spare time?'

'Erm, well, looking after Mum took all my spare time.' He patted my hand sympathetically and I didn't want to move away. The contact was nice. 'And I paint and draw. It's the only thing I'm good at.'

'Are you any good?' I was surprised by his openness.

'I am very good. I want to be an artist.' I said it out loud to someone I hardly knew – the deepest secret I hadn't even said out loud to myself or to Mum or Aunt Maude. He just nodded.

'Can I see some of your pictures?' he asked.

'Maybe,' I said.

'Sunday, we could meet here in the day if you like?' I smiled and nodded and thought I would pack a picnic. He wouldn't expect that.

'I have to go to the hospital first. Check Mum's ok.' He became serious. 'Of course. D'ya want me to come wid ya? I don't visit my gran 'til next week but I'll come wid ya if it helps.'

'No I'm fine. They might not let me see her. She's still, well, you know…'

'Sedated. Aye I know. Took weeks to get Gran talking again then she wouldn't stop. Still doesn't make no sense though,' and I shuddered at the thought that Mum would be sedated forever, or may have lost her mind completely. He saw the cloud cross my face. 'She'll be grand. They're good in there and there's all kinds of new stuff they can do now. You just have to be patient. That's why they call them Patients!' and he smiled at his little joke. 'No seriously though, it'll take time. She'll come round.' I nodded and took a deep breath. 'Sunday. 2.00? I'll be here. Why don't you bring a picture and I'll bring a poem? I write poems but I've never shown anyone.'

My pictures were all over the school and the house, in public, owned by whoever wanted to see them. But not the sketches. Maybe I'd bring my sketchbook.

It was dark by the time I got home, elated, and re-ran the conversation in my mind and out loud to the spirits of the house and wondered what Mum and Aunt Maude would have made of it and whether I would have told them. I sat at the table and drew his face a hundred times until I thought it was almost right. The blonde brown hair highlighted by the sun and cut short at the sides and back but just a bit too long on top. The deep set grey eyes, light at times and then dark and reflecting his mood changes. The fine straight eye brows, the bone structure sharp beneath a pale skin, the hint of a moustache which he must have shaved for work. Where did he work? I forgot to ask. Probably a desk job. Clean hands, not worn and calloused. A jacket and tie. Not a labourer. A spy? I laughed at that. Was he real? The curve of the mouth, smiling and curling up at the edges and tight and straight when he talked about the war. Hardened. Why? I forgot to ask. Nothing soft in his face. All clear and firm but changing with his mood, with the conversation, light and shade; his eyes changing colour, his lips hardening, his eyes dancing or hard, his jaw set firm and then a laugh and his lips curled upwards again… and again… until I captured his essence so far. There was a lot more to know about T'Ash. I signed it 'Scarlett' with a flourish, the first time I had signed that name.

What was his real name? He hadn't told me.

Chapter Two

We were lying on the picnic blanket under a tree. Cliché I know but I think this is a real bones memory and not a dream.

'You're Irish,'

'Well spotted.'

'How did you end up here?'

'The War,' and we laughed.

'How?'

'My pa came to fight for the English. There was no work in Ireland and no money and they was offering good money so we ended up here. Ma and me followed and the others stayed with Granny in Ireland 'til after the war and then they all pitched up and now Granny's in that place and the rest have all gone. I'm the baby.'

'How many of you?'

'The last of twelve. They didn't all make it. Only seven of us left.' Seven or twelve, I couldn't imagine having that many siblings.

'Are your parents still alive?'

'Aye. He made it through the war and got shipped back here via the port and stayed and got de-mobbed and a pension and then got odd jobs in the town…' he petered out and I stopped asking questions. I had touched a nerve. 'He's the one who should be in bloody Severalls, not my granny.' I propped myself up on one elbow to look at him. He had a faraway look but the anger was very close.

'Do you not get on with your Dad?' I found that sad and difficult. I loved the memory of my father but I could hardly remember him; just the safety of the big, round hugs and his bulk and the deep man smell of tobacco and sweat and oil paint. Mum and Aunt Maude were thin and smelt of lavender and soap and clean clothes and never of sweat or oil paint and whilst that was a different comfort, I knew now how much I missed the safety of his size and smell.

'Oh aye, we get on fine when he's sober; for about 5 minutes a day. Ma's a saint to put up with him. Says she'd be better off as a widow.' I thought about it. How would Mamma and Papa have fared if he had lived? I remembered so little and relied on the unreliable *'dreams'* which felt real. How real they were, I had no idea. Mum would know. She was the only person left who would know. 'Aye, they hate each other and I'm stuck in the middle. Soon as I've got enough saved, I'm off. I'm only staying now for her. She still needs me, and the money I bring in.'

'Where to?' I asked, thinking and not really thinking that I could go with him and how odd that we were both stuck with our Mothers.

'America. I've got a brother who went there after the war and a sister as well and other family. I want to go to America and be a writer...' Wow. What a great plan but I didn't say it out loud. I said,

'Could you take your mum with you?'
'She won't leave him.'
'But they hate each other.'
'Aye, so they do.'
'So why do they stay together?'
'They must.'
'But why?'

'Why d'ya think?' He had a habit of answering a question with a question. I shrugged. 'Catholic,' he said. 'You?'

'No', I said and crossed my fingers superstitiously.

'Protestant then? You know we'll never marry if you're a Proddy, but then I'll never marry anyway. Not the type,' and he laughed. It wasn't funny to me. I hardly knew him.

'I'm not really anything,' I said, 'although Mum and my Aunt went to St Michael's on the hill so I guess that's Church of England, but they never made me go.' I didn't even know if I was baptized.

I told him snatches of what I remembered; about Mum and Jellicoe and Pa's studio during the war; about coming back to England and my uneventful childhood with Aunt Maude in Grandpa Quinn's house....

I was looking up into the summer sun and the effort of retrieving the memories triggered it; that and the talk of Catholics. A flash and a haze passed my eyes and I knew it was happening. I was going to have a fit and I was outside with T'Ash and vulnerable. I lay back and closed my eyes and pretended to doze – let it pass, don't fight it, go with it....

Downstairs beneath the studio is the apartment we live in. Mum in the kitchen boiling something – carrots? Maybe carrots or some other roots and Jellico sailing in, full of energy and slapping a pigs foot on the counter and Mum's shock.

'Where did you get that?'

'Don't ask. Thought you'd like it,' and Mum looking at her and muttering 'thanks, some meat would be great. Are you eating with us?' and Jellico perches on the table and looks insolently at Mother.

'Love to,' she says as I watch from the other side of the table painting pictures with watercolors on the scraps of paper Pa lets me have ...

'Thought you might not eat pork,' Jellicoe says and Mum goes still and the air changes and I want to cry but don't dare and sit still and try to disappear.

'And why would that be?' Mum says

'No reason,' says Jellicoe and then Mum comes to the table and puts her face close up to Jellicoe's.

'You shouldn't say things like that. It's dangerous.' Jellicoe shrugs and Mum goes back to cleaning the pigs foot and puts it in the pan with the roots.

'Your mother. Ruby Quinn? Where was she born? Latvia? Lithuania? Ruby Quinn. Nee Rosenberg?' and Mum turns around with a pan in her hand and Jellicoe slips off the table like a cat and out of range and Mum's swipe misses her and tips my paints across the table and I scream and the water spills and I burst into tears. I still feel the deep sobs wracking at me and Pa comes in and sweeps me into his arms and sees the situation but doesn't know why and Ma says very low and quietly to Jellicoe,

'Get out,' and Jellicoe smiles and leaves and runs a hand over Pa's shoulder as she goes and I flinch although she doesn't touch me, but I feel the danger she leaves in her wake. Pa holds me close and says,

'Never mind we can paint another picture. Let's do it together shall we?' and begins to tidy up and sets me on his lap and gets some paper and we paint together but the danger is unleashed and they both know it and I don't know why.....

'Scarlett? You ok, Scarlett wake up for God's sake.. wake up...' and I did and the sky was too bright and my head ached and I sat upright and just managed to rush over to the bushes and was sick.

'What the hell's up? You ok? Let me get you home. You want a doctor? I can call a doctor if you want? Are you ill?'

'I'm fine. I'm fine,' I lied, everything in my body aching and weary and needing to lie down in a dark room. 'Migraine. I get headaches,'

'Jesus it come on so quick. I thought you'd had a fit but you just passed out in a trance. Was it a fit?'

'No. No. Just a headache. I'll go home now, thanks', and I started to pack up the picnic but he insisted I sit in the shade and he packed it. When he'd done, he took my arm.

'Come on, I'll take you home. Sure you don't need a doctor? My big sister Mary had fits. It was terrible ...*epiplectic*... that's it... that's what they called it...' and I realized I had been steered out of the park.

'Which way?' he said.

'What?' I said through the haze and the headache and trying to hold onto the images from my *'dream'*.

'Which way, where d'ya live?'

'I'm fine now. Honestly. I'm ok,' I said.

'You're as white as a sheet and shaking. I'm getting you home and into your bed...' he stopped abruptly and laughed and let go of my arm..

'No, no sorry, not that, I don't mean that. Jesus you don't think that do you...is there anyone at home to look after you?'

'Mrs. Walker, my neighbour. I'll get her to come in.'

'Good. I'll take you to your door. Jesus I didn't mean anything else, nothing bad....' and I smiled at his apology and thought it would be hilarious if I didn't feel so bad.

'It's not far. Stockwell Street, in the Dutch Quarter, just off the High Street. I'm fine from here,' I said as we passed the George Hotel.

'The Dutch Quarter, of course, but I never knew a Dutch Man live there. You, you're half Dutch. Hark at me, I'm rambling again. My ma would say I'm talking Double Dutch. Ha! Ignore me. I get like this when I'm anxious. You are OK aren't you? It looked like a fit to me and it scared the bejeysus out of me.....' He petered out and I had to laugh although it hurt my head. He made me laugh when I was feeling at my worst. That can't be bad.

I'd had bits of that 'vision' before but never like that. Never so clear. It was a clue to the stuff I didn't know which was far more than the stuff I did know. But I pushed it away. My life was moving on. I was rewriting it for myself, and T'Ash was the only sketch I had drawn on my new blank canvas.

Chapter Three

Wow. That was amazing but I know where she lives now. At first I just felt sorry for her because I'd seen her up at Severalls and I knew she was upset and then when we got talking and she told me her story, well you know how it is. My life is littered with stories about the war but hers is so special. It's like she thinks she only exists in terms of what happened to her folks and she hasn't had a chance to grow into her own skin yet. And I recognize that because I am busting out of mine and I really want to get on with it but I am trapped by my ma and everything and I fantasize at times about *him* dying. The man who calls himself my father but is nothing but an idle drunk who is weak and broken and then I think about Scarlett's story and how her Da is like this giant hero in her life. But when you dig down a bit I bet he isn't really and I wouldn't like to be the one who makes her see that and tells her the truth after all this time. But maybe I can shed a light into the darker corners and be there for her, and just hold her and support her.

And that's another thing and I will have to go to confession next Saturday as I do every bloody Saturday whilst I am under my mother's roof but this time I will have something real to confess and I will delight in it and enjoy doing it and would love to see the face of Father

O'Reilly as I describe to him in detail my thoughts about what I want to do with her. All those beautiful things. How can they really be 'impure thoughts?' It's just nature isn't it? It's natural to like someone so much that they make your body react with a will of its own and in a way which the priests think is shameful. Well it's not. It's beautiful and I will think these thoughts as much as I like. They can't control what I think.

So to start with I will stroke her pale cheeks, and they will be soft and creamy underneath my fingers and she will let out a little breath like a sigh like she wants me too. And then I will lean in closer and breath in her scent – I got a bit of lavender and soap and something else from her hair like freshly washed lemons and her soft brown hair will fall over my face and I will inhale her forever. Her fine broad brow and straight nose beneath closed eyes; green; they were green eyes she's got there for God's sake and how can I resist that? Brown hair with hints of auburn and green eyes and the palest creamiest skin – flawless like a statue. I am not even sure she was for real......

But to kiss her on the lips... this is where the Priest would really start to blush now, when I take her face in my hands and gaze into those fathomless green eyes and brush her pale pink lips with my hungry ones and taste the sweet almond of her breath and put my arms around her and pull her to me so that her breasts.... Nooo... no I can't go there... it is too real and then I would really have to confess something and I don't have the words to say it. Yet. But it will happen, I am certain of that. She is so different. Like no-one I have ever seen before and she has wrapped herself around my mind like an obsession and I think about her all day and every day since I saw her and I can't get her out of my dreams.

And then there was that fit thing which she had, so like my poor Mary who had the epilepsy for all those years until she was put away with the Aunts in Ireland because Ma had too much to do with the rest of us and I haven't seen Mary since I was a child. But Scarlett's fit wasn't like that; it was quiet and more polite; less boisterous, like herself, merging into the stones of the old Castle and not drawing too much attention to itself. But like the Castle, you can't really ignore her. She is an orchid in a garden of weeds; she stands out; she walks like a queen and has a kind of self possession which means that she doesn't need people. She is like a strong willowy sapling blowing in the wind, rooted firm and going with the flow and just being what she is. She is an artist; I know that because there are so few real ones about. I can tell by how she is. But she is vulnerable and I will swear to protect her now. It has become my job if you like, whether I like it or not and, well, I am pretty sure that I like it just fine.

Chapter Four

The spring sunshine warmed the buds and shoots and blossomed into the most intense time of my life. So much happened that I hardly believe it was all real. A sequence of events; Aunt Maude died, Mum had a breakdown and I met T'Ash all since I had turned 16; it was not surprising that I was restless like a missile fired into an unknown world and ricocheting off experiences. Mum was still in Severalls and now they were talking about an operation which would help her 'once and for all'. I would be lost and totally alone without T'Ash.

T'Ash's Grandma, Ida, who was now a permanent inmate at Severalls Hospital for the mentally ill, had a chalet along the estuary of the river, through Stour Wood. You reached it by train on the branch line to Harwich and Dovercourt Bay, and T'Ash held my hand and chatted carelessly about the landscape and its history.

'Manningtree, now, that's a really interesting place,' as we changed trains at an intersection to head to Harwich on the branch line, not Ipswich on the main line. 'The Witch-Finder General, Matthew Hopkins lived here and hunted out his witches, or should that be 'haunted?' Some of the houses here abouts are you know. Haunted. So is the chalet, but only at night. Anyway he hangs them, the witches, on the green at Mistley, just along the tracks there.

The next village....they hung, they didn't burn....' and I let the green of the landscape slide by as we left buildings behind, with T'Ash's comforting monologue and the ribbon of water winking through the trees.

He told stories well. He always had a story to tell and he had peopled my lonely existence with his tales of history and places and people he knew or maybe just made up, I didn't really care. Sometimes I listened to him and other times just sort of absorbed his presence to warm the very cold places inside me.

This had been his idea, a day out, a day off from the ritual trauma of visiting the hospital. There was little point in going to see my mother; she was sedated and wheeled from her locked ward to see me and she would smile and pat my hand but all conversation was gone, but only for now, the nurses assured me. *'She is sedated for her own comfort and will come back to you when she is stronger'* they said. But each visit she seemed weaker, older, more frail, and it took all of my youthful inner strength to not burst into tears in front of her and the nurse. I did the first time and was chastised like a spoilt child for misbehaving.

'How is this going to help your poor Mother, seeing you so upset. She's fine and happy and eats well....' said the large nurse who took me aside leaving Mum in the corridor in her wheelchair.

'But she is a shadow; a ghost; she barely exists! What have you done to her? What have you done to my mother?' I wanted to shout back, but I was too well behaved and so I shut up; stifled my feelings and saved it all for T'Ash who waited for me in the garden, a beautiful serene place which seemed not to belong in the Asylum. T'Ash came with me on every visit and I never asked him to, or asked him why. At first he said he had to check his Gran was still alive and he was sanguine, even humorous in the face of her condition.

'Mad as a Hatter, like most of the women in my family,' he laughed. 'More interesting that way.' He let me cry and rail against God and the universe and everything, and when I was spent and sobbing, he just held me until I was comforted and then held my hand and walked back with me all the way into town and to the Castle Park and sat and let me tell him about my mother and then held my hand and took me home. That's all. We didn't even kiss. We visited regularly as the spring wore on and Mum got no better, but at least I knew what to expect from the visits and it became a duty which I got used to. And I had T'Ash beside me. I loved it when he talked in his soft, mocking Irish accent and made me laugh when I wanted to scream at the injustice of the world.

We were the only passengers to get off the train at a little rural station called Wrabness, and he mocked the word as only T'Ash could; making up other words starting with a 'silent' W, making me laugh as I hefted the large picnic basket and placed it carefully on the platform. He carried a hold-all with blankets and 'emergency supplies' he said with a pirate accent. 'In case we get shipwrecked or press ganged or worse.'

'What's worse?' I asked out of breath as we headed from the station down a track which led into the woods.

'Scoffed by Ghouls,' he said throwing down the hold-all and raising his arms to chase me, and I obliged by screaming and dropped the picnic basket and ran only a few steps until he caught me easily and swung me in his arms and laughing and out of breath we fell onto the mossy undergrowth just beside the path. There was no-one about and he held me closer and raised my face to his and kissed me. It was gentle and natural and seemed right and then he stirred and I felt his urgency begin to grow and then I responded to that and felt a deep down stirring in the pit of my stomach and something burst and I was hungry for him. I laced my fingers through his hair, longer at the back than when I first met him, and he pressed me down into the ground taking his weight on one arm and his other hand slipped underneath the strap of my dress and cupped my small breast and I gasped and raked my fingers down his back. He pulled back and looked at me, his eyes half squinting in the dappled sunlight and he was beautiful to look at; his hair backlit and a halo of light, his eyes deep with desire and hooded; a hint of colour flushing his pale cheeks just below the high cheek bones. He rolled onto his back and let out a long groan.

'Holy-jeysus-shit,' he said panting, his arm thrown across his eyes.

'What? What is it?' I asked anxious that I had somehow hurt him.

'I want you so bad. It's never happened to me before. Not never.' I rolled beside him and looked down into his anguished face, his eyes closed against the sunlight.

'I want you too,' I murmured moving close and stroking his chest.

'I kind of got that idea,' he said, propping himself up on one arm and moving a stray hair form my face. 'But not here. Come on. You'll love where we're going,' and he sprang to his feet and helped me up and sprinted back along the path for the bags and set off at a pace, carrying all the bags and I had to skip to keep up with him.

The path meandered through the woods and under the railway line and then opened up to a vista of mud flats and the sparkling ribbon of light which was the Stour. A faint heat haze blurred the opposite bank and to the right, where the river was broadest, were the ports of Harwich with Felixstowe opposite. Boats large and small ploughed the water and I realized how ignorant I was of the world beyond Stockwell Street. I had no idea what these boats did although I could just about tell a ferry from a fishing boat. I had no idea what the birds were which waded in the mud on the tidal estuary; or the trees and plants around me, or the peninsular opposite. I could paint them, but I couldn't name them. I would ask T'Ash. He would know.

We scrambled down the small bank which led to the beach and hit the gravel with a crunch and T'Ash turned left along the shore line and rounded a bend and stopped and I caught up with him. There built into the cliff face were some mini houses on stilts; wooden frames with pointed roofs and wooden shutters, painted blue and green and yellow; just five or six in muted colours, nestling in the lee of the cliff, proudly facing the river and I swear they smiled at us.

'Just here. The far end,' said T'Ash, and sprinted the rest of the way, sand and gravel flying, swinging the picnic basket and throwing the hold-all over his shoulder.

'Come on. It's great. You'll love it', he shouted above the breeze which barely ruffled the surface of the water and whispered its secrets to the trees on the bank. I stopped and looked as he ran on. It was a serene and idyllic place and I wanted my memory to hold the image for later when I would paint it. I had my sketch book with me of course, but the colour and the light and shade were what mattered. The sunlight on water and muted tones; and the breeze. How could I paint the breeze whispering promises of love and T'Ash's laughter? I closed my eyes to take it in and then ran the rest of the way as T'Ash had put down the bags and was struggling to open a padlock.

His hands shook slightly and he shivered although it was a warm day. I said nothing. I just took the key and opened the lock and stepped back to let him open the door. A smell of must and damp and sea and summer washed over me and I closed my eyes and inhaled it deeply.

In my memories, smells are always the most evocative and when I think back to that day, it is the smell of the chalet and the close smell of T'Ash which hits me and sends my body back into the muscle memory and the deep bone memory of the moment. You would think that as an artist I would tell of the shade and the light and the colour of the little nest which was to be our haven from reality. But now, I can only feel that every fibre of my body ached for his closeness and words evaporated and the tide lapped at the shoreline and sucked itself away as we coiled into each other, inside and out and all thought evaporated in the sense of the moment.

That was it. That was the moment; the transition from our sheltered childhood into the adult world and we lay, side by side on cushions on the floor, and listened to the hearty chorus of angels which sang loudly as our breath stilled and our hearts drummed out a tattoo. It was in reality a chorus of wading birds who had witnessed our dance of consummation and wondered what all the fuss was about.

T'Ash was eerily silent. When I could move again, I turned to face him. His eyes were closed and he had a look of pain not joy etched on his face. I stroked his face gently and he opened his eyes, as if startled to see me there. Anxiety welled in the deep pit of my stomach fuelled by sudden doubt. What if he regretted it? If he now walked away from me? Was I 'too easy,' a notion I had heard muttered at school but taken no account of? And what of pregnancy? The whole reality of the adult threshold we had stumbled innocently across washed over me like a cold shower and I struggled to my feet and grabbed at clothes which lay strewn across the floor. He leapt to his feet and took me gently in his arms and wrapped a blanket around me and nestled with me on the couch which was built into the side of the chalet.

'Don't go. Don't move. Don't change anything. This is the most perfect moment of my entire life. I want to savour it.' He gazed into my face and the intensity which blazed from his slate grey eyes held me transfixed and I can't remember how long we stayed there, entwined on the couch, but when I came to again it was dark and T'Ash had lit some lamps and was moving about in the small space and I smelt the unmistakable smell of bacon frying.

The chalet, like a caravan, was compact and well equipped for overnight stays. There were two couches which doubled as beds, a kitchen unit and a small table and two chairs. At the end of the row of huts was a toilet and basic washing facilities, to which we had a key. I wanted to live here forever and to forget the past; my parents past and my dull, slow start in life, and create a new life here; T'Ash and me and the wading birds.

He turned and smiled at me and handed me a cup of tea and it was hot and sweetened with condensed milk. I cradled it silently and hugged the blanket closer over my nakedness. He had half dressed again but was barefoot and his shirt was unbuttoned and I felt an overwhelming desire rise from the pit of my stomach like an ache and in the lamplight and the steam from cooking, he looked like an Angel and I held the memory to paint later.

Our passion knew no bounds that day or the days which followed. We could not be apart, except that we had to live in the world and go to work. We talked of running away together, to America, or London, and in the fog of the next dawn on a quiet Essex estuary, we pledged ourselves to each other forever and he gave me a ring he wore which he said had been his grandmothers. I still wear it.

And so we were lovers and reckless all that spring. Insatiable together and obsessed apart. T'Ash, being older and wiser (and Catholic) knew how to take 'precautions' which I may well have disregarded in my state of total obsession, and he always brought with him something he called a 'French Letter'. I got through my work as best I could and so did T'Ash. I felt certain that my mother would notice when I went to visit her the following Sunday. Surely it was etched on my face and I could barely meet her eyes. I was transformed and it must be plain to all who knew me well. I needn't have worried. She had slipped further into herself and although she knew me and acknowledged me and asked if I was eating well, she barely noticed much outside of her own, trapped pain. It hurt a bit but I was released from parental censure and liberated to live my reckless life unchallenged.

Chapter Five

T'Ash came to my house after work and we ate together like a married couple and made love in my mother's big bed and he taught me to play cards – cribbage, which I struggled with but soon got good at and offered a reasonable challenge. He also brought a board game, well worn and a bit tatty, called 'Monopoly' and told me about all the places in London which were on the board and we fantasized about going there one day. It wasn't far; just along the train track.

After an evening together, playing games, eating and always making love, he went home to his mother and I ran the gauntlet of clicking tongues when I passed neighbours in the street and gossip which stopped abruptly as I walked by. I didn't care. My happiness was unique and they, the sad and lonely women could not claim me into their fold; and besides, we had plans, T'Ash and I, to go out and conquer the world.

But before we could he was curious about my past; and so gradually as the evenings wore on, we talked about my story, as far as I could remember, and he sat silently cradling a cup of hot tea in his hands.

I told him of the time just after Aunt Maude had committed suicide.

'Why did she do that? It's a mortal sin you know,' he said.

'She had a baby during the war. She wasn't married although she planned to marry her soldier when he came home on leave. He never made it back.'

'So you have a cousin then?'

'Yes. James.'

'So where does he live?' I remembered what Mum had told me in the days before her breakdown; '*so many babies lost,*' and I had no idea what she was talking about. So often her memories of the past washed over me and formed the background wallpaper to my life. But now that she could no longer remember things, it seemed to matter more.

'When we got back from Holland, Aunt Maude was happy that we had survived. She didn't know about me until Felix got in touch to say we were coming home. Mum was married before the war, so she could keep me. James would be a year younger. She just named him and handed him over at 7 days old. She bottled it up, apparently, until she saw me; she didn't tell Mum about James for ages after, and then, on my 16th birthday, she fell apart and she killed herself. Took a whole bottle of pills. Mum really thought she was over it.'

'So who's Felix?' he asked and I struggled to remember; it came to me in images; a flashback memory; a fragment like a piece of a torn banner which blew in the wind and flapped outside the window of my father's studio: a Nazi flag which my mother hated but my father said was necessary and kept us all alive; I could still see the pictures clearly in my eyes:

Looking down on the street; here; Stockwell Street; not the studio; and a car outside; a rare thing, a car calling on us and a man; the man from Holland; Felix unloading things; Mother's things; possessions from Holland; and taking them down to the cellar; the cellar always locked. But I couldn't see his face.

'Have you been down to the cellar? Do you know what this man unloaded down there?' he asked. I shrugged and felt a pang of guilt at my lack of curiosity.

'I went down once with Mum but it was dark and cold and she said there was nothing there of any importance just some old papers and stuff. But I saw some pictures. Canvasses still wrapped up. She never opened them.'

'Do you want to have a look now?' I felt fear creep over me in the familiar wave of anxiety.

'It's dark and I'm not sure if the light's working.'

'Have you got a torch?'

'Erm, somewhere.' I found it in the cupboard under the sink but the batteries were dead.

'Never mind,' he said, 'another time,' and I breathed a sigh of relief but when I was alone that night, the thought of the cellar and the canvasses haunted my dreams.

Next day, we met in the park after work but it was a cold wet night so we hurried home and I made dinner and then he reached into his duffel bag and put a torch on the table and a box containing a light bulb. It was a silent challenge, so I wiped my hands and reached into the kitchen draw and put the cellar key onto the table next to his offerings. He took the key and the torch, handed me the light bulb and took my hand and like Hansel and Gretel we began our journey into the darkness of the cellar.

Behind the door lay the secrets of the past and the key to my future. I giggled as the light overhead flickered on and off and T'Ash lit the torch and changed the light bulb and in the 40 watt light we stumbled down the stairs into a low space which mapped the rooms above. There was a brick arch separating the two sections and a brick pillar in the middle which supported an oak beam; bare old brick walls; salt marks where the damp had risen; boxes stacked against the walls; two trunks and old suitcases; a broken raffia chair; a box spilling broken lampshades and bits of a broken house; old books smelling damp and musty; clothes and old curtains which I didn't want to touch.

Through the archway were a dozen or so canvasses stacked against a wall. T'Ash let out a deep breath behind me and I realized that I was holding mine.

'Wow,' was all he said. 'Where do we start?' Curiosity finally got to me about the same time as the dust caused me to cough and sneeze and we laughed together as he picked up a box, blew the dust off the top and opened the lid. It was papers. Old stuff. Not at all interesting, at least to me, but T'Ash was a clerk in the archive office of the Town Hall and this was heaven to him.

'It's all here you know,' he said opening box lids and peering inside. 'Your entire history is here. Wow. I wish I had something like this.' Then, alongside the wrapped canvasses he found a wooden suitcase and prised open the stiff hinges and stood back in awe. 'This is gold dust,' he said peering at documents. 'This stuff looks like it relates to those pictures....' and his voice tailed off.

I was drawn towards the side walls where the canvasses were stacked. I counted them. 13 canvasses all wrapped in cardboard and brown paper and sacking; some of them, the larger ones encased in rough wooden pallets made into crates. They were stacked against the wall where above, the kitchen range would be, so although it wasn't warm, it kept the damp out and so far there was little sign of damage. I wanted to tear the wrappings off and see what we were left with. I had images in my mind of canvasses I thought I remembered, like the one of Jellicoe naked with her arm over her head gazing candidly at the viewer. The one I had inadvertently copied from a deep root memory. I made it into a picture of myself, two years ago and had got into trouble at school. I was almost expelled when Mrs. Davies confiscated my sketchbook and sent me to see the Head Master. I thought he looked too long and too eagerly at the naked form of my pubescent body, but I was powerless to say anything and when my mother got my sketchbook back, our relationship had changed. Not because I was growing up and had drawn myself naked, but because she knew I was an artist and that I had my father's talent.

I turned away from the paintings; and joined T'Ash who was delving into boxes and I started to leaf through some papers.

'No. Not like that. Don't mix them up. Keep them in order,' so I dropped the letter I was holding as though it had burned my fingers.

'It's in Dutch anyway. I can't understand it.' T'Ash carried on reading the document he held.

'This is really important. It looks like this is part of the Resistance.'

'What's that?' I asked a bit sulky now because I just wanted to unpack the canvasses and look at them but my excitement was quelled by fear. I felt the familiar nausea begin to rise and the throb at the base of my skull, on the right hand side, like the fear was worming its way in to eat my brain alive and panic began to rise in the dim, cold space. The walls felt too close. The ceiling was too low and I found myself barley able to breathe.

'It was the guys who fought against the Nazi occupation. They were brave and risked their lives to undermine the Nazis. This is important stuff, Scarlett.'

'Leave it,' I said and my voice was faraway and not really mine at all and T'Ash noticed. Hearing him say my name, here, surrounded by my past, by Beatrix Prins, not Scarlett, or Betty Quinn, I felt the panic rise and I ran for the stairs stumbling over a box which had been moved into the centre of the small space. He was there beside me, holding me, helping me up, saying things but I couldn't hear and like a frightened animal, I fought him off.

'Leave me. Leave it alone. Let it rest....' or something like that as I stumbled up the stairs running from the ghosts which we had unleashed and were now inside me and I would carry them with me to the end as my mother did, living with the ghosts and talking only to them.

I awoke with the pink light of dawn and found myself in my bed, half dressed and my head throbbing, mouth tasting of soot and my body had the familiar ache which came after a fit. I was alarmed. I remembered only the flight from the cellar, and I lay back on the pillow and knew that I wasn't able to go to work today. A movement in the corner of the room disturbed me and T'Ash was by my side, stroking the hair from my face and his pale anxious face peered into mine.

'You're ok. Thank God. I didn't know what to do. Who to call. You said you were ok and needed to sleep but I stayed anyway.' He had sat all night in the chair in my mother's room, the blanket which had covered him discarded on the floor. He had sat by me and waited for me to wake up.

He made me tea and said he would tidy himself up and get to work but be back at dinner time and would let the Bakery, where I worked, know I was ill. I heard him crashing around in the scullery and water running and then the front door slam and the house groaned and settled itself into is habitual silence. I lay still and listened but there was nothing to hear. The fear had subsided and the ghosts lay still and I was rational in the warm light of another dawn. I thought of T'Ash; of his devotion and my love for him and I knew that whatever happened, I was no longer alone.

I decided to go to the hospital and see Mum. I had neglected her since T'Ash and I had become inseparable. I would go to the hospital and I would see if she was able to talk to me and I would ask her.

Who is Felix?
How many babies?
How did Papa die?
Did you kill him?

Chapter Six

From the doorway, I stopped to look at her. Mum was propped in a chair in the dayroom, no longer a danger; no longer on the locked ward. There was a book open on her lap but she wasn't reading it. She stared blankly into the room and ignored the ceaseless chatter of an old lady next to her, who was knitting a long, long yarn in many coloured wool, the sort you re-use, as Aunt Maude would: unravel a jumper, rewind it and rework it into a scarf or hat. She was telling a long, long story to my mother and neither seemed to know that the other was there. The nurse breezed in beside me and hustled me across the room.

'You have a visitor Marianne. Look who's come to see you? That's coming on well Gertrude. Is it a scarf for your granddaughter? Millie don't get out of the chair dear, I'll fetch help,' and she bustled away with a small squeeze of my arm and an air of purpose. The book slid to the floor and I picked it up and laid it on the table beside Mum. It was *Gone With The Wind*. I bent forward to kiss her cheek which was cool and papery where once she'd had furry plump cheeks which I thought were like a peach and smelt of Nivea Cream. That was when I was small and she smiled sometimes and all was calm in the little house in Stockwell Street.

She didn't react at first and then her hand went to her face and she touched the spot I had kissed and turned her blank stare on me and I saw the struggle cross her face; the struggle to remember and the pain at not being able to and then the light. A very small dim candle light of recognition shone from behind her eyes, masked with tears and then a half smile and then a hand over her mouth to shut out the realization. She looked around the room and then at me and took my arm and pulled me to her and held me in an awkward bony grasp and cried. I gently pulled away and drew up a chair and took her thin cold hands in mine.

'Betty,' she said and her voice was hoarse with lack of use and I baulked at the use of my old name; a name long gone which was never really mine. I could move forward as Scarlett; Beatrix and Betty were the ghosts now.

I smiled and pulled out the chocolates I had brought her and her face brightened; she looked almost well and 'normal', except the eyes. I looked closely into her eyes and despite the dim light which now burned there, I saw the shadows flicker and the doubt and fear lurking just behind the light. I placed the chocolates on top of the book and took her hands again and began the ritual of small talk which was about the weather – it was turning cold again and had rained; about the neighbours: Mrs. Bracknell had had another baby girl; and Mrs. Hunter, two doors down was still hanging out her husband's pyjamas on the washing line, even though everyone knew he didn't actually wear them.

'I didn't know you knew about that,' and she almost giggled. I couldn't tell her that I had not been totally deaf when she and Aunt Maude sat in the parlour of an evening, sewing or knitting and gossiping and the story of Mr. Hunter's sleeping naked, as told by Lighthouse Lil (and we can only imagine how she knew) was so shameful that to dispel the rumours, Mrs. Hunter, Ethel to those who knew her well, would hang out two pairs of men's pyjamas every week on the washing line for all to see.

As I said it to Mum, I realized that I wasn't supposed to know such scandal but she seemed not to care too much. She turned in her chair and looked at me directly and said,

'You are all grown up, Betty. Please be careful. Don't get caught out like Maudie did. Don't give them reason to gossip,' and she choked the last bit back and turned away. I sat staring at the floor. She knew. How did she know? Was it tattooed on my forehead: 'Scarlett Woman' and I stifled a laugh at the irony. I wondered; if Aunt Maude were still alive and the three of us still together in Stockwell street, would I have met T'Ash? Would I have been able to have a lover? I could never have brought a man home under my mother's roof however liberal she might be, and certainly not with Aunt Maude there. So I was free. I was liberated from their world and I was exploring my new life with abandon and alacrity.

'*Be careful. Don't get caught...*' the words echoed around in the silence until Gertrude threw her knitting across the room and began to rant that they had taken all her babies away and she couldn't knit another one because they would take that one as well and they were Princesses of Spain. Mum's face closed and she retreated back into her mind until two large nurses came and escorted Gertrude from the room.

I took Mum's hand and rubbed some warmth into it and said very softly,

'Mum, who was Felix?' I saw the mind working again as she tried so hard to come back to me.

'Felix? Felix Van Gelder? You mean Doctor Felix?'

'Yes', I prompted, having more information than I'd had before. 'Yes Doctor Felix. Was he a friend of yours?' She chewed her bottom lip and I could see the struggle of her mouth trying to make the words which her brain refused to acknowledge and I felt guilt that I was clearly causing her pain.

'Yes,' she said quietly. 'A good friend to all of us,' and she fell silent.

'How did Papa die?' I said quietly, looking at the floor and she pulled her hand away and tried to stand. I helped her back into her seat and rearranged the blanket across her legs and put an arm around her bony shoulders and tried to calm her.

'It wasn't Felix's fault. It was her, that ....*whore*,' and she spat out the word and a nurse in the corner of the room looked up and headed towards us.

'Now you're not tiring your mammy out, I hope,' she said in an accent which I thought must be from the North. 'It's nearly dinner time and that means time for her medication and a little rest, isn't it Marianne?' and she patted Mum's hand and looked at me disapprovingly and walked slowly back to her station in the corner. Mum let out a long, deep shuddering breath which vibrated through my body and leaned towards me conspiratorially.

'It's the medication, love. It makes me drowsy and I can't remember things so I'll tell you this now before they dope me up again. It wasn't Felix's fault. He'd TOLD Jellicoe instructions for Papas new pills because we never liked to write things down. We were supposed to remember things. His medication was hard to get in those days; everything was, and she got him the pills but he wasn't supposed to each cheese and other things. I can't remember now; or drink. That was it. No alcohol. And if she told him she didn't tell me and he would ignore those things anyway and so when I could get food, we couldn't waste it; it was the *Honger Winter*, you know and lots of people were starving... but you see, it reacted with his pills and he... he had a stroke or something and it was all because she didn't tell us what Felix had said. Felix told me later when we left...'

'Did he come to England with us,' I said, breathless, keen for information whilst it flowed.

'No. Not then. Later. He brought your father's things from the studio...' and then she stopped. She had said too much.

'In the cellar?' I prompted and she looked at me disdainfully as though she had no idea who I was or why I was talking to her. She may have learned it from 'Queen Gertrude' whose knitted babies were Princesses of Spain.

'Just some old papers. When I'm out of here, I'll clear them out. It doesn't do to hold on to the past.'

'But I remember Felix. I remember him coming to the house one night.' I could see her struggle.

'Well yes of course. He knew you. He met Maude. He helped us to get home.'

'Where is he now?' I asked.

'I have no idea. Gone with the rest of them I should think. He wrote to me for a while, but I never replied. We had a new life in England. We were English and the war was over and me and Maude, we wanted to forget. It was much better that way.' She turned her candid gaze on me again and said, 'Leave it love. You have a future ahead of you and when I get out of here we'll move. Those new houses in Shrub End? I'm sure we can get re-housed by the Council. I will get better, I promise,' and the tears began to spill silently down her cheeks and the nurse came over and took me gently aside and said it was time to go. Marianne needed her medication.

'When can she come home?' I asked.

'Oh it'll be a while yet. She has an assessment at the end of the month and the Doctors will let you know.'

'But she doesn't seem to be getting any better,' I said, holding back the emotion which threatened to swamp me.

'Oh but she is pet, don't worry about that. This is a lot better. She can sit up and talk to you and feed herself and look, she even likes to read books now. She's a lot better than she was, and she's safe. That's the main thing. She can't hurt herself. But...' and she paused as though she shouldn't say the next bit and leaned in conspiratorially. 'This may be as good as it gets and she'll need constant medication and care. But it's early days... Now off you go. Say goodbye to your mammy and we'll see you again at the weekend maybe, with that handsome young man of yours?' and I flushed red and had no idea that they had seen T'Ash and me together because we went to separate parts of the hospital when we arrived and met afterwards in the gardens.

'Yes. At the weekend,' and I hugged Mum and gently wiped the tears from her face, and I turned and fled from the look of despair which followed me all the way home.

But now I knew. Forbidden food. Pa had died because Dr. Felix had changed his medication. I guess he got whatever he could get his hands on in a blockade, but gave a warning which Jellicoe knew and Mum didn't. Mum let him eat and drink whatever she could get and innocently, she thought she had killed him.

I felt the headache returning and hurried home in time to meet T'Ash on my doorstep with pies for our 'dinner' which is what he called our lunchtime meal. We called it lunch. I flung myself into his arms, shamelessly on the doorstep and didn't care about the twitching net curtains or the pyjamas hanging in another courtyard.

I told him what Mum had said about Dr. Felix and the pills and the forbidden food.

'Wow. What a great story. Can I use that? I mean, I don't want to be disrespectful or nothing but I could really use that idea. Forbidden food, taken with medication as a murder weapon.'

I dropped my fork to the table. 'Do you think it was murder?'

'No of course not. I also don't think it's true at all. I think it's just the first level of truth.'

'The *what?*'

'The first level of truth, you know. That's what spies are trained in. Three levels of truth if you're captured. The first two levels are cover stories or partial truths, rehearsed until embedded in the subconscious in the hope that it will be enough.'

'T'Ash this is serious. This isn't some stupid spy novel you are reading, or worse, writing! This is my life.' I got up and took my plate to the sink, scraping the remains of my half eaten pie into the bin. He put his fork down.

'No actually it isn't. It was your parent's life and yours is something else. This is maybe somewhere in your dim and distant past but it isn't your life Scarlett. Now, you either want to know the truth or you don't. Either way, life goes on. But I'll tell you one thing for certain. When I go to see my gran and I see those other people in there, the one thing they have in common is that they are haunted. The truth is locked up inside of them and they daren't face it and they get on well enough until one day it rears up and swamps them. Look at your Ma now. It was only when your Aunty Maude died that she fell apart. She couldn't hold on to another ghost until she had laid the others to rest. And I'll tell you something else as well, if you want to hear it. I'll tell you this. When I saw you run away from that cellar last night I knew that you have to confront this stuff and know what happened. Not for now or for some years to come but for eventually because it won't go away you know and you'll have no peace until it's sorted. Secrets and lies will always come back and haunt your nights if not your days as well and you end up joining them, the parade of lost souls and they take you away with them before your time and you end up in a place like… well … you know what I'm saying.'

I sat heavily into Grandpa Quinn's chair and let his words fall like pearls before pigs. He was right. I knew he was right, but my demons were my own property and I wasn't ready to share them.

'Three levels of truth?' I asked, eventually.

He nodded. 'I just don't believe that he died of eating cheese, although I can see how cheese could be a murder weapon in a thriller.' I laughed at his outrageous take on it.

'But it sounds plausible to me,' I said thinking of my poor mother wrenching the memory from her deep well of trauma.

'Oh, aye, so it is,' he said enigmatically. 'Partial truth. Not all of it. There's a lot more in those *'visions'* things you get…..' I shrugged.

'Maybe they're just nightmares. There's nothing to say what really happened.' He moved over to my chair and took my hands away from my face and held them warmly in his.

'Look,' he said. 'I've witnessed your funny little turns and you know, to me, they ring true. It's your soul trying to let it out; to lance the pain.' His face was close to mine and his words soft and gentle and I knew that he would write it all down in his notebook when he went back to work and it made me smile. At least I was giving him material for a story.

'So what is the truth then?' I asked and he stood up.

'No idea, yet, but there may be clues down there,' and he pointed to the cellar and I buried my face in my hands again and groaned and he took me in his arms, hugged me tight and said he had to get back to work. 'Oh, by the way, I got a book for you from the library. I thought you'd be laid up in bed, off sick for a few days. I didn't expect you to be up and about and gallivanting across Colchester,' and I smiled at the mild reprimand which didn't suit him at all.

'The *'funny little turns'* are brief and quite rare and I recover very quickly'.

'So I noticed,' he said without reproach and with some relief. 'But anyways, I got you a book. It's about painting,' and he left it on the table and was gone leaving a huge T'Ash shaped hole to fuel the rest of my day without him. And a book about a Dutch Artist I had never heard of called Vincent Van Gogh.

Chapter Seven

Walking to work was easy these days. I had a spring in my step and I was beginning to break away from the tyranny of my mother's rigid Catholicism and my father's outrageous hopelessness. *I was tasting freedom and its name was Scarlett.* I pulled out the notebook and jotted that down in case I forgot it by the time my mind was numbed by trays of papers for filing.

Scarlett had told me about the confiscation of her sketch book at school. I would kill anyone who touched my notebook.

But the boxes of papers had to be dealt with and I thought of the boxes in Scarlett's cellar. If she would let me go through it all and sort it out and maybe find some answers, but she wasn't ready just yet and anyway on first glance they were mostly in Dutch or German or something and I certainly couldn't decipher them alone. I know that when I first met her I was a bit of an idiot, trying to impress her and imply that I was a spy or something equally juvenile. But I was absolutely right that I can find things out. I have an analytical mind, you see, and I can also make some leaps of imagination which more often than not fill in the gaps in the picture. Then you know what you are dealing with and you can record the evidence, the hard facts, and build a case around it, with whatever else you imagine, forming the backdrop to it.

That is why I am sure that '*death by cheese*' is probably not a true memory and that we will need to dig a bit deeper to work this out. I am pretty sure that some of Mrs. Quinn's – Marianne's – memories are jumbled up like a jigsaw puzzle and all the pieces are there, but we have to be patient and work from the evidence, which is in those boxes and paintings. I will move things on a bit I think. Maybe plan a visit to the National Gallery. Scarlett will love that and I find it hard to believe that she has never been. Looking at paintings will definitely get her curious about what is really down there in her cellar.

And now we had more details about Doctor Felix Van Gelder. Maybe I could look him up, trace him through his war record, but my resources are limited and I would have to use an international archive for that and I don't have that kind of access – only to Mrs. Higgins' planning permission for an extension onto her guest house in Old Heath, or letters of complaint from Mr. Johnson about his neighbour's dog. Who was I kidding? But at least we had a name. Doctor Felix Van Gelder.

Chapter Eight
Amsterdam Spring 1956

The moon cast long shadows in the darker places around the canal and the water moved sluggishly and lapped at the pier. The body floated on the oily slick, face down and heavy, clothes billowing around it like sails. It reminded Jellicoe of the downed airman during the war which Felix had been so keen to save and protect. They all thought he was a good man, Felix; a hero. She knew better and she would prove it. But for now, a body floated on the canal in front of her and she saw an opportunity to move her plan into the next phase.

People were running and pointing and a siren sounded somewhere. She kept to the shadows and waited for her chance. Torch lights flashed down the slope and the steps were filling with people coming to help. What could they do? The woman's skirts spread out and held her afloat, face down. She was clearly dead. Another whore from the red light district, not willing or able to face the life the war had left for her? Another story of damage and destruction and despair. Another footnote written up as a four inch column in the paper; suicide or misadventure would be assumed although they would still check for obvious signs of murder; strangulation, stabbing, or a gunshot wound.

There were so many guns in circulation a decade since the liberation, and still no one really knowing who to trust.

Jellicoe had been running for too many years; running from ghosts and from a past long buried under the rubble of war. Fear could not release its icy grip on her heart, not now that she had her daughter to keep safe. She had been making ends meet, paying bills, moving from place to place, always one step ahead of the shadows, until the day dawned when she awoke into a different light and the shadows were fading and the grip of fear relaxed. The prison door was ajar but it was a prison of her own making in the shape of an oubliette, and she had long forgotten why she had dug such a deep hole and willingly thrown herself in. She could only plead protection of her child. The hormones of motherhood had swamped her and the flow of love was too overwhelming for the new landscape which the war had re-drawn.

There was a ladder she could use to climb out of her oubliette; a small fortune tied up in Max Prins's legacy, the paintings which were left unsold in the chaos at the end. But she had lost, and to the victor, the spoils. Felix had taken everything and taken care of everything, as he had planned to take care of her and her daughter. Felix didn't do sharing and he didn't take unnecessary risks, and by her own assessment, she was an unnecessary risk. She knew too much which made her a threat.

Now that the world was once again at peace, the threat was to his reputation and possibly even his liberty. Even in war some things are illegal, justifiable though they may seem at the time. And so she continued to play dead and hide in the shadows until she deemed it safe to come out.

She had left her daughter with relations in Philadelphia. Jan and Irina Lansaar were a childless couple about her own age. Jan was the son of her father's cousin which was close enough for her to call them family even though they had never met until recently. Unlike her father however, this branch of the family were staunch Calvinist but they would do what was required of them; raise Johanna and keep her safe whilst Jellicoe unlocked the fortune and the future.

And then it would truly be over and they could move on in peace. She would join her daughter again soon, if she could get her plan to work, and why shouldn't it? More audacious plans had worked only a decade ago in the war. She had been part of that and knew about things which Felix would rather she didn't.

The body had been pulled from the water now and a doctor was checking for signs of life. There wouldn't be any, or any marks of murder. It was a suicide or an accident because Jellicoe had witnessed the woman falling or rather staggering into the water and now was the time to step forward.

Earlier this evening she had walked along the top path and seen the woman below weaving along the tow path and then she heard the splash and looked around to see if there was anyone else. There wasn't and so she went down and could see that a young woman, mousy blonde hair, 5'7" more or less was unconscious in the water. She wasn't going to save her alone and so she stepped back into the shadows and realised that this was the chance she needed. She had heard of it before. Unidentified corpses washing up in the sluices of the locks and blocking the gates; it was not unusual and there was often little scrutiny. She could take her chance now to send out a message to those who still hunted her: *Jellicoe Du Pont is Dead.*

Chapter Nine

That weekend, we decided to have a day out. T'Ash didn't work Saturdays and I got one Saturday a month off, so we went to London to the National Gallery. It seems strange to think that I had never been out of Colchester except the occasional visit to Ipswich for Christmas shopping, a day out on the bus which included lunch in the Lyons Tea House and a look around the big stores. We occasionally went to the seaside; to Clacton on a sunny day, again by bus, and had fish and chips on the pier and put pennies in the slot machines. But I had never been to London and I was excited.

I dressed with care in the dress I had for my birthday and which I had hardly worn since. Aunt Maude had made it for me; my first grown up dress, made with new cloth bought on the market and not one of her old ones cut down. It was a stiff calico cotton print of yellow and lilac flowers, cut with a full flared skirt and a tight fitted bodice. Mum gave me her pearls which Pa had given her when they married, and bought me stockings and a new headscarf in yellow to match the dress. I was a grown up overnight and I had loved the feel of the stockings and the flared skirt and the excitement of leaving school and starting my first job in the bakery.

Now, the dress hung loose where I had lost weight. I also had a new pair of shoes which I had saved up for and my dark navy coat was just about presentable. I wore the yellow headscarf and a pair of Mum's navy gloves and T'Ash let out a whistle when he met me at the train station and spun me around to get a proper look.

'You look gorgeous,' he said and chastely kissed my cheek. We were in public and T'Ash for all of his radical ideas and poetry, was old fashioned.

I was excited, sitting beside T'Ash in a train carriage heading to London for the first time; to the National Art Gallery. We chatted about what we would do when we got there; how we would get from the train station to Trafalgar Square, using the London Underground trains, a concept I found equally terrifying and exciting. T'Ash had maps and plans and a London Gazetteer, which was a Street Atlas of London in which every street was printed and named. I let him lead the way and steer us through the maze of London. I was in a daze as we emerged at Leicester Square and walked passed St. Martins Church into Trafalgar Square, approaching the Gallery from behind. It was like the pictures I had seen of it and I stopped to take it in. As T'Ash read from the guide book and pointed out landmarks, I looked up to the pillars and porticos of the National Gallery and laughed out loud.

Trafalgar square was crowded with people; some hurrying through; some in suits and smartly dressed, some tourists speaking foreign languages and even some coloured people: Caribbean, African; Indian: Chinese. Faces I had rarely seen before and I wanted to draw them all. I wanted to be here; to live in the vibrant heart of the world where life beat to a faster rhythm and the pulse raced and the tide of people, all types of people, ebbed and flowed around us and was never still at the beating heart of a city alive with its fast flow of images, ideas and thoughts.

T'Ash said later, when we were home and in my bed, that he could hear the stories murmured in the footsteps and on the wings of the pigeons as they scavenged for the crumbs given generously by the tourists or casually dropped from picnics. I felt the same and my sketch pad, a new one brought especially for the occasion, burned a hole in my handbag and twitched excitedly waiting for its virgin pages to be ravished by ink and lead.

We had made an early start but it was mid morning before we arrived in Trafalgar Square and we were both hungry so we bought tea in a small café on a side street run, I thought, by Italians, and we sat at a table on the pavement outside, under an awning, to drink it. Then we found a bench in the square and ate some of the sandwiches I had packed and we sat in the weak sunshine, muffled in our coats, chatting excitedly, pointing out to each other the fights of two pigeons over one crust, or the small child wheeling his arms about and chasing the birds; the lovers holding hands silently, looking sad as they strolled halfheartedly across the square, or young man climbing the statues of the Lions to impress the girls laughing on the ground below and taking a photograph.

I had packed my mother's Kodak Brownie and asked one of the girls to take a photo of T'Ash and I side by side, at the base of a Lion, T'Ash's arm draped casually around my shoulder, both smiling at the camera. I have it still. It has travelled with me and reminds me of the day my life began. The 'Monopoly' board had come to life and I had really thrown a six to start and the impact was excitement and a sense of purpose. I was going to live here in this city and go to Art school and paint every day and feel more alive than I could ever imagine.

But how did you begin to do things like that? Did you just turn up and show them your pictures and they would say, 'Ok we like you come in', and there would be a huge well lit studio, not unlike my father's attic with painters silently working away all around it and I would be shown to an easel and given some oil paints – lots of them – as many as I wanted, and I would paint? I had no idea of how the world worked and had no one to ask, except T'Ash.

Inside the gallery was another world. I walked up the stairs and discarded the guide which T'Ash had thrust into my hands as he planned our route.

'Ok. Shall we start with the early works, you know, your Renaissance, Rococo and Neo-Classicals; your Dutch Golden Age and Genre paintings will be in that lot; and then work through to the Impressionist and Romantics and the pre Raphaelites, and then Post Impressionists, Art Nouveau, Modern and Abstract stuff, although to be honest I don't really understand what that's all about.' I had no idea what he was talking about. My mouth was open in awe and I was barely there. I walked up the stairs and turned left and ignoring T'Ash completely wandered alone, lost in a maze of canvasses some bigger than my front parlour, which held you at bay with their religious themes and grandiosity, and others so small and detailed that they drew you in, intimately to see their detail. The colour and the scale; the light of the painting of Jesus before Pilate; and the Turners.

I came at last to the 'Modern stuff' as T'Ash called it and I had to sit to catch my breath. I took in the movement of the Renoir and the sedate lines of Cezanne; the romanticism of Millet and the wild other worldliness of Rousseau. And then I saw T'Ash sitting opposite a picture of a chair with a pipe on it, not unlike the broken chair in the cellar at home. I sat next to him breathless with excitement.

'Would you look at the that? The chair is almost alive.' He said. I looked and understood what he meant and leaned over to see the name of the artist.

'Vincent Van Gogh,' said T'Ash. 'He went mad and cut off his ear. That one over there,' he pointed to a picture of a cornfield; swirling yellow corn; trees which spiraled up towards the light blue sky; more vibrant than anything I had ever seen. 'He painted it in an asylum, in France.'

I looked into T'Ash's grey eyes and saw the sadness etched there. 'He only sold one picture in is life and died poor. Now his paintings are all over the place and priceless, and bloody Hitler classified him as 'degenerate'. Can you believe that something so amazing could be 'degenerate'. But no one really cares enough.'

'You do. You left me a book about him,' I said gently touching his arm.

'I admire his struggle', he said, and we sat in silence for a while and absorbed the works around us.

It was dusk when we left and we had very little to say. There were so many paintings in so small a space. So many artists and this one place told the history of art through the ages and I knew that I had left a little bit of my soul under the great dome of that place, and I would be back.

I took out library books about the history of art; I read everything I could and began to be familiar with the terms T'Ash had used and gradually the movement of art as a reflection of its time made sense; and then I studied techniques; the use of colour and light and texture and movement on a still frame; how some artists like Renoir used the frame differently, and I learned about the golden section and the Renaissance and things I had taken for granted like perspective. And then I began to copy some of my favourites; Van Gogh was one because I felt that his pictures were not only paintings of scenes or people or things: they were a reflection of himself on the canvas.

The library book T'Ash had left for me had a picture on the cover of a bright yellow corn field with a pale blue swirling sky and the picture seemed to animate before my eyes. I turned the pages and discovered more; swirling colours; blue and gold; and dark skies and streets with cafes. There were few colour prints and those were separated with tissue but even the black and white reproductions expressed his personality. This was his soul on the page and I was drawn in.

I took out my paints and began to copy the pieces I saw there. There was a black and white picture called '*The Gleaners*' and I recreated it in my own colours based on what I had seen in the rest of the book and the gallery. It absorbed me totally and I pinned the finished pieces to the kitchen door and the walls, and stepped back to see that they brought vibrancy and colour back into the sad little house. I painted after work, studying in great detail how the brush strokes worked, how the colour moved on the page, how he made me feel.

And then as the paintings I copied covered the walls of the kitchen and the hallway, I was drawn back to the cellar stairs. If art reflects the times it was painted, why did Papa recreate the old world?

I sat and waited for T'Ash and decided that this weekend, we would unpack the canvasses and then I would know. I would remember, and then I could move on and start my life without the baggage from other people's cellars.

Chapter Ten
Amsterdam Spring 1956

Felix folded the newspaper, placed it on the table and removed his half moon reading spectacles. He sipped the last of his coffee and placed the cup silently back on its saucer. His tapered fingers tapped the newspaper. It was almost a week old, and he had missed the small item on the bottom of page 6 until Ben had drawn his attention to it. A two inch column told him that Jellicoe Du Pont – she had reverted to an earlier alias, he noticed – was dead. Drowned in the canal near the dock in the red light district. The story felt *'unlikely'* thought Felix. Yes that was the best word for it. That or *'improbable'*. He read it again to be certain.

'The body of a young woman, was pulled from the Oudezijds Achterburgwal at 2.00am on the morning of 3rd May. She was identified at the scene as Jellicoe Du Pont by a close friend, named as Anika Went, who believes that the deceased was suffering from personal difficulties and was severely depressed at the time she went missing. Both were working in De Walletjes and shared an apartment at Bloedstraat. Police are not treating the death as suspicious and are not looking for anyone else in relation to this incident.'

Yes, unlikely, he thought. Jellicoe may be many things, but as far as he knew she was not, and never had been working in the Rossa Burt, the red light district of Amsterdam. And it was unlikely she could be depressed. She had too much savoir-faire for that and would not allow herself to be. He had very little idea of what had happened to her after she fled; there was chaos and other priorities to follow up and then the trail had gone cold and it didn't seem to matter anymore. His contacts would have told him immediately if she had resurfaced so close to home. He would get Ben to ask questions in the right places and get to the bottom of this.

For some reason, someone, and he guessed it was Jellicoe, wanted him to believe she was dead. That could simply be so that she no longer wanted to look over her shoulder all the time, or, knowing Jellicoe as he did, it meant that she was after something. He knew Jellicoe very well, so first he had to find out if she was playing games with him and if so, it was fairly obvious why.

It was time to recover the paintings, hidden in a cellar miles away in a small town in Essex, England. Even Jellicoe would never think to look there.

Chapter Eleven

We cleared some space and I laid sheets along one wall to stand the canvasses on. T'Ash brought a claw hammer, a small saw, some scissors and a Stanley knife. We cracked open the crates like it was Christmas morning and I stood the canvasses carefully on the clean sheets along the empty wall of the cellar.

Like Hansel and Gretel caught breaking bits off the gingerbread house, we held hands and slowly stepped away from the wall as though the revelations stacked there would cause it to explode. I was torn between laughing and crying, a heady mixture which threatened to overwhelm me.

'We have our very own National Gallery down here,' said T'Ash quietly. We carried the 13 canvasses carefully upstairs and placed them around the kitchen, silently, reverentially. T'Ash pulled out his notebook and began to make a list.

'So what have we got then? I'm guessing these are your Ma and that Jellicoe woman he painted?' and I nodded.

'She turned up one day when I was quite small and became his model. But I think it was more than that. I think she was his Mistress. Mum hated her and I never really liked her. She smelt funny....'

'Smelt funny?' said T'Ash looking up from his notebook.

'Hmmm,' I said. 'Like she was from somewhere dangerous and I hated her as a child. I think she brought trouble with her.'

'So what have we got?' asked T'Ash

'13 paintings. Of course, these were the pictures he didn't sell, the ones left behind for Mum to take back to England', I said. *For Dr. Felix Van Gelder to deliver to the house in the dead of night.*

The names of the paintings were on labels on the back, with some other marks and gallery stamps. I didn't see any signatures which I could read. The faces of the women were familiar: and there was also a child, a small girl who appeared a few times. I assumed that was me. T'Ash began to make notes as I read out the titles on the backs of the paintings.

'*The Apothecary*,' I said stumbling over the unfamiliar word and then stepping back to look at it. The kitchen was cramped and full of pictures so there wasn't much room to get any distance, but this is what I saw.

It was an interior, with a man, long dark hair, in robes of his profession, leaning over a table mixing compounds. There was a flask and a pair of scales and some weights, like he was weighing his life.

Next was *The Fallen Woman*: a biblical epic. The Man (the same man in nearly all of these pictures, his face obscured, but there was something about the bulk and the set of his shoulders and the long hair, curling at the nape, in which I saw a memory of my father, Max Prins. The man is behind the woman and holds her in a passionate embrace, his face hidden in her neck; she is half naked and has her eyes closed, leaning into him. She looks very like I remember Jellicoe. The background is strewn with visual allegory of corruption, guilt and sin.

Next was *Brother Jude* in which a shadowy figure dressed as a monk stands in the background looking at the artist; it is a self portrait of Max Prins, looking... what exactly? His gaze is directly at the viewer; direct, pleading, asking for help, understanding? Deep sadness gazes at me and moves me.

'These three are all in the style of Dutch Masters. 18th century, I'd say. They look pretty old,' said T'Ash.

'17th Century. Dutch Golden Age.' I said quietly looking at the first three pictures and losing myself in the details.

'Are you sure your Pa painted these?'

'Pretty sure,' I said frowning at the paintings and letting a memory buzz around me, going into that place in my head where I shut out all distractions so that I could feel the answers.

'If he didn't we are sitting on a goldmine. Either that or a lawsuit, depending on if they were looted....' I let him speculate. My mind had already moved on to the next painting.

'Lady's Maid' the label said. Two women: the tall dark haired woman is the Maid, standing behind the fair haired 'Lady' who is seated in splendour on a high backed chair which looks like a throne. The 'Maid' holds a tray with a jug and goblets on it. A mirror on the wall reflects the rest of the room and in the background, a man of some importance sits at a table facing the women and looks clearly at the Maid. His face is blurred as he is a shadowy figure in the mirror. The Maid is looking at the Lady with loathing.

Next to it, in random sequence, is *The Prince Betrayed:* It is an angry painting and the largest of them all; it portrays a dark and brooding scene of a battle with close up gory detail of limbs hacked off, heads rolling, swords thrusting, but the centre of the picture is where the eye is drawn. A shaft of light illuminates a wounded man, clearly the *'Prince'* of the title who wears a gold circle on his head and lies wounded on the ground, supported by another knight. The wounded 'Prince' holds his chest and his eyes roll upwards towards the robed figure of a Monk whose smile is just visible beneath a cowl covering much of his shadowed face. A sword covered in blood has just fallen from the Monk's hand and his other hand is open and covered in blood. This picture disturbed me and I felt nauseous and rushed outside to the privy in time to be sick. When I came back in, T'Ash had finished his list and was making tea.

'You look a bit pale; do you want to go for a lie down?' he asked, but I shook my head and carefully moved the paintings which I had already seen into the hallway to get a better look at those stacked behind.

'I want to see them all,' I said and my voice sounded very small even to me, almost like it was coming from a distance. T'Ash looked uneasy.

'Are you sure it's not upsetting you too much. I mean, it can wait 'til later?'

'They've waited long enough,' I said and turned the next picture to reveal its title.

Maid's Folly was a picture of the same two women in front of a dining table and guests who all looked important. This time, the roles are reversed and the maid is the shorter, rounder blonde woman with the beginnings of a smile on her peasant face. She offers the *Lady* a large platter with a Hogs Head, complete with apple in its mouth. Several of the guests look shocked, whilst the Lady, who is tall and dark, holds a hand to her breast and recoils. It made me smile. Someone was playing games.

Peasants was a picture of a darkened interior with a lighted lamp on the table. Two peasant women looking pale and drawn are peeling vegetables. A little girl sits on the floor of the shabby room and eats the peeling which falls from the table. The fire grate is empty and the women are wrapped in shawls. The pretty little girl is dressed in rags and barefoot. The picture feels cold and bleak and made me sad again. In a departure from the other paintings, this picture looked more like the style of Victorian Realism which I had come across in one of my library books.

The next painting was a surprise; a medium sized canvas tucked away behind the others portrayed a pregnant Jellicoe dressed in 17th century costume, a dress I clearly remembered, smugly holding her huge bump and gazing happily out of the window. A man sits at the table with his back to her, shoulders hunched, smoking, his other hand clenched tight against the table edge. Light from outside casts the shadow of the window across his figure, creating the impression of bars, or prison. The painting is ironically called *'Confinement'*. The detail is stunning and the expressions and body language shout from the canvas.

'Reflection' is a canvas of a woman looking in a large mirror: She is in the same bright sunlit room with flowers on the table. Outside, it is dark and stormy and rain lashes the windows. The mirror reflects the outside storm and not the interior of the room. It is a physical impossibility and an allegorical conceit. The woman looks angry and challenging.

The next painting was another Victorian Realism. It shows a peasant woman in a shawl, outside at night, holding a child in her arms whilst looking over her shoulder, fearful and crying, surrounded by mist, rubble and darkness. I recognise the unmistakeable strong dark face of a young Marianne, although her head is covered by the shawl.

The final three were lined up in the hallway and so I moved them carefully into the front room to get enough light. I finally cracked, and let the tears spill.

A modern painting, in the style of Cezanne I wondered? It was called *'Reclining Nude'* and showed a woman lying on a plum satin bed, naked, arm behind her head looking at the viewer. I am pretty sure she was Jellicoe.

'Beatrix Asleep'; a crib; a sleeping baby and a hand with a distinct ring on the third finger; a signet with a ruby in it, rocks the cradle. It is painted with love and tenderness, the brush stokes caressing the plump pink cheeks of a sleeping infant.

'You still look like that when you sleep,' T'Ash said and he kissed my wet cheek and hugged me close

The final picture, and his magnificent face which I feel as though I have known for a thousand years, stared back at me, looking defeated and in despair. It was clearly a self portrait of Max Prins. Chess pieces spill across the table and the Queen has fallen onto the floor. There is an empty glass and wine stains on the table and the scales and weights of *The Apothecary* mixed in with the chess pieces. He called this one *'Check Mate'*.

In addition to the canvasses, T'Ash had spread the folio of loose sketches and drawings across the front room rug and was looking carefully at them.

We stood in silence again and listened to the rain dripping from the eves and splashing against the window sills. We heard a car go by outside, its tyres hissing on the wet cobbles. I heard my shallow breathing and my heart pounding not with the fear or anxiety which usually made my heart thump; this was excitement. I stuffed a hand in my mouth but couldn't contain the laugh which ripped itself out of me despite the tears, and then I couldn't stop and T'Ash who had also been holding his breath, laughed as well and it was infectious and soon we were both laughing and crying as the canvasses watched aloof all around us.

I went back into the kitchen and pointed to *'Confinement'*.

'That's it. That's what I couldn't remember. Jellicoe had a baby. It was at the end. There was confusion with the liberation and Pa was shot...'

'He was WHAT?'

'He was shot. I'm sure he was. There was blood and shouting and Mum pushing me hard out of the room so I fell and cried and another man, Dr. Felix I think, but I don't remember – he scooped me up and handed me to someone and then there was more screaming and Jellicoe was on the ground and Felix rushed out and an ambulance came and then the soldiers…..' It was a jumble, half remembered, triggered by the image of Jellicoe's swollen belly. I looked up and saw that T'Ash was scribbling away in his notebook. He was writing it down.

'Your Ma will know,' he said quietly. 'You have to ask her.'

'I can't. She gets too upset.'

'You must before she loses her mind completely.'

'She won't . She's getting better.'

'You mean they're doping her up more?'

'No I mean she's calmer.'

'More manageable? Aye, that's what they do. They'll turn her into a cabbage so that she's quiet. But they won't cure her, because by the time they've cut out all of the stuff that's hurting her, this stuff,' he said waving his arm around the canvasses, 'she'll be a vegetable. No memory. No thoughts of her own, no need to think anymore. Calm and safe and almost dead. That's what they've done to my gran in there. It's what they do. They'll operate and take away that bit of her which hurts and rip out her soul.' He was getting agitated.

'No. They are just calming her, making her better.' I was horrified at the thought that the woman from these canvases, young and very much alive, would no longer be able to feel or think or even care very much..

'We have to get her out of there. Bring her home.'

'Oh yes and confront her with this lot? That will really help. You didn't see her, T'Ash. You didn't see her pain and how much she was hurting. She almost died and there was nothing I could do. She's better where she is, for now anyway.'

'So what about this? What about the story it tells?' I was angry now.

'You know what? You can just make it up. Tell your own story, because I don't want to know anymore. Not if it hurts this much. It killed my father and destroyed my mother and I know enough to move on. I want my life T'Ash. I have to live my life not theirs and if that means packing this lot away again and leaving Mum safe where she is … yes SAFE…. and cared for,' my voice was raised as he tried to interrupt me… 'then I will do that and I will go to London and go to Art school and be my own artist, not my pa, and not living with the ghosts as Ma has done. They are all dead.'

'But their echo is still here Scarlett. Their lives mattered. We have to tell their story.'

'Why? There are so many stories from the war. All tragic. All shrouded in mysteries and enigmas. Why is this one any different?'

'Because it is your story and you need to know before you can move on or else it will come back to haunt you.' I threw his notebook across the table at him.

'Then write it. Tell me a story. Tell me what really happened there in that studio because no-one else can tell you if you are right or wrong.'

'But they can. Has it not occurred to you that some of these pictures are modern like your father's own hand and others look like old masters? Are they all his? Did he paint them all?'

'I told you, he painted in the old style. He liked to recreate the old settings. I remember him mixing paints. I remember that, like it was a game; and playing in the studio; it was like a dolls' house; and costumes: he had a rail of costumes and I wanted to dress up as well when I was bigger.' T'Ash was silent. I knew the look which came across his face when he was thinking. He turned and left the room and went back down into the cellar, and I filled the kettle to make tea. I had become very English in my childhood and it was a comforting habit to make tea when things got stressed.

I was pouring tea when he came back into the kitchen carrying the wooden suitcase and laid it on the table. I pulled the table cloth from under it as the dust cascaded onto the old scrubbed wood below.

'Careful,' I said and sneezed.

'Sorry, but this is really important.' It was full of old papers and documents and some photos. 'I think it's in here.'

I rolled my eyes and sipped the tea. 'Good luck with that,' I said.

'No really. Look, here, a bill of sale from a gallery in Geneva; another receipt for the purchase of canvasses.'

'Mum said he was a dealer as well as a painter. That's how he made his money. It's always been hard to make money as a painter.'

'Not if you are as good as he was. Do you realise what this means?' I shrugged and drained my cup and reached for the pot. T'Ash sighed like I was a recalcitrant child at the back of the class. I rubbed my eyes partly from the dust and from exhaustion and emotion.

'Who was buying paintings in Amsterdam in 1943?' he asked me pointedly. I could see where he was going with this and it was all a bit too much. 'Where did the paintings come from?'

'He painted them himself. I was there. I saw him.'

'All of them? You know that he painted all of these and others?'

'Of course there were others. He had to sell them to keep us all. I told you. It was how he earned his money.'

'So. He was a dealer and a painter?' He was pacing the small room and firing off questions like a Barrister in court.

'Yes,' I said stubbornly and folded my arms. He put down the piece of paper he was holding and came around the table and put his arms around me. I refused to respond and remained stubbornly mute and rigid. His tea remained untouched in the cup and a brown skin had formed on the cool surface. He spoke very quietly close to my ear.

'He painted Dutch Masters, or versions of; and who did he sell them to? Who was buying?' He let the question hang. 'And if he didn't paint them himself, if some of those canvases are real, then who did he buy them from? Who was having their precious works of art taken from them?' Put like that, I could see the layers unfold and I could feel the safety of my father's memory cracking wide open.

'Coll –abor –ator....' I chanted and felt the harsh slap from my mother.

'He was either selling looted paintings, probably from Jews, to the Nazis, or, if he painted them himself then he was a forger,' he said like a closing argument.

'Which is worse?' I said hopelessly overwhelmed. 'A collaborator and thief or a forger?'

'So why was he shot?'

'I don't even know for sure that he was.' T'Ash gave me a long look; what Aunt Maude would have called 'an old fashioned look.'

'No maybe he wasn't. Maybe he was killed by Dutch Cheese. But only if they shot the holes in it and missed!' I laughed and so did he although it wasn't remotely funny. There was a silence now which had filled the small room, the suitcase and the paintings absorbing all real life which was suspended somewhere else. 'It's all in here, I think,' and he tapped the lid of the wooden suitcase.

'And Mum's memory?' I said. 'She won't get better now. They are saying she has senile dementia, but she's too young for that, so they don't want to operate because she isn't dangerous. Something called a Lobotomy?'

'I know. They do it to dangerous patients who rant and rave and think they are the Queen of Sheba. But the quiet ones like your mum, like my gran, they'll just let them sit there, lost. So long as they are quiet and eat a bit and go along with what the nurses tell them to do. It's a tragedy. She'll only come home you know if they chop half of her brain out and then she'll be a cabbage,' he said quietly and took my hand.

'Unless we can unravel all this and maybe we can help her?' I said, the upward inflection sounding imploring. He moved closer and kissed my cheek.

'If you want my honest, I think it's a bit late for her, but I think that we need to find out for you. For your sake…'

'Do you think I will end up like her and your Gran? Is that what you're saying?'

'No. Just that it will give you peace and maybe help with the fits… you know, the 'visions'. And don't you want to know anyway?'

Of course I did and I knew that without medication the fits or visions, call them what you like, would not heal of their own accord. And besides, I had a memory of my father; a larger than life picture of a man who loved me and spoilt me and protected me and made me feel safe. I hadn't really felt safe since he was taken away and if my memory of him was false, then I needed to know and not be held in the safe arms of a deceitful childhood. My life would be a lie forever and I could never hope to escape the past.

I crouched beside the painting he made of himself and let out the breath I had been holding in for too long.

'There are clues here as well,' I said quietly and between us we would no doubt be able to create a story from the paperwork and the pictures. But where was the truth and which were the lies?

It was late and T'Ash stayed the night and we lay in the big bed and held each other close and both lay wakeful most of the night watching the changing shadows cross the ceiling as the traffic ceased and the town fell silent and we heard each other's breathing. He moved against me and whispered in my ear.

'I really want you.'

'It's too risky,' I said, moving into him, pressing my body along his length.

'I'll be careful,' he said and rolled on top of me and our intimacy was a great release of the emotion we had both lived through today.

Chapter Twelve

Work today was a bit of a washout except for the new guy, Wilf Brown who was tagged into my section in Records and who is a foreigner although I have no idea where he's from so I guess Brown is a made up or changed surname from something foreign. Happens a lot now and the poor guy can't help where he was born, or who his father is, any more than I can. He speaks prefect English and only a small hint of the foreigner on the *'th's'* which he says a bit like Mickey, my sister's little one says *'De'* instead of *'th'* so it could just be that he's never learned it properly and we are all hoping that Mickey will grow out of it anyway and maybe Wilf just never did and has a grown up speech impediment. I'll ask him if I get the chance. He doesn't speak much though, which I like, so I can get on with thinking up stories and right now, thinking about Scarlett.

Mr. Robinson, head of Records smacked me on the back of the head as he walked by earlier.

'Stop daydreaming Mr. Ash and get on with those papers. I need them before Christmas.' The others sniggered of course and as soon as 'Jammy' Robinson – he would be 'Golly' but we saved that one for the coloured guy who works upstairs in accounts – as soon as Jammy was out of earshot the taunts began.

'So what's her name?'
'Have you done it yet?'
'Course he hasn't, he's a virgin,'
'Bet he hasn't plucked up courage to kiss her yet.'
'*Crockett*' AKA Davey Thomas came over to my desk and said in a loud whisper,
'I can get you French Letters when you're ready,' and carried on past me to the filing cabinets on the back wall.
'Don't be silly, Crocks. He's a left footer. Catholics don't use them things, so I've heard,' replied Rick AKA *Stick* because he was so tall and thin.
'Have you seen her Stick?'
'No one has. She's just another one of his stories.....' and so I got up and dropped a heavy box on Stick's desk and let him cough on the dust.
'Jammy wants these sorted and filed by dinner time,' I said and walked out to the gents, heart pounding and fuming. What did they know about anything? About love especially and about the ties that now bound Scarlett and me? The story we were unraveling bit by bit. What could they possibly know with their smutty talk and their stupid ideas. I had to get away from this job soon. Take Scarlett with me to America where I could be a writer and she would be able to paint and no one would think we were strange.
I sat in the cubicle for a while and calmed meself down with thoughts of escaping and when I came out, Wilf was taking a pee. He didn't say anything as I washed my hands but I caught him looking at me in the mirror. He is older than us lot by about 10 years and we all wondered why he was starting at the bottom in a junior role but there were loads of people in the last ten years who had been denied their education because of the bloody war and were now doing jobs they wouldn't have done if wasn't for Adolf bloody Hitler.

'So got yourself a girl?' he said in his funny accent, but kindly and with a smile. I shrugged and dried my hands on the wet towel which hadn't been changed for a couple of days.

He patted my shoulder as he walked towards the door and said, 'Good for you. I am very pleased for you. You deserve a nice girl in your life,' and he left me standing there wondering how he knew anything at all about my life and why he should care.

Chapter Thirteen
Amsterdam Spring 1956

The breeze stirred the leaves and Jellicoe walked West in the late afternoon, lifting her hand to shield the low angle of the sun from her eyes as she adjusted the brim of her hat to prevent it from blowing away. The leaves swirled randomly and scattered beneath the wheels of passing bicycles tumbling to gain the best advantage.

She caught her reflection in the window of a shop, windblown but fine, holding onto her navy velour hat with the feathers in the side, her curled blond hair neatly holding its own in the wind. The face beneath, pale but strong, the youthful bloom transformed into a confident maturity. Her red coat was buttoned smartly to the top and leather gloves covered her manicured hands. Strong expensive navy shoes with matching handbag completed her outfit. She clutched the bag closer and smiled to herself. A well healed modern Dutch housewife out shopping on a windy afternoon. Why would anyone suspect that she carried a gun in her Dior handbag? But then, they didn't know that she going to meet Felix.

Felix Van Gelder left his club and walked east away from the setting sun, his long shadow mimicking his confident gait. His umbrella, little use in this wind, rolled up as a walking cane to add length to his already long stride.

Ben had done his job well, he thought as he squared his shoulders into the blustery conditions. He was heading for Maison De Bonneterie where he knew that Jellicoe would take tea in the afternoon.

She was renting a house a stone's throw from him just off the Prinsengracht posing as a wealthy war widow of which there was no shortage these days, but he wanted to know more. Where had she been? Where was her child, born in the chaos of the liberation? Why did she run? And most importantly, why did she want him to think she was dead?

Jellicoe walked up the monumental staircase to the first floor and waited to be shown to a table she had reserved in the window where she would take tea.

'I am expecting a guest,' she said to the waiter.

'Of course Mrs. Van Der Meer. Tea for two?'

'That will be lovely. He will be here shortly.' Felix would be surprised that she was expecting him. Surprised that she too had surveillance and could trace him and find things out. There was only one piece of information missing and she would, no doubt persuade him to tell her where the pictures were this afternoon.

She had a good hand to play. She knew a lot about his activities during the war and she also knew that he would not like some of it revealed now that he was a respected member of the Netherlands Institute for Scientific Research.

As always, she lit a cigarette and then took a paperback from her handbag. It was an American writer called Raymond Chandler and she loved his sparse style and quick, tight plots, populated with *femmes fatale*s and brisk dialogue. To a casual onlooker, it appeared that she was simply reading and smoking but she had in fact not seen a single word of the page in front of her. Her eyes though lowered were lost in thought and she was remembering why she had been so vulnerable to Felix's charm.

They had met at a party in a Swiss house in the summer of '39, and she fell for his easy charm and charisma. She also detected in him silent and dangerous depths and that was exciting. He was a Doctor at a private clinic and spent his time between Holland and Switzerland, he was fluent in five languages, and in his spare time, he was an art collector and occasional dealer.

He was in the drawing room of the house which belonged to a Swiss Banker named Yves Giraud, standing in front of a large black Art Nouveau fireplace admiring a portrait of a 17th century nobleman, reputedly a Giraud ancestor. Yves Giraud had invited Felix for his opinion on the painting. Jellicoe sidled up beside him, glass in hand and looked at the painting.

'A bit of a clash of style there,' she said, sipping her vodka martini.

'Hmm', he said, not taking his eyes off the painting and then seemed to notice her.

'The Art Nouveau fireplace and the Old Master painting. Most houses these days, it's the other way round. I love the way the Swiss are always so unconventional,' she said. He laughed.

'Yes. Very good. I hadn't thought of it like that. Felix Van Gelder,' he said holding out his hand.

'Jellicoe Du Pont,' she said, instinctively using a false surname, just to tease, but also because she could. Because it didn't matter.

'Du Pont? But I detect a Dutch accent.' They were speaking French. She smiled.

'How very observant of you and how remiss of me to let it show.' He smiled and indicated that they should sit and be better acquainted. By the end of the evening, they left together having discussed Art, Politics and the possible outcomes to a Nazi invasion of Holland. By next morning, they were even better acquainted having made love all night in Felix's hotel and travelled back to Holland together.

Felix paused on Rokin and lit a cigarette in a doorway. It was a good opportunity to check if he had been followed. He stood for a few minutes, waiting, smoking, watching a barge glide sluggishly along the grey canal in front of him and decided that the rear entrance to the store would give him greater advantage. She didn't know he was coming and the added element of surprise would give him precious moments to assess her. If she saw him approach she could choose to escape or to compose herself and invent a story. Either would give her the advantage.

He walked down the alley beside the store and in through the kitchen entrance. Interesting that she should take tea here when it had been such an important part of his network a decade or so earlier. Scores of Jewish staff members had died during the Occupation, but he still knew people here and that was how he had traced her so easily.

Pieter the waiter smiled as he saw Felix slip into the kitchen and Felix removed his hat, saying nothing.

'Table four in the window,' Pieter said and Felix replied with a slight incline of the head and slipped away almost unnoticed by the other kitchen staff who looked up momentarily bewildered by the presence of a gentleman in the kitchen and then looked away, knowing better than to ask questions. A lovers tryst no doubt with Pieter as facilitator.

Jellicoe felt a hand firmly grip her shoulder and before she could leap to her feet, he was there beside her, holding her firmly in her seat, his mouth stretched into a rictus which could be mistaken for a smile if you didn't know Felix.

'How lovely to see you again,' he said loudly for the benefit of fellow diners,' and bent as though to peck her cheek, but his hand still gripped her shoulder. She tried to compose her face and not wince under the pressure. His breath smelt of mint and tobacco and the past and she felt the handbag slide from her lap into his free hand. She made to grab for it but he swiftly released her shoulder and swung around to sit in the seat facing her, taking her ungloved hands in to his still gloved ones and the bag had vanished from sight.

She looked shocked, he noticed. She had been expecting him, that was clear as the table was laid for two; but she had been watching the front door and window, as he expected, and now she looked thwarted rather than surprised. He glanced around the room still holding her hands and noticed the man by the door hunched into his shabby grey overcoat, trilby hat perched on the table, a coffee cup on the table in front of him. He was reading The Daily Post open at page 6 with the notice about Jellicoe's death facing out. He nodded towards Felix without appearing to look up from his newspaper.

Gently, a smile still pasted on his face, Felix released her hands and slipped something into his overcoat pocket. He then removed his gloves and lay them beside his hat on the table.

'You look better than I was expecting, considering your recent 'accident',' he said with his usual sardonic elegance. She glared back at him as Pieter approached the table carrying a tea tray set for two. 'How kind of you to order for us both. I wasn't sure if I had remembered to confirm I was coming?'

'Darling, I was certain you would be here. A little bird told me.' He twitched his mouth in a gesture which could have been the start of a smile, but he knew never to drop his guard to smile at a cobra, particularly one who carries a gun in her Dior handbag. He was pleased that his instincts were as strong as ever and not too rusty, even if these skills had had little use since the war.

'What do you want, Jellicoe?' he asked as Pieter left the table. She lit another cigarette and the tea tray lay like a chasm between them.

'I think you know that.'

'Tell me,' he said, not taking his gaze from her face. She was older, certainly but still a remarkable looking woman. The round softness of her youth had given way to a sculpted tighter face, leaner and more convincing. The wide apart hazel eyes seemed darker and the hair beneath her hat was shorter and curled. Her make-up was refined and sensuous; pale pink lips and a hint of blush was all it took. The features had changed little, but in the attitude beneath them, he read anger, greed and determination. She took a long drag on the cigarette and made little attempt to blow the smoke away. She was not going to play nicely. 'I thought you had died; drowned in the canal as a common prostitute.' She snorted and a flash of anger momentarily warned him. She looked at him candidly.

'Then why did you bother to look for me if you believed I was dead?'

'Hmm. Let me see.' He began to rattle the cups onto the saucers and made ready to pour tea. 'You disappear from the Nuns Home with the baby you were going to have adopted, without trace for 13 years, and then you show up as a prostitute in the docks area and pretend that you have died in a way which will get published as a notice in the paper and drawn to my attention.... Milk or lemon?' She ground her cigarette aggressively into the ashtray.

'Why were you so sure it was fake?'

'Because I know you well, Jellicoe. I vetted you. I worked with you. I watched every nuance of every expression in that face which you turned so charmingly on Max. I knew every thought in your head, how you would manipulate a situation to your advantage, work both sides, play for yourself. I wasn't surprised that you disappeared when the child was born, but I was surprised that you took her with you. I didn't see you as a natural mother.' She shrugged. 'Johanna. A pretty name,' he said and she looked startled that he knew so much. She blanked her face to give little away. 'Where is she?' he asked, quietly, dropping lumps of sugar from the tongs into each tea cup. A fleeting moment of fear crossed her face and then she regained her neutral composure.

'Safe,' she said, taking the cup he offered with two hands so he couldn't see them shaking. In the intervening years since she had been 'away' she had forgotten his power and his ability to control the situation. She had grown soft in comparison, although still determined. He shrugged. 'She is of no consequence at the moment. So. Why are you back now?'

She sipped the scalding tea and put the cup back onto its saucer, composure restored.

'I want the paintings, Felix. The ones Max left in his studio. I know that you have them and I know their value.' He nodded sagely as though this was what he expected.

'So. The paintings. Hmmm.. You *assume* I have them. You *assume* they are valuable and so you have added up *assumptions* and for reasons of which you have not yet enlightened me, you expect me to hand over Max's legacy? Are you forgetting he has a wife and daughter?' She slammed her hand on the table and the cups rattled in the saucers. The sugar tongs danced out of the bowl and landed on the floor and there was a temporary lull in the conversation level around them. She didn't seem to care. Pieter came over and quietly picked up the silver tongs and replaced them with a pair from his apron pocket and moved swiftly away. Over by the door, the man in the grey overcoat spilled his coffee on the table thus diverting Pieter and the customer's attention from 'Table Four'.

'How could I forget? Are you forgetting he has another daughter who needs to be provided for?'

'And a former mistress with expensive tastes,' he said eying her in a way which was rude by any standards and below the belt for a gentleman such as Felix. It wasn't wasted on her.

'Whatever I did, I did it because you asked and I thought it was going to help.'

'Until you switched sides.'

'I took risks for you Felix. It was a dangerous time.'

'Where have you been.'

'None of your bloody business. Where are the pictures?'

'Long gone,'

'I will find them.'

He smiled. 'I doubt it.'

'Where's Marianne? Back in the UK I guess. I can find her as well.'

'So why didn't you? Why the subterfuge?'

'I needed to test you. See if you still wanted to kill me.' He patted his overcoat pocket where her gun sat safely out of her reach and raised an eyebrow. He leaned in close.

'No longer my style. The war is over Jellicoe.' She leaned in to him.

'But the spoils have not yet been divided, Felix, and I know a great deal about what you did and how. Your methods were dubious even in war, and there are still those who want reparation.'

'You would incriminate yourself,' he shrugged.

'I was under duress, pregnant and in love; you forced me.'

'You would still go to prison.'

She shrugged. 'It would be worth it to see Johanna a wealthy woman and secure for life.'

He stared into her eyes and saw real love and realized that for the first time in her selfish life, she cared more about someone else. It was a powerful motivator and she had handed him a trump card.

Chapter Fourteen

Mum came home again in June, as the roses bloomed and wind blew from the West and took with it the freedom of my life with T'Ash. I became a full time nurse for her and we lived on her small pensions and with state help. T'Ash and I had put the canvasses back into the cellar in the certain knowledge that Mum would not venture down there. She was totally passive and happy to sit and listen to the wireless in the evenings; to read and knit during the day and to help prepare vegetables, butter bread and other small tasks.

I signed up for drawing classes for the Summer term at Evening School and although it wasn't stimulating or challenging, it was something to do out of the house with other people. I would meet T'Ash afterwards – he was doing a writing course – and we would go to the Three Crowns and have a drink and hold hands.

Mum had met T'Ash and he came for a chaste Tea on Sundays when he wasn't visiting his Gran in Severalls, after going to Mass and having Sunday dinner with his parents. Mum was pleased that I was 'courting' and I would see her gazing fondly at me with damp eyes as she sighed and asked when I was seeing Tarron again.

'Wednesday night,' I said for the umpteenth time. She knew that but she would ask over and over. 'At the Evening School.'

'Yes of course. Is he coming for tea?'

'Yes. Sunday, Mum.'

'What day is it?' and so it went, night after night until I was almost screaming for release.

T'Ash felt equally trapped and we made a plan to escape to the chalet in Wrabness for the occasional Saturday night.

'Dad'll be drunk and won't know I'm not home and Ma won't make a fuss. What about you?'

'I'll put Mum to bed and make sure she's had her medication and she'll sleep through the night.' I was reckless with anticipation.

He had 'borrowed' the suitcase full of papers but there was an unspoken agreement that we didn't talk about it again. Not for a while and not in the few precious hours we snatched together. We talked instead about the future, about where we would go and what we would do.

'We'll have to be back early,' he promised, and so we found ourselves, at the train station early on Sunday Morning, T'Ash kissing me goodbye and sprinting home to change for Church and me setting off briskly up North Hill and slipping in through the back door before Mum woke up.

We were in the Three Crowns one Wednesday and T'Ash looked distracted.

'I have to tell you something. It's important.' I noticed that his face was pale and he was wringing his hands in a way he never did. I was alarmed. I had never seen T'Ash troubled like this. 'My Da tried to throw me out of the house last week, after I stayed with you all night. He was not impressed.'

'What happened?'

'He said I couldn't treat the place like a hotel and that if I was going to go out.... well he used words I can't tell you... but if I was going to live that kind of 'debauched' life then I could do it somewhere else. He wanted to know where I'd stayed.'

'What about your Mum?'

'She stepped in and said I had a right to my own life and that it was my home and I wasn't going anywhere.' His voice was full of pain and anxiety.

'What happened?' I asked again, laying a hand gently on his.

'He was drunk. He hit out and hit her, so ...I hit him.' He looked at me in pain as though he had committed patricide. 'I didn't want to hurt him. I didn't mean it. But Mum.... well she's put up with it for too long and ... she shouldn't have to and I promised her I'd get her away from him and then we had a letter from Kathleen in America; in a place called Brooklyn in New York, and .... I promised Mum we would go there and get right away.... and then I thought about you.... well about us....and I don't want to leave you.'

'So are you going to America?' I was in shock.

'Only if you come as well...' The enormity of the choice hit me like a cold slap in the pit of my belly and I knew with certainty that I couldn't just go.

'I have to stay here. I have to look after Mum. I want to go to Art School and be an artist.... and anyway, your Mum will be uncomfortable with our...relationship...'

'I thought about that,' he said excitedly. 'We'll get married. Mum will love you...'

'I'm not Catholic. I thought that mattered.' I said coldly trying to put some distance between this mad scheme which was running out of control and my racing heart which saw him slipping away. He waved a hand in the air as though it was nothing.

'You can convert. It's not hard. People do it all the time. The church loves converts,' and he stopped when he saw the set determination of my face. 'What's the matter? I can arrange it all. By the time we have the papers to go to America we can be married and ... well maybe your Mum can follow us afterwards. When she's well enough...' and he petered out and I saw the excitement flop out of him. 'I've done it wrong, haven't I? I should have proposed to you and got a ring and done it properly. I'm so sorry. I just rushed in and got carried away with myself, but I can't stand living in that house for any longer than I have to. And I can't leave Ma there with him. I just can't.'

I let the silence sit for a while, but inside I was churned up. There was no way I was going to 'convert'. From what? I didn't even believe in God so why would I become Catholic for the sake of appearances and to keep the paperwork in order? I didn't believe in any of it. My belief was in my new passion which was my painting and I was going to pursue that. I was going to Art School. But I didn't want him to leave. I loved T'Ash as I had never loved anyone – well, since my father, and that was so long ago, I held only the faintest memory. Was it real? Was he the giant I felt deep in my heart, that I clung to in my desolation? I didn't really know, but whilst T'Ash was here I felt safe again and warm inside, but his scheme was all about him. It made no mention of my situation. It seemed like I had to follow him or... what? Maybe he could follow me?

'You could move in with us,' I said quietly. 'You could rent Aunt Maude's room for a while, until Mum is better and then we could go to London. That's where the Art Schools are.' He was shocked.

'I can't ask you to live in sin. It's not right and Ma would be horrified. But we could get married and they have Art Schools in America and Kathleen will get me a job with her husband Jimmy in the hotel where he works and maybe your Ma can come out later when she's really better?'

I just stared at him in disbelief. Deep down, I knew that I would never go to America but I couldn't say it there and then because it would mean the end for us. We would be finished and he would go and I would be bereft and left here with Mum; looking after her, maybe in one of the new Council houses in Shrub End, and never getting to start my life. It was all too much to think about but I had to be practical.

'When are you going?' I asked coldly, moving my hand away before he could reach out and touch me.

He shrugged. 'Mum wrote back to Kathleen and said she will come next year when she has saved enough. I've got the forms for our passports and we must register with the Embassy for emigration, but it's not confirmed yet. I don't want to leave you,' and he looked at me with desolation in his eyes and I felt the tears well up and spill down my cheeks and when we parted that evening, we clung together although we had never felt so far apart.

T'Ash moved into Aunt Maude's old room as a 'lodger' when things at home had got much worse for him. His rent money helped and of course, we could be together when Mum took herself to bed early and slept the sleep of the living dead. But I knew that the clock was ticking for us. The applications were at the Embassy and Kathleen had promised money to help with their fares. It was only a matter of time. T'Ash went home to see his mum after work every night 'to check for bruises,' he said. 'If he lays a finger on her, I swear I'll kill him,' and I let him rant and buried the anxious pain which threatened to rise up and swamp our snatched happiness.

Time hung heavy and T'Ash reported that the paperwork for the emigration was slow; his Ma was less eager to go now that things had settled down and he promised me that on my 21st we would get married and then go to America together because in his fantasy world, my mum would be well by then and I would be free of parental consent. I think we talked like this because it all seemed so far away that there was little reality in our future plans and we were content to rumble along quietly as we were.

Chapter Fifteen

Mum seemed to be getting better and I decided that I could get a part time job. It would help me to save for an uncertain future; whatever T'Ash's plans, I had a vague notion of my own. By the end of June, I was taken on by The George Hotel as a receptionist, working evenings and the occasional weekend. T'Ash was able to keep an eye on Mum in the evenings and I had days free to take care of her. It restricted our time together, but it gave me some independent life again.

It had been a scorching day a few weeks after I had started which led to a wet summer night, and the roll of thunder threw up the next landmine. It had been slow all evening and we were waiting for the last guest to check in.

'He was due in earlier, but the Ferry's delayed. Bit stormy out at sea apparently. That's what you get when it rains on St. Swithin's day. But I just had a call from Barbara in Harwich to say it's docked and the train's on its way. Should be here in half an hour. I've put him in a single. Top floor. Room 204,' said Janet, desk supervisor, as she put on her coat and handed over to me for the evening shift. 'He's a Doctor something or other….. Don't know if he speaks English, but probably, they all do don't they, the Dutch?' I smiled inwardly and tried to remember a few word:

'Hello. Welcome to The George....' *'Hello. Onthaal aan George....'*

'How long is he staying?' I asked.

'Hasn't confirmed. Couple of nights maybe, then on to London; back next week for one night. That's what I was told by Kathy in reservations. So just keep the booking open, but you could ask him when he checks in.'

'In English,' I said. 'My Dutch is a bit rusty!'

'Mine too. None existent. I'm off. Have fun. You might as well leave after he checks in. John is on nights and he can take care of everything else. It's a wet night, but I've still got plans!' and she pulled an umbrella from 'lost property' and headed out into a summer storm.

The guest arrived at 9.30 with the twilight. He was a middle aged man in a smart grey Mackintosh, removing a fedora hat to reveal a good head of steel grey hair and a chiseled face, still handsome with the unmistakable look of an educated European. The sort of well heeled customer we expected at The George.

'Hello. Onthaal aan George....' I said and was greeted by a beaming smile and a stream of incomprehensible Dutch. I held my hands up.

'Sorry I'm a bit rusty! *Spreekt u het Engels*? Do you speak English?'

'Of course,' he said perfectly accented and his smile wrinkled the corners of his eyes and narrowed slightly.

'A young English woman who speaks Dutch. How unusual. Where did you learn?'

'Oh, I was born there, but I've lived here all my life. My father was Dutch. I grew up speaking only English I'm afraid.' He shrugged.

'Why not? The whole world does,' and he held out his hand. 'Dr. Felix Van Gelder,' he said and I froze to the spot. My heart missed several beats and my hand rushed to my throat, a protective gesture, as I looked at the hand written card in front of me for confirmation. I hadn't thought to check his name. How many Dutch guests were we expecting tonight anyway? I managed to compose myself and take his hand.

'*Onthaal aan George,*' I said and my voice was little above a whisper. He shook my hand firmly and held it a moment too long and his eyes never left my face. I handed him a registration card so that I could hide my confusion.

'Do you know how long you will be staying?' I asked and tried to make my voice as normal as possible. His gaze lifted from the paper he was signing with his gold fountain pen, and I felt his eyes bore through me as though he could read me in English or Dutch or any other language.

'Tonight. Possibly tomorrow but I will know in the morning. I hope to conclude my business in Colchester and travel up to London. I will be back next week before I take the ferry home.' He was very still and his voice was low and my hands trembled as I took the card from him and reached behind for the key to room 204.

'John will take your bags to your room, Dr. Van Gelder,' I said and was proud of the steadiness of my voice, but my shaking hand betrayed me as I handed him the key.

'Thank you, Miss..?' and he held onto my hand until I supplied a name. My mind was racing. He would know the name Prins and I needed to play for time. Talk to T'Ash. Warn Mum? *Beatrix Prins…Betty Quinn….*

'Scarlett. Scarlett Ash,' I said loud and clear and he released my hand, nodded politely and turned for the stairs.

By now it was gone 10.00 anyway and almost my leaving time, and I ran home without regard for the rain. I crashed through the front door, dripping wet and found Mum and T'Ash huddled together in the parlour, well past Mum's bed time. They were playing cribbage and both looked up, startled as though they weren't expecting me.

'You're early, *Beatrix*' said T'Ash running a hand through his hair which had grown longer in recent months and there was definitely a smile in his voice, where my real name sounded unfamiliar.

'I finished early,' I said, looking from one to the other perplexed. Mum looked totally well again. 'What are you doing?'

'Oh Tarron is just showing me how to play cards. I'd forgotten you see. I used to play with your Grandpa before the war, before I went to Holland,' and her voice sounded wistful and trailed away. She looked up at me innocently, like a child discovering new toys. 'We were having a lovely chat about the old days.' I glared at T'Ash.

'Is this wise?' I said emphatically.

'Your ma was telling me about you as a little girl. I can never hear enough stories about you. Beatrix has a lovely ring to it,' he said and leapt to his feet, planting a brief kiss on my wet cheek. 'But look at you all soaked through. Go get out of them wet things. I'll put the kettle on. He turned to Ma and lowered his voice to a gentle sing song which you would use for infants, or invalids or the terminally insane.

'I'm going to put the kettle on, Ma Quinn. Would you manage a cup of tea now?'

'Oh yes, thank you Tarron. I'd love one,' and she turned her attention back to her hand of cards as though I wasn't there, counted on her fingers, laid a card on the table and moved the pegs randomly around the cribbage board and smiled to herself. 'That's got you,' she said to her invisible partner. I followed T'Ash down the dark hallway into the kitchen.

'What are you doing, talking about the 'old days?' She's not well enough. It might trigger a relapse.' He busied himself getting the tea things out and laying a tray.

'Where d'ya keep that tea cosy thing? The blue knitted one. I like that one,' and he was rummaging in the cabinet and drawers and the cupboard built into the wall.

'T'Ash. Listen,' I said, my voice more shrill than I wanted it to be. 'Listen to me. Dr. Felix turned up at the hotel.' It had the desired effect. He put the tea pot he was warming back on the hob and let the kettle whistle until I reached across him and turned it off.

'Dr. Felix?' he said.

'Dr. Felix Van Gelder. He was a friend of Mum's during the war. He brought us back here...'

'Yes yes I know who Felix is,' he said, and turned back to ladling tea leaves into the warmed pot. He was hiding something, I could tell by the way his eyes looked sideways and he didn't make direct contact. 'Anyways, you go and get out of them wet things and I'll have the tea ready...' I moved closer and turned his face to mine and made him look at me.

'Tell me,' I said quietly.

'Ok. I've been reading the stuff in the suitcase and his name kept cropping up so I just asked your Ma and she told me...'

'You asked Ma? How could you? She is so fragile...'

'Yes and no, Bea.'

'Scarlett,' I said defiantly and he took hold of my shoulders and pulled me to him.

'It's time for some truth,' he said. 'I know a lot more about your story now and I was going to wait to share it with you. Your Ma, well her mind is forgetful but only the recent stuff. She can't remember what she had for dinner but she remembers the war like it was still happening. Maybe for her it still is and that is part of the problem. We need to help her to get out of that trap and the only way is to talk to her about it. To let her talk and to remember.'

'No,' I shouted pulling away from him. 'No. She doesn't need to remember it all. They told me at the hospital. She needs to forget. She needs the medication so she won't dwell on it all the time and let it eat her up inside. She needs to be calm and looked after,' and I brushed the wet hair from my face and realized I was shivering. T'Ash was stirring the tea and pointed the spoon at me.

'They are wrong. I know they are. They turned my gran into a cabbage with their medication and their *never-talk-about- it- all and don't- let-her-remember-because-it-will-upset-her*, and she may as well be dead. Your Ma has a chance and through playing cards with her and very gentle chatter, she is coming to terms with things. It's a struggle and she may relapse a bit but at least she will be alive. Are you sure it's not your fear of what you might learn that makes you not want to know?' and his face was flushed and he was really angry. But not half so much as I was.

'My fear? What do you know about that? It's nothing to do with that. I am protecting her, that's all. That's what we have to do. And are you sure that it's not just that you want a good story out of his for your precious novel? What's your motivation T'Ash? And more importantly, what's your REAL name if we are going for the truth?'

'Alfie. Alfred Tarron Ash,' but it wasn't T'Ash who spoke. It was my mother's voice from the doorway. 'I heard raised voices. Everything alright? Shall I take the tea through?' and she was as well and as sane as I had ever known her as she took the tray, a little shakily, and walked steadily back down the dark hall to the parlour. T'Ash threw down the tea cloth and glared at me.

'So now you know. No big secret. I told her my name simply because she asked me. It was all part of a conversation, you know, asking questions and listening to answers and just telling it as it is...' and he marched past me to steady Mum in the hallway and take the tray from her.

I dried my hair roughly with a towel and brushed it through and put on my long white cotton nightgown and yellow dressing gown, a gift from Aunt Maude when I was younger, brought too big so it would fit me forever.

My life was happening in multiples again. Nothing happens and then several things in one evening. Was T'Ash right about Mum getting better by talking about it? Was it really me who didn't want to know? And what should I do about Dr. Van Gelder?

When I came back downstairs the game was drawing to an end and T'Ash was declaring Mum the undisputed victor and she beamed like a child, shuffling the pack with a dexterity I didn't know she had. So much I didn't know, but I needed some time alone with T'Ash to talk about Felix.

'You look so much better Mum but you mustn't tire yourself.'

'I'm not tired love. I feel much better. It's a shame we had to hand our wireless in to the Germans though. I'd have liked some music, but I think your Pa has one hidden away somewhere. We could get Radio Oranje and the news in Dutch?' And she looked at us and realised that it wasn't quite right and her confusion was painful. I threw a hard glance at T'Ash who was rubbing his hand across his face.

'Now Ma Quinn, you know that's a bit confused don't you? That's all over and the Germans have gone. You're in England now and Beatrix is all grown up.' She looked at me, her eyes huge in her gaunt face and I saw that tears swam there.

'My baby. Safe. That's all that mattered. Too many babies lost...' and she looked bewildered again. It was too painful for me to witness.

'Look what you've done,' I hissed at T'Ash as I crossed the room and crouched beside her chair to hug her.

'There was no food left you know. It was hard to get food to keep you alive. And it was so cold. I never thought we'd get out alive.'

'We did. We're here. It's all over. It's in the past.' She looked at me like I had slapped her.

'Oh no love. It'll never be over. So many friends who didn't make it. Thank God for Felix....' T'Ash and I exchanged anxious glances. Had she heard us in the kitchen?

'Beatrix has something to tell you about Felix,' said T'Ash defiantly and glared harshly back at me. Mum looked up expectantly.

'Has he got your Pa's medication, only it wasn't my fault. I didn't know he couldn't eat those things and she did it on purpose. He took her baby away you know...'

'Whose baby Ma?' I asked, greedy for information.

'She was a whore. She had no right to be there. But we had to help her, me and Felix. She had her baby and Felix took it away. A lovely little girl. Johanna, I called her, but I couldn't keep her. I had to look after you and we had to leave, and your Pa.....' She looked at us horrified at the memory which was running in her mind and then her eyes clouded over and she became vacant again like the door had slammed shut against the pain. She stood up slowly and shuffled to the door and headed for the stairs and I had to steady her and help her to climb. She should have had Aunt Maude's room downstairs but she would never sleep in the room in which her sister had died.

'That's it, nice and slowly. We've tired you out playing cards,' I said gently.

'Oh yes. I always could beat your Grandpa and I still can....' I gave her her medication and she was as gentle and compliant as a child and I put her to bed, stoked her hair away from her eyes and made a note that I would wash her hair and trim it neatly tomorrow, if she was well enough. If Dr. Felix didn't turn up, or maybe in case Dr. Felix did turn up. I turned off the lamp and saw T'Ash silhouetted in the doorway, leaning one hand on the door jamb and gazing forlornly at us.

'She'll be ok will she?' he asked.

'Yes,' I snapped. 'I gave her her medication,' and I brushed past him toward my own room. He grabbed my arm.

'We have to talk about Dr. Van Gelder. I am not sure your Ma should see him....'

'Oh, that's good of you to admit,' I hissed, whispering so as not to disturb her. He held his hands up defensively.

'I know, I know, but I still think I'm right. Listen, when It's just the two of us and we are playing – she can't remember the rules by the way so it's a bit one sided – but when it's just us two and we chat, it's no big stress for her to remember the little things, not the really tough stuff, that'll come later, but then with you....'

'Oh so it's my fault is it?' He hushed me and took my arm and steered me in to my room and shut the door. He flopped on to the bed and patted the mattress beside him.

'Come and sit down. You must be shattered. I didn't mean it's your fault like you're doing something wrong. I just mean that she sees you so differently – she remembers the struggle of keeping you safe; the heartache; your Pa... and with me, it's different don't you see? I'm not involved emotionally. She can just talk about it or not, and it doesn't matter. I keep playing cards and let her move the pegs about in some random order and count her scores in her own unique way and she'll just say things and I'll respond and ask a gentle question.... and she's ok.'

'But she's not better and you are pretending she is and it's like the Mad Hatters tea party,' I said exasperated.

'But you saw for yourself how much better she was tonight.'

'Until I turned up and ruined it,' I said harshly. He took my hand.

'You didn't ruin anything. Maybe she'll be able to talk with you in a while, when she's stronger.'

'But not to Dr. Van Gelder?'

'No. When I saw how she was with you.... I think it'll be worse with him. No. We have to stop him from coming here. That could set us back to square one.'

'So what do we do? He knows where we live. He brought us here. In fact, I think he may have recognised me, but he didn't say anything, just looked a bit suspiciously,' and I told him of the encounter.

'Scarlett Ash. I like it. Has a ring to it.... but seriously, why didn't you tell him who you are? He must be here to see your Ma and you.'

'I don't know. I was taken by surprise. I didn't know what to do,'

'So you instinctively lied?' I opened my mouth to reply and couldn't. I was too tired. 'I played for time,' I said.

'Ok. Do you want to see him?'

'I have to if I'm working at the hotel.'

'I mean, does Beatrix Prins want to see him?' and my name sounded like a song on his lips. I shrugged. Of course I should talk to him. He would know things that the wooden suitcase would take years to uncover. I had to see him.

Chapter Sixteen

Next morning, T'Ash and I strolled hand in hand into the George Hotel breakfast room and saw Felix sitting at a table alone, reading the Times and finishing his coffee.

His face was long and lean, his hair thick and grey and trimmed very neatly and he wore round glasses on the end of his nose which gave him the air of an intellectual. His long legs were crossed as he sat sideways at the table and leant across to stub out his cigarette in the ashtray. I took a deep breath and approached the table with T'Ash a few steps behind. Millie who was on breakfast duty intercepted me.

'Erm, can I help? Oh, it's you, Scarlett. I didn't know you were on duty this morning.'

'I'm not,' I said. 'I need to speak to Dr. Van Gelder,' He looked up at the sound of his name and his face closed to give nothing away. He folded his paper without taking his eyes off me and placed it carefully besides his cup.

'Erm, well, I'm not sure you're allowed in the breakfast salon,' said Millie, her flat Northern vowels betraying the veneer of 'posh' she was trying to portray. Felix stood up.

'Miss Ash. How lovely to see you again. Would you join me for coffee?' He looked at a very flustered Millie who was ringing her hands at the lack of propriety. Staff didn't join guests at their table.

'Shall we adjourn to the lounge?' I said, as it was a public space and anyone, even I, could come in for coffee if I could afford it and if I so desired. He cracked a small smile.

'Coffee for ...' he looked up and saw T'Ash.

'Alfred Tarron,' I said, thinking quickly and making a cursory introduction. 'Dr. Van Gelder.' I didn't want Felix to think I was married to T'Ash. He raised an eyebrow in a face which I guessed was trained to give little away.

'I can't stop, I have to go to work. Nice to meet you Dr. Van Gelder,' and they shook hands. Felix turned to Millie

'Coffee for two then, in the lounge please,' he requested politely and her lip quivered as though I had bested her. It was a small gesture but he noticed. 'Miss Ash and I are related,' he said quietly moving closer to her so that T'Ash wouldn't hear, and she breathed a sigh of relief as propriety was not breached.

He knew, I thought as I led the way into the lounge, he knows who I am. T'Ash took my arm as we reached the door of the lounge.

'I've got to go. Will you be ok?' I raised my eyes in a gesture of *'of course I'll be ok. What do you think is going to happen in the sedate lounge of the George Hotel at 8.30 in the morning with a perfect European gentleman and Doctor. Unless he has a gun.'* Of course I would be ok. At least physically. I had no idea what I was going to say to him and emotionally I was in turmoil.

We settled in wing back armchairs by the open fire grate, full of fresh flowers for the summer months, and he steepled his fingers and removed his spectacles.

'Miss Ash,' he said, quietly. 'Scarlett...' it was a question, an accusation and challenge all in one. 'What a very colourful name,' and he turned his gaze directly on me. I blushed and looked down at the patterned red and blue and gold carpet which I had not really noticed before. But then, I had never sat in the lounge before with a predator from my parent's past.

The coffee arrived, Millie looking at me with disdain and made a point of addressing Dr. Van Gelder directly.

'Will that be all Sir,' she said, her posh voice polished to perfection.

'Thank you,' was all he said with a slight incline of the head and then a flicker of a smile cracked his solemn face and he turned back to me.

'You must be used to these English hierarchies,' he said. 'I think we have offended her sense of propriety,' and when I looked up his gaze was kind and he was almost smiling properly. 'So, what is it you wish to talk to me about?' and he expertly poured coffee, sipped it and winced. 'I must get used to drinking tea in England. The coffee is terrible even in the best places.' I didn't really notice. I hardly ever drank it but I said nothing. The small talk was killing me. I didn't touch my cup.

'Beatrix Prins,' I blurted. 'That's how you will remember me,' and I looked directly at him. The light which flooded his face transformed him and I realised that his guard was thoroughly breached. I thought he was going to jump to his feet and hug me but Millie may have thrown us out so he reached across and took my hand in his and I realised that for a moment he couldn't speak. Then he regained some of his earlier composure and sat back in his chair.

'I was almost certain,' he said chastising himself. 'I can't trust my instincts as much as I once could and I thought that maybe it was just the fanciful wish of an old man, but it is truly you? After all these years? I am so glad to see you so well...' and the emotion in his voice touched me and I felt the tension flood out of me and I was laughing out loud, not caring what Millie or any of the others might think. Several of the early staff, obviously alerted by Millie of the scandal of a member of staff in the lounge with a guest, had peered round the open door to see for themselves. I no longer cared, even if I got the sack, meeting Dr. Felix was like a door had opened and there was only joy and light behind it.

'So why the subterfuge and false name?'

'Oh, I was just, erm, taken by surprise,' and I explained that Mum and me had reverted to my mother's maiden name, Quinn, so as not to appear 'foreign' in post war England. He smiled and inclined his head in acknowledgement.

'And how is your mother?' he said sipping the coffee. I paused. I didn't know what to say.

'That's why I'm here. When I realised last night who you are, I felt certain that you would come to the house,' he nodded and replaced his cup on the saucer.

'How did you know about me?'

'Mum ...mentioned you from time to time. I just always knew about you and I remember coming back here, to Stockwell Street, and you coming to the house...'

'You remember that?' he asked sharply and then his voice softened. 'You were so very small. Remarkable that you remember that. And a little Dutch I remember from last night,' and he smiled kindly at me. 'That is partly why I am here; to see your mother, and you, of course,' and he patted my hand affectionately, like an Uncle, I imagined, although I had never had one. I had no relatives except Mum.

'She can't see you,' I said and then wished I had said it better. His face closed again and he looked at me as though he could see through all of the layers and the pretence and the lies and go straight to the truth. I didn't know it so well then but I felt uncomfortable under his gaze.

'She can't see me, or won't?' he said.

'Oh she doesn't know you are here.' Again the same look, only this time quizzical, and in the look, the unspoken thought, 'tell me more.'

'Well, it's just that she is ... ill...' and told him about her breakdown and her time in Severalls Hospital and her recuperation. 'So I think that she mustn't talk about the old days too much. It upsets her,' I said and realized that I was talking to a Doctor who had known Mum in her younger days when she was well and whole and beautiful. He sat back in his chair and steepled his fingers again in thought. I sat silently looking at the cold coffee, untouched. Rain was splashing onto the windows outside and the High Street was lively with a morning in full swing; shoppers, workers, cars and buses; horns and shouts. Inside, a long silence which echoed down the decades. He took a deep breath and looked directly at me and spoke quietly and kindly.

'It might help her to talk to someone. Whatever it is that caused her trauma, I may be able to help. I am a Doctor after all,' and he smiled kindly at me and then became business like. 'Yes I am sure I can help her. On the continent we have done a lot of research into mental illness and trauma. There is a lot of it about after the war.' His amber eyes seemed to blaze with fury. 'Talking about it, facing the truth may be the only thing which can save her.'

'But at the hospital they said to keep her medicated, that her heart might not stand another relapse. No, I need to keep her calm. You have no idea what is it like when she is in despair and there is nothing I can do,' I stopped abruptly as I realized my voice was raised and Millie was back in the room rattling cups on the nearby serving counter and obviously trying hard to listen. She could not help but hear what I was saying. Felix glanced at Millie and went across and said something which sent her scurrying from the room. He was back in his seat and took my hand.

'There are different views in how to treat mental patients,' he said moving very close so we could not be overheard. 'As I said, I have been working with trauma patients in Holland. There is a lot of suffering everywhere, and I am sorry that you have not had the support you need to help your mother. Will you let me help you, both of you? Can you trust me as a friend?' I couldn't speak and I was aware that tears had begun to flow down my cheeks. He handed me a handkerchief and sat closely until I was composed. 'Now tell me about the young man I met just now and we will have a hot drink to cheer us. I ordered tea from your inquisitive colleague which I hope will be better than the coffee. I don't blame you for not risking it.'

We talked about life in England and my school days and work, and I realized that I was telling him far more than he was telling me and the morning was moving on rapidly and the lounge was filling up with shoppers having morning coffee.

'I have to go soon. I can't leave Mum alone for too long,' I said but there was so much I still wanted to know. 'Can we meet again, before you go back?' I asked and lowered my eyes so that he wouldn't see the need there. 'There is so much that I would like to know. Mum is not clear about things and I have not been able to ask her very much.' He stood and helped me into my raincoat and held my gently by my upper arms.

'Of course. I want to get to know you much better, Beatrix. May I call you Beatrix? It suits you so well,' and his enlightened smile was back and he embraced me affectionately. 'I won't come to the house just yet. Maybe you need to prepare your mother a bit for the shock.' As he escorted me to the door he added, 'I have to go up to London this afternoon on business. I was here to see your mother and you were right in thinking I would come to the house. I will be back here next week. I have a room booked for Tuesday and am planning to take the Wednesday ferry from Harwich. Maybe I can meet your mother then?' It sounded like a request or a question but I knew it was a statement.

'I thought you were staying tonight?' I said.

'Change of plan. I will check out this morning and hope it doesn't upset your paperwork too much.' There was a smile in his voice and I tried to hide my disappointment at losing him so soon after meeting.

'I will write to Marianne and say that I am visiting England and would love to visit her. I will keep it light and unthreatening. You can judge her response and let me know when I come back if she is able to see me.' I nodded and shook out my umbrella, not feeling that I could trust my voice if I tried to speak. 'By the way, does she still have any of the paintings your father left?' Of all the unexpected things which happened, I wasn't expecting that.

'Erm, in the cellar, I think there are some… we never go there… Aunt Maude was adamant that the past was the past and let sleeping dogs lie…' I petered out and he patted my arm affectionately.

'Well, so long as they are still there. We can talk much more when I am back next week,' and he hoisted my umbrella and handed it to me in a gesture which said that this meeting was over. For me, however, it was far from a conclusion and a week was too long to wait for it to unfold.

The letter from Dr. Van Gelder arrived two days later and I held on to it, unsure what to do, until T'Ash came home. I had done a lot of thinking since I had met Dr. Felix and what he said made sense. I decided to try to speak to her doctor again at Severalls. If I could get a clear idea of her condition, give Dr. Felix some medical jargon to work with, we would know better what to do.

'I still say she shouldn't be meeting him. It would set her back. Look how well she is now and she is talking a bit about the past when we play cards. She even asked if I could teach her Monopoly last night, Lord help us,' and T'Ash laughed, cutting another slice of bread to mop up his gravy. The letter lay unopened on the table between us. Mum had eaten earlier and was listening to the wireless and dozing in the parlour. 'Mind you, if all the places on the Monopoly Board were canals and stuff, you know places in Amsterdam, now that might help to get her talking a bit. I'll mention it to Dr. Van Gelder. It might be good for therapy....' and he wrote it down in his ever present notebook. I got the feeling that T'Ash was still interested in the story he could write rather than the impact on its major players and I sensed a veil, like a gauze of separate interest had descended between us. I also noticed that his notebook was full of arrows and diagrams and a red line which joined several of the pieces of his puzzle together.

Chapter Seventeen

'The hunger winter – 1944-45. Somehow we managed without fuel or much food. I had Beatrix to take care of. I had to get food for her and I always made sure she had something; Max would feed her his own food and we went hungry, but not often. We ate what we could find but I was always resourceful. And Jellicoe; she knew people – Germans. I always mistrusted her but Max was convinced she was working for us. She wasn't....'

I was standing in the doorway after work and Mum and T'Ash had the Monopoly board in front of them. She was holding the Chance Cards as though they were playing cards and T'Ash was sitting opposite her, leaning forward, holding her other hand. I didn't want to speak in case I broke her lucidity.

'I managed to get a lot of sugar beet which was also rationed and I heard, from neighbours when I was out, that some families were eating flower bulbs. We never did and I always managed to get enough sticks of wood to fuel a stove to cook on and to heat us. Many were not so lucky and the Jews' empty flats were vandalized for any scraps of wood which could burn. I bought some from Van Jolsen; and I knew for certain that it was dear old Reuben's flat; our friend. We tried to save him; he was a friend of Max's, an Art dealer; we tried to save him but there was no way.

Max would have been arrested and then where would we be? But I recognized Reuben's kitchen cupboard doors even chopped for firewood. He had been so proud of them and painted them himself. I wept as I set a match to them but we had to eat.... and then Jellicoe came in with a pig's foot and I thought we would all be well fed tonight what with the roots I'd managed to get but she was playing her stupid games again .... I never trusted her after that and I was right. He should have listened to me....' Silence. T'Ash and I held our breaths. This would have tipped her over the edge in the past. I was tempted to comfort her, tell her it's all right, no need to go there now, it's all over, but T'Ash warned me off.

'I'm listening to you, Ma,' said T'Ash quietly.

'And then later a great crashing sound and next day, Reuben's house had collapsed. Not only the cupboards and fittings had been stripped; they had also taken floors and rafters and staircases. Anything which would burn. Survival of the living. No time to dwell on lost friends......' She was dry eyed and lucid, talking about it as though she was talking about a shopping trip to Ipswich. And I thought that T'Ash and Felix were right, she needed to talk...

'But then it was over, right? The Allies came and you was liberated?' T'Ash was trying to move the story on. She looked up blankly at him as though she was just waking up.

'What? What was I saying? Oh yes, all that... it was all a long time ago. I don't remember now,' and she shook the dice and threw a two and a three and moved her counter, the Top Hat, about twelve places backwards and handed the dice and cup to T'Ash. 'Can I buy Vine Street? Where is it anyway?' T'Ash ran a hand through his hair and took the dice cup from her and looked up and smiled a half smile; apologetic? wistful?

'Yes, why not? It's in London, Ma. Why don't you put a Hotel on it as well. Look, Bea's home, I'll go and put the kettle on,' and Mum looked up and smiled at me and

T'Ash escaped to the kitchen. Mum lowered her voice as I kissed her cheek.

'I seem to be doing very well in this game, but I don't think Alfie is concentrating tonight. He's a bit distracted,' and she placed about six wooden 'hotel' replicas on her newly acquired property and began to search though the cards for the title deed.

'I think she's well enough to get Dr Van Gelder's letter, T'Ash said as he made the tea.'

'Tomorrow,' I said. Tomorrow morning would be soon enough and I was keen that she sleep well tonight.

Next morning, T'Ash left early for work and I delayed getting up until I heard that he had gone. Mum would sleep until I woke her with a cup of tea and I had time to reconsider. We had about three days before Dr Van Gelder was due back in Colchester and even if Mum refused to see him, or was not well enough, I would see him, and I felt excited at the prospect.

Mum looked at the words on the page and her eyes were swimming with tears.

'It's from Felix,' she said with an air of incredulity. 'Felix. After all this time. I thought he was dead as well.'

'What does he say?' I prompted her and she handed me the page.

'Not a lot. He's here. He wants to see me.' I took the letter and saw the neat copperplate which I knew he had written with his gold fountain pen. I could see his studious, handsome face carving the letters into the quality vellum with grace and ease. No mention of meeting me. No betrayal of our 'secret' meeting. I was intrigued by him and there was so much I wanted to know.

George Hotel, Colchester, July 31ˢᵗ 1956
'My dearest Marianne.
Many years have passed since we last met and I have thought of you often in the intervening years. I hope that the memory of our

parting is not too distressing for you to consider seeing me again when I return to Colchester on Tuesday 4th. I have new information concerning our 'mutual friend' which may be of interest to you.

Please contact me at The George Hotel if a meeting is agreeable to you.

I trust that you and Beatrix are well?
With Fondest Regards,
Felix

As I thought it would be, neutral and enigmatic. He was teasing us with more mystery, hooking us in. It worked on me, but Mum seemed unconcerned.

'Who's your 'mutual friend'?'. She shrugged. 'No idea. Could be anyone. So many people, I've forgotten most of them.' So what was Dr. Felix playing at? He knew she was ill. He knew her memory was in shreds and her emotions ragged. He was her doctor once. Why was he provoking her?

'Mum, it's from Dr. Felix. He wants to see you.'

'I don't think he does, love. I think he just wants the paintings,' and she said it so matter of fact and so 'sanely' that I was left speechless. 'They are your legacy. Don't let him have them will you? They're in the cellar. I meant to tell you about them one day but I never seemed to get round to it. Now you know,' and she stood up and left the room, steadily and strongly as though her illness had fallen away. I wanted to shout after her, 'No I don't know, you have to tell me,' but I was completely speechless. I put the letter down, took the key from the kitchen drawer and went down into the cellar.

I looked at the paintings again. Were they valuable? Was I mistaken in thinking that Pa had painted them or were they really original masterpieces in which case they were looted.

The evidence was in the wooden suitcase which I found in T'Ash's room and carried it into the parlour where there was a table. I heard mum moving around upstairs and shouted up to her. 'Would you like some tea?' but there was no reply, so I went up and found her at her dressing table, fully dressed and applying makeup, not manically as you would expect, but quite sanely and rationally. Her hair was combed and although it needed a cut and a perm, it was tidy. She was her old self again and my heart broke for her. She caught my eye in the mirror and the sadness of ages was reflected there. I couldn't speak.

'I'm just popping out love, to see Felix,' she said and my heart stood still. I know people talk about their heart missing a beat or skipping or racing; I am not quite sure what mine did but it could have been all of the above. I felt it drop into the pit of my stomach. This rational calmness, saneness almost was hard to understand and I hoped that it was almost lunch time and T'Ash would drop in to make his usual hurried sandwich, check all was well and run out again. I knew he would today because of the letter but I needed him now. I needed to know what to do.

'Would you like me to come with you?' I asked, stalling for time. She didn't answer, just applied another layer of powder and a slash of lipstick which was garish against her gaunt face and I realised that she was nowhere near well enough to see Felix. I crouched beside her at the dressing table and said quietly,

'Mum, Felix isn't here until next week. I'll take you to see him then. He's in London at the moment.' She turned sharply to me.

'How do you know that? He didn't say that. He's at the George,' and then I saw a flicker of light and reason crash through her damaged mind and with great lucidity she turned to me.

'Of course. He's at The George. You've seen him. You knew he was here.' The effort was almost too much for her and she slumped in her chair. 'So you're in on it as well?'

'I'm not in on anything Mum. He turned up at the George. I checked him in. We had a chat. I told him you are not so well at the moment, but he said he would love to see you.' She was drifting again and had a far off look in her eyes.

'Is he still handsome?' she said.

'Oh, yes, he is,' I said quite firmly. Old enough to be my father but still handsome I thought. Handsome where T'Ash was 'pretty'. A young Peter Pan. A boy next to the man. I hadn't thought about it much and now wasn't really the time.

'He always was more handsome than his brother,' she said and turned back to the mirror and combed her hair. 'He's your Godfather, you know although he didn't believe in God. Funny really isn't it? He promised to look after you. Fat lot of good he's been,' and she threw the comb down, knocking a jar of Nivea cream off the dressing table and it landed upside down spilling onto the floor boards. Mum was getting upset and my radar was on alert. It was my job to make sure she didn't although it wasn't always easy. I picked up the jar and the smell was evocative of kinder warmer days when I was young and Aunt Maude was still here; innocent, irresponsible days gone forever and so quickly evaporated. Was it always going to be like this now?

I went into my room and took some of Mum's 'calming' medicine, *Largactil,* from my bedside drawer. I kept all of her medication hidden for obvious reasons. I couldn't watch her day and night and look what happened to Aunt Maude out of the blue; how that triggered this new nightmare of Mum's breakdown? I shook the bottle and carried it through to Mum.

'Time for your medicine before lunch,' I said with my 'cheery nurse' voice. I had developed several different voices when dealing with Mum. There was Nanny talking to small child; stern teacher when she was being totally unreasonable and kind friend when we cruised in neutral times. I had ceased to be her daughter. I was now her carer, nurse, jailor.

'How about a little lie down and I will go and make lunch?' I said and she swallowed the foul smelling liquid and allowed me to help her onto the bed, remove her slippers and cover her with the eiderdown.

'Have you got any of that vegetable soup left? I liked that,' she said drowsily.

'I'll make some more,' I said, glad of something to do, and half pulled the curtains to darken the room so that she could sleep a healing sleep and recover.

I put the wireless on in the parlour and turned it up so that I could hear it in the kitchen as I chopped carrots and onions and whatever other vegetable I had left over. Leek and turnip and celery all went in. There was music playing, gentle and soothing on the Light Programme. I put the soup onto the back gas ring and sat in Grandpa Quinn's chair as echoes and images drifted through my head.

Click - clack. I hear my mother's footsteps, ricocheting off the cobble stones, piercing the darkness and I want to shout in delight, or burst into tears but I know that either will attract attention and I should be asleep. The footsteps stop and I hear voices; my mother talking to a German soldier. I strain to hear their conversation but only whispers reach the open window of my tower and I don't understand it anyway. The flag outside whips the content of their voices away on a sudden breeze sending a bat flying into the blackness. A shiver runs through me and I clasp a hand over my mouth to stop the scream from escaping. The voices stop, momentarily, and I step back from the window in case they can see me and then the voices continue briskly, and the red and black flag lies still again and I hate it in a childish way, because my mother does.

Something roused me. The front door had creaked on its ancient hinges, or was it just the music finishing, replaced by a news report? I smelt the soup, a good strong healthy food which would make Mum well. She would never be hungry again.

I stood up still drowsy and realized my face was wet with tears, which I wiped away with the sleeve of my cardigan. I had heard something. But what? Maybe it was the front door. T'Ash was home. I called his name. Nothing. I went into the hallway and he wasn't there. It was silent and I thought I had imagined it so I went back into the kitchen and added lentils to the soup and thought about waking Mum in plenty of time to enjoy lunch.

I went through to the parlour and turned the wireless off and sat at the table to go through the wooden suitcase and found that T'Ash had already sorted the paperwork into categories, bound with elastic bands or bulldog clips which he must have taken from work, or just held together with a folded document as a file. I was careful not to undo his sorting and laid out the bundles in order. There were photographs, letters, receipts and bills of sale and something T'Ash had labelled 'Provenances', a few papers in Dutch and English which were the stories of the pictures. There was a large envelope with 'ID' written on it in T'Ash's hand and in it were passports, identification papers, ration books, birth certificates. A bundle held together with a bulldog clip was pages of lists, in Dutch; names, I thought and another page of items. Another envelope said 'Misc.' in T'Ash's writing and contained scraps of paper; fragments; numbers which could have been phone numbers; names, addresses; messages, baffling and meaningless unless you knew what it was. Dr. Felix would know.

On the largest envelope was T'Ash's neatest handwriting. It was all here, a plot relating to the pictures and linked by a line drawn in red ink; reminding me that my red line had refused to show for over a month.

Chapter Eighteen

This time I did hear the unmistakeable click of a key in the door and T'Ash call out.

'Mmmmm. That smells great. What's cooking?' I leapt up, feeling guilty that I was going through the papers in the wooden suitcase, and checked myself. This was my property. I had a right to see what was in it. I went to meet him in the hallway and he swung me in his arms and kissed me fondly.

'You've sorted out the papers in the old wooden case,' I said as I stirred the soup and tasted it and laid the table with the fresh crusty loaf T'Ash had brought in with him. He sat at the table.

'I hope you don't mind. I just needed to see what was there. It's amazing stuff, don't you think?' I felt unreasonably irritated. Amazing or not it was my stuff and Mum's.

'Amazing if you like mysteries,' I said coldly.

'You know I do,' he replied, equally coldly.

'So have you got your story yet?' I said ladling soup into a bowl for him as he cut bread.

'Yes I have, as a matter of fact. I have got a story. I'll tell you about it tonight if you like, after tea.' I looked at him coolly again.

'I'm working. Maybe tell Mum. She can let you know if it's true or not.'

'What was in the letter?' he asked, ignoring my sniping and taking a bite from the buttered bread.

'Nothing much,' I said. I didn't want to tell him about the 'mystery information.' He would add a whole new chapter to his novel and somehow I was beginning to resent my mother's life being peeled open. She was vulnerable enough.

'I have to go and wake Mum. She'll need something to eat,' I said.

I don't know if I screamed or shouted or simply thumped on the floor but T'Ash was running up the stairs and holding me by the time I realised what was going on.

'She's gone,' I said in despair and flopped onto the side of her unmade bed. Details flashed by me in what was an instant but seemed like a lifetime and T'Ash was holding my shoulders and asking me things.

'She was dressed but no shoes. Her slippers have gone from where I left them, so at least she has her slippers on,' I said helplessly.

'I'll check the hall for her coat,' said T'Ash running back down the stairs and I followed, words stumbling over each other in my haste to find her.

'She wanted to go and see Dr. Felix. Maybe she's at The George? I should have checked. I heard a noise but I thought she was asleep. I should have checked.'

'Her coat's still here. I'll go to the George and check and if she's not there I'll call the police. She shouldn't be out on her own and in her slippers. Check the yard and the back. Check the cellar, all over, ask the neighbours. I'll be back soon as I can,' and with the briefest peck on my cheek, he raced out of the house. I knew she wasn't here but I checked anyway. The cellar was the obvious first place; I had left the door unlocked and panic rose again. '*Look what happened to Aunt Maude*' my head was shrieking at me, *'and it will all be your fault'*. But she wasn't there. I tried the back yard and the entry behind it; no sign; she was long gone; how long since I heard her? Half an hour perhaps. How stupid. I should have checked.

It felt like a hard punch to my stomach, like I was being beaten by an invisible hand which held me totally responsible for a vulnerable deranged woman in my care, out in the world, bewildered, alone and cold. I doubled up in pain in the alleyway where Lil found me, steered me back into my own kitchen and served me a bowl of my hot soup which I couldn't touch. I had made it for Mamma, so that she would never be hungry again.

'They'll find her love, she can't have gone far,' said Lil soothing and I had to believe her.

Time slowed and it was an age later when T'Ash crashed through the front door and there was a Policeman with him. I went to meet them and found that my entire body was numb. She was dead. Clearly I had killed her by neglect. I could barely breathe.

'They found her,' said T'Ash, his voice grown up and gravelly. She's ok,' and I burst into tears and threw my arms around him and her steered me into the parlour followed by the Policeman and closed the door on Lil who was hovering in the hall.

'Sit down,' said T'Ash. I sat, wondering why he wasn't joyful. 'She's safe now, Beatrix,' said T'Ash. 'She's back in Severalls, on the locked ward and sedated but she is safe. They committed her and you, as next of kin, should sign the papers.' He looked kindly at me and I knew that if he could he would spare me what was to come. 'Except that you are under age so it will have to be a solicitor who signs until you come of age. Unless.... does she have any relatives that you know of?' I shook my head. Aunt Maude was the last. And me. The Policeman stepped in and looked at me in a fatherly sort of way.

'You see Miss, we picked her up at The George Hotel. She went there to meet someone but she wasn't making a lot of sense; speaking in Dutch as a matter of fact, and the receptionist saw that she was a bit, well, not quite right and was wearing her slippers and all, and they called us. They didn't know what else to do. She seemed very agitated when they couldn't understand her. She kept saying *Brother-in-Law* in English and a Dutch name. She was quite insistent but they had no one of that name there and frankly, they just thought she was a bit, you know.....' I looked from the Constable to T'Ash and his face was drawn and closed.

'She went to meet Dr. Van Gelder,' I said.

'Yes that's right and there was no one there of that name but you see, if she has a brother-in-law, maybe he will be her next of kin, until you reach your majority that is. Anyway,' and he sounded brusque now 'I have been asked to check it out, meanwhile she's sectioned and ordered to remain incarcerated in Severalls.' He saw the look of anguish cross my face. 'For her own safety,' he added hastily.

'Can I see her?' I said in a small voice and the Constable glanced at T'Ash. 'That's a matter for the hospital, Miss,' he said gently. 'So what can you tell me of this 'Dr. Felix Van Gelder' character then?' and he took his notebook out and looked at us both optimistically.

I clung to T'Ash like a life raft for the weekend which followed. After visiting the hospital, we were told that we would be able to see her on Sunday. We sorted out paperwork and waited for Dr. Felix.

In the middle of the night I awoke with a gasp, thudding heart and heat pouring from every part of me. Wrestling free of T'Ash's liberal embrace I sat bolt upright on the edge of the bed my breath coming in gasps.

'What is it? What's the matter?' he said in a bleary voice more asleep than awake. Something buzzed around my head like an irritating wasp in the summer. Buzz, buzz, dive bombing my mind, trying to provoke a response. Breathe in, count to three, out count to three, in.... out.... it's nothing just the heat. Calm down. Cool down, breathe....I got my breathing under control and walked over to the chest of drawers to pour a glass of water. It was cool out here and the bare boards were dusty, testament to my haphazard house-keeping skills but I wasn't going to be a housewife anyway. I was going to be an artist and go to art school and then I felt a cold slap across my face and I remembered something Mum said. Had she said it for real or was it in my dream? If she had said it, how real was it considering the state of her mind? I was wide awake and reached for my dressing gown, and tiptoed barefoot downstairs.

'It was about the paintings,' I said to T'Ash as he stumbled down the stairs fifteen minutes later, seeing the bed empty, the darkness of the darkest part of the night. Knowing I was 'unsettled'.

'What about the paintings?'

'She said Dr. Felix would want them. But they were my 'legacy'. I wasn't to let him have them.'

'Did she really say that?' and his voice went up; incredulous.

I snapped back. 'Well I don't think I dreamed it.'

'What else did she say?' he asked gently, comforting.

'That Felix was more handsome than his brother.'

'Or his brother's uncle's cousin! We don't know who his brother was.'

'Guess,' I said, throwing a photo of my father onto the table. I had taken it from Mum's bedside table. 'She went to the hotel to meet her *brother-in-law*?' He looked closely at the portrait; taken in the studio; *Artist Max Prins, 1932* stamped on the back; a handsome face, strong, smooth lines of a young man, still with a head of thick dark hair. A long face, smiling amber eyes deep set above high cheek bones. A hint of a smile which was enigmatic and wistful. He looked away from the camera to his right, into a light which gave hope to his expression.

A publicity shot probably; a rare capture of a man who mattered, who was already, long before I was born, a 'somebody.' Or if not yet, then on the way to being so. It was optimistic. It was in contrast to the sketch I placed on the table next to the photo; a page torn from a sketch book which I had found in the suitcase in the envelope labelled '*misc*.' This was another face staring out at the viewer, eyes blazing with challenge; hair line receding, dark hair lighter, longer, wispy. The face leaner, softer, ragged. Max's self portrait expressing something of the life he was now living; *To Marianne, December 1944,*' in his hand across the bottom. A self portrait full of his skill, of longing, and despair.

'This photo looks a bit like Felix, I can see that but it doesn't prove anything,' T'Ash said. 'He could be Max's brother but I don't understand why it would be such a big secret. Although if he is your uncle, with you being under age and everything, that's going to make a difference.' I shrugged deeper into the folds of the woollen blanket, knitted in multi coloured squares by Aunt Maude, and drew my knees underneath me in Grandpa Quinn's chair.

'What about the paintings though? If they belong to Ma and he gets control of her affairs...'

'Then they belong to you in trust, I think. We'd better check that out. Shall we hide them?'

'Where?' I said, gesturing around the small house. 'Besides, he doesn't know for sure we still have them.'

'I'll think of something,' T'Ash said, sipping his tea and pulling the notebook from his overcoat pocket.

It seemed a long time until Felix Day, as Tuesday had become in my head. We hadn't exactly arranged a meeting but T'Ash agreed that I should go alone. He tried to coach me in how to deal with the situation; to be cool and to listen; to talk as little as possible; to ask more than I say; to get answers, not to give information.

'Think Mata Hari,' he said enjoying his role of spymaster. I understood the theory but I also knew myself quite well by then.

I dressed with care. I put on makeup, something I rarely did, and then wiped it all off again and applied a hint of pale lipstick and took a long look in the mirror. A young, emotional girl, looked back at me; a girl I knew was prone to painful 'petit mal' fits which stung like barbs and triggered migraine attacks; a fanciful dreamer who was still sitting in the wings, waiting for her life to begin. I was a girl of no experience, little real education and a lot of dreams. I was no match for Dr. Felix Van Gelder, the enigma, the intellectual, cool, well travelled man who had known me from birth, and who would, I was certain, treat me like the child I clearly was. However much I had grown into a woman, now openly (and scandalously as it transpired,) living with T'Ash.

I counted every step between home and the George to drive out the needle of pain which was beginning to stab its way into the base of my skull just above the hard bony bit on the right hand side.

Felix stood as I entered the Hotel and embraced me with affection and then ordered tea.

'I am afraid my mother is unwell,' I started to say but my eyes filled up and my voice cracked and he put out his hand to comfort me.

'How unwell?' I told him and he paled and sat back and exhaled sharply.

'I need to speak to her,' he said

'You can't. She's, well, she's gone...' and I felt the tears prick again but sipped the tea; part distraction part comfort.

'I have experience of working with mental health patients. It is my speciality. I will at least speak to her doctors.' How could I say to him that she had retreated permanently into the landscape of her mind where she dwelt with shadows and ghosts; no one could follow her there. How could I say to him that speaking about him had triggered her final collapse?

'She read your letter. She was coming here to meet you, but her mind went. She cannot be persuaded to relive the past, it's too painful.' He nodded

'There are things then that you need to know. If she is incapable and you are not yet of age,' he raised an eyebrow in acknowledgement of the fact that he had known me all my life. 'You must appoint a solicitor, although the hospital probably have already.' I nodded. These things seemed unimportant in the great big landscape of my own desolation.

'This is important, Beatrix. There is a considerable fortune sitting in your cellar and I know for sure that people in Holland are looking for it.' I dropped the spoon I was toying with and looked at him.

'They are not there anymore. I looked. They've gone,' I said, remembering my coaching with T'Ash. *Don't tell him where they are until we know more.*' 'They are not worth that much, surely? My papa painted them. I remember some of them in the studio.' Felix's eyes narrowed, the way my father's had when he looked closely at a subject he was going to paint.

'What do you remember, Beatrix?' and the tone of his voice was harsher, only a little, but in my state of impending migraine I was aware of even the smallest changes around me. I could smell the coffee from the table next to me and the strawberry jam they were spreading on their toast. I could hear the clatter of a teaspoon from across the room. I was brittle, spun from glass and felt that if he touched me, however lightly, I would shatter. I knew that if I talked I would put off the worst of it, the nausea and vomiting which I had to delay at least until I could get home.

T'Ash had said listen don't talk but I told him more or less what I could remember anyway, and about the 'visions' which may be memory or fantasy I still didn't know at that stage. My tea had gone cold and a tannin skin had formed on the top. The smell of it forced a sudden wave of nausea to hit me like a slap and I rushed to the ladies room, just in time.

When I returned, Felix was standing by reception with my coat and bag in his hand and took control.

'I'll take you home. We'll talk more when you are better.' I tried to protest but he simply stroked my cheek, slipped my coat around my shoulders and escorted me home. He knew where we lived of course. He could have come anytime but it was not what we had planned, T'Ash and I. We wanted to keep him out of the house and to get him to tell us things. I had failed in my mission as Mati Hari and it made me laugh out loud as he took the key from my shaking hand and steered me through my front door.

Chapter Nineteen

The house was pretty much as he remembered it. Opening straight from the narrow cobbled street, it was dark, quiet and at least 400 years old with overhanging gable and a hint of must and old dust.

He helped Beatrix into her bed and removed her shoes and encouraged her to drink water.

'Dehydration is a large part of headaches,' he said. Then silently he set about his task; a thorough search. She had said that the paintings weren't here but he needed to know how long they had been gone, if there were any clues. Any trace he could detect would help.

Marianne's room was the only other room upstairs. A picture of Max on the bedside table had been removed from its frame. It had been taken in a studio; *Artist Max Prins, 1932* stamped on the back. There was also a framed photograph of Beatrix in her cradle and he remembered the canvas which was painted from it.

Downstairs, the cellar door was locked as he presumed it would be. He moved silently down the corridor, not turning on the light in case he attracted neighbours, and came into the small back kitchen. This was different. The old chair was still there in the corner and the room looked like a relic from an earlier age, but was now festooned with pictures; mostly watercolours, sketches and a couple of oil canvases. He moved into the light from the small window to see better. The Castle Keep; lots of sketches of Tarron Ash; Colchester High Street in the snow, looking like a Christmas card; or perhaps a Hans Breughel? And then, something else. Impressionist versions of Matisse; Van Gogh; and Picasso.... all exact; all clearly copies. All, he assumed, painted by Beatrix. He picked up the sketchbook which lay on the old chair in the corner and flicked through the crisp, bulging pages of ink wash and watercolour. Her life was here.

An old lady, wrapped in a blanket made of knitted squares, sitting in this corner, the detail exquisite; the ravaged, haunted face of a once beautiful woman gazing sadly at him.

This was more than he had expected. This was extraordinary. He had come for the paintings but it looked as though he was going to get an Artist's Apprentice as well. He smiled to himself and lit a cigarette and then rummaged around in the kitchen cabinets for an ashtray. There wasn't one so he used a cracked saucer instead, white chipped china with red roses on it and a once gold rim around the edge. It had seen better days, like this old house.

His own house in Amsterdam was old and valuable but had been modernised. He looked around the dingy kitchen and passed through to the back of the house looking for a bathroom as there wasn't one upstairs. There was a tin bath hanging in what he assumed they called the 'scullery' or 'pantry' or 'utility room'. His English was good but too many nuances evaded him sometimes and he wasn't sure what this was called. So, an outside toilet then and a tin bath in the kitchen. All very pre-war and primitive but not uncommon in the UK as he already knew.

He went back into the kitchen and opened the right hand drawer of the dresser. The left one held cutlery and the right one was a jumble of kitchen detritus. A large key and been pushed under some papers which he expertly sifted and replaced exactly. They were mostly about Marianne's Pension, and some books which would give her state benefits, that sort of thing. Nothing here he needed, just the key to the cellar.

The light was dim down there but his eyes adjusted quickly and he stood at the foot of the cellar stairs and inhaled the musty air. He pulled on his gloves from practice but one look at this place told him that the dust had lain for decades. *'Not a great place to store paintings,'* he thought. *'I should have come for them sooner.'* There was a broken wicker chair, not unlike Van Gogh's in his famous painting, and a box full of seemingly broken household things; a lamp, a broom, some old dolls and a few suitcases. A cursory sift through these showed up little but old clothes smelling of damp and a bedspread which was rotting at the folds. He replaced everything carefully and clapped his hands to shake off the worst of the dust. As his eyes adjusted he could see further into the corners of the cellar. Around one wall, there were marks where the dust had been disturbed. Lines in the dust were all that remained in the spot where he had placed the pictures himself 13 years ago, and sheets thrown in a heap in the far corner with barely a mark of dust on them. Recently then. The pictures had been moved recently. Why? And where to?

A last inspection and he saw clearly imprinted a rectangle of dust where a box or suitcase had been removed. The others which were scattered around the cellar had simply been moved around and he could see by the marks, that they had been dragged out of the way or simply opened, rummaged and left.

He silently climbed the stairs, turned off the light and locked the cellar door. He went into the middle room where a single bed had been pushed behind the door and clothes folded over the back of a chair. A suit hung on the back of the door and a few folded pullovers were on the end of the bed. This must be Tarron's room, maybe Maude's old room? Reasonably tidy for a single young man, he thought. A suitcase full of clothes was pushed neatly under the bed and Felix explored it thoroughly and professionally without disturbing anything.

In the front room, there was a bureau in the corner by the window and a vase of dead flowers on a dining table covered with a clean yellow cloth. A box game of Monopoly was on a shelf in the corner with a few books, including a Dutch –English dictionary, and judging by the dust along the top, rarely used. The rest were mostly romances and some art books from the library. Overdue he noticed. Matisse, Picasso and Van Gogh with the few colour plates which were copied so exactly in the kitchen.

The bureau contained more paperwork which was routine and domestic, relating to Marianne's sister's death; deeds to this house, which he noticed belonged to Marianne and would now belong to Beatrix when she was of age, if Marianne didn't improve. Birth certificates; no passports, so he would have to sort that quickly if his plan was to work. And still no trace of the paintings.

He sat in an old brown leather armchair and steepled his fingers in his customary gesture.

The paintings were not here, clearly, but the evidence suggested they had been moved recently, and that space on the floor in the thick grey dust could be the shape of the wooden suitcase with the provenances in it.

How much did Beatrix know, he wondered? She knew something about him, but true to her training, Marianne had said very little and was now incapable. That was good. Beatrix was still a blank canvas with blurred and unfocussed memories.

He silently left the house, taking Beatrix's front door key which he had slipped into his pocket earlier. He took a taxi to the hospital to visit Marianne, but had only been able to see her through the glass. She was sleeping; in an induced state to keep her comatose and calm. He had been told by a Dr. Steans, Marianne's physician, that she had been given a new drug with which Felix was familiar. His research institute had run many of the trials.

'It is a Phenobarbital which will induce a prolonged narcosis,' he was informed.

'Yes, it is a powerful sedative. She will be unable to speak or think very much until she is stable,' replied Felix.

The further prognosis was that she would not be coming out of Severalls for a long time. Her general health had suffered as a result of prolonged nervous exhaustion and she was in the safest place.

In the taxi back to Stockwell Street Felix made a mental list and ticked things off in his mind, straightening his thoughts. His return to Colchester had proved surprising and he needed to regain control of his plan.

Marianne was incapable and may never recover and she was possibly beyond his help.

That made him Beatrix's only relative and very likely, as she was under age, her Guardian. She knew where the paintings were, he was certain of that, so why the subterfuge? She also proved to have a great talent which he had not expected and would be a bonus. A new idea was beginning to reshape his original plan. But she was also suffering from trauma: the headaches, those 'fits' she described. She was still a child in many ways, and malleable. Still young enough to mould.

There was something else which would complicate everything. He didn't know her well; he had only recently met the woman she had become, but there was a look about her; a look which he had seen a thousand times in a thousand different faces of the women he had known as patients, lovers, and during the war, colleagues in arms. A blush, a vague blossoming like new spring life behind a veil of vulnerability. She was protecting a secret, he thought which she may not even admit to herself yet. The eyes were the clue; secrets were visible in the eyes if you looked hard enough. Time would tell if his instinct was still as strong as ever, but he would not be at all surprised if Beatrix was pregnant.

Chapter Twenty

Later, there was a gentle tap on the bedroom door. I had been sleeping under the bedcover fully clothed but my shoes had been removed. The curtains were half drawn and the light suggested late afternoon. It must have been almost time for T'Ash to return. Dr. Felix came in and sat on the bed and handed me a glass of water and a pill.

'Here, take this. It will help with the pain and the nausea.'

T'Ash had concocted this whole theory about Felix; he was a spy; he was a murderer; he was a Resistance leader in the war; and he said there was some evidence in the wooden case to support his claim. I dismissed it as his novelist fantasy. Even in my confused state, however, I was aware of Mum's belief that Pa had died from 'the wrong food' alongside his medication from Felix. What if it was 'the wrong pills' which finally killed him? I sat up and took the water and sipped it and set it down on the bedside table but I wasn't going to take any pills until I knew more. I shook my head and he frowned, took my pulse, felt my forehead and looked into my eyes.

'There is medication which can help your condition,' he said quietly. 'You should see your doctor,' and he placed the two innocent looking pills on the table next to the water. 'Pain killers,' he said. 'For later if you don't want them now.' I sat back against the pillows and laid my arm across my eyes. The light was still too bright although I knew the room was darkened.

'He was my Brother you know. Well, half Brother. Max and Felix. We had different fathers, and it wouldn't do during the war for us to appear to be related. There was too much at risk.' He looked at me and smiled. 'That makes me your Uncle, Beatrix, as well as your Godfather. Did your mother tell you that? I guess I am your only living relative?' I turned a painful gaze on him. It hurt to open my eyes.

'His brother?' he nodded. 'Uncle Felix?' I said and he smiled.

'I would prefer 'Uncle' to 'Doctor' Felix,' he said. So I had been right about that. What else did I need to know?

'Did Jellicoe have a baby? I remember a baby.'

'Yes. A girl. Johanna.' He said. 'You were a baby yourself then. I can't believe you remember that?' I ignored the question. Memory, I think now, is a strange thing; how much did I remember because I saw it? I know that I have a very developed visual memory, but how much do I 'remember' from photographs, paintings and sketches and from my mother's stories, even though I hardly listened to her when she used to ramble on in the old days. Something must have gone in.

'Do you know where she is? Johanna.'

'She was adopted.'

'Is she my sister? Half sister?' He took a deep breath.

'There is no proof who her father was, but Max told me, privately that he believed she was his daughter. He was proud of that, in his own twisted way, but we can talk about that later. There are more immediate issues which we need to address.' I closed my eyes again and lay further back into the pillows. 'Those pictures could be very valuable in the right hands. You could be a very rich woman Beatrix, but we need to act fast. There is nothing left for you in Colchester, and you deserve a life. You have a very great talent. I couldn't help but notice the paintings around the house. Yours I assume?' I nodded but only slightly. My head was still fragile. He leaned in closer and his breath was barely above a whisper. 'You have his talent. You are a natural and I know that your father would have wanted this for you. I would fail in my duty if I did not help you to truly become his daughter.'

'They are not here,' I said quietly.

'I know. I went down to the cellar to check. Nor is the suitcase which contains the evidence to unlock that fortune. Forgive me but this is really important. Do you know where they are?'

Of course I knew. T'Ash and I had taken them out, over the weekend to the beach chalet. His cousin Sean was roped in to help with his van, armed with a toolbox, Yale and padlock. The paintings were now securely locked and weatherproofed, as best we could, in T'Ash's chalet. 'Uncle' Felix would have no idea where to look.

'The key to the cellar. How did you know where it was?' He smiled a tight smile at my naivety and leant closer in.

'During the war,' he said, quietly, 'there was a Resistance in Holland against the occupation. We all had to play our part. I learned a lot of skills which have served me well since then,' and he placed a warm hand over mine. 'We all leave a surprisingly long trail as we stumble through our lives, Beatrix, and if we listen and look and see what is going on around us, it is not hard to follow. Don't worry. I'll find them,' and he patted my hand. 'I will come back later to see if you are well. I would very much like you and T'Ash to join me for dinner at the hotel if you are well enough. Think about it, Beatrix. Your whole life is ahead of you and there is a fortune which is yours if you remember where it is.' He slipped out silently and I wondered if he had learned that with the Resistance as well.

Chapter Twenty One

We met at the White Hart hotel at 7.30. By the time T'Ash got home, I had washed and dressed with great care and was wearing makeup. The pills had helped and I was feeling almost fully recovered. I smiled at my childish suspicion that Felix might try to harm me, but then, here he was, a fairy Godfather turning up in my life promising me a fortune. It was worthy of T'Ash's fiction although I still doubted the happy ending.

I had borrowed one of Mum's dresses; navy crepe de chine, the only smart dress she had; scoop neck, fitted bodice, flared from the waist in eight gores, calf length, with petticoats to hold it out. There was a long navy sash which I tied artfully and made my waist appear slimmer than it really was. The black patent heels fitted perfectly. That was one thing my mother and I had in common, our shoe size; I looked in Mum's mirror and almost saw a younger version of her looking back; a younger version which only existed now on canvasses in T'Ash's beach chalet and if Felix was right and the pictures were valuable, then we should do something about it. I felt a familiar wave of panic rise in my throat.

I sent T'Ash to the George to report that I was too sick to work tonight and to ask Felix if we could meet somewhere else. It was T'Ash's recommendation as he had never been to the White Hart and it was a place frequented by *Bohemian Artists*.

As we entered the lobby, Felix was waiting and he gasped when he saw me, but recovered quickly. He kissed my cheek and whispered, 'You look so like your mother,' and I knew that I looked like his memory of her. 'But from what I have seen of your art work at the house today, you have your father's talent.'

'So you are heading back to Amsterdam tomorrow then?' asked T'Ash as we waited in the bar for our table. Uncle Felix was drinking red wine, T'Ash beer and I had orange juice.

'That depends,' said Uncle Felix as a waiter approached to show us to our table.

'Depends on what?' asked T'Ash without much preamble or social grace as the waiter handed Uncle Felix the wine menu. He perused it slowly then chose a suitable red and handed it carefully back to the waiter before turning his attention to T'Ash with a look which I found daunting. T'Ash defiantly returned the gaze.

'I went to Severalls this afternoon and spoke to Mrs. Quinn's Doctor.' T'Ash tried to protest but Uncle Felix continued. 'I am a specialist in mental health and I am probably closest kin of age.'

'So is that going to make a difference now?' I asked

'Yes,' Uncle Felix said simply and turned his attention to me. 'I am so glad to see you are feeling better. Did you take the painkillers?' I nodded self consciously aware that I hadn't told T'Ash that bit and feeling the tension rise between the two of them.

'Did you see Mum at the hospital?' I asked quietly.

'No she was sleeping,' he said and took my hand. 'It is not good news, Beatrix. She is unlikely to improve much now. The revolving door policy of her coming in and out was worth a try but they don't want to risk it again. They believe that they can keep her calm and safe in there. They are now talking about permanent incarceration for her own good.'

'So she'll end up experimented on. ECT, drugs? They'll turn her into a cabbage, like my gran. They should have just had her put down like a sick horse, all the good it's done her in there.'

'I am sorry you have had a bad experience Mr. Ash, but that is not very helpful right now and things are changing, slowly, but they are changing and for Mrs. Quinn,' he still held my hand and was looking intently at me, his gaze flicking only briefly to T'Ash. 'For Marianne and for the future there will be better provision. It is early days but there is a lot of research into other therapies. The new medication is, frankly, less brutal but it does have some side effects. But your mother will be cared for and there is a new dawn, Beatrix, it is fast approaching and I will do everything in my power to ensure that she has the very best care. You are free of that burden. Think about it. You are free now,' and he quietly slipped me his snow white linen handkerchief which I held to my face as I hastily made a retreat from the table to the ladies room.

As Beatrix left the room, Felix placed his knife and fork purposefully on the side of his plate. He was not going to eat any more of the meal. He was fairly indifferent to food anyway and only ate when he was hungry. His appetite at this moment was for information, not food.

'How did you meet my niece Mr. Ash?' T'Ash paused, fork midway to mouth and then looked a bit startled.

'Erm, well... I saw her up at the hospital. My gran's in there.'

'So I gather. And are you sleeping with her?' T'Ash blushed to his roots and spluttered on the lamb stew he had just put in his mouth. Felix laid a hand gently on T'Ash's arm. 'I am not judgemental but I need to know. It may matter in due course...' T'Ash shrugged.

'We are always careful. I know what I am doing.'

'No doubt. But she is a minor and soon to be my ward. The current 'arrangements' will have to change until provision can be made for her.' T'Ash began to raise his voice and objections but Felix simply pressed harder on the wrist he was holding.

'I want to marry her. Will you sign for that?' T'Ash said belligerently shaking himself free of Felix's grasp.

'No,' Felix said simply. T'Ash waited and when nothing else was forthcoming he said,

'No? Is that it? No? Why not? What have you got against me? You don't even know me!' and T'Ash was aware that his voice was just a little too loud and a bit slurred. He said it again, quietly and carefully just to make the point. 'You don't even know me...'

'Precisely,' said Felix. 'Perhaps I should have said *not yet*, until we get to know each other better. Beatrix is going to be my priority.' Then he stood up and smiled over T'Ash's shoulder as Beatrix returned from the ladies room.

I don't know what T'Ash and Felix talked about but when I returned, having applied fresh powder and covered up the worst effects of the red rimmed eyes, T'Ash was behaving like a spoiled child. It could have been the wine and beer he had consumed, matching Felix glass for glass, and T'Ash was no drinker. With an alcoholic father, he was virtually teetotal. I felt the tension rise again as the *Pears Belle Helene* were served with cream.

'So what about these pictures then?' T'Ash said stabbing a pear with his spoon and draining his glass. I was seeing a belligerent, slightly boorish and juvenile T'Ash tonight.

'Yes, the paintings,' said Felix, unperturbed. 'Of course they still belong to Mrs. Quinn, until Beatrix is of age, unless of course they have been sold by the rightful owner, in which case there will be a trace which I can follow. I will find them for you, Beatrix,' he said patting my hand again and turning his attention to the pears.

I saw T'Ash shift in his seat beside me and felt how inadequate we both were playing adult games in a very real and grown up world. I think of Felix now as a friendly assassin who lobbed dynamite into the middle of our lives and blew T'Ash and me apart, but in the process helped us both to realise our juvenile dreams.

'So I won't be returning to Holland tomorrow,' he said, placing his spoon carefully on the dish. 'There is more business to attend to here than I had originally planned for. I think we have worn you out, my dear, you are looking pale again. May I suggest we adjourn and let you rest? I will come to see you tomorrow if that is agreeable?'

His use of English was flawless, old fashioned and virtually accent-less, although there was an undertone which gave away his 'foreignness' as Aunt Maude would have said; and he was my uncle; an uncle I never expected to have or knew about. I was less alone than I believed myself to be and I felt comforted by his presence. I was glad he was staying. I wanted to know him better and I knew deep down that I was falling for his charm and the security he brought me. He was the closest to my beloved Pa as I could get and I wasn't going to let him go too easily.

'The pompous, arrogant bastard. Who does he think he is swanning in here and upsetting you like that?' T'Ash and I were in the kitchen and he slammed the kettle onto the hob. 'I'm telling you, I don't trust him one iota. Next thing he'll be using them new drugs they've got now – he said didn't he? *'phenobarbitols for a prolonged narcosis.'* That's what he's planning. He'll drug you and get you to talk and take those paintings. How do we know he's your uncle anyway?' and he was pointing the spoon from the tea caddy at me.

I was slumped at the table, my hands fighting a losing battle to hold up my head. I looked at T'Ash with eyes washed clear from the tears I had shed for my poor mad Mother, lost to me now for all time. I saw the angry contorted face of a thwarted boy who thought that he had been so clever and outwitted Dr Felix. I saw 'Uncle' Felix's eyes; deep with love; for me or for the Mother he saw in me? Or maybe for his Brother, long dead, who had sparked this whole scene, rippling down the years, echoing into the next generation; his unresolved death; his mysterious life in that studio; his illegitimate daughter still in Holland; Johanna, my sister; and all of it adding to my mother's decent into madness and my disturbed 'visions' and migraines. It could only end when the truth was finally understood and accepted and not just told; and that had a way to go yet.

I saw a thin red line running unbroken from Max and Felix – *Max Prins, Artist, 1932*; through Marianne and Jellicoe, more triangles and deceit; more betrayal and secrets; down to me and then Johanna, the end of that unbroken line; and I had to follow it to the very end.

And T'Ash? He was a tangent; he was not part of that unbroken line and he was trying to break it. I saw it with all the clarity of a vision:

I saw the line, carmine red; the colour of the Nazi flag and of blood; whose blood? Pa lying dead in a pool of blood, the red line going back into a time before I existed; and running away from me in the other direction, into a future which I, the small child hiding behind the skirt of a strange woman who smelt funny and who held me tightly could not grasp; a future I couldn't see but felt with fear which embedded itself and was part of the line; and the woman's face; wrapped in white cloth with a black veil; she was a nun and I was taken away to a quiet place which was all white and soft and clean until my mother came to claim me back and we fled along the red line and I knew I had to follow it to the end.....

T'Ash was shaking me and stroking hair from my face.

'Scarlett, my darling. Are you ok?' Scarlett? Who was Scarlett? She had already left. 'Is it one of your turns? I said you shouldn't take them pills from him. It could have been the pills. You haven't had a 'turn' for ages. Are you ok?' I shrugged him away and moved to the sink and splashed water on my face and drank a cup of cold water.

'I'm going to bed. It's been a long day,' and I walked out, and closed my bedroom door firmly on him.

Scarlett Ash died that night, just as Betty Quinn had met her end when T'Ash strode so unexpectedly into her life with his Irish blarney and his stories of adventure and smelling of pear drops.

Chapter Twenty Two

The door closing was the only sound I heard. It echoed down the stairs like a sound effect in a second rate film, and reverberated around my head like shock waves. The door closed. Quietly it clicked too, and she was gone from me. No lingering goodnights. It was the calm and quietness which was so surprising: a door slamming, a murderous screeching quarrel would have made sense, but the clicking of the door and the silence did not.

Then, things started to happen so fast I couldn't keep up. One minute she was there in my arms and then it was like she was wrenched away and I was left holding dreams and fragments of herself. But Love surely doesn't evaporate with the mist. You see, that is where Dr. Van Gelder is wrong. And also where he is wrong is that some lives are small and some, maybe like 'Dr. Felix Van Gelder, Hero of the Resistance', are colossal lives; brilliant, lighting up the sky and chucking ripples of fireworks down the ages and my Scarlett, Beatrix, Betty, she is getting the fallout and she doesn't even know it, which is why I have to write this so that one day, posterity will unravel, revealing itself in all its glorious Technicolour and light up her canvas and make her real again, and then I can hold her, really hold her in my arms forever.

But there is work to do first. She is slipping away from me as he tugs at her unravelling past – not even hers, but her parents and she can't let go of the threads because she fears that like her mother, she will unravel as well. But she won't. Not if she becomes solid and holds onto me and then we can tie off her loose ends and begin to weave our own lives together, in America. And I won't let my mother and my family get in the way of that by way of her not being Catholic and everything – we will just have to make that bit work out.

First he changed the locks, so that was my last night as Bea's 'lodger' and I had to go home to my ma. My things were packed and he arranged with me to collect them one dinnertime and Scarlett wasn't there. I hadn't clapped eyes on her; I needed to be sure that she was ok, and then he tells me they are going to Amsterdam. He didn't say when. I suppose he is still trying to get the paintings back. Will Bea tell him where they are?

I left her a poem I wrote but I don't know if she'll get it before she leaves. If he will let her have it. All I know is that he has turned up in her life and taken her away from me and threatened me – he actually threatened me with court action if I didn't go along with his scheme and all along he only wants the pictures and I don't know if he really wants her anyway.

So, this much I know. There are thirteen paintings and the paperwork. reveals something of the activities. There were receipts, letters, bills of sale. I had them translated by Wilf at the Council. Turns out he was Dutch, spoke flawless English and had lived here since before the war. He was a bit too interested so I said that they were documents found in an old ladies attic and the family wanted the Council Archive to have them. Before I handed them over, I needed to log what was there. That was my job, you see, to keep track of documents and source information for officers. It was dull and involved me having to type reports. I would much rather have been working for the local paper but that would come, in America. I would be a writer; start local, maybe writing about the Irish Community in Brooklyn, where we were heading. But first I had to join up the clues of Beatrix's life. She had got me involved and now I was right in it up to my hocks in this suitcase full of papers and canvasses. And if she didn't want to know anymore, I still had to find out. I still love her. I still want to be with her but the Doctor has forbidden it and I want to know why and what he is hiding. He has stolen her away from me just as we were getting close. I want to marry her. To take her with me to America, but he would never sign for her to marry and she is still too young.

Wilf seemed interested as well and he knows a fair bit about Dutch Art, so when I get to know him better I might get him to help me unravel the clues.

Then, when Dr. Van Gelder turned up at my work and asked to speak to me, I was dumbfounded. There he was, bold as brass in the foyer of the Council Offices, looking suave and debonair and me in my shirt sleeves and sleeveless pullover with inky fingers where I had just changed the ribbon on my typewriter, feeling dishevelled. I ran a hand through my hair which I knew was curling in the damp weather because it flopped over my forehead and I nearly stumbled down the last few stairs as I tried to straighten my tie. I felt like I was going to see the headmaster. As he looked up and saw me, his gaze was – what was it? Intense. Piercing. Determined. Whatever you would call it, I knew that it was trouble for me. He inclined his head. I ran inky fingers through my hair again.

'Is she alright? Scarlett – Beatrix I mean. Is she ok?' I blurted clumsily.

He shrugged. 'As far as I now.'

'So what then?' I asked, a bit irritated now and wanting to stand my ground.

'I need to speak to you. When are you free?' It was coming up to lunchtime but I wanted to go round to Bea's and check she was ok.

'Tonight, after work,' I said, and turned to go back upstairs.

'How about now?' he said, crossing his hands in front of him, his black leather gloves menacing and I imagined the weight of the iron fist inside the soft leather. I hesitated. That was my mistake. 'You have a lunch hour. I know. I checked.' That irritated me beyond belief. How dare he check up on me? He must have seen the look in my face as I turned back to look at him.

'I will be at the George,' he said and walked out.

The George Hotel was about two minutes walk from the Town Hall and Bea's house was a quick five minute sprint in the opposite direction. I ran back upstairs, and found Wilf flicking through my notebook.

'This your novel?' he asked. I snatched the book from him and muttered something about it being 'private property' and shoved it in my jacket pocket as I pulled it from the hook on the back of the door.

'I have to go out,' I said. 'Back after dinner.'

'What will I tell Jammy?' he shouted as the door slammed and I shrugged as though it really didn't matter. And it didn't. Whatever Van Gelder wanted it was more important than Jammy, Wilf's curiosity or even my job right now.

I sprinted round to Bea's house and found the spare key to the back door under the mop bucket, but she wasn't there, and my overactive imagination kicked in. I checked the cellar, and the rooms of the house. Maybe she was at the hospital? There was no chance I would get there and back in my lunch hour and besides, I needed to know what Felix wanted. So I sprinted back around to the High Street and into the foyer of the George. The smoky warmth and smell of food hit me and made my nose run. I rummaged in my pockets but didn't find a handkerchief, so sniffed and felt the well heeled surroundings begin to press in. I was in a tweed jacket and the elbows had been reinforced with leather patches. My hair was a mess and I hadn't had time to wash my hands. I looked quickly around, saw Felix facing away from me at the bar and sprinted through the lounge to the Gents at the back. I had a quick spruce up, tried in vain to put a bit of gloss on my scuffed shoes and dampened my hair down to tame the worst of it. The ink wasn't all going to come out, but I scrubbed my hands as best I could and wished I had leather gloves. I felt wrong in here with all of these ladies in hats and gentlemen in fine suits and highly polished brogues. It hadn't occurred to me before. I just got on with my life and fitted in where I was. I couldn't fit in here though, and I realised that was exactly why Felix had wanted to meet me here at lunchtime. He also seemed certain that I would come. I was about to turn and walk out and thought that I would meet him tonight somewhere else, but then I would have to wait to find out what he wanted. He turned and looked directly at me across the room and I realised that he had been watching me in the mirror all along. I felt warm very suddenly and knew that my face was flushed. To turn and run now would be defeat so I squared my shoulders, ran a hand through my hair, and crossed the room.

'What do you want?' he asked brusquely. I stared at him. 'To drink?' he added patiently.

Caught off balance again, I muttered 'Just half a pint. I have to go back to work.' He gave the order, quietly to the man behind the bar then turned back to me, glass in hand. Gin and Tonic I guessed.

'We have a table booked. I've ordered wine.'

'How did you know I'd come?'

He shrugged. 'Because you want to know what I have to say.'

'How can you be so certain of that?' He looked at me; no that's not quite right; he looked right through me and over me into a world which he inhabited and where I could never join him. Then his gaze fixed on me like a bullet and pierced my defences.

'You have some property which belongs to my ward. It is valuable to her and I need to ensure it is safe.' I was about to protest but he held up his hand, now glove-less and spotless with long piano players fingers. He wore a heavy ring on his little finger, like a signet ring but with a ruby in it. I thought I had seen it somewhere before. 'I know that you have seen the documents and the pictures and that knowledge itself could be dangerous.' Then he leant towards me and I felt his breath warm on my ear. He was about the same height as me and slim but with a powerful build and his grip on my arm was like steel. His voice was low and I wondered if Bea had ever seen this side of him. 'There are others who want those pictures and who shouldn't have them. There is a lot at stake. This is not a game, Alfred.'

'Who are you?' I said and pulled away and my voice rose. He sipped his drink and looked coldly at me and I swear his lips didn't move as he spoke again.

'I can find the paintings, and when I do, I will make sure that you are in the frame for theft of precious artefacts....'

'You're threatening me. Bea would never let you... She knows where they are...'

'She is in a fragile state right now and I don't want to put pressure on her.'

'How fragile? What have you done to her?' and I wanted to strangle him with my bare hands but he was quick and put a restraining hand on my arm and gripped like a vice.

'Stay away from her, Mr. Ash.' I saw two men in the mirror pushing through the bar towards us. One I recognised as the Manager. He stopped in front of us and Van Gelder surreptitiously released my arm.

'Everything alright Doctor Van Gelder? I hope this ... person.... is not disturbing you?'

'I'm leaving,' I said and Felix turned his back on me.

'Your table is ready, Sir,' said the Maitre D as I felt another grip on my arm and the Manager was steering me away from the bar. I shook him off.

'I'm going,' I said, slamming my glass on the bar and watching it slop everywhere. The couple nearby leapt back to avoid being drenched. 'But you can't stop me seeing her,' I shouted to his retreating back and heard him say to the Maitre D.

'No, a small domestic matter. I'll be dining alone.'

'Thank you, Sir', was the last I heard as I turned and fled the Hotel, and sprinted back to Stockwell Street to see Bea. She still wasn't there so I sat in the parlour on the lumpy sofa and stared into the empty grate and willed my fury and impotence to create a spark which would ignite the ashes.

Then I decided that I had to go to the beach chalet to make sure that the paintings were still safe and I would sleep there whilst I thought about what to do next.

Chapter Twenty Three

This country was grey and drab and the summers fade fast, she thought as her heels clacked on the old stones of the Dutch Quarter. Hard to believe it was the Capital city of a once proud Roman Empire in Britain. What did they call it? Camulodunum? Something like that. The Romans must have been devastated to be posted in Colchester, when they could have been in Rome or Spain or Gaul. She would have a holiday in the south when this was sorted, before she went to America to be reunited with her daughter.

Jellicoe's plan was that she would track down the fortune and reclaim her daughter from the Puritanism of her Father's family and they would travel deeper into the land of freedom, heading West to California and Hollywood where they would finally live out loud.

It had been a long journey but now she was ready to confront Felix and make him pay for what she had endured in the years since the war. But for now, she held the aces and the pictures were almost within her grasp.

Wilf was a treasure. She could not have done it without him. He had photographed all of the relevant documents in the battered brown suitcase which the stupid boy with the strange name – Tash, or something like that – had taken from the old house in which Marianne had ended her days. Ok she wasn't dead yet, but as good as.

Jellicoe had visited the hospital and seen Marianne in the day room, through the glass door. A frail old lady staring out of the window. She had been difficult to recognise until the nurse pointed her out. Marianne turned her head at the sound of the door opening and her blank eyes stared at Jellicoe then for a fleeting moment came the recognition and the scream, which echoed down the corridor and reverberated in Jellicoe's head as she ran from the building. What had she expected? Forgiveness or revenge perhaps? But then neither was really necessary any more.

And the girl – Beatrix. Jellicoe softened as she thought of the small child she had once resented for taking Max's attention; the small tyrant who could do no wrong in her father's eyes, who had grown up here, in this dreary town; but at least she had been loved by her mother and English family. She was English now, not Dutch; a young woman with a lover and her life ahead of her and a father she could claim along with his inheritance. She tried hard not to think about her own little girl, growing up parentless as she herself had endured. She found it hard not to hold on to a little resentment of Beatrix.

The van pulled up outside her lodgings at twilight, shortly after people in this country sat down for their evening meal which they called their 'tea'. It was too early to go yet and there was still too much light and traffic and too many people out and about. Wilf and Arturo jumped down from the cab as she wiped the condensation away with her sleeve to peer through the windows of the guest house; a shabby place run by a Mrs. Kane, on the north side of Colchester. Wilf had been staying here since he came to Colchester a few months ago to work for Jellicoe, and Arturo joined him only yesterday as his 'cousin'. As Jellicoe was fair, despite the dark wig she was wearing for this trip, she would never pass as Arturo's relative; he looked too Hispanic, so she became Wilf's older sister on a trip to visit their aging Aunt who was in Severalls hospital. When she mentioned it to the landlady, Mrs Kane's lips pursed and she sucked in breath and shivered as though Jellicoe had said that her Aunt was practicing witchcraft.

The three met in the small front 'parlour' as Mrs. Kane called it, not a word Jellicoe was familiar with but Wilf explained to her. He had grown up in England. His parents left from Rotterdam for London before the war but he had never forgotten his roots or language, and although he was evacuated to the countryside with other children during the war, he believed that his father had kept some contacts in The Netherlands. When Jellicoe contacted him to find some information for her, it didn't take him long to work out that it related to the war; and she was paying well.

Mrs Kane provided an evening meal, which was served in the 'parlour' at a small table set for three in the corner of the room. Tonight she served something called 'shepherd's pie' which Jellicoe had never heard of but which consisted of tasteless minced meat with watery mashed potatoes and tinned peas. She had little appetite but the men ate heartily and had second helpings of the suet pudding and custard which followed, seemingly oblivious to the lumps and texture of glue. She hoped that with all of this food on board they would be ready for the task ahead.

'That was lovely, Mrs Kane. Thanks. By the way, we will be going out tonight. There's a new film at the Palace which my sister won't have seen. I wonder if you could leave the door unbolted? We shouldn't be back too late,' said Wilf as the plates were cleared away.

'Oh that sounds lovely,' said Mrs Kane and then addressed Jellicoe as though she were herself an inmate of Severalls. Jellicoe had also noticed this trait in the British people she had met; first a distrust of foreign accents, then they would speak very slowly and loudly at you in an attempt to help you understand their complicated language. And because the British could never imagine speaking anything other than English, they just didn't get the fact that 'foreigners', especially Dutch ones, had no problem speaking other languages.

'Oh- that - will – be - nice -for – you - Mrs. -Vogel,' she said slowly and carefully, using Jellicoe's nom de guerre, Mrs Margot Vogel, war widow and teacher in Deventer, a small town in Holland. No one was likely to check and the guise was working well. There would be no trace that Jellicoe had ever been in England. With her dark wig and dowdy clothes, the woman smiling at the absurdity of Mrs. Kane was unrecognisable as Jellicoe Willem, mistress to the German Director of a chemical plant, Ipsmar Internationale, based in Geneva.

They left the guest house at 7.30 and Arturo and Jellicoe took all of their belongings with them. Wilf left an envelope with payment for his visitors and a note to say that they had to travel urgently to London but he would be back later when he had seen them safely onto the train.

They headed north out of Colchester on the Old London Road heading for Harwich, but before they reached it, they turned left down to the estuary and through a small village whose name was totally unpronounceable to Jellicoe, even with her excellent English.

It was dark in the woods even at this time of year. Jellicoe stayed in the van to keep watch and wished she still had the small gun in her handbag which Felix had 'liberated' when they met. But this was England in peacetime and she very much doubted that carrying a gun would endear her to the authorities, should she be stopped. Besides, shooting someone in this quiet wood, other than Felix, would be quite wrong. Wilf knew what to do if anyone got in their way. A heavy club was quieter than a gun and effective enough to get them away.

Round one in this fight had gone to Felix, but she was sure she was in the lead on round two. Thanks to Wilf's investigation, she had found Marianne and Beatrix in Colchester. Following T'Ash was easy. He was supremely unaware like many people who had lived their lives in safety and plenty. He was soft around the edges and she knew that he would never stand up against Felix. Or her.

She hoped the pictures were not too badly damaged by damp or neglect: she had not factored in costly restoration processes which would take time and money, both of which were running out fast.

They had crates and tools in the van ready to pack the paintings – she knew from Wilf that there were 13 pictures and she was glad that she wasn't superstitious. Wilf had told her what he could remember of the list in T'Ash's notebook and some she could guess from her memories of the hundreds which Max painted or bought or acquired during her time in his studio. She guessed at the sizes the pictures would be and had ordered crates from a packing firm in London delivered to the Port this afternoon and loaded by Wilf and Arturo before they picked her up. They were booked onto the crossing on the SS Amsterdam from Harwich tonight.

It was the kind of operation she had missed since the war but now her life had shifted purpose and it was very simple; she wanted her daughter to be safe and provided for. Her own parents, now dead, had backed the wrong side and lost everything and so she had no inheritance of her own, and was reliant on what she could make of her life alone, and she was getting a bit old for the oldest profession. Legitimising herself mattered so that Johanna could be proud of her. Her past would be rewritten or simply deleted from all records so that she could be reinvented. Sleeping with men for information was fine when there was a cause you believed in but in peacetime it was simply sordid.

A noise from down the slope startled her and she stopped daydreaming and listened. There were voices and a scuffle, some shouting and then silence. She got out of the van and keeping the beam of her torch low, listened hard. Wilf and Arturo were used to this sort of operation but it was difficult to move soundlessly, carrying heavy objects, in a dark wood at night.

Two sets of footsteps approaching. Hasty whispers. Then Arturo appeared out of the gloom and spoke to her in Dutch.

'The boy was in there. He didn't see Wilf but I had to deal with him.' She set her face to neutral. She didn't care about the boy one way or another, but in peacetime, murder was not acceptable. 'He's ok. He'll have a bit of a headache in the morning though,' and he smiled ruefully and handed her a small crate wrapped in plastic. She took it from him reverently, dying to see which painting it was. 'They are nearly all in crates and we found this,' he said as Wilf held up the battered brown suitcase. She smiled the kind of smile which wraps itself around you in a hug.

She was relieved that the packing was appropriate and would assess the damage at the other end. Now all that she had to do was pack them into the large shipping crates, ready to be craned into the hold of the SS Amsterdam for the overnight sailing. She would be travelling first class, Arturo second. They would ignore each other so that if one of them ran into trouble, there was a chance the other would get through and deliver the pictures to their destination, a warehouse in The Hague where she would collect them and drive down through Europe to the South of France. It would be easier there to sell the pictures, and in the suitcase, she hoped, were the provenances.

Chapter Twenty Four

Felix was at the hotel when the first phone call came through. A knock on his door and the receptionist summoned him to the booth in reception.

'Dr. Gelder speaking,' he said, often dropping the 'Van' in the UK.

'Dr. Gelder. This is Dr. Ritchie from Severalls Hospital. I am the duty doctor this evening.' He paused for a reply but Felix remained silent. He always preferred to listen than talk. 'Your sister in law, ... er. Mrs. Quinn, has taken a turn for the worse I am afraid.'

'How worse?' said Felix without too much emotion.

'To tell the truth we don't really know how much the incident has affected her. From what I understand, a woman turned up at the Hospital this afternoon. The nurse reported a dark haired woman, 35 – 40 years old with a foreign accent asking to see Mrs. Quinn. She registered as...' there was a pause whilst he checked his notes and Felix tapped impatiently on the black Bakelite phone casing. 'Ah yes, Mrs. M Vogel. Said she was Mrs. Quinn's sister-in-law so I wondered if she was a relation of yours? I believe that Mrs Quinn has Dutch relations other than yourself?' It was a question rather than a statement.

'No. There is no sister-in-law,' Felix said firmly.

'That's interesting because Mrs. Quinn took one look at Mrs. Vogel and started to scream. It took three staff to control her until she was sedated.'

'What happened to the woman?' said Felix already a few steps ahead of the Doctor.

'She ran away. No-one saw her go, she just fled. I am sorry that she got in but Mrs. Quinn has made improvement and was in the day room and the visitor seemed very ...kind.'

'What time was this?' he asked. The doctor paused again to check his notes.

'Erm, let me see; there was a change of shift shortly after so it would have been around 3.30 this afternoon.

'And what has happened to Mrs. Quinn?'

'Oh yes of course, well, she is sedated now and back on the locked ward. The visitor didn't get close to her or cause her any physical harm, in fact from what I gather, she barely entered the room. Mrs. Quinn has been calm and controlled recently and she has never shown these violent outbursts until today. It was a surprise for the staff who know her well and we feel that this woman must be of some significance to Mrs. Quinn's past?

'How is Mrs. Quinn now,' Felix asked again, not wishing to divulge any more than he had to about his suspicions as to who the intruder might be. The Doctor took a deep breath which sounded weary to Felix and he felt a moment of sympathy. It was not easy dealing with mental patients all day, every day.

'Well, she will remain under surveillance and we will make another assessment tomorrow. There is really no need for you or her daughter..' again Felix heard the rustle of papers as he checked his notes and his impatience grew, 'Yes, her daughter, Beatrix, to be alarmed or to rush over here, but we felt the need to let you know.'

'Let me know when she is conscious and able to talk. I am sure she is in the best hands. Thank you, Doctor

Ritchie.' And Felix hung up. There was no point in going to visit Marianne, she wouldn't know he was there. And Jellicoe was here. She had fulfilled her promise to trace the pictures and she had found Marianne. What did she intend? Maybe she knew where Beatrix was. He felt that Jellicoe would stop at nothing to get those pictures and Marianne and Beatrix were vulnerable. At least Marianne was safe for now, in a locked ward, but Beatrix was alone since he had warned T'Ash off from seeing her. He made a quick decision. He would bring Beatrix here to stay at the hotel where she would be safer. He ran up the stairs and took his overcoat from a peg behind the door. By instinct, he checked his inside pocket which was hard to detect; wallet, identification papers, passport, and he smiled to himself. During the war he had taught the women in his 'cell' to have their papers and some cash stitched into the lining of a handbag, or hidden somewhere in their clothing in case of sudden flight. Old habits had never left him despite the years of peace. He hurried back down the stairs, putting his hat on as he left.

'Dr. Van Gelder, another call for you. You are popular tonight.' His jaw tightened. 'I'll put it through to the booth; it's from a call box,' and the phone he had recently put down rang again.

'Felix, it's me. T'Ash. There's been a break in. They got the pictures. You've got to come now. I'm hurt... ' and the pips went.

'Where are you T'Ash? T'Ash!' And the line went dead.

Felix slammed the phone down and the receptionist looked up surprised.

'Where did you say that call was from?' he said more aggressively than he should. It wasn't her fault and he saw that he had alarmed her. She checked her notes.

'Erm, the caller said he was in a call box in Wrabness and to hurry, he didn't have a lot of change.....'

'Where's Rab-Ness?' he said urgently leaning on the desk. She leant away from him.

'Erm, well it's along the estuary. A little village.'

'Do you know where the call could have been made?'

'I think there is a phone box next to the pub. There is only one. I don't think there is another one in the village.'

Felix took a deep breath.

'Thank you. I need a taxi. Urgently.'

'Oh, outside. I'll get John to call one,' she said as he hurried to the entrance.

The village was in darkness, except for some lights at the far end of the main street. He saw T'Ash outside a village pub, which had a trademark red English phone box outside, as the receptionist had suggested. T'Ash was slumped on a bench and Felix prayed he wasn't too late. He quickly assessed that T'Ash was conscious, but cold.

'Why didn't you wait inside the pub?' Felix said as T'Ash tried to stand up to greet him. 'Let me have a look at that wound.' He parted the bloodied hair and saw a deep gash and bruising. T'Ash winced and cried out in pain.

'They would have taken one look at the state of me and thrown me out as a vagrant especially with my Irish accent and I didn't want to draw attention to meself. I hoped you'd find me. Ouch....'

'Ok. It's not too serious but I can't tell if you are concussed. I'll call an ambulance, but before it gets here, I need to know what happened, T'Ash. Can you remember anything?

'Pretty much all of it but there isn't much to say. They got the pictures, Doctor. I'm so sorry...' he said drowsily and closed his eyes. This wasn't going to get them anywhere so Felix crouched in front of T'Ash still slumped on the bench and shook him by the shoulders.

'I know it wasn't your fault. Just tell me who? How many?'

T'Ash was struggling to speak and his voice was slurred. 'Two. I think there were two blokes. I'd just made a cup of tea with me camper stove and was going to try to get a fire going on the beach – there's no heating in the beach chalet - and I heard a noise round the back and I thought it might be the fox who lives along the estuary – seen him a lot round here – and anyways, as I turns to look, this bloke, big guy, comes at me with a stick and whacks me over the head. And there was another one – if I think really hard I might know who he was – you know, the way he stood, his body language, all that... but his face was covered, both of them, faces covered with scarves.

'Next thing, I am unconscious on the beach and my hands are bound in front and my head hurts like I've been run over by a train and I can't move a muscle and then I hear them talking.'

'What did they say?'

'No idea. It was foreign... and then I heard a woman's voice some way off. She was foreign as well. But one of the men, not the one who hit me, said something in English. It was very quiet but I was trying to listen hard and I was surprised to hear that he spoke English so well.' T'Ash closed his eyes as though he would go to sleep, too tired to say anymore. Felix shook him awake.

'What did he say, T'Ash. In English. What did the man say?' T'Ash opened his eyes painfully and looked at Felix, unfocussed and probably concussed. 'It's ok. I'll call an ambulance. You will be ok. Can you remember what he said?

'Yes, he said, *Time and Tide waits for no man. Or woman,* and he laughed.' The effort had exhausted him. Felix could do without being involved in this, but he had to make sure T'Ash was safe. He slipped into the phone box and called an ambulance and then went back to T'Ash.

'T'Ash I have to go after the paintings. Just tell them you were attacked at your beach chalet..'

'It's my gran's....'

'Yes, yes, ok. But don't mention the paintings. Do you understand that? Don't tell them about the paintings.'

'But the police can help you get them back,' said T'Ash.

'No. I can do that and I don't want you to get into trouble, ok?

'How come I'll be in trouble? I didn't steal the pictures...' and he tailed off as realisation dawned on him. Felix patted his arm.

'I will get the paintings back. I have a good idea who has them, but I have to go now. If you mention this to anyone, you are involved. Culpable. Do you understand? I think it best if you leave immediately. For Ireland and then we will sort out your passage to America...' That had T'Ash's full attention and he was upright again and defensive.

'What about Bea?'

'I will tell her something. She will understand. And she will follow you as soon as she is able...'

'I won't go without her.'

'You have no choice. I press charges for theft of my ward's property and claim that you colluded with Jellicoe to steal valuable works of art belonging to the Dutch people. You would be facing a very long sentence.' T'Ash fell back onto the bench aghast, his head still hurting. He tried to clear his thoughts. How could he play a game against this man?

'Who are you?' he said to Felix.

'Right now, I am Beatrix's Ward and it is her interest I am prioritising. I will pay your passage to America, via Ireland. You can get that far by the end of the week and wait in Ireland until your emigration papers are sorted. I will contact you there.'

'I'll never see her again.'

'When she is of age, she can choose to join you.'

'But I still love her.'

Felix leant in close and his voice was low. 'You will forget her in time. She has a new life waiting for her and I know that if you truly love her, you will let her take her opportunities. I will make sure that you have some money to start you off in the States. I am trying to help you T'Ash.' T'Ash stood up and roared with rage and threw himself at Felix.

'I don't want your fucking money,' he yelled as the older man side stepped, grabbed T'Ash's arm and wrenched it up his back holding him in a vice. T'Ash was crying with pain and frustration.

'But you may change your mind when you arrive in America penniless. You want to be a writer. You want to go to America. I am offering you that opportunity. Don't be a fool T'Ash.' He slowly released T'Ash's arm and let him fall gently back onto the musty carpet of dead leaves. Then he crouched beside him. 'But first I have to get those pictures back. Will you help me?'

'Fuck off.'

'If you don't want to help me, then do it for her.'

'The pictures are for you. I know that. It's all about you getting your hands on them pictures and nothing at all to do with her. You don't even know her. I do. I have been trying to help her. Why can't you just leave us alone?' Felix was running out of time and patience. He heard the Ambulance bell clanging in the distance and could see it's lights from the main road.

'I have to go,' he said checking his watch. 'But I will tell you why I can't leave things as they are and it has nothing at all to do with pictures. It has everything to do with the law and with the future of my niece, Goddaughter, ward. The State are putting forward the argument that she is at risk here of 'moral corruption' or some such; she cannot continue to live in the house with a man without an adult there, even if he were 'the lodger' rather than 'the lover'. As she is technically under age, the law would frown upon it and the neighbours may not tolerate it. And I put forward the argument that her mental health is at risk because of the trauma she has suffered and her medical records support that. I made a promise to her father and that doesn't end because she is sixteen and wants to marry a man of.... how old are you, T'Ash, twenty?' T'Ash leant against the side of the phone box and shook himself free. 'So you see, you need permission too, before you can marry her.'

Felix felt the fight go out of T'Ash and helped him gently back onto the bench. I would rather have him on my side, he thought, but removing him to the other side of the world will do the least damage.

He had asked the taxi to wait at the other end of the lane and now Felix walked away along the shadows towards it.

'Harwich Port. Can you get there quickly, I need to catch the night ferry? I will make it worth your while,' and the taxi driver laughed.

'Cutting that a bit fine sir, but I'll do me best. No traffic this time o' night and I know the porter on duty. He's me brother in law,' and he pulled off quietly taking a back road all the way.

Felix sat back in the car and felt weary but could not allow emotion to cloud his thinking. First, he had to ensure that Beatrix was safe. If he was right in his assumptions, and he hoped that his instincts were still functioning, Jellicoe was behind this and he believed that the woman at the hospital was her. Knowing the way she operated, he felt certain that she would leave on the boat with the pictures. But what about the two men? Would one of them go back to harm Beatrix? They had only immobilised T'Ash and he was more of a direct threat so the chances were unlikely. Still, he would need to warn her. He pulled a notebook from his pocket which had a silver pen attached and wrote briefly:

'I have an unscheduled appointment with our old friend in Amsterdam tonight. Please ensure you have a 'vellig' *evening and I will send you further details tomorrow.'* He had no envelope and knew that the 'postman' would read it. He tore the page from his notebook, folded the note into quarters and wrote Beatrix Van Gelder, 35 Stockwell Street, Colchester, on one side. Marianne had kept her Dutch dictionary and the use of the Dutch word for *'safe'* and his surname, would alert Beatrix to be careful. He would send her a telegram from the boat and book her into The George.

He reached over to the front seat and said, as casually as possible.

'I wonder, also, could you deliver this note to the address on the front? I can't leave my niece worrying about me, can I?' and handed the piece of folded paper to the driver who shrugged and slipped it into his top pocket. It was too dark to read the address.

'It's in Colchester. I will pay you the appropriate fare in advance, if that is agreeable.'

'Fine by me Gov. I'll pop in on my way home and enough said. Then that's me done for the night. Cost you a bit more than a first class stamp though,' and he laughed at his little joke and Felix laughed with him, but there was little mirth in the sound he made.

Chapter Twenty Five

Felix found Jellicoe's first class cabin quite easily without having to bribe anyone. He poured himself a drink and sat down to wait whilst she finished dinner. Despite the dark wig and glasses and the pea jacket and trousers, he recognised her immediately. There is always something about the way people move; a tilt of the head; a gesture of the arms; the length of stride or simply their posture, seated or walking.

She was on the middle deck where dinner was served in the first class dining room. She seemed wary, her head titled to the left, listening, looking around the lighted deck; something of the woodland creature about her; fragile; anxious; alert. She didn't see him although he knew, that like a feral animal, she sensed danger.

He was tempted to join her for dinner and surprise her, but he needed this business to be conducted in private and he had the element of surprise.

He was happy to wait here in her cabin and doze in the brittle way he had learned years ago, which snapped him awake as soon as his sixth sense alerted him to action.

'Where are the paintings Jellicoe?' In the dim light, he saw a mixture of expressions cross her face. After shock and a moment of fear, defiance was the one he recognised as her greatest strength. He spoke quietly.

'We are trapped on this boat until tomorrow. We owe it to each other to conduct our business in a civilised way.' She tried to run away but he blocked the doorway. 'It is stifling down here and there isn't enough room to ... negotiate. Shall we go on deck?' and he steered her through the open door, taking her arm tightly in his and letting the cabin door swing shut behind them and they sauntered, like lovers, arm in arm along the rocking corridor of the boat.

At the ship's rail, the noise of the engines was drowned by the sound of the water churning below.

'We leave together. Those paintings are going to be driven to my secure lock-up,' he said.

'You won't get away with this.'

'With what?'

'I should have those paintings.'

'They belong to Beatrix. She is Max's daughter and heir.'

'He has another daughter. She should have half.'

'Where is Johanna?' he asks.

'You think I would tell you?'

He shrugged. 'I don't need to know. I would not of hurt a child anyway but I think you know that.'

'You would have given her away for adoption.'

'The nuns would have found suitable parents.'

'I am a suitable parent. And I would never have seen her again.' He turned to face her directly.

'How do I know that she is Max's child? You refer to her as 'your' daughter.'

'How do we know Beatrix is Max's daughter?' She put her face close to his and spat out her words.

'Why do you doubt it? He never did.'

'And he didn't deny that Johanna was his. But he didn't live to see her. I loved him, Felix. I just wanted to be with him and our baby.'

'But he already had a wife and child. You knew the deal.'

'She didn't deserve him.'

'She saved your life. And your daughter's.'

'And you would have had no scruples about finishing me off, because I knew too much. I still do. I have been hiding from you for over a decade, Felix. So go on, finish it now.' She stepped away from him and held her arms out like a crucifix. Her coat caught the wind and billowed around her.

'I am not a murderer Jellicoe, as well you know. I save lives, I don't take them.' She moved closer to him again so that she could laugh in his face.

'You never used to have such scruples.'

'That was war. Different rules apply and we were fighting for survival. It's over now. Can we have peace do you think?'

'Whatever we did in the war, crimes were committed. Admittedly with good intentions but I still know far too much for your comfort, Felix.'

'Yes. But you won't say anything because it won't be in your interests. You are too heavily implicated and wherever your daughter is, she needs a mother. I hope you will be a good mother to her. I hope you made the right decision, Jellicoe.' She sat on a bench by the rail and his eyes didn't leave her.

'We were lovers once, Felix. I haven't forgotten that you enticed me to your brother's bed to serve your cause, and I did that for you. But you didn't intend that I would fall in love with Max did you?'

'Frankly I thought you incapable of loving anyone, but I have to admit that it complicated things,' he said pulling the cigarette from his pocket and offering her one. They smoked in silence.

'Have you ever been in love Felix?' He blew smoke over the ships rail and watched the waves churning below.

'Yes. Just once.'

'And?'

'And nothing.'

'Now there is no one left to love?'

'Oh yes. There is still someone.' She looked at him and waited. 'Beatrix. I love her like a daughter. I will do anything to ensure her happiness and secure her future.'

'You have another niece,' she reminded him. He was silent.

'Yes. I suppose I do. So I will do you a deal.' He paused for a few moments and watched the churning grey waves in a sea of blackness all around them. 'I will sell the paintings and set up a trust fund for Johanna's future. She will have a portion of the value of the paintings invested until she is of age. Until she is 21.'

'Half,' said Jellicoe.

'You are hardly in a position to negotiate,' he said. 'The majority will go to Max's *legitimate* daughter. A portion, to be negotiated, to Johanna,' and she recognised the firmness in his tone. He would not bargain further and she was amazed he had mellowed sufficiently to consider any sort of deal.

'Why should I not just keep them all? I know how to sell them. I have the provenances.'

'Because I will ensure that are labelled forgeries. No self respecting gallery will touch them.'

'You will bring the whole thing crashing down.'

'Oh no. I am not so stupid. I have put measures in place to protect me, and Beatrix of course, from any fall out.' Was he bluffing? What sort of measures? What had he done?

Felix watched intently as Jellicoe stood and looked over the rail at the churning sea. She couldn't believe that she had once wanted to end it all, that she could see no way to continue her life when Max died and Felix held her prisoner until her baby was born. It was Sister Maria Roma who had helped, who had enabled her baby to be taken safely out of Holland with Jellicoe, fragile and sore from the birth, by simply leaving the door unlocked. That was all it took and her life had meaning again.

'I don't want to fight you Felix. What's done is done.'

'Why did you go to see Marianne in hospital?' She looked surprised that he knew about that, but then Felix always knew about everything. 'Did you wish to harm her?' She shook her head.

'I wanted to know how Max died. I was unconscious. I remember gunshots and fainting into a pool of blood except that it wasn't blood it was water; my waters had broken and Max was going to kill me and Marianne stepped in front of me. I think I wanted to thank her.' She turned her face to Max and he could see the hurt there. 'When I saw her, in that hospital, she looked so old and lost. She's gone, Felix. I didn't even get near her. She just started screaming and set off some of the others and then it was mayhem. I just ran away. It's time to stop running.'

'And time to stop playing games. Do you agree to my proposal?'

'What is the alternative?'

'The pictures belong to Beatrix. She will have the proceeds from all of them.'

'I have them now.'

'Yes. In the hold of this ship. One call from the Captain and we will be met at the Hook of Holland by police.'

'Then no one gets them.'

'The rightful owner will.'

'They will be destroyed as forgeries.'

'Restored to the rightful owner, Miss Beatrix Prins, legitimate daughter of the deceased, Max Prins, as worthless paintings in the style of.... There are no signatures on any of them. It is not a crime to paint *'in the style of...'* only to claim that they are by someone else. We were always very careful.' She let out a long held breath.

'No signatures?' He shook his head. 'But the provenances?'

He shrugged. 'I have copies if I need them in the future. I can wait. Another decade will make little difference now.'

'So, the paintings are ready to sell as works by famous artists but not signed?'

'I have someone who can sign them should that become necessary.'

'Who?'

'A restorer in Amsterdam.'

'Ben Van Mueller,' she said categorically.

'You know him?'

'I know of him.'

He was impressed. 'Do you want to work with me, or against me?'

She chewed her thumb nail. 'I can't win. They are of little value as copies of famous works by a little known Dutch forger.'

'He wasn't a forger. He was a Master.'

She was surprised by the vehemence in his voice. 'So what you are proposing to do with them is still a crime.'

'In a good cause.'

'Another good cause. Is Beatrix your new 'cause?' It is still no less a crime.' She turned back to look out at the blackness and felt the cold air and spray slap her face.

'Will you work with me or against me?' She considered the offer. She was literally between the devil and the deep blue sea, except that the deep ocean beneath them was grey and churning white foam and not the warm turquoise of the oceans she would retire to. And the devil himself was behind her, mellowed with age and not nearly so bad as her memory painted him. She shivered and he draped his coat around her shoulders. She stood and held out her hand. They shook on the deal and he stepped forward and kissed her gently on the cheek. She shivered again in the cold north wind.

Chapter Twenty Six

We are sitting in the parlour, Felix and I, as the crates are loaded into the van. I am in my travelling clothes and the suitcases will go with the van. I have a large, overnight travelling bag which is all I will need until we reach my new home. In the front window, the back of a grimy sign saying *'To Let'* cuts out most of the feeble light.

It is the start of Autumn and I am leaving England for a new 'temporary' life as the Ward of my Uncle Felix. Technically an orphan and not yet twenty one, I had a choice. Stay here as a ward of court or go to Holland with Felix to begin my training at Art School there. It had all been sorted out remarkably quickly and efficiently. Felix knows how to get things done.

The fact that I was born in Holland smoothed the argument for me to return to my native country with my only living relative, only relative that anyone counts anyway. Mum is a shell and no longer exists as a legal person. Johanna could be my sister but I have no idea where she is. And what of James, my cousin, Aunt Maude's son, also out there somewhere? Would I ever meet either of them? Could I inadvertently marry James and not know? Would I meet Johanna in my new home and not know her? Become her friend at Art school? My head was racing so I stood up and paced the room and began to count the boxes of crates on the pavement outside. Felix put down his paper, glanced at me and smiled.

'Where's T'Ash? I thought he would come to say goodbye,' I said peering through the grimy window.

Felix folded his paper, put his spectacles in his top pocket and looked fondly at me.

'I wanted to spare you this, Beatrix. I didn't tell you because I thought that it would upset you more. I have helped T'Ash to escape from the police and a possible prison sentence.' I gasped and sat down.

'What? How? What has he done?'

'Well, the pictures were in his beach chalet and he was attacked trying to protect them.' I was about to protest that I would not have pressed charges and that I was equally culpable, but he held up his hand to silence me.

'The people who attacked him said they would come back for him and press charges against him. T'Ash called me in a panic. He was injured, and I called an ambulance and helped him to get away. I decided that in your interests as well as his own, I would get him a ticket to Ireland where he will be safe until he can finalise his emigration to the States.'

'Who? Who attacked him? Where are the paintings?'

'They are safe now. And so is T'Ash.'

I flopped in a chair and put my head in my hands. I had missed T'Ash since that last night when he had been a bit drunk and boorish and, yes, totally selfish; but he was still my T'Ash and I thought I would never see him again. Felix was beside me now, speaking very softly in my ear, as though he had read my thoughts.

'You will see him again Beatrix, if you want to.'

'It's just that...well, it's just that...' I wanted to tell him about my doubts; about the changes to my body; about my fear that T'Ash and me hadn't quite been careful enough, but I needed to be sure. I would be able to talk to T'Ash which is why I needed him here with me, not on the other side of the world. Even though Uncle Felix was a Doctor, I could not find the words to express my fears to him; my mother was incarcerated and incapable and I had never felt more alone.

'If you really hate your new life, you can come back here you know. This house will still be yours. Or you could choose to join T'Ash in America. You will be a wealthy woman by then, Beatrix. I think you will blossom in Holland like the spring bulbs. It will be spring again and the flower fields are a joy. You will want to paint them '.

When I am twenty one I can choose to come back. Felix has assured me of this, and I will be free to marry T'Ash if he will still have me. The back door is still open even though it stretches so many miles into the future that I cannot possibly see that far. And it is what may happen in the next six months which concerns me far more right now.

Something catches my eye on the floor between the bureau and the fireplace and I reach into the crevice to retrieve the battle ship token which T'Ash had always favoured when we played Monopoly.

'You know, during the war, Waddington of Leeds were still making Monopoly sets and the Secret Service adapted them as 'gifts' for prisoners of war, distributed by the Red Cross,' Felix said quietly behind me. 'They contained concealed maps and real cash and small tools to help escaping prisoners.'

Escaping prisoners. Was I now a prisoner? Would I need concealed maps and cash and small tools to get back to T'Ash? I slipped the token into my pocket with the folded paper: the poem T'Ash had sent me. I had sat day after day waiting for him to come back and then I got a letter: not even a letter; just a poem and no T'Ash. I felt the net tighten around me, and I closed my eyes to ward off the rising panic.

Part Two

Unravelling

Amsterdam 1956-1957

Chapter Twenty Seven
Amsterdam Autumn 1956

My new life dawned warmer than the days before it and I awoke full of the joys of early Autumn, happy to greet another day of new sights and sounds, and then the nausea hit me and I made it just in time to my indoor private bathroom and was sick. I ran a hot bath and lay there for a while eyes closed, enjoying this turn of my life from pauper to princess; wrapped in a warm robe, freshly laundered by Mrs. Vries, Uncle Felix's housekeeper. I sat by the window and made a list to marshal my thoughts and fight the rising bile, but the words wouldn't come. I was never one for words; it was T'Ash who could fashion a poem from clouds and weave words into gold. I doodled instead and the charcoal line followed its curving path to become a likeness of myself as a princess joined to T'Ash, a cavalier; and behind us, in the background, was the face of my father, or Felix or both; the face of Judas in the scene from his painting. The background filled up with tall thin buildings which could have been towers but was most likely the view of the street outside. In the far, far distance, was a field of flowers. The sunlight hit the flowers and they glowed golden; a shadow crossed the path of the princess like a finger of doom, and her belly was swelled full with child and the cavalier had ridden off into the distance, and was disappearing into the field of flowers.

What began as a morning sketch turned into an obsessive all day frantic painting in my studio, interspersed with breaks to eat the pastries Mrs. Vries had left and to make coffee which made me nauseous so I asked for weak tea instead.

The light had finally gone from the studio and I had barely dressed or made myself presentable when I heard Felix at the foot of the stairs. He knocked on the open door.

'May I come up?' he asked politely, respecting my privacy. I stepped back from the canvas and thought that I should cover it but the paint was wet and anyhow, it was my statement; it was the words I could not speak.

Could I get back to Colchester; to T'Ash? But he was a million miles away. Should I write to him? What would his mother, a good Irish Catholic say? What would we have done if Felix had not intervened? I knew the answer before I framed the thought; but what about here? How would Felix react? I felt panic rise inside me; I was in a foreign country and Felix was the only person I knew, and I was beginning to realise that I didn't even know him that well after all. Which left Mrs Vries; would she help me? I had barely spoken to her as my Dutch was as basic as her English although I believe she understood more than she could speak.

Felix bounded up the stairs like a man half his age and embraced me and stepped back to look at me properly.

'You are looking a bit pale. Not unwell I hope?' and I felt the full force of his professional scrutiny, like he could see through me. I felt embarrassed, ashamed and couldn't make eye contact. 'Maybe a tonic. I will make something up for you myself,' and then his gaze shifted and he glanced sideways at the painting I had almost completed and a low whistle escaped his lips.

'I hope you have not been overdoing it,' he said, slipping his spectacles onto his nose and moving closer to inspect the incriminating painting, his focus totally on the work. This was something I noticed about Felix which separated him from T'Ash and at this point in my life they were the only two men I knew, apart from teachers who didn't count. Felix and T'Ash. My gaze was on Felix's face, lost in the painting, and I realised that I hadn't breathed out since he had entered the room.

The momentous events in life turn on a breath of silence or so it seems to me, and that was certainly true of that encounter with Felix.

'Good, yes, exceptional,' and then he noticed the female figure, her swollen belly, her resemblance to me and he paused and in that silence, that single moment, I knew that I had told my secret, shouted it from the rooftops and there was no going back.

Slowly he removed his glasses, took my arm and steered me downstairs to his library. On the way, he ordered tea from Mrs. Vries. We sat in leather arm chairs opposite each other, by the fire which burned small but beautiful in the ornate grate surrounded by old blue Dutch tiles. It was comforting. I was glad to be seated after my marathon painting session and realised that I had neither sat nor eaten much all day. Daylight had gone and he lit a few side lamps on the tables around the room.

'We need to talk about your future,' he said, quietly, still moving about the room like a cat, as I slumped, exhausted, confused, beyond anxious. Simply resigned. I said nothing.

'Your training course will begin after Easter, after you turn 17, if you still wish to take it up?' He had secured me a place at the Institute of Fine Art, based on the portfolio of my work. When I arrived, I had an interview which seemed to be a formality and which gave me the impression that if Felix Van Gelder suggested I should come to this school, then they would take me regardless, although they were quite positive about my work. I realised that he had influence in many areas.

I stared into the flames, feeling dumb and dull and stupid here in this lovely room with the world at my feet and Felix prowling as my future turned to ashes in the fire. He crouched in front of me and said, not unkindly,

'Do you want to tell me something, Beatrix?'

No I don't want to tell anyone anything. I want it to go away, I don't want it to be real,' I screamed in my head. He stood up as Mrs. Vries brought in the tea and cake and I was suddenly ravenous. He set the tray on a small table between us poured the tea and offered me cake, with a small smile.

'Have you eaten today?' he asked.

'A little.'

'Well you must keep up your strength. I know that your father would spend many hours at his easel and forget to eat, much to your mother's chagrin.' He had my attention now. I wanted to hear more about this and I looked up suddenly and he caught my look and his face softened with sympathy.

'He once said to me, *'My legacy is my paintings, and Beatrix. She will be a very great artist one day. We need to nurture that talent. Take care of them for me if the war goes badly....'*'

'And did the war go badly?' I asked, my voice tight so with emotion and lack of use.

'Yes and no. There are always casualties in war and there are no winners however the history books choose to weave the stories. What matters now is Max's legacy and whether you are prepared, or able to realise it.'

The silence hung for a while. Fire spat and crackled. Shadows danced and the fire and lamp light did not dispel the shadows from the corners of the room.

'I have my own life to live. I cannot relive theirs,' I said, nursing the teacup and replacing it on the saucer with shaking hands.

'And what have you in mind?'

I shrugged. 'I thought I knew, but now I am not so sure.'

'You were sure about going to Art School when we first met. I am sure that you have a very great talent and so does the Institute. I think you know it too. Being an artist isn't something you do, Beatrix, I am afraid it is who you are. It has chosen you.'

'I must have a choice as well,' I said defiantly.

'Yes you do. You choose to be who you are or to deny it.'

I looked down at my hands. 'Sometimes the choices are not so easy and things happen....'

'So tell me what has happened and I promise that we will find a solution. I am sure that it is not so difficult.'

'It is the worst thing ever,' I said and I knew that we were taking about the same thing.

'Will you let me help?' I nodded very slightly and he moved closer to me and took my hand.

'Right now this seems like the worst thing that could ever happen in your life. Believe me when I say that I have seen it before. Many, many times but you know, women are tough and life goes on and you will be able to get through this and move your life on. You are still very young; you have a fantastic life ahead of you and my sworn duty to your father is to see that you have the best life you can have. So let me help you.' I was ready to succumb totally to his reasonable tones and the cosy room conspired with him to reassure me.

'I will need to check you out, or find you another physician if you prefer to talk to someone else. We will get you registered at the clinic. Don't worry it will all be very private and discreet and we, Mrs. Vries and I, will keep you safe here until... until your time and then I know a very safe place where your baby can be born.' He had said it. He had called it a baby, and I was appalled at the reality of my situation. I was going to have a baby. T'Ash's baby and Felix was going to help me. Relief flooded through me.

'What about the Institute?' I asked.

He smiled one of his lopsided half smiles which could have been regret, or cynicism or even uncertainty, but that last one was unlikely in Felix. 'They will wait. There is no time limit on talent which often refuses to follow rules. They will wait until you are ready for them. There is also another option.' He let it hang. 'We could begin your training now, a distraction if you like, over the months to come. You will need something to occupy you and I fear you will find it dull here without the friends you would make at art school. I would enjoy helping with the History of Art and how to read paintings,' he looked over his glasses at me and his eyes were smiling, 'and my dear friend Ben is the best technician I know. He is an alchemist and learned from the very best. He will teach you all you need to know about paint and light and how to breathe life onto the canvas.' His eyes were shining with a fervour I was to associate with his passion for Art and it ignited something inside and I smiled back and then laughed and we both laughed and he said quite simply,

'You see. It is never quite so bad as it is painted.'

Chapter Twenty Eight

Felix had business to attend to.
'I will be away for a few days,' he said to Beatrix. 'Mrs. Vries will take care of you. Enjoy the delights of your new home, but don't overdo it,' and he patted her cheek, as she sat up in the large comfortable bed, the coffee he had brought up for her on a tray by her side.
'It is so early. It's still dark. Where are you going?'
'Don't you worry about me. I do still have work to do but I will be away from the city for a few days, in Delft.'
'Oh, I would love to come. Vermeer painted a very famous view of Delft...and so did.. what's his name?'
'Van der Pol?' They both came up with the name together and laughed.
'Well you can see that picture in a museum but for now, I have to go alone.' She lay back on the pillows flushed and he felt an unusual surge of love and affection for this child who had been denied him for so long. What mattered was that she was in his care now, and he would do everything in his power to be a father to her which meant protecting her from everything , especially the silly boy who made her pregnant and went to America, writing dozens of letters, which Felix intercepted. All the mail went to a post box and letters from T'Ash, passionate declarations of undying love, went in the fire. And the letters she asked him to post

to T'Ash? After he read them, the same fate. He had to protect her. It was his responsibility to be midwife to the rare and special talent which the world needed and would be frittered without him.

And he loved her. He realised that since his brother died, his feelings had been numbed and finding Beatrix again had been like the Spring sun warming the earth and giving new life to the dead bulbs beneath the soil. She had brought him back from slumber and reawakened his passion for his cause. His new cause which was Mental Health reform.

Change was coming; he had been to a conference in London earlier in the year where they had discussed a new act which would supersede the Lunacy Act of 1890 with a more modern, Mental Health Act. He hoped that it wouldn't be too late for Marianne. They would no longer use brutal programmes like Insulin Shock Therapy and strait jackets, although Intramuscular Largactil with side effects such as tics and twitches, would continue. He fervently hoped that Marianne would benefit from the new treatments which he could support through his research programme.

At least she was better off than Max had been. Felix had needed Max and worked hard to keep him alive, and for his part, Max had a great appetite for life. Some of the drugs Felix got hold of were early versions of Chlorpromazine, now with the trade name 'Largactil'. This had a very dramatic effect on reducing agitation, psychotic or manic episodes, and was what Marianne's doctors had prescribed for her; but he was in no doubt that Max's health had suffered from the antipsychotic drugs administered during those dark days when the only medical trials were Nazi experiments. The Nuremburg Code of 1947, after the war regulated pharmaceutical research and was still in place. During the war, especially the blockade towards the end, they were fortunate to get any medication and that mostly through Jellicoe's contacts with the Nazi officers she courted. The antipsychotic drugs caused Max's hands to shake and he developed nervous twitches which people put down to the war.

Beatrix was proving herself to be a very useful apprentice painter, and she was still so young and dependent; far too young for the responsibility of parenthood. Her current condition, although a setback, was only temporary and then her focus would have to be on the work. A child would distract her. In everyone's interest, not least her own, she could not be allowed to keep her child.

Chapter Twenty Nine

I twisted the ring on my finger; the one T'Ash had given me in the beach chalet a lifetime ago. Mrs. Vries suggested I wear it on my wedding finger 'for appearances'. Felix had made no comment. That was one of the things I loved most about Felix; he was not judgemental; no histrionics followed, and no lectures; no 'disappointment' or emotional blackmail, just support and practical solutions and I grew to love him unconditionally and wholeheartedly and he replaced the gap in my life which T'Ash had created with his departure.

I heard nothing from T'Ash. Not a single letter reached me and I felt that he had deserted me totally and started his new life in America, and with Felix gone away for a few days, I felt lonely for the first time since I had left England. I thought about my mother. Felix had updates from the hospital and promised that we could visit, 'when I was well again,' a euphemism for when I was no longer pregnant.

After the first of many short break's away on business, slowly, slowly, Felix began to manage every area of my life. He set up an appointment with an obstetrician friend; he managed my diet; my rest time and my training.

On weekday mornings, I would sit with Felix and study books about Art, and we would sometimes stroll around the streets for a while and he would point out sites and views which I might not have noticed and he would sit and read whilst I sketched. His comments were always positive, but he always got me to look and look again and I was learning to see more than I had before.

'The light is very interesting this afternoon, don't you think? You have captured it well in this sketch, but the shadows could be more expressive,' or 'Yes, I see what you are trying to do here but I think the drama is in the background, don't you? Maybe reduce the foreground?'

To look, to see, to interpret and to express myself. That is what I was learning on the streets of Amsterdam and from the books Felix and I poured over until Mrs. Vries brought our tea and then I was allowed some recreation.

At the weekend, we would visit a museum and look at real paintings by the great masters.

'The whole of civilisation in contained within these walls,' Felix proclaimed portentously as we entered the Rijksmuseum for the first time. 'You can trace the history of our culture in these halls,' and my art history lessons continued. It was one such Saturday morning, when I had the option to go to the market with Mrs. Vries or to come here. Felix was meeting someone; he never said who and I never met them, but at the entrance, he said that I should wander alone for a while and absorb the works and we would meet in one hour in salon thirty two.

I found him there, alone, sitting on a bench in the middle of the room, gazing at a small canvas on the wall opposite. He stood up when he saw me and guided me towards it. We stood in silence as I took in the Dutch 17th century landscape and then he steered me towards the seats in the centre of the room. The salon was deserted apart from us and a security officer, idly gazing into space by the door to salon 33.

The picture was a view of a street corner in Amsterdam. In the foreground was a tall house and an avenue of trees ran away into the background. It differed from the sketch I had done earlier in the week in that a man approached the door of the house on the left, where a woman stood in the courtyard. It was enchanting and I wanted to reach out and touch it. Even the light was as I had sketched it, the same time of day, 300 years later. It was accredited to Jan Lievens with whose work I was unfamiliar.

'That painting saved many lives once upon a time,' he said. I looked at him curiously and felt excitement at the thought of the history lesson I was about to receive. I loved Felix's stories of the pictures we looked at in books. He made them come alive with meaning; hidden meanings and allegory. His voice was low and mellifluous and I leaned in towards him, threading my arm through his, like a small child eager to be told a story.

'I mentioned to you once that I was in the Resistance? I was an early recruit, young and idealistic and very patriotic. I hated Nazis with a passion and I hated what they did to my country, my people, turning friends, brothers against each other. And I had Jewish friends; Doctors, Intellectuals, Artists; the flower of European knowledge and learning, like the Moors of old; wiped out by the fear and prejudice of the bigoted.

'Max remained neutral at first although he was no lover of bigotry either, and as an Artist he knew a lot of Jews, homosexuals, gypsies; he was a *bon viveur* and hedonist and welcomed interesting people to his studio. But he also didn't want trouble; it was too much effort for him; too political he said, and it got in the way of his work. He just wanted this stupid war over; people to stop killing each other, but he had no idea that he, we all, had to DO something to make that happen. In many ways he was like a child. Whatever he wanted, he wanted 'someone else' to take care of it so that he could simply focus ALL of his attention on his Art. And on you.' His voice had changed when he spoke about my father and when he quoted Max's words, I could hear the petulance he described. His tone was irritated, indulgent and regretful.

'He was a creative maverick, an adulterer and a consummate copyist, and it was that particular talent which he alone could bring.'

'You recruited him because he could copy paintings?' I wondered if this had something to do with the picture we were looking at.

'We needed money Beatrix, and we knew that the Nazis would pay well for works of art if they believed them to be great masterpieces. One good sale of a small Italian, Dutch or French *'Masterpiece'* and we could get half a dozen allied airmen out from behind enemy lines. We had links through France, across the Pyrenees, all the way to Gibraltar. Spain was 'neutral' but Fascist, and we had friends amongst the anti fascists, who were suffering after Franco won. This small picture saved many lives.'

I looked again at the painting in front of me. 'He copied that?'

'Not exactly. It is all his own work. Jan Lievens, shared a studio with Rembrandt in the 1620's but he was not so well known by the 1940's. He painted mostly portraits, but there was anecdotal evidence of lost allegorical pictures and some landscapes. We filled in the gaps and 'found' them. Because of the studio system there were difficulties with attribution during this period, and then, 1630 something, Lievens went to England, which also suited our purposes and clouded the attributions and traces of provenance. The experts in 1943 chose to believe that this work was authentically Jan Lievens. And that is where the 'crime' comes in. You can copy great works with impunity, but if you claim that they are by someone else, then it is forgery. Your father never did that; we did it for him.' I let that sink in. My father was innocent. He was not a forger.

'But surely he must have known?'

'I told you, it was a team effort. Max could paint like any great artist living or dead. He had a rare gift. Reuben was an alchemist and could age the pictures. He knew how to bake the canvasses to create the craquelure - the lines on a painting when it ages. He found old canvasses, authentic 17th century; he created original pigments. I simply needed leverage to enrol Max to the cause.'

'What did you do?'

'I sent in Jellicoe.' I gasped and stood and walked away from him and back again.

'Jellicoe? She almost destroyed my mother!' I shouted at him. 'And Mum said that Jellicoe worked for the Germans! She betrayed you.'

'She did, in the end and that was my misjudgement.' That Felix could call such a catastrophic turn of events a 'misjudgement' said a lot about the man I was dealing with.

'She worked both sides. I knew that, which is why I recruited her. Firstly I needed to get Max on board and Marianne was having no success. Second, Jellicoe knew the right people who could reach Nazi high command in the Country.'

'She sold the pictures?' he nodded.

'I made the provenances, she sold.'

'But she turned against you all?'

'Yes.' He looked defeated, then regained his famous composure . 'Jellicoe fell in love with your father. It wasn't supposed to happen, but it did. She was a professional. She was supposed to stay neutral.' It sounded cold to me, like Felix expected people to turn off their emotions for the good of his cause. Alarm bells rang deep inside me and I felt T'Ash's baby turn a somersault. I had to sit down.

'Tell me about Jellicoe,' I said. He came and sat beside me and put his arm around me.

'That is a whole other story for another time. Right now, it is lunch time and you must eat something.' My arms were wrapped protectively around my swelling belly.

'How did that picture by Jan Lievens end up here anyway? Surely you didn't sell it to the museum?' I asked over lunch of grilled fish and salad in a restaurant on the Keizersgracht.

He moved in closer to answer me as discreetly as he could, looking around. There were few people in the restaurant to overhear.

'After the war, the Dutch were relentless in their pursuit of 'Collaborators,' and hungry for justice for those who had died. 20,000 civilians died during the Hunger Winter from starvation and hypothermia. We lived quite well, because we were well connected and because of your mother's skills at getting food, Jellicoe's connections; your fathers talent; my links. But it made us a target and the term 'Collaborator' was being thrown around and the press wanted blood. There were of course those who did deserve to be punished, and those, like us and all the rest of the people who had worked tirelessly and risked their lives and died for our cause; they deserved justice as well.

'The Allied Art Commission was tracing and repatriating items looted by Nazi occupying forces; not just paintings; there was gold and jewellery and even furs which were valuable, and mostly stolen from the Jews. There were warehouses full of supplies stolen from shipyards and train depots. We had won the war and I was keen to win the peace as well and to protect all of those who had worked with the Resistance.

'So I led the Commission to that one small painting, sold to a Nazi officer in '44 and they loved it, reclaimed it as a National Treasure and now it hangs, with other works of your father's in the hallowed halls of the Rijksmuseum. He would be so proud.'

'There are others?' he smiled his secretive, half smile again.

'Of course. I will show you all of them, but not today.'

I was bewildered. 'But the war was over. Why did the deception have to continue?'

'That painting would be destroyed if they knew the truth and after Max died,' he paused and I saw the real emotion in his eyes. 'After your father died, I felt the need to protect his legacy. To shout to the world that he was a great painter, and that he was not acknowledged in his lifetime.'

'But no one knows it is him. It is not signed Max Prins....'

'That doesn't matter.' He had his zealous face on and I knew not to challenge him. 'It is the same painting; it is glorious, the others even more so. It saved lives. It is a tribute to his memory and many of us, those who fought against the darkest evils, come to the Museum to pay secret tribute to him and to all of those who gave their lives. It is our memorial and a snub to the so called 'experts' who think they know best and who act as 'gatekeepers' to our culture. The work is the same; the name doesn't matter. Those who know, know, and those who believe, follow. And those who neither know nor believe, don't care.' I was following his logic, but I was still young enough to have an ego.

'I would want my name on it,' I said quite categorically. 'I would want everyone to know that I had painted something in the Rijksmuseum.'

'Is that so important to you?' he asked indulgently.

'Yes,' I said emphatically, otherwise what is the point?'

'In our case there were many 'points' as I have explained.'

'I know that there were then. But what is the point in keeping up the pretence now?' I asked. I wanted to be proud of my father the famous artist with works hanging in famous galleries. He leant in close and conspiratorially and sighed.

'Do you know that there are thousands of pictures in famous galleries around the world which are not painted by the person attributed to it and that a whole evaluation of authentication is being done as we speak? New works turning up all the time, looted mostly in Europe during the recent dark days. In England, your National Gallery collection was sent to a slate quarry in North Wales to keep it safe. Besides, forgery is a crime, even in wartime. Not so serious as Collaboration, which they could have charged us with if we were selling real art treasures, punishable by death. Forgery however would have meant imprisonment for all of us concerned, and dishonour to your late father, his paintings destroyed. That is why I was keen to have them back. I didn't want the evidence to be so casually left in a cellar, although they were safe for a while. Until someone discovered where Marianne had fled to.'

'Who? Who discovered that?'

'Jellicoe,' he said with a hint of a smile, 'and she still knows too much.'

'But it is all over now, surely the truth can be told?' I said.

'It is never truly over, Beatrix, as you will discover,' he replied. This lesson in Art History though, was over for now.

'And besides,' he said, 'whose truth will finally be told?'

Chapter Thirty

After a few weeks had passed, I said to Felix, more casually than I felt,

'I haven't heard from T'Ash.' T'Ash hadn't written. Not one word. Felix looked at me directly and took my hand.

'No,' he said with a sigh. 'I am afraid that T'Ash has, how do you say in English, *absconded?* I looked at him aghast. I didn't understand. 'I contacted him and told him that you are expecting his child in the Spring and his reply, well it wasn't very positive, I'm afraid.'

'Let me see the letter. I want to see it.'

'I.... telephoned him in America. I know where he is working and I spoke to him. There is no letter, Beatrix. He has broken all contact with you and I am truly sorry. I thought that if you do choose to go to him when you are older, he should know the situation. He should have a choice as well.'

'Why?' I said sitting heavily in the nearest chair. He knelt gently beside me and spoke quietly and kindly.

'Why do you think?' I shook my head and felt the tears streaming down my face. I couldn't speak. I couldn't believe that T'Ash had abandoned me so totally. 'He is with his family in America. They are Catholic and would not accept an illegitimate child. He had to choose between you and his family who are all he has in a foreign land. An illegitimate child would simply complicate things.' He patted my hand and handed me a handkerchief. 'It is for the best,' he said distracted. But it was hard to take. T'Ash had abandoned me? I didn't believe it. I couldn't. I would write to him again at the address Felix had given me, in America, and this time, I would post it myself.

Chapter Thirty One
Ireland 1956

It was a slow dawning. It took me a while to work things out but when I did, my head virtually exploded. It was all there in front of me in my notebook and the rest was in my head. No not in that made up sort of way where you just invent a story and it is kind of real but you know deep down that it's not and it just keeps tugging away at your brain until you write it down. Listen, I mean *really* listen deeply with your heart not just your ears, and then it dawns. It is literally like that; like the dawn lighting up a landscape you knew was there all along but couldn't believe it in the dark and the fog and didn't trust yourself to believe it anyway. But I had a lot of time to brood on it on that crossing over to Ireland and then the weeks waiting with Aunt Ida in the farmhouse away up there in the country and there was nothing else to do except to read my notes and write to Bea and walk the hills, and it was bitterly cold and usually wet and it got dark so early.

There was still no word from Bea and I was getting worried. I had written to her every day since we left for Ireland. She would have replied at least once, I know she would but I hadn't received anything. Maybe her letters had gone on to my *care-of* address in America; c/o Kathleen. But then I would never know since I never made it to America. I would have to write to Kathleen and get her to send them on. I was sure Bea had written. It would be unthinkable that she wouldn't.

One afternoon it was too wet and dark to go out and Ma was in the kitchen with Ida and her daughter Philomena and her little boy Jack was raising merry hell because he was hungry, or cutting a tooth or had a nappy rash or some such lore that women know all about and is a mystery to the rest of us. Anyway, I goes upstairs to lie on my mattress in the room I was bunking down in with Callum and Kevin and Niall, Aunt Ida's youngest three boys, all out working the fields all day and Tommy who was still at school. So I lay down for a bit and drifted off and I came the closest I have ever come to one of those 'vision' things which Bea had all the time and scared the wits out of me, but I knew mine was just a dream and that I must have dozed off.

It was the paintings I saw and they came alive, and the whole cast of Bea's story were there and in those pictures they told me their tale. There were 13 pictures and I woke in a sweat with the fear of God in me and 13 at the last supper and the final image of blood and sacrifice.

It went something like this......

There is a man in the 17th century robes of his profession, his long dark hair trailing as he leans over the table. The table has all the tools of his trade; mixing compounds and flasks and a flame, like a Bunsen burner and he is holding a set of scales and some weights in his other hand. He is weighing compounds and mixing his medicines. His face is younger, but long and lean and the long hair could never disguise the look in his eyes. The hard steel look which Felix had fixed on me so many times and battered me into this defeated state. Like a film, the picture runs on, and in the corner of the room, Jellicoe lies on a bed, naked, her arm stretched above her head gazing at the *Apothecary* whilst he holds his weights and looks at the us, the viewer.

The scene shifts and Jellicoe is upright, naked and in the throes of ecstasy, whilst a man holds her from behind and fondles her breasts. In the 'dream' or vision or whatever it was, I have to admit that I was aroused now and I may have groaned out loud. It was an erotic scene, biblical in its allegory, with all the trappings of 'sin', corruption, guilt and hell scattered in the room.....I tried to focus on the people but my own arousal blurs the image and I feel the guilt and corruption rip through me like an orgasm and there are tears on my face, but I want to know more. I am not going to surface yet. This was a new form of reality. *The Fallen Woman* is clearly Jellicoe but I can't tell who the man is. His face is buried in her neck and the light is falling on his hands, large and strong and holding her breasts with fervour and passion. It could be Max or Felix. I don't even consider that it could be anyone else except one of the players from my small cast of characters.

In the background, a shadowy figure dressed as a monk stands watching the scene. *Brother Jude* is looking at the artist. The picture is a self portrait of Max Prins, looking... what exactly? His gaze is direct and piercing. Pleading for help or understanding? Deep sadness gazes at me and makes me sympathetic and supportive. Why? And then the answer comes to me; Brother Jude is the artist's brother, Judas. The man who will ultimately betray him.

Then the women put in an appearance, fully clothed, both of them. Marianne, tall and dark dressed as a Maid, standing behind the fair haired 'Lady' Jellicoe who is seated in splendour on a high back chair which looks like a throne. The 'Maid' holds a tray with a jug and goblets on it. A mirror on the wall reflects the rest of the room and in the background, a man of some importance sits at a table facing the women and looking clearly at the Maid. His face is blurred as he is a shadowy figure in the mirror. The Maid is looking at the Lady with a look of pure hatred and I see the eternal triangle. The man and his dutiful wife and the cuckoo in the nest. Later I will ask myself why she put up with it. Why would a woman put up with her husband's mistress under the same roof and I get the only answer which makes sense. It was a war, a difficult time and they were fighting a common evil by whatever means they could.

The two women are now standing in front of a dining table with guests who all look important, some in military uniform of the 17th century Dutch Guard. The Maid this time is the shorter, rounder, blonde Jellicoe with the beginnings of a smile on her pleasant face. She offers the Lady, Marianne, a large platter of a Hogs Head, complete with apple in its mouth. Several of the guests look shocked. The Lady, who is tall and dark, holds a hand to her breast and recoils at *The Maid's Folly*, but it is clear from the allegory that there was no 'folly' but intention to cause harm.

And then a 17th century picture in the style of Vermeer or Pieter De Hooch. A painting of a pregnant Jellicoe – smugly holding her huge bump and gazing happily out of the window. A man sits at the table his back to her, shoulders hunched, smoking a pipe, other hand clenched against the table edge. Light from outside casts the shadow of the window across his figure, creating the impression of bars, or prison. Was he unhappy about Jellicoe's pregnancy? The light around her and the darkness around him, give a clue to how they feel about this situation. The picture is called *Confinement* and the shadow of the prison bars make it clear that they are both trapped.

And then, a crib. *Beatrix Sleeping* as a baby and a hand with a distinct ring on the third finger; a signet with a ruby in it, rocks the cradle. I know that ring to be on Felix's hand and I feel that if Felix rocks the cradle, whoever the child is, no good can come of it. So why is Felix rocking the cradle? Or did he take Max's ring?

We are in a 12th century battle scene by the looks of it, like a crusade picture by Uccello; Italian influence I am pretty sure even in a dream and in reality I had memorised the titles and descriptions so well. Only now was I seeing them come to life like a film in my head.

This is a busy picture and wherever I look there is close up detail and gore; dark and brooding scene of limbs hacked off, heads rolling; swords thrusting, but the centre of the picture is where the eye is drawn. A shaft of light illuminates a wounded man, clearly the 'Prince' or maybe *Prins* of the title *The Prince Betrayed*: he wears a gold circle on his head and lies wounded on the ground, supported by another knight; the wounded man holds his chest and his eyes roll upwards towards the robed figure of a monk (brother Judas?) whose smile is just visible beneath the cowl which covers much of his face. A sword covered in blood has just fallen from the monks hand. His other hand is open and covered with blood.

And the picture dissolves to a Self portrait of Max Prins: old, looking defeated and in despair. He looks at the chess pieces spilled across the table. The Queen has fallen onto the floor. An empty glass with wine stains on the table and the scales and weights of the Apothecary mixed in with the chess pieces and a thin red line of blood or wine washes the white squares red and I feel it pour across my face, wet with blood.

Check Mate. I hear the laughter and the rattle of rifle fire and leap to my feet in turmoil and remember that I am in Ireland in a farmhouse with leaky roof and the rain pelting down outside is dripping onto the bed I am lying in and onto my face and sounds like rifle fire as it clatters the tin roof.

Check Mate. That was it. Jellicoe fell in love with Max. She tried to betray Marianne for being Jewish. Bea remembered this through her 'visions' and now Max had confirmed it in oils. Max was angry about the pregnancy. *And Felix killed Max.* He lurks throughout the pictures like a menace, betrayal stamped in every image of him by his half brother. Max's paintings were narratives, each a story in itself, but put together, they make a longer narrative of love, war and betrayal. I ran a hand through my hair and had to keep asking why? Why would Felix kill Max and not Jellicoe? I know that Jellicoe is alive. I am sure it was her in the beach chalets, and she has the paintings. Felix told me. So Felix murdered Max. Why? And is Beatrix now in danger?

I have to warn her.

Chapter Thirty Two

My art technique lessons were to be started by Ben Mueller who was taciturn and sullen where Felix was charismatic and charming. From the start I got the impression that he didn't really want to teach me anything at all and it was only after he saw a Van Gogh which I was copying that his attitude softened.

We first met at Felix's house where an outline of what I was to learn was drafted; or at least, insisted upon by Felix. It seems I was to learn how to mix pigments from raw materials; I asked Felix if Ben was the alchemist he had described.

'His nephew,' he said. 'Old Reuben himself died sometime after '44 in a concentration camp. We tried to keep him safe but they got him in the end. We managed to get Ben out to Britain with the Kinder Transport but old Reuben refused to leave and worked with us for as long as he could.'

'That must have been very hard for you.'

'It was. It was difficult times and when Ben came back, there was nothing left for him. The house had gone, collapsed after being looted for firewood and then burned to the ground. But Ben had learned his uncle's trade and we could still use him.'

'Why were you and Pa not rounded up for the labour camps and German factories?' I asked.

'My, what a lot of questions!'

'I'm sorry. There is just so much that I don't know.'

'Ignorance is sometimes bliss. There are things it is wiser, safer, not to know. But that is an easy question to answer. I was a Doctor and needed at the hospital here. Nazis got sick as well and I had friends in high places. Your father, well.... Max simply lied about his age. He made false papers and added ten years to his age and with his medical record they decided he was too old and sick to work, so he stayed.'

'Was he sick?'

'He wasn't a well man, but at the start of the war we exaggerated his condition and by the time of the occupation, I already had a use for him. I needed him here so he developed a terminal illness overnight. It was quite tragic of course.' He smiled at his own cleverness, but I was still not convinced.

'But he did die before the war was over. How did he die?'

'Not of a terminal illness that's for sure. It was an accident, Beatrix, simple as that. They happen in war you know although it is hard to believe and people always look for another reason.'

'Mum said he ate the wrong food.' He smiled at me, his indulgent smile.

'Yes, that's also true, but not what killed him. He was taking medication for headaches, violent migraines which rendered him incapable for days. He also suffered from depression, not an uncommon ailment in an artist. In simple terms, the medication caused hypertension, high blood pressure. It was early days for those drugs, called MAO inhibitors, and we didn't really know all of the side effects and it was hard to get medicines but I managed to get these, illegally of course, from a German laboratory via contacts in high command, courtesy of Jellicoe. They were prescribed for a Nazi Officer so I tried them on your father and they helped enormously. But....'

'He wasn't supposed to eat cheese,' I said. 'T'Ash called it *'Death by Cheese'*! He thought it was a good plot for a novel.'

He smiled, wryly. 'T'Ash would, but this was serious. Not only cheese; other things as well, but they have revolutionized the treatment of a wide variety of conditions, including depression, panic attacks, phobias, and manic depression. They are now licensed and there is a lot more research happening in Germany and elsewhere. We may yet see more effective treatments for mental illness. We are so close. On the brink.' The fervour was back in his eyes, but I still didn't have an answer.

'So that's not what killed him? I thought that I remembered it and that's what Mum said. She blamed Jellicoe,' I said.

He smiled at me. 'It was all a bit of a tangle,' he said. 'Food was hard to get and we ate what was there. One of the side effects, fatal if untreated, is *'malignant hypertensive crisis'*, brought on by eating food rich in an amine called Tyramine. This includes aged or cured foods, such as salami, yeast extract...and cheese; especially mature or blue cheese. But Max was a law unto himself and never took any notice of doctors. Even those who cared about him.'

'So what happened?'

'Max suffered a heart attack, but a mild one and he recovered. He was very sick for a while and it was a lesson to him. He slowed down the high living. You were very young at the time, so you may well only remember the Max who stayed in his studio and painted obsessively and never went out.' It was true. All of my memories are of him in the studio.

'Aged or mature cheese could be a risk, but so also could badly kept meat, fish or poultry; in fact most food which is old, fermented or spoiled. And remember when this was?'

'Yes. I know. The *'Hongerwinter'.*' He sighed and I realize I sounded disrespectful. How could I ever know what it was like to be hungry, to live in fear and to risk my life every minute of the day? 'Sorry. My mother talked about it a lot.' He smiled indulgently at me.

'It seems like another world and a long time ago, now. But it was very real, Beatrix, and if you are to understand the choices which had to be made then you need to really know the context within which we operated.' He said it quietly and sadly as though he had made choices he wouldn't make now, as though they had been made by someone else; different times; different places; different people. Or just the same people and only the circumstances changed?

'But you experimented on my father?' I continued. Would he do the same thing now for a different *'cause'* I wondered? Once you have a crossed a line, can you really step back over it? I had the feeling that Felix was still living his own private war.

'We needed him to paint, and we needed to keep him calm. He was a risk when he was left untreated. You have to realize that many lives depended on us all keeping quiet. Max was always a loose cannon and he suffered from anxiety, phobia and depression. We didn't know the side effects at the time, as I said it was early days and the world was in chaos – all research was aimed at winning the war by fair means or foul. The Nazis invested huge amounts into their laboratories but mostly for their own purposes.'

'To keep people quiet or compliant so that they could play their part?'

'This was different.'

'How? Just because it was 'the goodies' and not the 'baddies' doing it?'

He look at me with one of his stone cold hard gazes which I had seen reserved for others and never, so far directed at me.

'How could you possibly understand? How would you feel if those you loved disappeared, were sent to concentration camps, or shot in front of you simply for saying something they shouldn't? Or for delivering leaflets to give Dutch people information about what was going on in their own country? The Resistance was the only force we had to fight evil and it was evil, Beatrix, make no mistake. Your own mother, and you were at risk if they discovered the truth about your Grandmother Quinn.'

'Nee Rosenberg?' He nodded.

'They changed it to Rose in the early part of the century but there was no disguising their Lithuanian, and former religious roots. How could putting you and Marianne into a concentration camp be justified? What danger could you possible pose to a regime as strong as the Nazis?'

'That is why they were so strong,' I said quietly, and he nodded, sadness overwhelming his solemn face. I raised my hand gently and touched the lines which etched their sorrow into his careworn features. He took my hand, turned it over and gently kissed the palm and then patted it. After a deep breath, he said,

'It is over now. Here we are at peace. We won, and even though I lost far too many friends, brave people, it was worth it and I would do it all again to fight those who would deny us liberty. Art cannot survive without the oxygen of freedom and challenge and we used our skills and Art to fund the fight for freedom. Oh yes. It was worth it.'

'So it was an accident, then? My pa's death. Was he shot?'

Felix sat heavily and let the air out of his lungs with a deep sigh. 'Who told you that?' he asked.

'It is one of my memories. I remember a quarrel and a gunshot and Pa in a pool of blood and Jellicoe screaming and a baby.... somehow there was a baby as well. Was that Johanna?'

'Yes it was Johanna but it was not all at the same time and there were always gunshots in those days. This memory is confused, Beatrix.' He said it almost like a warning.

'So how did it happen?' I insisted.

That was when Ben was shown in by Mrs. Vries for the first time and my answer would have to wait.

Chapter Thirty Three
Liverpool 1956

The quayside was crowded as it always was. Me and Ma were finally off to America after months of biding time and waiting for paperwork and not knowing where Bea was or how she was faring. I was back in England; the boats sailed from Liverpool but the accents on the dockside were almost all Irish. I felt at home here.

Kevin, Aunt Ida's oldest was coming with us. He had saved his money from his labouring, what he didn't tip up to his Ma, and got himself his papers sorted and wanted to be off with us. I had helped this last week and given him the balance on the ticket. He was a few pounds short and he swore he would pay me back in America.

'When I am a rich exporter,' he said with a twinkle in his laughing eyes. He was always laughing, Kevin. He would do well in America. His music and his laughter needed more space to be heard and it was a big country. I was delighted; it suited my plans completely to have him along; I don't think I could have done it otherwise. I could see that Aunt Ida was distraught, though, as I guessed Ma would be if she was waving me off with the possibility that she would never see me again.

I felt a lump in my throat and flushed despite the cold air and the mufflers and caps we wore. You could see the steam of our breath as we gathered around, waiting to board. I had to take my chance. I had to choose between Beatrix, alone and vulnerable with a possible murderer in Europe, or Ma, travelling to be with her family, who would take good care of her and see out her days in comfort in the land of plenty. Now I had Kevin to take care of Ma on the journey, I just had to say goodbye. I had slipped a letter explaining it all in her bag. She would find it when she unpacked in her cabin. Now I took Kevin aside.

'I am not going wid ya,' I said resorting to the rural Irish I spoke with my family.

'Whaddya mean? You've gotta come. You've gotta ticket an all...'

'And so have you. But there is something much more important I need to do. I'll join you in a few months when I have tied up some loose ends.'

'Have you told your Ma?' I shook my head.

'I don't want to neither, she'll make a fuss. Cover for me. Tell her I got on already and I'll see her in her cabin. There's a letter in her bag. Tell her....' I welled up. How do you tell your cousin, whom you have only recently met, to tell your Ma that you love her, when you could just cross the quayside and tell her yourself?

'Tell her Beatrix is in danger and I have to go get her. But I will join her. Later this year. Yeah? You make sure she knows. She will see me again. As soon as I can,' and I patted his arm. 'Take care of her on the journey. And have fun yourself,' and I turned and melted into the crowd, my bag slung carelessly over my shoulder.

'Yes, but wait. Tash. Wait up....' and then he was gone and I was running away from the quay and towards the trains. I was travelling East, not West and it felt totally liberating.

Chapter Thirty Four

'These are precious and rare,' Ben said. 'Hard to get and very few people know how to do this now.'

'How do you know?' I asked.

'I was taught,' he said, 'and I am showing you not because you need to know how to do it, but because you need respect for colour and light and you need to know how paint works when it's wet and when it dries and not take it for granted. You will be a better painter if you know these things.'

I doubted it, but I was fascinated anyway. I loved colour but I had never thought of where it came from. I thought it was simply squeezed out of a tube. But Arturo showed me how to make massicot from lead and tin to make a brilliant yellow. Green came from celadonite and ultramarine, that exquisite blue which Vermeer used so sparingly but to great effect, came from lapis lazuli and was rare and hard to get hold of.

'If you want to learn from the Great Masters you have to understand their tools,' he said by way of justifying what we were doing and I trusted that and grew to love these sessions. Ben warmed to me after a few meetings and we chatted more as he mixed and explained what he was doing.

'Ores and metals are heated to extract the colour,' he explained. 'Clays are roasted. But this brilliant white; I have strict instructions from Felix that you are not to mix this one.' It was lead which he oxidised in jars of weak vinegar and then collected the white powder and added clay as a base. 'Zinc White has replaced it and is safer. It has a different feel to it. A brilliance which zinc never quite reaches. And this,' he added, holding up a lump of ore which looked dingy and grey. 'This is a substitute for the very costly aquamarine. We roast the cobalt ore to produce an oxide and melt with quartz or potash and pour it into cold water,' he instructed, as it disintegrated into a blue powder.

I mixed the massicot to make a lustrous powder and showed Ben. He grinned and took it from me and continued to mix his jar of lead oxidised in weak vinegar. Ben passed me a lump of rock.

'Vermillion, made from cinnabar, mined in China; nowadays, commonly called "China Red." Vermillion was a more common name in the 17th century, but it has a mercurial base. It gives warm hues from a bright orange-red to a bluish red.'

I touched it and rubbed my fingers with it. It felt coarse and was a little dull. I could not believe that this would make such vibrant colour.

'This one needs to be ground for a long time. Larger crystals produce duller, less orange hues. You can grind it for me, but the mercury base is also dangerous in ... in your condition,' and he turned away embarrassed.

The painting consumed me and I became even more obsessive; I was either learning to be an alchemist with Ben, looking at the world through the eye of an artist with Felix, studying his books about the history of art, or, spending long hours on a stool, painting, as my father had done. I had truly come home.

Chapter Thirty Five

Nothing had changed in Colchester except that the streets were lifeless and the air itself seemed dead. There was no vibrancy to any of it since Bea had gone. I decided that I would stay at the little house in Stockwell Street for a few days, if it was still empty. I wouldn't go home to Da. That would be too much. He had not taken well to losing Ma and he thought it was all my fault.

'Filling her head with your bloody nonsense,' he had shouted at me. 'What's Americky got that we can't get here. Hey, you tell me that much then...' and on and on he ranted but we just left anyway. I practically dragged Ma out of the house, thinking he might well attack me and there would almost definitely be bloodshed. I had avoided him in the last few days before we left, but now I was free and things had changed; I had changed; and I was here for a purpose. I needed more information before I went blundering in accusing Felix. Look what had happened last time? I needed to be better prepared if I was going to outsmart him this time.

He had stitched me up good and proper hadn't he? I had no choice. By the time I went home and packed a few things, he had already booked my passage to Ireland. He seemed to know how to do those things and because money wasn't an obstacle it happened fast. But then there was the wait for the visas and the passports. Even Felix couldn't speed that up so we stayed with Aunt Ida, hidden away like criminals, me and Ma who had never done anything wrong. But Felix had made it clear to me when he got back from his mysterious 'trip' that if I didn't go, the police would be on the door step and I would be in the frame for a serious offence and well, I just wasn't going to take that risk. So I caved in and I went and I took Ma to safety and I felt so bloody angry that if I went anywhere near my Da or Felix bloody Van Gelder I could have killed them.

I walked up the long hill from Colchester Station and turned left along the High Street, passed my former place of work and turned left again towards the Dutch Quarter.

It was twilight by now and the lights were on in the shops and as I turned into Beatrix's street, I saw the unmistakeable glow of lights behind the closed curtains upstairs in what was, until only a few short weeks ago, her bedroom. My heart sank. I stopped across the road and saw that the '*to let*' sign had gone and there was clear activity inside. I heard a child's voice and a mother shouting and a dog barking and I stood on the outside, looking in; a warm glow of family life which I had abandoned to take a wild goose chase back here. My spirits slumped and I realised that I was hungry, cold and tired. I turned around and headed back to the High Street and found a cafe, warm and steamy and ordered pie and chips and a mug of tea. I needed somewhere to stay. I had some money; Felix, true to his word had been very generous and I had cashed his cheque before I left. I had enough to stay in the George if I wanted to but somehow that felt uncomfortable.

I looked out of the steamed up windows and saw a familiar figure walk by. There was something about the walk and the turn of his head as he waved to someone, on his way home from work. I leapt up from the table, leaving my pie half eaten and my bag cluttering the floor and ran to the door.

'Wilf,' I shouted and he turned and I saw alarm cross his face and then he was acting pleased to see me. He came back and stepped inside the warm cafe.

'Shut the bloody door. It's freezing out there,' shouted the cafe owner from behind the counter, so I almost dragged Wilf in and summoned the sullen waitress to bring us more tea.

'You seemed surprised to see me,' I said being deliberately jovial. I had seen the look and after my revelations about Max's Paintings, I had developed a radar if you like; but it could have just been cynicism. He saw my huge bag on the floor.

'I thought you'd left,' he said matter of fact.

'I did. I came back. Couldn't stay away.'

'Would they not have you in America then?' he said and stirred sugar into his tea. I returned to the serious subject of my pie which was cooling rapidly and ate carefully whilst I thought this through. It was him. I was almost sure of it. His voice, his mannerisms. It was him. And he spoke Dutch.

'Ah well, you know what they say, *Time and Tides wait for no man*,' and I watched the confusion cross his face. '*Or woman*,' I said as an afterthought. I laughed, chewing vigorously and pointing my fork at him daring him to laugh as well. Slowly, he did and I could see him wondering if I knew. It was the kind of forced laugh I had expected.

'So why are you back?' he said, recovering his composure and sipping the tea.

'Sorry you'd probably have preferred a pint but I had to eat. Been travelling all day,' and I finished the rest of my pie and chips and sat back, satisfied, taking the advantage. I had learned a lot from Felix. 'So why am I back? Just a small question of some unfinished business here,' I said and fixed him with a stare.

'Still writing the novel about those paintings?' he said and there was a hint of challenge and mirth in his voice.

'Nah. Forgotten all about that. But there is a friend I have to see. As I said, loose ends.'

'Ah well, doesn't do to dwell on things,' and he wanted to change the subject but I was going to press my advantage.

'See, the thing is, I got a whack on the head before I left; some thugs attacked me in the woods.' He looked back at me blankly. 'But it made me "imagine" things.' There was a silence and the fryer sounded loud in the background. The waitress clattered dishes and the chef shouted 'egg and chips table 5'. Life went on around this still point where we sat isolated and things happened in slow motion. A plate crashed to the floor. The waitress screamed; the owner shouted 'sack the juggler' and people laughed and our frozen moment was shattered. Wilf shook his head distracted.

'Yeah. I heard something about you being attacked. Wondered why you never came back to work your notice....' I leaned forward and spoke quietly as though there was only us in the room.

'You see someone I care about, the only person I really care about in the world could be in danger and I need to get her away from the man who has taken her.' He leaned back and looked confused.

'No, mate, sorry. I am not going to get involved in this...'

'You already are,' I said and rubbed the sore part of my head which had now healed. He folded his arms.

'I don't know what you are talking about.'

I shrugged. 'I think you do. I need to get Beatrix away from Felix Van Gelder.' I watched his face carefully. There was a flicker, a twitch. Bea would have been better at this; she read faces better than me. He rummaged in the pockets of his jacket and pulled out a packet of cigarettes and offered me one. I shook my head, not breaking eye contact. He took a cigarette between his teeth and struck a match with a cupped hand, the way they did in films. He shook the match, reached for the ashtray and inhaled, tipping his head back to blow the smoke upwards.

'Supposing I knew what you are talking about, what's in it for me?' I shrugged again.

'There's no bounty here. There is justice. The pictures you helped to steal are Beatrix's legacy. Only she should have them. Not Jellicoe, not Felix not anybody else. But the way it is now, Jellicoe has the pictures and Felix has Beatrix. And she is just caught up in the middle and I am not sure she is strong enough to cope on her own.' He leant forward.

'And you want Beatrix back,' he laughed. 'So go get her,' and he stood up to leave. I put a hand on his arm.

'Wilf, wait. I trusted you. No one else knows anything about this. You are the only one I confided in, and I could press charges for assault.' He laughed and put his face close to mine and spoke through his teeth.

'Prove it.' Then he sat back in his seat to consider what I had said. 'You lied to me. The rest, I worked out for myself. And Jellicoe will pay me well.'

'So it was you?' He shrugged. 'How much has she paid you then?' I asked. He pulled away.

'She is waiting to sell the pictures. Then she will pay me in full.'

'And you are sure she still has them?' I raised an eyebrow and let what I thought was a cynical smile escape.

'You just said she does!'

'And how would I know? All I know is that Felix went after them that night on the boat. I've been away don't forget. And how can you be so sure that she will pay up? From what I've heard of her, she is not the most trustworthy character in this story.'

'It's not a story T'Ash. This is real life.'

'Oh, is that so? So let me tell you my version of 'real life' and you can tell me if it's a story or not.' I waited for him to speak but he just ground his cigarette into the ashtray and sat back and folded his arms. He gave me an *I'm waiting to be impressed* sort of look.

'Ok. So first thing. You turn up in the council offices just as I am making headway with my research and act as 'translator'. Coincidence or plot twist?' he shrugs. I nod and carry on.

'So did Jellicoe send you?' Impassive; same look.

'Do you still work at the council?' Nothing.

'Oh that one's easy. I can just go in and ask.' I say

'So do it.' He says. My guess is that he doesn't.

'So what are you still doing in Colchester?' I ask.

'Same as you. Loose ends.'

'If you are waiting for Jellicoe to stump up, you'll be here for several lifetimes.' He nodded, drained his mug and prepared to leave.

'I'm in no hurry. Nice to run into you,' he said and left.

Chapter Thirty Six

The bump was huge in my slender figure and distorted me. Felix had tried to interest me in my condition but when I showed little interest he decided that at least I needed to be educated about what was happening to me. He supplied books and tried to engage me in conversation about the birth; about where my baby would be born; about what would happen afterwards. I blanked it. I couldn't cope and he would look at me though narrowed eyes and nod, silently. He prescribed a medicine which was a 'tonic' and would help me to cope with the changes of emotion and I took it unquestioningly, indifferent to what happened to my body, only interested in the canvas I was working on, anxious to get back to it.

But my body would not be denied. My breasts were larger and tender and Mrs. Vries had kindly supplied me with more appropriate underwear. My bump was quite noticeable and hard and felt like an intrusion on my still girlish shape. I did my best to ignore it and to ignore the fluttering and movement of the small life inside me, but I could not ignore the heightened emotions I was undergoing. I missed my mother deeply. This was the time I needed her but she was gone from me as well. Like T'Ash and Maude and everyone else. I clung to Felix in a sea of isolation and channelled this emotional outpouring into my work. The burgeoning life inside me inspired my most creative works and I was prolific.

One day I caught the tail end of a hasty conversation between Mrs. Vries and Felix and they turned silent when they saw me. She scuttled away muttering and Felix took me by the arm and guided me into the dining room. He had arranged for me to see a doctor at the hospital for regular visits and there was a team of midwives attached, whom I saw monthly. I knew from the books Felix had supplied that my time was close and that I should really be prepared, but I was in denial. I wanted to shut it out. I didn't want to have this baby and if I could sleep the sleep of innocence and wake up to find it gone, I would be content to continue my studies as an artist.

'You will soon be approaching your due date, Beatrix. We have to prepare you for the next stage.' He must have noticed the closed look on my face as the shutters came down and he sat beside me and took my hand. 'I have made arrangements,' he said quietly and slowly, 'for you to be admitted to a small hospital in Delft, a town I know well and where there is a private clinic staffed by nurses. It is like a home and you will stay until your baby is born. You will be well taken care of.'

'Why can't I just stay here? I can't paint in a clinic in the middle of nowhere....' I felt a cramp and stood to overcome it. I was shouting and even in my hyper emotional state I knew that I was being unreasonable. He soothed me as he always did.

'You are young and healthy and there should be no problems for you and under normal circumstances, staying here may have been the best option. But this is not... normal circumstances is it?'

'Why not, why can't I stay here?' and my breathing quickened. 'And anyway, I haven't finished my painting. It is still in Ben's studio and he is going to show me how the ageing process works next week. I need to be here,' I said firmly.

Felix passed me a glass of water and settled me back into my chair. 'The painting will wait. It will be something to look forward to when you come home, and it won't be long. A few weeks and then we can get your life back on tracks.' I breathed deeply a few times, felt the cramp again and let it wash over me.

'What about the baby? Where will it live?' I asked belligerently.

'It is all taken care of, Beatrix. The baby will be well cared for. At the home in Delft, they have expertise and will find the perfect family to raise your child. Believe me it is for the best.'

The child inside me kicked. I felt a small foot press against my abdomen and I held my breath and just stared at it. It moved again; another foot? A hand? My hands responded tentatively and I stroked those places through my loose woollen dress and I swear the baby answered me. I was in awe. I had seen the pictures and I knew that the 'bump' was by now, a baby.

Too many babies... all lost...' My mother's voice came back to me and in that moment, I knew what all women must know; that hell would freeze over before they would take my baby from me.

Chapter Thirty Seven

T'Ash. My first love. He was Peter Pan, eternal boy, a sprite, a spirit, an angel. He strode into my life strong with charisma, and smelling of pear drops, wearing an ethereal beauty which was both male and female and I wanted to paint him and to hold him forever. He is gone now and remains just sketches in my notebooks.

My Dearest T'Ash,
Many months have passed and my life has changed forever. I have no idea now where you are or whether you will receive this letter, but I am compelled to write it anyway.
My life here has been all that I could have hoped for. I am painting every day and learning new techniques which make my work so much more real; Felix says that I am maturing as an artist and will be even better than my father, which is hard to believe. I don't know if he has got Pa's pictures back yet but he doesn't tell me much of what he is up to.
Felix told me that you didn't want to have anything to do with the baby but I feel sure that if we were to see each other again, you would feel differently. I am close to my time now. By the time you receive this our child may be born. Felix wants to give it away for adoption but I will never let that happen. I cannot keep the baby on my own. I need help. I am sure that Mrs. Vries won't help me and there is no one else, except Ben, my Art tutor. I have made no new friends here, and

in my condition, I have not really had the opportunity. Felix promises that after the baby is born and I am recovered, we will go away for a while. Art galleries around Europe and then in the Autumn, I will go to Art School and meet new people.

I feel a warmth and a love for the child growing inside me when I remember that it is our child, T'Ash. We loved each other once. Could you find it in your heart to love me again?

I enclosed a self portrait with bump, sealed the envelope and addressed it to: Mr. A. T. Ash. c/o Mrs K. O'Malley, 1276, Station Street, Brooklyn, United States of America.

I was drenched in confusion and frustration as I wrote these words to T'Ash. I had to be bold now. I could feel the baby move. It was becoming real and in my heightened emotional state, I felt my love for T'Ash as though it was still new. How could I keep this child, mine and T'Ash's?

I needed a plan. As much as I loved Felix and longed for the life he was offering me, his life had no room for my child and he would have to chop off my right arm if he wanted to wrench this baby from me. I would have to try to persuade him to include it in our joint lives, but I wasn't optimistic. His version of my life did not include the baby and T'Ash's version of my life would be spent in America. I wanted to stay in Europe with my baby and my painting.

I sat back in the armchair and sipped the weak tea Mrs. Vries had left for me. It was almost cold but sweet and comforting. I would need to step up and take control. I could no longer depend on those who had their own versions of my life, but in reality I was totally at the mercy of Felix, my ward, patron, uncle, jailor. He was offering me my dreams on a plate but the price he asked was high. The cost would be my child and I now knew that it was a price I could never pay.

Chapter Thirty Eight

I found somewhere cheap to stay up in the North of Colchester so that I could visit Marianne. She was the person I needed to speak to, if she was able, and besides, I wanted to check her out. She was all alone now and no one would visit her. I just hoped she remembered me.

I was shown into the day room by a very harassed nurse who said they were a bit short staffed because of the flu and she hoped I didn't have it because some of the patients were very vulnerable. I managed to persuade her that I was in rude health and so she went off to find Marianne.

I stood by the big bay window and looked at the landscape. The garden was wearing its threadbare winter livery but I liked to see it in all seasons: as a kid I was dragged to visit my gran and I would play around in the trees and even the small farm they had here to be self sufficient. But at thirteen I went into long trousers and I was deemed too old to fool around outside and I had to sit like a grown up and watch my ma talking to her ma like she was now the child. It was all upside down somehow.

A couple of old people sat in chairs, one reading, one just looking at the floor and my heart broke for them. These were people who had lived lives and lived through two wars and raised families and loved and laughed a lot, but now, I saw only emptiness behind their eyes. Their souls had fled leaving just a shell of brittle bones and hurting limbs. I took out my notebook and jotted it down and when I turned around, Ma Quinn had been wheeled in silently behind me and was looking at me intently.

'Now don't go tiring her out or getting her too excited, do you hear? She is due her medication in half an hour so I will come back, alight Marianne?' Ma Quinn nodded without taking her eyes off me and her gaze was compelling. I touched her arm gently and said,

'Hello there Ma Quinn. How are you keeping?' She smiled a smile as enigmatic as any that Leonardo could have pasted onto the face of his Mona Lisa.

'I'm not too bad today thanks Alfie. Are you going to give me a kiss?' Delight, shock, joy, flashed through me and I bent to kiss her and pulled up a chair to sit beside her.

'Where's Bea?' I haven't seen her for a while.' How much had they told her? Did she know that Bea was now in Holland with Felix? When Bea left, Marianne had been a cabbage and not known anyone. Hell, this was going to be a lot harder than I thought. I needed to take it gently and see how much she remembered.

'Oh she's grand and sends lots of love.'

'That's nice,' she said and smiled placidly and folded her hands demurely into her lap. 'Only the last visitor I had was not welcome,' and a look of total distress came across her face. I patted her arm.

'Oh dear, I hope I am?' I said.

'Oh always, Tarron. Or is it Alfie? I get you confused sometimes with that other young man who was courting our Bea.' I sighed and just patted her hand again and said, 'Oh both. I don't mind which one you call me.'

'Well you can't be both. That would just confuse me,' she said firmly. 'I have enough trouble remembering as it is.'

'What are you remembering Ma?' I asked gently.

'T'Ash. That's it. We played cards a lot didn't we?' and her face lit up at the memory.

'That's right Ma. We played cards.'

'Shall we play now? Is that why you came? I'll see if I can get a pack. But it's hard to find a full deck in here,' and I wanted to laugh at the unintended pun, so I just filed it away to use later.

'No Ma. Maybe next time.' She leaned in conspiratorially.

'Thing is, Mrs. Watson takes all the Jacks out of the pack and rips them up. Says they are the Devil and they will get her if she doesn't destroy them. And Mrs. Adams, Margery, she keeps the aces in her pocket so she can always cheat. I tried to teach them that game we used to play, what was it Alfie?'

'Cribbage Ma,' I said and wondered how she could teach it as the rules seemed to evade her. I needed to change the subject but at least she was lucid. 'So who was your unwelcome guest then?' I said and her face flushed and set in the frown of a small child. She was looking distressed so I gently touched her arm.

'It was her. That whore. She wore a wig and tried to look different but it was her. I know it was.' She looked at my puzzled expression and tutted loudly. *'Jellicoe,'* she whispered conspiratorially.

I had no idea whether this was true or not. I would ask before I left. Had Jellicoe really been here? Why? But then if she had been in Colchester the night the pictures were taken, why not visit Marianne?

I didn't want to push it that day so I left her to her nurses and medication and went back to my digs and wrote to Beatrix.

My Dearest Love,

I saw your Ma today and she is surprisingly well. I will visit her again tomorrow, but for now I was delighted to find her lucid. I reassured her that you are well and happy and fortunately, she has no *real sense of time, so she has no idea when she last saw you. I say this in the fervent belief that you are well and happy but I have no news of you still. I wish you would break your silence and send me word. I will hold you always in my heart and I will come for you on March 1st 1961. Wherever I am in the world I will look for you. Wherever you are in the world, I will find you. I will keep faith with you and not give up....*

The next day I visited again and Marianne was pretty much the same. We chatted a bit, warming up to what I really wanted to know.

'You know the paintings, Ma, in your cellar?' She looked at me with a cold stare so I just rattled on. 'Well I took a peek at them and you know I think they may be valuable. It would bring in a bit of money you know if you sold them and maybe you could stay somewhere like a nice private nursing home?'

'I like it here thank you,' she said and sniffed and turned away from me.

'Well then, maybe they would be helpful for Bea, you know? Give her a bit behind her to set her up?'

'Are you planning to marry her, because if you are, I would forget about what she might get for those paintings. They are worthless now. There's no market for them anymore. I kept them for her because Max painted them and asked me to. I haven't the slightest idea how to sell them. '*Her*' and Felix took care of that side of things and I never saw a penny.'

'Were did the money go?' I asked quietly.

'Where everything else went. The bloody Resistance....'

'And Max painted all of them?'

'Of course he did. No one else could paint like him.'

'So Max painted and Jellicoe and Felix sold them?' She looked confused.

'Why are you asking me all these questions? I thought I'd told you all this before.'

'Of course you did Ma.'

'Why do you need to know anyway? It was all a long time ago now.' I nodded agreement. What exactly *did* I need to know? Maybe I just wanted confirmation that my version of events was true. Ok, here goes.

'So what Bea still wants to find out is, who killed her Pa?'

'He's not dead,' she snapped back. 'I saw him. He came here to see me. A while ago now...' Ok, so that was how it was going to be.

'Ma, don't you remember that Max died at the end of the war?'

'How can I bloody forget. He was my husband. I should never have let her in.'

'So he is dead then?' She turned to look straight at me and I swear I have never seen her look so intense or so sane.

'Oh yes. Max is dead. But he's not Bea's father.' She stopped suddenly and looked at her hands and wrung them together and I saw that tears were running down her face. Was this the truth? The third and final level of truth? I saw one of the nurses look across at us and I thought that at any moment she would come over and tell me to leave, and dope Ma up again and then I would be no nearer than I was now.

'Who is Bea's father, Ma?' I asked very quietly.

'Felix.' She said equally quietly and sighed and looked out towards the gardens. 'You see, I told you. It doesn't do to keep too many secrets. I kept them all this time. Bea doesn't know. Or Felix. He came here to ask me when I was ill last time but I pretended to be asleep so he couldn't talk to me. I wouldn't tell him anyway. I wouldn't give him that satisfaction. Not after what he did. Max deserved her. Felix didn't.'

'What did he do? What did Felix do?' my voice was barely above a whisper and I didn't want to break the spell.

'It was mayhem and she was responsible really. Saying she loved him, she loved my Max and she was having his baby and she would tell the Nazis about my mother who was half Jewish. I never knew it and we grew up here as Catholics, believe it nor not. Bea was baptised in Holland. She is a Catholic too but when we came back, we just didn't keep it up...'

'So what happened, the night Max died?'

'She threatened to expose me and that would have meant Bea as well and we would have been sent to a camp so Max tried to kill her. I stepped in. I couldn't let him kill her if she was pregnant could I? Should I have done? I often wondered. God knows she deserved it but she was working with us until then, until she wanted Max all to herself. She was useful. She knew a lot of Nazi officers and 'worked both sides.' That's why Felix wanted her dead as well. She knew too much. But I persuaded him, both of them that it was against nature to kill a pregnant woman. I could not have them do that, whatever she had done. Max went mad; he got dangerous and was going to blow our whole little cell apart; his baby Beatrix was threatened and so was I. It unhinged him. He loved me as well, you see. I like to think it was both of us.'

'I am sure he loved you both. I've seen the pictures Ma. You look lovely in those pictures. I can see by how he painted you that he loved you. But you put yourself at risk. Surely getting rid of Jellicoe would have been safer for you and Bea?' She shrugged.

'It was all but over by then. The end was close. We knew that liberation was on its way so the threats were empty. She could have done it any time in the previous couple of years but she didn't. She knew I was keeping them all alive.'

'How?'

'I got information and food. I'm not proud of it but I did have to do things.... just to keep us all fed. In the end I was no better than her. Max thought Bea was his daughter and she was in every way that mattered. But I know that Felix is her father. He was always irresistible. When I realised that he seduced me so that I could get Max to join the 'cause' I was devastated. I thought we were going to leave together; go back to England out of harm's way with our unborn baby. But he always wanted to be in the thick of it. He didn't care too much about me after all and I was a fool, but I stayed loyal to Max even though he was hard to live with. Felix was staying to fight and persuaded us all to join in. Then later, when Max wouldn't listen to me, he sent in Jellicoe. Those last years were hell and she just complicated everything....'

I was unsure about asking her to relive hell again but not talking about it had already caused her more than enough pain.

'So what happened?'

'Max attacked Felix. They had a fight. Felix was younger and much fitter so it was a very uneven contest.' I sat and waited and her mouth worked itself, chewing at the words she could not bring herself to speak.

'I told you this before, T'Ash. Felix killed Max. He shot him. He had no choice in the end. We were all at risk.'

That was it. That's what I needed to know. Max was shot by his brother as I had worked out from the pictures. But how could Max have known that? He painted them before he died so he must have felt his brother's betrayal long before. His betrayal in love as well as war.

'What happened to Jellicoe?'

'Felix took Jellicoe away to the Nuns. She went into labour and he put her in a home until her baby was born. I thought he had gone back to kill her. I thought she was dead until she turned up here. I wish I'd had the courage to talk to her. To explain it all. To forgive her. But I can't. I saved her life. Risked mine and Bea's. But I could never forgive her.'

Chapter Thirty Nine

I pace Ben's studio, paint brush in hand, thinking hard. It is uncomfortable now and Ben is uncertain about me coming here. I am trying to remember something important. Didn't Jellicoe escape from Felix with her baby? How did she do it I wondered? Would she help?

'Do you know Jellicoe?' I ask Ben innocently, returning to look at the canvas again. He is surprised by my question.

'Erm, Jellicoe who?' he asks, clearly stalling for time.

'You know. The woman who modelled for my father during the war.'

'I wasn't here during the war,' he says and goes back to mixing his paints. I stand in front of him, bump pointed directly at him, making him feel uncomfortable and stare until he stops and looks at me.

'What?' he says. 'I told you. I was in England. I only came back when it was safe. I was just a kid.'

'But you know who she is, right?' He shrugs and reaches behind him for a jar of white clay to mix with the madder.

'Heard the name,' he says.

'From Felix?' I am greedy for information. 'Go on. You can tell me. You see, I grew up hearing all these names and stories about the war and these amazing people and now I am actually here, well it is all coming alive for me. It's not just stories anymore. And I want to be able to tell my child all about those times...' I let it hang like a wish in the air. He puts his pestle back in the bowl and covers the contents with a cloth and busies himself with tidying.

'Aye. They were interesting times, that's for sure. But a lot of people got hurt and don't like to talk about it. Bit of a hornet's nest if you know what I mean.'

'I know,' I reply sympathetically. 'I remember Jellicoe so well though even though I was only a babe at the time. She lived with us and used to look after me. More like an Auntie than anything else. I'd love to know what happened to her.' His reply sounds like 'hrumph,' or something and he looks towards me. I give him my sweetest most innocent smile but Ben isn't much of a talker, not like T'Ash who has the gift of Irish blarney. Ben is taciturn. Tall, like most of the Dutch people I come across, light brown hair and that extraordinary Dutch face full of character and expression; high forehead; ski slope nose; strong large mouth; a face I recognise from a thousand Dutch Renaissance paintings in every gallery in every city in the world. If it wasn't for my condition I may have found him attractive but there is something else. I love T'Ash. Always will and no man will ever match up. Ben catches me staring at his face with the intent gaze I have which I don't always realise I am inflicting on people. I shake it away.

'Sorry. I was miles away. Thinking about Jellicoe and the early days in Max Prins' studio.' He is alert now and I realise that in order to get information from him I will have to give some so I tell him an anecdote about Pa and the first time I tasted chocolate. Jellicoe is in that story: the story of how she strolled into my father's studio in broad daylight and announced:

'I'm Jellicoe. I want to be your model.'
'What?'
'I want to be .....'

'Yeah, Yeah. I heard you the first time. No.' and Pa threw himself back onto the daybed by the wall. She moved indoors and rested a small bag of food on top of him. He sat up.

'Where did you get this?' he asked, pulling out fruit cake, chocolate and a bottle of wine.

'I know where to get things,' she said ingenuously. He called me over and lifted me onto his lap and wrapped his arms around me and broke off a piece of chocolate.

'Beatrix has never tasted chocolate, have you sweetheart?' he said and he popped a piece into my mouth whilst I kept my eyes suspiciously on Jellicoe. She stared back at me so I turned away from her and buried my face in his warm shoulder which smelt familiar and safe. The bitter sweet chocolate was strange and I knew I should love it, but I didn't and I haven't eaten much chocolate since.

'Yes, I've heard stories about people starving, and freezing...'. and he walks over to the bench carrying two cups of tea. 'Let's hope we don't go through it again,' he says and is not going to say anything more. I sigh.

'Jellicoe had a daughter, my half sister, and she will be the only family I have, apart from Felix. It would be great to have a sister to share my.. well... just great to have a sister right now. I could really use someone my own age. Some female company. Mrs. Vries doesn't say much.' I hear him make a tutting sound of agreement and let his breath out in a controlled way.

'I thought Jellicoe's daughter had gone abroad?' he says not making eye contact. I seize on this piece of information.

'Has she? Where to? Maybe I could write to her.' He shrugs. 'Come on Ben. I need someone to talk to, or else it will have to be you and I don't think you want to hear about what happens when my waters break and whether the baby is lying breach or how many centimetres dilated I will be! God I miss my mother so much!' which is true. Talking about it like this, I realise how much I really miss

234

her. She would have been so kind and gentle and supportive, and T'Ash and I would be together under her roof and damn the nosy neighbours. Ben has flushed to the roots of his tawny brown hair and held up his hands in submission. I have succeeded. Even in a more open society such as Holland, people don't talk much about childbirth and men, never, unless like Felix they are doctors. He gets over his embarrassment and looks directly at me. Through me.

'Are you sure you know what you are doing Beatrix? From what I hear, Jellicoe is pure poison.'

'Says Felix?' He shrugs. 'Besides, she knew me when I was a baby. She has her own child so she may have changed? Being a mother changes something in you, I know it does,' and the acting gives way to real emotion and although I hadn't intended emotional blackmail, it works. He tears his eyes away and moves over to the workbench and pulls out a well thumbed notebook. He finds a stub of pencil on the bench and rips a corner from a sheet of scrap paper and copies from his notebook.

'Don't tell Felix I gave it to you. Seriously, Bea, I don't want any trouble.' He holds the scrap of paper at arm's length to emphasis his point. 'It is a phone number where you can find her. Felix asked me to track her down when there was some bogus item about her in the press. It is not an Amsterdam number, she lives out of town. And if Felix finds you have it, tell him you found it on my workbench, understood?' I nod, keeping my eyes on the scrap of paper and wanting to snatch it from him. He grunts and hands me the number which I carefully fold and slip into the pocket of my painting apron.

Chapter Forty

Felix paused on his way to collect Beatrix from the studio, needing to take stock. She was coming along well; her first real painting complete and already almost as good as anything Max could have done. The only part missing, before they could age the canvas was to add the signature. He had asked her not to sign it yet. Did she know what they were doing? In her current condition it may well be better if she didn't; he couldn't afford mistakes now. His reputation was blameless and he was respected professionally and personally. But his campaign for mental health reform would never succeed without research, and research needed funding and to the Government, however sympathetic, mad people were not a priority. They didn't vote. He thought retrieving Max's paintings from the damp little cellar in Colchester would do it, and it would be a very good start. By the time Bea went into 'confinement' the first of Max's masterpieces would be restored and rediscovered. A *Pieter de Hooch*. Not the Vermeer yet: that would have to wait because Vermeer's *Catalogue Raisonne* had been re-attributed since the end of the war, and his works were harder to pass off these days.

He thought about the other artists whom Max had studied and whose work he captured so sublimely that the experts were totally convinced. The Nazis to whom they were sold were only too eager to believe those expert views. There were three or four by Nicholas Maes which Jellicoe had sold via her contacts to Herman Goerring. They were oil on oak rather than canvasses; small domestic scenes with models who would not be recognised, and Max, being a perfectionist had studied the artist well. He had understood the use of the reddish tones of Maes earlier works and perfected this in the domestic scenes. The portrait of a 17th Century Gentleman, closer to a Van Dyck than a Rembrandt, which Max completed shortly before he died, filled in the gaps of Maes' later works, the period after 1660, when Maes used greys and blues in the shadows. That painting was now in a private collection, Felix believed, in America.

The paintings which Felix had now were the ones which had not been sold in Max's lifetime for a number of reasons, not least because the 'models' were recognisable then, although looking at the paintings again, Felix was convinced, they would never be recognised now. Also Max painted faster than provenances could be invented, paperwork forged, a trail and history created, and they couldn't risk flooding the market. His judgement about the timing and placing of the work was as much a skill as any other part of the process and he was calling on that skill to guide him now.

He would begin this re-launch of Max Prins' work with *Checkmate*: the self portrait of his brother who depicted his feeling of betrayal as allegory in so many of his works. Who became deranged and dangerous and had to be silenced. There was too much at stake to let sentiment get in the way.

Check Mate by 'Pieter de Hooch'. The brush work, style, pigments, canvas; all crafted with expert care. The paper trail was in place and he was certain that it would pass authentication. He was also certain that it would cause a bit of a stir, by which time he would reveal that he had a few other paintings he wished to sell. Ben would need to work fast to complete the restoration, mostly cleaning, but even in their current state they would sell for a fortune. The paintings would not appear on any list of looted art works and would not be traced to any original Jewish ownership and Max was careful to craft his paintings in a way which filled a gap in the oeuvre of a particular artist.

Checkmate was un-catalogued but there had long been debates in the Arts press about De Hooch's missing years. All artists leave gaps in their trail of work which leaves possibilities and vacuums to fill. They were simply fulfilling the expectation of the experts by providing what they wanted to see.

He had let the market settle after the turmoil and upheaval of war; let the Allied Art Commission have its time in the spotlight. But then he had been prompted into action by that small article in the paper about Jellicoe's faked death. Spurred into action by four incidental column inches. Now was the time to act.

That was the extent of his plan until he discovered the truly remarkable talent of his niece. He was testing her with her first painting. An 'old master' was much harder to reproduce than a modern or impressionist painting and so far she had passed the test.

She would become his new Max. She would take her father's role and together they could make a difference. She even had a vested interest in his cause as she knew the pain of mental illness first hand. But he would take it slowly, gently and gain her trust and love.

The baby was a complication but it was all in hand and he was not going to make the same mistake again. He let Jellico slip though his fingers. He would be more protective with Beatrix.

He had arranged for Beatrix to be sedated at the clinic, where the doctor would perform a caesarean section and the baby would be taken away before she could know what had happened. She could not bond with a baby which she didn't see. And the tears would dry soon enough. She was still young and resilient and had shown little interest and even less sentiment for her unborn child. He was doing her a favour and he was sure that it was for the best all round.

Chapter Forty One

It was a week before I summoned the courage to make the call and I had to wait until both Felix and Mrs. Vries were out of the house. It was a dull, wet morning; Felix had left after breakfast for his clinical duties at the research centre and Mrs. Vries had shopping to do on the market.

'Would you like to come with me? If we wrap you up warm you will be fine. The fresh air will do you good,' she said, rather like Matron in a boarding school. She was a good woman and I knew her to be kind, but I hadn't warmed to her. There was a professional distance about her which I knew I could never breach, even if I wanted to, and I wasn't sure that I did. I coughed and shivered and put on a small voice.

'I'll stay here thank you Mrs. Vries. I am not feeling too good this morning,' and I rested a hand lamely on my bump and looked at her through lowered lids. If I had done this with Mum or Aunt Maude, they would have hugged me, or at least patted my head or rubbed my shoulder, and discussed at length whether I was coming down with something, and laid a cool hand on my forehead to check for temperatures. I felt again the pain of loneliness and what I was missing; but the professional matronly Mrs. Vries simply nodded and said, 'as you wish. I will leave you some biscuits for later and make sure you drink your milk. Dr. Van Gelder is quite clear about those instructions.' A tight smile softened the otherwise terse delivery and she left the room. I waited until I heard the downstairs door close and her key turn in the lock and then saw her climb the steps from the basement and turn left down the street towards the market, hoisting an umbrella as soon as she cleared the steps.

I was aware of the silence. Of the mantle clock in the dining room. Of the creak of a solid old house. Of the muted light flooding in through the front windows and making patterns on the parquet flooring from the rain which barely had the impetus to trickle down the panes. I was aware of the metallic taste in my mouth and the bile which was rising in my throat, a recent occurrence as the baby sat high and squashed my stomach up between the ribs. I sipped the cool milk which was from a Friesian herd and was creamy and sweet, and which was delivered for me daily to add calcium and protein to my bones. I felt cold despite the fire burning warmly and high in the grate and I sat for a while in the silent room and wondered about the wisdom of contacting Jellicoe. Could she help? Would she? What exactly did I want from her?

To keep my baby, as she had done. To find T'Ash again. To live my own life. But what about the plans to go to Art School? To meet other young Artists? To be a part of the world and to travel Europe?

Handing over my baby to anonymous faceless people was too high a price to pay. If the worst happened, then I still had my house in Colchester. Maybe Ma would be better and she could come home and T'Ash could move in and all would be well. Another generation to sit in Grandpa Quinn's chair.

The sad quiet depressed world I had waited so eagerly to escape now seemed like a safe haven.

I looked around at the rich and opulent surroundings of this house, this mansion on the Keizersgracht, one of the best locations in Amsterdam. The cloth of gold and the world at my feet, offered in love and good faith and I was about to trample on my own dreams. I hugged my baby bump tightly, found my resolve which was driven now by something I had never known before; maternal love, and I stood and strode purposefully into Felix's study, closed the door and lifted the telephone handset and dialled the number on my scrap of paper.

Chapter Forty Two

It was time. Felix was to introduce the art world to the 'collection' he claimed to have inherited from his late industrialist grandfather. Han De Groot was born in Holland but made his fortune in Switzerland as a pharmaceutical industrialist. De Groot was indeed Felix's paternal grandfather although he had abandoned his wife after World War I. Werner had died after World War II at the age 80. So far the story was true. He was not, however, an Art enthusiast, in fact, if the stories Felix heard were true, his paternal grandfather was a very wealthy philistine and Nazi sympathiser. More than sympathiser; a part of his vast fortune had helped support Hitler's rise to power.

He had met his grandfather once on a visit to Berne before the war, and the experience had justified Felix having no further contact.

The knowledge of this helped to goad Felix into his work for the Resistance, to redress the balance of good and evil as he saw it, which any family holds within it. He took his mother's surname of Van Gelder to put as much distance as possible between him and De Groot, but now, he needed a basis for Provenance for the paintings and the stories he had used during wartime would need to be refreshed.

Forging the documents was easy; ensuring that the canvasses, nails, pigments and finish of the paintings were not anachronistic was a simple matter of science; pure chemistry at which Ben excelled. He was certain that those elements were in place and the fewer who were involved, the greater the chance of success. His small 'cell' had spent years in the early days of the war perfecting their techniques and subsequently had made even greater improvements.

Getting the story of the provenances right was the hardest part and he had always been good at inventing a likely scenario, so the story he intended to tell the gallery owner whom he had selected to launch the first of his 'collection', was this:

One of De Groot's friends in the 1920s and 30s had been a well-known art dealer and collector named Albert Stofer. Months after Adolf Hitler came to power, Stofer fled into exile in Paris; he had a Jewish background although no one knew at the time. He took with him what he could of his collection. (So far, this was true). According to Felix, Stofer sold many works which he couldn't take with him, legitimately to De Groot and Felix had the (forged) documents to prove it. De Groot hid the paintings in his country home in Friesland, safe from Nazi plundering. The pictures remained there until his grandfather's death in 1947 when Felix, the only remaining grandson, inherited the house and its contents. Only now was Felix able to authenticate the paintings and wanted to sell them. Felix would also maintain that his grandfather had no idea what he had purchased; he was not interested in Art but saw that his old friend was desperate, and that he could score a bargain.

The experts had a whiff of a 'great discovery' and a chance to make a name for themselves and Felix understood people. He knew how to read, and then to meet, their expectations. If they had suggested that

Vermeer had a period of his work missing and they thought he had perhaps travelled to Utrecht and Italy and been influenced by the Carravagistas, then Max would supply such a canvas. A religious scene would fill the gap and the 'experts' would be delighted that their predictions had been true. They would publish papers and enhance their profile; and the Nazis would be delighted to buy a part of the Nations Art treasures.

Checkmate was to feature in an auction of Dutch Art in April 1957 and would be on view to the public from the end of February.

Statements of authenticity from leading authorities were essential before offering the paintings to auction houses and galleries, and so Felix invited De Graaf, expert on the Dutch Golden Age, to his house on Keizersgracht to look at a painting from his grandfather's collection which in his humble opinion was a De Hooch.

In the catalogue, De Graaf praised the artist's use of colour and the gallery notified its customers that De Graaf had confirmed the work's authenticity and had checked the documentation and provenance back to its original owner, with subsequent catalogue entries of its sale in the 18th and 19th centuries in London. To bolster his hoax, Felix had pasted on the back of the frame, a label from the Stofer Collection. And so the provenance of *Checkmate* was duly identified in the auction catalogue as:

Albert Stofer, Amsterdam; Han De Groot Berne.

And the stage was set.

Chapter Forty Three

There is a small cafe on Rembrantplein. There are many cafes on Rembrantplein but this is the one where Jellico had asked me to meet her. I am nervous and despite the warm spring air, I feel deeply chilled. My coat is fastened up to the neck with a large collar which adds width to my shoulders and takes the eye away from the bump. It is an A-line style which hides most of my condition, but there is no escaping the reality. I twist T'Ash's ring on my wedding finger and approach the cafe carefully looking at the women's faces. An older couple, not unlike Mrs. Vries, are gossiping and taking little notice of their surroundings. A few tables are taken with single men, older and reading the paper, smoking pipes. The younger men will be at work. I push the door open and step inside to be met with the smell of coffee which appeals to me at that moment, and cigarette smoke which doesn't. I look around the large salon.

How old will Jellicoe be now? Could that be her in the corner by the window sipping a small coffee and lighting a cigarette? She is paying little attention to her surroundings and then she turns the newspaper over, takes a pencil from her handbag and begins to fill in the crossword. She is about the right age, late 30's or possible even 40. I only know that Jellicoe is younger than my mother. Surely not so young for the responsibility she took during the war? But this woman is heavy set with dark hair and has slipped glasses onto her nose as she continues with her crossword clues. She chews the end of her pencil, stubs out her cigarette and looks across the room. She looks past me but I decide to take a seat opposite her as she is the most likely to be Jellicoe, although I can see little resemblance to the woman Pa painted, and loved. I have a moment of panic. What am I doing here? This woman ruined my mother's life and set a train of events in motion which have led me here, without T'Ash and in a foreign land. I have Felix which is something. He has become the father I never knew, but right now I really need my mother and the woman I am about to meet had all but destroyed her life.

A waiter approaches me with a smile and as I order a milky coffee, a woman slips into the seat opposite me.

'Straight black for me,' she says, her voice heavy and gravelly. 'Hello Beatrix. My word. You are all grown up.'

Chapter Forty Four

'Don't be alarmed. I didn't mean to startle you,' Jellicoe said more quietly and gently and Beatrix took a deep breath of relief. She was like a startled rabbit, thought Jellicoe eyeing the young woman in front of her.

'I'm sorry, I didn't see you coming... I was looking for you...' Jellicoe patted her arm and sat back in her chair to look at the young woman she had last seen as a small child. She recognised the child in the woman facing her and felt a pang of guilt and regret that things hadn't turned out differently. But they were different times and as Felix had reminded her, different rules applied. And of course, having her own child, loving her own child more than anything in the world, even more than Max, had changed her. But she wasn't here for sentimentality. She was here for information. She had waited in a doorway opposite and watched Beatrix approach. It was a hangover from the old days but she knew it worked. Wait and watch and then use the element of surprise. She felt in control.

'Just as well I saw you then,' she said removing her gloves and adding them to her handbag.

'How did you know me?' Beatrix asked and Jellicoe laughed. A real, heartfelt laugh. Beatrix was barely a woman and yet, even an untrained eye could see that she was blossoming as only a woman can. This child was pregnant and that changed things.

'How did I recognise you?' Did the girl not realise how much she resembled her father?

'Instinct?' Jellicoe said and pulled out a photograph from her handbag. She placed it on the table and saw confusion and then recognition cross Beatrix's face as she looked at the photograph. The picture was taken around the turn of the century. A beautiful woman in a long dark skirt looked intently out at the camera. Her gaze was piercing, direct. There was a smile tugging at the corner of her full mouth and the long dark hair was piled high on her head. Her eyes were dark. On her lap was a small boy dressed in a sailor suit, a solemn expression on his infant face, his hair tumbling in long blond curls. Behind her stood an older child, about ten years old, Beatrix guessed, but even then she could see the self assurance in the handsome child who would grow up to be her father.

Even allowing for the period, there was a distinct family likeness; something about the set of the jaw; the dark hair and light eyes; the challenging gaze. Beatrix always thought that she looked like her mother, but maybe she was much closer to her father than she realised; and closer still to this woman.

'My grandmother?' Beatrix said, as a question and statement at the same time. Jellicoe nodded.

'Sakia Van Gelder, formerly Prins. Nee De Groot.' She said as Beatrix turned the picture over to read the inscription on the back.

'Saskia with Max and Felix, 22 June 1913.' She read. 'I've never seen a photo of my grandmother,' she said a little in awe.

'It's for you,' Jellicoe said and offered no further explanation as to how or why it was in her possession and not amongst Marianne's or Felix's papers.

'What happened to her, do you know?' asked Beatrix, taking her eyes from her grandmother's face for a moment to look directly at Jellicoe.

'There it is,' thought Jellicoe, 'The famous Prins look.' She simply shrugged. 'Max told me she died shortly after the Great war. Influenza, I believe. Max was away at school and Felix followed shortly afterwards. They spent holidays with their grandmother in the countryside.' Beatrix was silent and staring at Jellicoe.

'I never knew,' she muttered. 'I didn't hear much about my father as I was growing up. Just about my Irish family.'

'The Quinns,' Jellicoe said as a matter of fact. Beatrix looked up surprised.

'Did you know them?'

'No of course not. But I knew that your grandfather was Irish and married a dark haired beauty...' It came back to Beatrix in a flash.

'She was Jewish. My other grandmother...' she said and flushed as she remembered Jellicoe's betrayal of Marianne.

'It doesn't matter anymore.' Jellicoe said, but Beatrix remained unsure, Her hands shook slightly as she turned back to the photo in front of her.

'Felix was so fair,' Beatrix said and Jellicoe shrugged.

'Small children often are. Even when the parents are dark. My daughter is fair, but then, so was I.'

'Johanna,' Beatrix said.

'So she knows about my daughter,' thought Jellicoe as she nodded affirmation. She needed to know what else Beatrix knew.

'You look like your father,' she said. Beatrix smiled shyly and looked down at her hands. 'Do you remember him at all?' Jellicoe asked.

'A little. I have photos and a few of his sketches and things, but not much.' Silence. Jellicoe looked hard at the girl opposite.

'Why are you in Amsterdam?' she asked. She already knew the answer to that but wanted to hear the girl's version.

'My mother is... well, she is... unwell and in hospital.....' Jellicoe patted her hand in encouragement. How was Johanna faring without her mother? She pushed the thought aside and felt a connection to this child in front of her. Sympathy? Maybe. Maybe something else. Maternal. A pregnant child without a mother. She could almost get emotional about it but that was not why she was here.

'So, Felix to the rescue.' It was a statement and not a question and Beatrix looked down at her hands again. The waiter brought the coffees and discreetly left the tray on the table beside them.

'How can I help, Beatrix,' she said quietly. There was no point in platitudes, in saying *there there it will all be ok,*' because this was going in only one direction and Jellicoe had an idea about where that was. Beatrix turned a naked face to Jellicoe, totally devoid of makeup or artifice.

'I heard, well Felix told me, and Ma, Marianne told me, that you had a baby, Johanna...' Jellicoe watched her shrewdly.

'And what else did they tell you?'

'That Pa, Max was her father and that...' Jellicoe squeezed her hands in encouragement and moved closer. The girl was speaking very quietly and was in danger of fading away. 'And that you loved him.'

'Did they tell you that Marianne, your mother, saved my life?' Beatrix nodded. 'I owe my life to your mother but she still hates me. I never got to say I am sorry. You can't help who you fall in love with, can you Beatrix?' Beatrix's hands went defensively to her bump. 'And did they tell you that Felix wanted me and the baby dead?'. It was hard to think such things of Felix, Beatrix thought. He was so gentle and kind. She jumped to his defence.

'Oh but they were very difficult times and people did all sorts of things that they wouldn't do now.'

'My, he has trained you well!' and Jellicoe smiled. She couldn't blame the child and there was no point in venting her anger against Felix at an innocent. There may be another way to get revenge on him. She turned to the coffee and began to pour adding milk to one cup and handing it to Beatrix. It was nice having coffee in the square with a young woman who could almost be her step daughter or niece. It felt normal, but a cloud crossed Jellicoe's face. There was little normality in her life and never had been.

'Tell me about the love of your life? Where is he now?' A little cruel maybe, but she had to know what she was dealing with.

'T'Ash. He is called Alfred Tarron Ash. I call him T'Ash.' Jellicoe knew all of this. She had seen him however briefly on a cold wet night on England's damp East Coast. She smiled encouragement at Beatrix who seemed reluctant to say much else.

'Where is he now?' Jellicoe asked.

'America. He hasn't even written. When Felix told him about the baby, he just ... ran away. I can't believe it. We were going to get married when I am of age; Felix wouldn't sign for me yet. He says I need time to think about it and that I have to train as an artist first and that has always been my dream....' Jellicoe started to pay attention. She had expected a long, girlish romantic outpouring about how much she loved him and how he used her and now he was gone... all too familiar.

'So did you tell him about the pregnancy?'

Beatrix shook her head. 'I wasn't sure. I waited too long to admit it and by then, T'Ash had gone to America and Felix told him. I thought he would come back but he hasn't even written.'

'And he went to America because?'

Beatrix wrung her hands. 'Well, he always wanted to and Felix paid his fare. He would have been in trouble if he stayed, over the paintings and everything...' she tailed off, perhaps remembering the part I played in that fiasco, thought Jellicoe.

'Why would he be in trouble over that?' she needed to prompt Beatrix into seeing beyond Felix's superficial charm. Beatrix shrugged.

'Felix said someone wanted to steal them. You...' she looked down embarrassed.

'That's true, but I wouldn't call it stealing. Max had two daughters. I wanted a share for Johanna.' Beatrix nodded.

'I don't even want them. He said he had to preserve them for me until I was of age, but they have caused so much trouble. I just want to move on now; to have my baby...' she tailed off and Jellicoe reached across and touched her hand again.

'And keep it?' Beatrix nodded and Jellicoe could see what she had to do. Help the child. Pay her debt to Marianne and get her own back on Felix. 'We need to get to know each other better if I am to help you,' and Jellicoe noticed a truly happy smile cross Beatrix's pretty face.

253

Chapter Forty Five

I was relieved that I had made the phone call and by the end of the morning, I felt the happiest I had felt for ages. Jellicoe was going to help me keep the baby. She would send her to live with Johanna for a while although she didn't say where, and I could go later; and she talked about the baby as 'she', and I began to as well.

We walked back around the square past the heart of the city, the Royal Palace. There were bicycles everywhere, some carrying a whole family and others, just the shopping. Little carts on the back held the youngest children and dogs often ran alongside their owners.

'So many bicycles,' I said to Jellicoe in amazement.

'Oh yes, and we still hold the annual butcher boy race on bikes. It is great fun, and a very good way to get around this city; but not in your condition,' and she took my arm and held me close.

As we walked we talked about my small life in Colchester, about T'Ash; but I found it too distressing and so changed the subject. I was aware that I didn't know Jellicoe very well and that all the warning signs told me to be wary. She was attentive and careful and seemed to be concerned, but I really wanted to hear her version of the story I knew so well.

'How did you escape with Johanna?' I asked as we approached the plaza along the canal to the Rijksmuseum. I was out of breath and she stopped in front of me.

'You must be getting tired. Let's go in here and sit down for a while then I must run to get my train.'

We entered the large domed hall and steered our way past the thin crowd of viewers to a bench in the centre of a gallery. We were in the Dutch Masters and sat opposite a Vermeer. I tore my eyes away to listen to her story but it will always be associated with that painting of *The Milk Maid*.

'Johanna was born right at the end. You were there to start with. Do you remember?' I shook my head. I wanted to hear her story not tell mine.

'I went into labour as the Allies approached and the Germans were retreating and the Resistance was continuing to make their life difficult. Felix had organised a safe house for me. It was one of the most dangerous things to do during the war; to hide prisoners. He feared, quite rightly that I would be in danger once the war was over.' I frowned. This didn't quite match up.

'I thought he wanted to kill you?'

'Yes, earlier, when I told Max I was pregnant and I wanted to marry him and threatened your mother.'

'And me,' I added, looking at the Vermeer on the wall opposite. The light from the window played so beautifully on the copper plate and created deep texture and depth in the bread and the table cloth. Jellicoe sighed beside me and turned to look at me. I tore my gaze from *The Milk Maid* and saw a hardness in her eyes. It was the same look which Felix had when he tried to tell me about the realities of those days; to tell me that I, born in a feather bed and protected by the bravery of those who preceded me, could never understand. But I was trying to.

'Felix believed that I had betrayed them and that we would be arrested as collaborators. I said that I would betray them all to be with Max; and Felix raised his gun...' She shook her head trying to ease the pain of the memory which was falling into place before my eyes. I took her hand and she smiled at the gesture as though she were indulging me.

'Marianne stepped in front of me...' and she was silent.

'Is that why you want to help me?' I said quietly.

'Yes.' She said simply. 'Beatrix, you have been told haven't you about what will happen? How you will know when the baby is coming? What to do?' I withdrew my hand and nodded and I think I may have flushed a little.

'It's just that nobody told me and I know that you have no mother around to help. That is also why I want to be here.'

'To finally replace my mother?' I said and then wished I hadn't. She stood up and walked around the gallery not looking at the pictures. I gazed at the Vermeer and wondered how he had managed to get her expression so gentle and yet so focused. I stood and joined Jellicoe on the other side of the gallery. She was looking at a Pieter de Hooch of a man sitting at a table laughing. I had studied this painting and knew it well. My eye was drawn to the room behind and the story which was unfolding just out of sight.

'I could never replace your mother and I should never have tried.'

'I know. I am sorry.'

'It's just that it was different then...'

'I know. Different times. Different rules.' She looked at me as though she was seeing me for the first time and nodded.

'Yes. Different rules. After being liberated, Dutch citizens began taking the law into their own hands, as they do everywhere after a war. Women who had relationships with men of the German Occupying Force, called

moffenmeiden were abused and humiliated in public, usually by having their heads shaved and painted orange.'
'Did this happen to you?'
'It would have done. The nature of our work was secret so we had little evidence that we worked for the Resistance. The cells were small and no-one knew more than a few members. We were not part of the Communist's CPN which organized resistance from the start of the war. Our small cell had a particular purpose which you may know about?' I nodded agreement. 'We had little interaction with other cells. At least I didn't. Only Felix seemed to know everything that was going on, and we believed he had worked for Intelligence services before the war. He led our cell. Anyway, my not so simple job was to sell to Nazi officers. I had to be seen to be on their side. Yes I would have been arrested as a collaborator.' We walked for a while and she continued with her story.
'That night, the night all hell broke loose in the Studio, my waters broke. The contractions were fierce. I think Marianne sent you for help?' I shrugged but I had a strong memory:

of fear and shouting and running. It still haunted my dreams; and then a gunshot and returning to see Jellicoe on the floor doubled up in agony with Ma's arm around her shoulder and Pa in a pool of blood with Felix leaning over him. The woman holding my head against her scratchy skirt so that I couldn't see and then hands taking me, picking me up and being carried away from Ma and Pa and lots of shouting and Jellicoe screaming....

I felt her hands around me and I was steered to a bench in the centre of the gallery and a Security Guard was talking to Jellicoe.
'Just a glass of water please, she will be fine.' Her voice was clear but sounded far away. I came to and stared with blank eyes into the face of the woman who had been my

mother's tormentor for my entire childhood; who had lurked in the shadows of my life; who didn't know that my doll had her name; and she was the one person now who would help me keep my baby because these were different times; different rules.

Chapter Forty Six

Felix received two letters in the post that morning, both from England. The first was official and was a report from Doctor Steans, from Severalls Hospital.

'Dear Dr. Van Gelder,
Please find enclosed a copy of the clinical reports for your sister-in law, Mrs. Marianne Prins, (known as Quinn.) You will note the results of the ECT therapy have been positive, as has the continuing medication on Chlorpromazine. She has shown signs of memory recovery and is calmer and more proactive, day to day.
I must emphasise however, as you will be aware, that her treatment is long term and such progress is not unusual in the early days of such treatment. We recommend that she continue as a long term patient in our care until prolonged recovery is evident.
I remain your faithful and obedient servant,
Doctor Robert Steans
Chief Medical Consultant, Severalls....etc...

Felix was unmoved. It was no more than he expected. When Beatrix had recovered from the birth and their tour of Europe, they would visit Marianne again and he would assess for himself whether to bring her here under his care as a private patient.

But there was work to do first. He had to ensure that *Checkmate* was a total success. He had to ensure that it got its share of media attention and that it would pave the way for the 'rediscovery' of the other lost masters.

The second letter however was less easy to file away in a neat and tidy box labelled, 'for later'. It was written in a hesitant scrawl, penned by a shaky hand.

My Dearest Felix,
I hardly know where to begin. I have moments like now, when the light is clear and the colours of my memory are so vivid that I am living it all again and sometimes it is a joy; I am almost back in the house in Amsterdam where we first met, when I was already married to Max. And then the darker days crowd in and they give me medication to calm me and block out those memories and then it is all lost to me again in the fog.

I am writing this painfully and slowly as I haven't put pen to paper for a long time and this may take a while to complete. Nurse McDonald offered to write it for me and they may well read it, but I will seal it in any case and hope you receive it intact. What I am remembering is intended for you only and I need to know if this is how it really was. I remember that back in those days, we would never commit to paper things of this nature but I am desperate to know whilst I am still able.

The seal was intact, although he knew that that meant very little when dealing with authorities, but it could have been read. He read on quickly hoping that there was nothing which could damage his plans.

First, is Bea with you? Please confirm. They tell me here that she is your ward. If so then that is good but I would love to see her. I dream that she is a baby again, but it is not her; it is some other baby, fair and smiling with curling hair and I love her as I did Beatrix. T'Ash has been to see me and we played cards, (I think we did, or we spoke about it?) And I wonder again why I have not seen Beatrix for so long? T'Ash told me she was fine and would come soon. Maybe she did come on my dark days and I don't recall?

And finally, I have known for a long time that Max is not her father, although he raised her and loved her as his own, and I believe now that he knew, in the end, the truth about us. I have had a great deal of time, alone in my head thinking about the paintings he left behind, and I know that behind the image he paints, Max told his own truths in a way which sometimes only he understood. Do you still have the signet ring I gave you for your birthday in 1940, just before the invasion? My father's ring that should have gone to Max except that his fingers were too wide and he said he couldn't wear rings whilst he painted?

He tells that story in his picture of Beatrix in her cradle. *Do you have it? Of all his pictures it is the one I would like to keep.*

Beatrix is your daughter not Max's as I think you suspected.

I believe that is why he was so angry with you in the end; I believe he was incapable of fathering a child, which leaves open the question of the parentage of Jellicoe's child. I know that I saved her life and I would do the same again, and maybe, like me she didn't know for sure until later. Or she claims parentage for other reasons? I can remember well enough things from those days, but my ability to sort and reason them into any sensible pattern has gone. For now I must leave that to your capable brain.

Max left the paintings to Beatrix. I assume you have them now? I pray that you do the right thing and love her as Max did, and I always have.

For old time's sake?

My love always, Marianne

There were blotches and tear stains and the ink was smudged. The corners of the pages were dog eared and he wondered how long she had taken to write it. It was heartbreaking and his famous composure cracked. He sat heavily in the hall chair and stared at the patterns of light as the drizzle from the window cast dancing shadows on the parquet floor.

It was as he had always suspected. With Max's condition, it was rare to father a child, let alone two. Felix could count as well and knew that he could easily have been Beatrix's father, but he would not deny Max his daughter or Beatrix her loyalty. How would she react now, in her condition to knowing that the most fundamental truth which she held onto, that Max, from whom she had inherited an extraordinary talent, was not her father? What if she realised it was all fake, like the pictures?

And what about him? Although he had suspected, he had never really known. At a practical level it made little difference: he was now responsible for Beatrix and she would be his heir anyway as he had no other children, siblings or partner. But at another level. Damn it. He had missed all of those years when he could have been there as she was growing up. They could have gone away, anywhere in Europe, as a family – he would have lived with Marianne if it meant having his daughter with him. His daughter.

Damn it all. He folded the letter and stuffed it into his pocket. How had this insane woman from his past rattled his deepest emotions which had remained locked away for so long? He mustn't let his feelings run away from him or the whole edifice would dissolve and he had worked too long and too hard to let that happen. He took a couple of deep breaths and paced the room engaging logic over feelings. As a *modus operandi*, it had served him well all his life.

Next, there was the question of Jellicoe. Could Max be Johanna's father? So here was a dilemma. He had done a deal with Jellicoe believing that Johanna was Beatrix's half sister and it was the right thing to do. But that agreement was now null and void. How would Jellicoe react, he wondered, when he delivered the punch-line:

'Max could not father children?'

Chapter Forty Seven

Marianne was feeling stronger. Since she had persuaded Nurse MacDonald to post her letter to Felix she felt herself gradually restored to something close to her former self. She knew that she would never fully recover, but her one single aim was to get out of here and live her life again with Bea in Stockwell Street. Nothing would bring Maude back. She was dead and so was Max and all the others from the war. But she had Bea and maybe Bea would marry T'Ash and have children and there would be another generation to run around in the little house in Stockwell Street. It would be more than enough.

Felix was very grand now. Even during the war nobody really knew much about what he did. He was the leader of their cell and they were disciplined; they had a job to do and too many questions, knowing things you shouldn't, could cost lives. That had become a way of life, she realised ever since; *ask no questions, told no lies* was a mantra but Bea was a questioning child, born into chaos, growing up in peace. Maybe that created a conflict in her.

Her final truth had been spilled. She had told Felix that he is Bea's father, so she had to find Bea and tell her, face to face. That was her mission.

Since she had begun to improve, she was allowed to walk in the gardens in the afternoon when the weather was nice, unattended, but a nurse was stationed on the veranda to keep watch. It was a new treatment which was being tested by Doctor Steans to give the patients some responsibility for themselves. His was the only voice in this place which believed that some of the patients could be restored to such an extent that they may, one day go back into the world and he knew that sooner was better than later.

This was Marianne's secret joy, to be allowed to walk in the gardens where she believed Beatrix had met T'Ash. The thought of young love made her smile; of her and Max so long ago; a different place, but the rules are the same. And look at what happened to Maude? Same rules different outcome. Maybe she would find James, Maude's son, one day, but that was a distraction. She could only manage to hold one thought and to grasp it with all her strength, what little she had, but it was growing every day. The medication was working and the little exercise she was permitted helped. She no longer felt quite so bleak and she could remember things for days on end; small things like T'Ash came to see her. She decided to keep a notebook and to write things down like T'Ash did. Not her story exactly but just events, things which happened so that she could keep track of the days. That and read newspapers, or at least scan the headlines and see what was happening in the world.

She was not mad. She had to prove to them all that she was sane; damaged yes; depressed maybe; her doctor had called it 'nervous exhaustion' once and that seemed like the best description at the time. The other word used was 'trauma' and she had suffered her share of that. The war years took their toll on a whole generation and her greatest sorrow was that Beatrix had been caught up in its wake. But Beatrix was free now and she would no doubt be an artist like Max, not a Doctor like her true father. Interesting how these things criss-cross through the lives of the generations, like her and Maude. So different in so many ways and yet ended up in the same place; the same traumas. War is a great leveller.

She sat on the veranda for a while and watched two fat doves pouting and strutting about the grass, pecking at the earth looking for food, and the sheer simplicity of it made her smile. She couldn't tell if they were male or female. Nature had never been a significant part of her urban life, but now she saw, with greater clarity than she had ever felt, that in nature lay the answers. The pure beautiful simplicity of life made far too complicated by people. The birds were happy to be birds. To eat, fly, roost, mate, nest, raise young and do it all again. Survive. Pass on the genes. That is what it was all about and why Max was so keen to accept that Bea was his daughter. His genes living on in this beautiful innocent creature who loved him unconditionally; who followed him around his studio copying his every move; learning how to be like him; how to be him. Was that it? Was that why Felix wanted Bea? To replace Max? Did the genes matter more in the end than how we are forged in our parents' likeness? The genes, hers and Felix's mixed together in Bea. Would Bea have children? She smiled at that and felt warmed by the thought of it. A daughter would be nice. A little girl to keep the genes flowing.

She watched the birds and let the thoughts float away on the breeze. Humans make things complicated, she thought. I must try to keep it simple.

She picked up The Daily Mail which had been abandoned on the seat beside her and turned the pages as a distraction, then something caught her eye. It was very small print and she wished she had her reading glasses with her. Her heart skipped for a moment and she felt the blood in her veins run cold.

It was a painting she recognised even though the reproduction in the newspaper was small and black and white. She knew that picture well. What was it? Her hands shook as she turned the paper to catch the fading light and read the largest print she could manage without glasses.

'*Lost Painting Hailed by Critics as a Great Master.*'

She closed her eyes and held the paper close.

'Please God, not again. Please don't let this be happening again.'

By the time the nurse found Marianne an hour later, she was frozen in her seat, newspaper clutched closely to her breast, staring at the open landscape before her. She was put to bed, sedated and didn't speak to anyone for a week.

Chapter Forty Eight

I tried to see Marianne again but they said she was poorly and couldn't see anyone. I insisted; I said I was her son-in-law so that they would know I was family and that it was important family business; well I was nearly and I would be as soon as I could get back to Bea and marry her.

'She cannot be disturbed by anything right now,' the nurse said quietly.

'Why what's wrong with her?' I know I sounded belligerent, but she was fine when I was here a few days ago.

'A relapse. It happens with her condition, and we did warn the family that this is not unexpected.'

'Why did she relapse? Did something happen?'

'We don't know,' said the nurse patiently talking to me as though I was a nuisance she could do without. 'Dr. Steans will see her again when she is stronger. We will notify her next of kin who will inform you of any significant changes. Now I am needed on the ward.' She looked at me kindly, possibly understanding my distress and touched my arm.

'It is good that someone cares so much about her. It can help with recovery if they are not abandoned, you know, and with her daughter leaving...' was she fishing for information? I was unsure how much to say so reluctantly I let her go, but I would come back every day until I could find out where Bea was. My letters went to a post box in Amsterdam. I needed an address and thought that Marianne must have it.

I could hang around here for ages and still not get the information I needed, so I would travel to Holland on the weekend ferry anyway, and hoped that Marianne would have improved by then.

I walked along the famous long corridors of Severalls, infamous not long ago when they were unglazed and nurses would bicycle from one end to the other, and I wandered out into the gardens, and the birds on the grass flew into the air at my sudden appearance. I let the sound of wings settle fleetingly on the spring breeze and walked through the long shadows of the budding branches of the trees. The long shadows cast on green grass, wet with dew underfoot and soaking through the hem of my trousers. I walked until I was across the field and sat on a wall and pulled out my notebook and began to read. It is all here. A red line which links my story; snippets like,

'The long shadows cast long shadows...' and I smile at the innocence of those days. And another one which makes me laugh out loud, in Beatrix's hand and I read it and clutch the book to myself and feel her there;

We were at the beach chalet. I said, *'I want to write your story as a novel.'* It was early days and I had no idea what would unravel.

'Ok,' she said. She was warm and safe and I could see the humour sparkling in those green eyes. She took the notebook from me and wrote,

'Once upon a time, there was a young girl who lived in a dark, dark house in an old, old town, in a cold dark place with a mother mad as a bag of frogs........' and she drew a sketch of herself as a princess and her forlorn mother, a black humoured attempt to see the funny side. There were a lot of frogs hopping about. I asked about the frogs.

'You have to kiss an awful lot to find a Prins...' she wrote underneath and then laughed her devil-may-care laugh and threw herself at me in a moment of true mutual passion. How did we lose that passion? Where did it go? How did I let it slip away from me? Well, I wasn't going to make that mistake again. I would find her and find out why and pray that I was the only frog she had kissed.

Chapter Forty Nine

Marianne feels the wind blow through the dark room and the sound of predatory wings swooping, and fear grips her. She cries out but knows that no-one will come. Emptiness fills her as the dark wings swoop once more and force her to reel backwards.

Doctor Steans sits beside her bed holding a folded newspaper in his hands. He has been watching her for some time and has noticed the signs that she is surfacing. The medication is being carefully withdrawn.

'Hello,' he says gently. She turns her head away and then looks around in confusion.

'Oh,' is all she can say.

'You were dreaming?' A statement or a question. Her mouth is dry so she can't answer. She nods slightly and finds that her head feels thick and heavy.

'Oh,' she says again and this time it is a groan more of realisation than surprise.

'Are you able to talk?' he asks gently. She shakes her head. He pours her some water and helps her to sit up and to sip the water. She lies back on the pillows exhausted.

'I will come back to see you later,' he says and moves away. She turns to watch him go and sees that he carries a newspaper and that there was something important she needed to find out. She wants to shout after him but her voice won't work. It is like a bad dream where you can't move or shout. She slumps back in to the pillows and closes her eyes against the hammering of her heart and the tears spill down her cheeks and the sense of loss is overwhelming.

Chapter Fifty

Wilf. It came to me in a flash. Wilf might be able to help but where was he? I had tried the Town Hall but he had moved on. Not even a week's notice. Gone.

I waited outside one lunchtime and managed to get in when Tommy on security was dealing with an elderly gent at reception who was trying to understand a piece of paper he had in his hand, which looked to me like a rates bill. He was ranting at Tommy that he had paid all his bills and never owed nobody nowt! So I took advantage and followed a group of former colleagues through the door, back from lunch break. I took the stairs and turned left then right into a warren of small offices, saw Jammy talking loudly to impress a stern looking woman in sensible shoes, and managed to avoid him by dodging into the gents and listening behind the door. I felt like a criminal and technically I shouldn't be there but then, technically, Felix had claimed Beatrix, my Scarlett, from me, and exiled me.

Was she at risk? Would Felix kill her too? Until I knew why he had killed Max I couldn't answer that. But I had to find her soon.

I heard Jammy moving away and opened the door to see Davie Thomas sauntering along the corridor with his usual swagger.

'Bugger me, look what the cat's dragged in,' he said and laughed, stubbing out his cigarette in the ashtray on the corridor. I quickly pulled him inside and he looked surprised.

'No mate, I'm not that way inclined,' and he held his hands up and prepared to defend himself, then he saw that I was serious and looked curious. 'Woz up wi you then?' he said. I took a deep breath.

'Wilf. Do you know where he lives? I need to find him. It's urgent.'

'Bugger me I had no idea he was that way inclined either, but then again...'

'It's not that,' I snapped. 'Nothing like that. It's...' I struggled for words. 'My girl, you remember?' He leered in an ugly way and I wanted to punch him. He moved over to the urinals and prepared himself.

'Up the duff is she? I told you I could help.'

'No. Not that. I mean... never mind,' and I made to leave.

'Norf Colchester. That's where Wilf used to live. Out past that new estate. Grimy little B&B apparently. He was worse 'n you for not givin' nuffink away.' He zipped up and pushed past me at the door turning back with one last thought.

'Janice in Personnel. She'll know. She might even tell you for a price, know what I mean?' He leered again and patted my arm. 'Good luck mate,' and left.

The girls in Personnel had always been quite good with me; maybe because I didn't chase them, and it wasn't difficult to lie; to say that I he'd lent me a book and I wanted to return it before I left the country. Yes, I was off to America to work as a journalist on a newspaper. Yes, really exciting, what I'd always wanted and an uncle had left me a bit of cash, yes wasn't that lucky just now when I could really use it and I just wanted to tie up the loose ends before I went....' I provided some distraction for them in a dull day and I got his address. I also realised that I had laid a false trail in case anyone came after me. Based in truth if not *actually* the whole truth. Level one.

I found the place not far from my digs, situated off the Mile End road and walked around for a bit wondering what to do. I wondered what Humphrey Bogart would do in a film and shook the thought from my head. I had to stop thinking like that; this was real and the outcome was important. That sort of nonsense had got me into trouble in the first place and now look where I was; lurking around outside lodging houses hoping randomly that a bloke who hated me would help me find my Scarlett.

Fortune favours the brave so I marched up to the door and rapped the knocker like I meant business. There was silence and then the sound of shuffling slippers down the hallway which was clearly not carpeted. These places were more likely to have oil cloth which could be swabbed down easily and was harder wearing. The door opened and a rotund, fierce looking woman glared at me. I could see beyond that I was right about the oil cloth. Before I could say anything she folded her arms and said,

'I don't buy anything on the doorstep. What are you selling anyway,' and she looked past me as though I was hiding my wares behind me. I looked around confused and said,

'Oh, no, no I am not a salesman.'

'*No Irish*,' she said pointing at the sign in the window which read "No Blacks, No Irish" all double underlined for emphasis. 'And I've got no vacancies anyway,' and she was about to slam the door. I always thought that 'foot in the door' was just an expression but I learned that day just how much it hurts against a robust and determined door slammer.

'Ouch' I yelled. 'Look I just need to ask if Wilf Miller is still staying here.' I said quickly before I suffered more injury.

'Who wants to know?' she said suspiciously, opening the door a little more and watching me hop about on one foot.

'I worked with him. At the Town Hall. We were both clerks.' She looked me up and down with distaste.

'Oh is that where he goes to waste his time and my rates money? He's not in.' And she was going to slam the door again but I managed to put my shoulder in the way. She backed off.

'Can I leave him a message? Please?' She shrugged and realised I was harmless.

'If you like,' and she stepped back and folded her arms again. 'But if you are one of them queers, I don't want no illegal activity in my house,' she added, checking up and down the street to see which net curtains were twitching.

'No nothing like that...' I muttered pulling out my notebook and hastily scrawling a note.

Wilf. I need to see you. Urgently. Where we met before. 5.00 today? T. Ash.' She took it from me, glanced at it and sniffed dismissively.

'I'll put it under his door,' she said and closed her front door quietly. I stood rooted to the spot, took a deep breath, and slowly made my way back into town.

By 5.00 I was at the same table I had been at when Wilf passed by outside. I ordered shepherd's pie and peas and realised how hungry I was. I hadn't managed lunch, spending the time instead lurking outside the town hall and in the gents, getting the information I needed. I just had to do this one last task, and then I would see Marianne again tomorrow and book my ticket to Amsterdam.

'What's all this about then?' asked Wilf as he slipped silently into the seat opposite me and laid his copy of The Times on the table beside him. I had finished my meal and was toying with menu cards, making my mug of tea last, hoping they weren't going to close too soon, hoping he might still turn up. The waitress was busy clearing away the final few tables and wiping things down. She was clearly getting ready to close.

'Cup of tea, love, he shouted to her. She looked daggers, tutted and stomped behind the counter.

'I didn't think you'd come.'

He shrugged. 'Why not? I might learn something,' he said. I hoped I would and so decided to get straight to the point. There was no use in trying to pretend we were friends. He reminded me of that as his tea was plonked in from of him and slopped in the saucer.

'Thanks love,' he said ironically then turned to me. 'Your head alright?' he asked as he stirred in sugar. He was probably trying to wind me up or simply remind me that he had the upper hand. I let it pass.

'I need to know where Jellicoe is. I don't want to hurt her but it is really important...' I told him the bare bones about Bea going with Felix and needing to get to her and her not answering my letters. My naked honesty seemed to surprise him. He dropped the tough act and looked directly at me, nodded slowly and let out a low whistle between his teeth then shrugged.

'I don't see that there's anything to lose by telling you. She employed me as you know to find out what I could about you and them paintings. Contacted me through some Dutch people my Dad knew.' He shrugged. 'Apparently she worked with my Dad during the war, but I don't know anything about that. Don't want to neither. What's done is done. Anyway, I helped her and she said she'd pay me but that foreign bloke got her pictures back. She said they were hers and I had no reason not to believe her and it wasn't too hard. You didn't hide them very well did you mate? I always knew you wasn't cut out for that kind of work.' He was leaning close and smiled at me, not unkindly and I felt the blow to my pride as hard as the blow to my head had been.

'Anyway. She had a number I called her on. In Holland. Long distance and all that but we had a phone we could use,' and he smiled again. 'She still owes me the money for that night,' he said. I was desperate to get that phone number.

'Do you have it? The number,' I said quietly. He didn't take his eyes off me but reached into his pocket and took out a small notebook, the sort the police would use, and detached the pencil from its holder.

'Security and translation services, that's my new line. Got a job with a Dutchman at the moment; ships 'antiquities' in and out of Harwich. I'm his liaison and driver. Good money, and I never did enjoy office work much,' he grinned and turned his attention to the notebook, scribbled a number, tore it off the pad and held it in the space between us. It was all I could do not to snatch it from him.

'If there is any comeback on this, you didn't get it from me, right? And there is no evidence that I was anywhere near Wrabness that night, remember?' I nodded. 'And if you see her, tell her she still owes me and the interest is mounting up.' He handed me the scrap of paper. 'Good luck, mate,' he said. Second time I'd heard that today. He stood up to go, then remembered his copy of The Times. He picked it up and had second thoughts, turned and handed it to me. 'Page 8. Anything to do with your Dutch friends?' and he left as silently as he had arrived. The waitress turned the sign behind him to closed, folded her arms and looked directly at me. I hastily counted out some money which I threw on the table, picked up the newspaper and left, driven into the dark evening chill by extreme curiosity.

Chapter Fifty One

Marianne was still sedated and I couldn't get them to let me in, so I got the next available sailing. I would have gone straight to Beatrix but she was with Felix and he had warned me off and I wouldn't have put it past him to have me arrested or something and then I'd be in trouble. I didn't think Bea was in immediate danger from Felix. He had nothing to gain by hurting her and he was her 'guardian'. But me? Well I knew a bit more now so I was a threat so I had to tread carefully. I must speak to Jellicoe first and find out what she knew. I hoped she would see me.

The ferry crossing had been a total nightmare and I was sick as a dog most of the way but at least I managed a few hours sleep in a chair. I was glad to get back on dry land. However did I think I was going to get to America in one piece? There'd be nothing left of me by the time we reached the New World.

So I got to Amsterdam and found a boarding house down near the docks. In daylight it seemed fine but then it got dark and I realised my mistake, but more on that another time. I had a purpose. I had to phone Jellicoe. I had changed money on the boat but because I had no coins I had to go and buy a beer and anyway, I was hungry having not kept much down all day, so I headed away from my lodgings towards Dam Square where I thought the cafes might be. It was all a bit strange but I managed to get a beer and some sandwich type thing which I pointed at as I didn't know what it was called, and I hoped it was really ham and cheese. It seemed ok although the cheese was a bit funny. I had coins now and they were burning a hole in my pocket. The waitress was clearing the table next to me and smiled.

'Are you English?' she asked in a cute accent.

'No. I'm Irish,' I said, ploughing through my sandwich, which was like a long fat bit of bread and hard to get your teeth into.

'Oh. Is that not the same thing?' she said. I sighed and finished chewing before I answered.

'No. Not at all. Totally different,' I said and took another bite. I was keen to get out to the phone box I had seen in the square outside.

'But you speak English.'

'Oh aye, so we do. Well, kind of.'

'Yes your English sounds funny,' she said and smiled at me and I choked on the words and nearly spat out my sandwich at the cheek of her, sounding like a total foreigner as she did, so I took a sip of beer to wash it down. I laughed out loud.

'Oh does it now?'

'Aye, so it does,' she said in an almost perfect imitation of my accent. She disappeared with her tray of table clearings behind the counter and I was left astounded. I played with the strange coins in my pocket and took them out to look at. She was beside me again.

'They look strange to you, no?'

'Aye, so they do. Can you tell me which ones I need to make a phone call?' She looked at the coins in my hand.

'Well,' she said, 'is it to England or Ireland?'

'No,' I replied patiently. 'Here. Holland. Amsterdam I think,' she was looking at me quizzically and I was getting flustered.

'Oh well in that case, not so much. Maybe just a few of these cents but then it depends how long you want to talk. Is it your girlfriend?' I felt myself flushing at her forwardness and right now I was not in the mood for flirting.

'My aunt,' I lied. 'I'm here for a funeral.' Well I had to stop the silliness and I thought that even foreigners would understand the seriousness of that.

'Oh, I am sorry for your decease.'

'Loss,' I said, automatically correcting her English. She looked at me with big round blue eyes, so different to the intensity of Bea's. She was virtually transparent. 'My *loss*. Not my *decease*.'

'Loss. I am sorry for your loss,' she repeated like a good student. I wanted to get back to the subject of my phone call.

'So two of these you reckon?'

'You will chat for a while with that. Would you like me to help you?'

'I'm sure I will be fine,' I said and handed her a fistful of change for the sandwich and beer.

'Oh no wait, it is too much,' she said.

'Keep the change, you've been helpful.' She smiled sweetly at me and said 'Goodbye and come back soon,' in her cute Dutch-English, and gave me a little wave. My God the girls were forward here and judging by some of the sights I'd seen near my lodging house, well I just hoped it wasn't rubbing off on my Bea.

The phone box took longer to manage than I had anticipated. Did I put the money in first and then dial, or dial and then wait? Trial and error and I eventually got through to a woman speaking Dutch.

'Oh Hello, Hellooo? I shouted into the phone. Incomprehensible Dutch came back at me. 'Do-You-Speak-English?' I said loudly.
'A Little,' she shouted back.
'I want to speak to Miss Jellicoe.' I said in a rush.
'Mees Jellicoe not here. I tell you phone. Name pleees.'
'Erm, my name, its erm... when will she be back.' And repeated it slowly and shouted and heard pips going and dropped the second coin into the box. So much for talking for ages.
'I not know. Your name pleess.' I struggled to get my name across and then the pips went again and I shouted. 'I'll call her back,' and hung up disappointed. How long should I wait? I don't want to get her into a bad mood with me before I spoke but it was urgent. I wished now I had been nicer to the waitress in the cafe. I had time to kill and would need to buy another drink if I was to have enough coins for that damned phone box.

Jellicoe laughed when I finally got through to her. Actually laughed like I was a complete idiot to be doing something so stupid as to phone her, like I should be passing secret messages hidden in newspapers on park benches. Or in cafes. Is that what Wilf had done? The thought hit me like a whump in the pit of my stomach. I'd have to scour the pages of that paper to check.

So after I'd arranged to meet Jellicoe in Dam Square – it was the only place I could be sure to find, I sat on a bench and went through the paper again line by line but I found no hidden clues or messages or phone numbers scribbled in the margins. Page 8 was after all, the only interesting bit and I had already read that a dozen times. I looked at it again.

Preview of <u>Checkmate</u> by <u>Pieter De Hooch</u>: This recently discovered Old Master will be on view at The Windmill Gallery on Tues 28th February: for auction 4th April 1957.

The viewing was Bea's birthday. I wondered about that. And there was a small repro of the painting in black and white which didn't do it justice.

Full colour catalogue available from.....

I was sitting on the bench and scouring the square, and stood up and paced up and down, and the dodged the bicycles – Jaysus, never seen so many people on bikes – and smelt the tempting smell of some sort of sweet pancakes cooking on a griddle but I didn't know what they were so I didn't know if I'd like it.

So this was Bea's world.

I sat again and imagined her walking around the corner; I saw her face in the faces of the people passing by; I saw the way she walked in a total stranger; I heard her voice in the chatter and babble that went on all around me and I thought I had seen a thousand ghosts. I felt her here. I could imagine her being at home here in this alien place with its funny street names and bicycles and open spaces and cafes around the square and I felt a pang of loneliness. Me, I was a fish out of water here; I felt uncomfortable and alien like I was on the edge of someone else's world. It was how I had always imagined Beatrix, from the moment I first saw her in the garden of Severalls almost a year ago when she looked like a fairy child who had just landed in Colchester and I did wonder, afterwards whether or not she was real or just a ghost from the Castle. She never really seemed to belong there, not really rooted, if you see what I mean. And now the winds had blown her home. This was her home. She was born here. Maybe her roots would take to the conditions here better than to Colchester? There was no way of knowing until I saw her but for now, I felt sad and lonely and as far away from Bea as I had ever been.

I turned round to survey the square again and found that a woman had sat beside me on the bench. I hadn't seen her approach or heard her coming and so I was startled by her sudden appearance. My mouth fell open in a gesture which displayed my surprise. I was staring at the woman from the paintings, albeit more than a decade later. She had fared better than Marianne who was unrecognisable now from the strong younger woman she had been. Jellicoe was still attractive in an older woman sort of way – in a way I had always imagined European women to be; less of drudge than my own Ma, God bless her, or Marianne, God help her... Jellicoe looked as though she needed no divine intervention; and I hoped that she would be helping me.

'Let's walk,' she said and stood up, after looking me up and down quite blatantly and then I remembered that not only was she a Dutch woman, and so far I had found them to be extremely forward, but she was *The Jellicoe* of the famous paintings and Resistance stories. She was the living legend which had haunted Marianne and whose charisma still rippled through the lives of those she had damaged. I watched her march away from me and she didn't even look back to check I'd followed her and I realised that she was in control and as always I was chasing this story, so I gathered up my belongings and ran after her and caught up as she reached a cafe on the far side of the square. I followed her in and she took a seat by the window, summoning a waiter as though she owned the place. Maybe she did. She spoke in rapid Dutch which sounded harsh and guttural and ugly and I wondered if my Bea now sounded like that as well. There was so much I didn't know and I was.... well.... a fish out of water. My lungs were busting and my heart racing and I was hyperventilating. I don't think I was making a good impression, which she confirmed with her next words, in accented English.

'So you are the lover boy Beatrix is trying to escape from?' I was dumbstruck. Who told her that? Who told her Bea was trying to escape from me?

283

'She's been forcibly taken away from me,' I blurted a bit too loud but I saw the crinkles crease the corners of her eyes and her red painted mouth stretched over perfect white teeth into what I thought must be her version of a smile. She patted my arm as though we had known each other for years and not only just met. I pulled my arm away. It felt dangerous being touched by her and I could feel Marianne's aversion. I wanted to cry for Ma Quinn stuck in that hell hole, locked in her own mind because this reptile in front of me had ruined her life and survived herself on the flesh of others. She saw me shrink away and I saw triumph cross her face. Maybe she thought I was afraid of her but I wasn't. If I'd had one of my ma's crucifixes on me though, I'd have held it up in front of me.

The waiter brought us strong dark coffee with little chocolates on a side dish but I couldn't face anything right now. She stirred sugar into her coffee and her gaze never left my face.

'So why are you here?' she asked eventually, probably getting a bit tired of toying with me. I took a few deep breaths to calm down and my voice came out sounding almost normal. Only a bit higher than usual. I coughed and lowered it to sound more serious.

'As you quite rightly say, I am here to find Beatrix.'

'Then why come to me? She's with Felix.'

'I know that....' I tailed off and she leant forward and her voice was softer.

'It's ok. I understand. Has Felix threatened you?' I nodded, not sure if I could trust my voice again.

'She is fine, Tarron,' she said and her use of my 'real' name sounded more foreign to me than the double Dutch she had spoken to the waiter. 'And she is still so young....' she waited for me to say something but I had learned to listen more than to talk; and I couldn't trust myself to sound sane.

'I wanted to marry her...' I blurted, eventually.

'She is far too young,' said Jellicoe dismissively.
'But why does he not want me near her?'
She shrugged. 'Felix always has his reasons. But it could simply be that he loves her.'
'Not as much as I do!' I said
'I should hope not. At least not in the same way. He is her uncle and several decades older than she is,' and she smiled to herself, shaking her head at the absurd thought and took a cigarette from her bag and offered me one. I shook my head. I still didn't get on well with smoking and I wasn't going to be distracted.
'No he isn't,' I said defiantly. She looked confused.
'He isn't what?'
'Her uncle.' Well that got her attention and she looked at me sideways as she blew the smoke away.
'He is Max's brother,' she said through a haze of smoke. 'Well half brother. Same mother.' I nodded and sipped the coffee nonchalantly enjoying having the upper hand at last. It was bitter and strong and was almost cold and I spluttered a bit, but recovered myself and coughed.
'Aye, so he is.' She looked confused and I thought that's it. Be Irish. She'll have to struggle then to get what it is you're saying.
'Sooooo...' she waved he hand about as though I wasn't making sense and she wanted a fuller explanation. I made her wait. I stirred some sugar into my coffee and watched the little bubbles rise to the top and took another sip without wincing this time; I knew what to expect. I placed the cup carefully on the saucer and looked her in the eye for the first time. She really did look quite normal in close up. A bit like my oldest sister Kathleen would look in a few years time.
'What if Max Prins isn't Beatrix's father?' and I raised an eyebrow the way Bogart would when he was being sardonic. She carefully placed her cup on her saucer and ground out her half smoked cigarette in the ashtray.

285

'What makes you say that?' she asked sternly.

'I was told.'

'By Beatrix?'

'Oh God, no. She doesn't know. It might tip her over the edge.'

'That depends,' said Jellicoe, piercing me with a look which could burn holes in the wallpaper behind my head.

'On what?'

'On who her father is,' she said. I thought, yes, fair do's. I waited and we sat staring each other out for a moment but it felt like a week and then I couldn't contain myself.

'Felix.' I said. 'And there's more.' She was shaken. I could see that now. She sat back and gazed at me bewildered.

'Who told you? How do you know this?' and her voice sounded like a German interrogator off one of those war films, like that Kommandant guy in the Colditz Story. Frederick Valk? He was German, or Dutch or something.

'Marianne told me. But I had worked it out for meself. The story is in the pictures. Have you looked at them, Jellicoe? Max told stories with his pictures. It's all there if you know what you are looking for.' She nodded silently.

'So Beatrix doesn't know?'

'No, she doesn't. I don't think Felix does either...' and then I kicked myself because I had just shown her my hand and she had told me nothing that I didn't already know.

'What else,' she said, placing a hand firmly on the table in front of her.

'What else?'

'You said there was more...'

'Oh, did I?'

'Don't play games with me, Tarron. Tell me what you know, or what you think you have worked out from the pictures, and I can help you to get Beatrix back. I know where she is, where she goes. I have seen her...'

286

'You have? How is she?' and I forgot about the coolness and the poker game and I just really wanted to get to Bea....

'She's fine...' she said and hesitated...

'But?'

She shook her head. 'But nothing. She is fine, happy, well cared for and she has a future here with Felix.'

'So when did you see her? Did she get in touch with you? Did she talk about me?' It was sounding lame so I tailed off. She raised an eyebrow at me and I realised she wanted tit for tat. She wasn't going to tell me anything unless I spilled. She leaned across the table and put her hand on my arm. This time it didn't burn a hole through the duffle coat I was wearing but it still felt warm.

'Tarron. I know about love. I have been there. And I know how you feel about Beatrix.' She paused for effect and waited for a response. I nodded so she continued. 'I can help you to get her away from Felix. To escape, the two of you. But you have to tell me what else you know.'

Now here was the bit I couldn't fathom. Could I trust her? Was she a viper? I had always thought so, but here she was offering me the one thing I wanted most. To be with Beatrix. I closed my eyes and felt the loss and the longing through my heart and soul, so if I was doing anything wrong, it was for the right reasons.

'Ok. So. Felix killed Max....'

'You know about that?' she said and sat back abruptly and my arm felt cold where her warm touch had been. I nodded. So I guess she knew all along.

'That's why I came. I was worried sick about Bea and ... him...' She waved the thought away as though it were cigarette smoke.

'There's no danger to Beatrix from Felix. I can guarantee that. But you? You know a bit too much, Tarron. I don't think Felix would like you to know that bit of the story.'

'Does Bea know?'

'Of course not. No-one does.'

'You do. And Marianne.'

'We were trained to keep secrets, and it gives me leverage.' I was alert. So Jellicoe had a hold over Felix because she knew all along. Like Marianne. What other secrets were buried in the rubble of war I wondered? And Jellicoe could use it for 'leverage' whilst for Marianne it became a burden which broke her. I was now on high alert. Jellicoe had become dangerous again. She leaned in conspiratorially and so did I.

'I will help you to get away,' she said.

'With Beatrix?' I added.

'Yes, yes of course. With Beatrix. But beware. Don't go near Felix until you hear from me. I am not joking Tarron. He is dangerous when he is under real threat and this news could damage him. Especially now.'

'The paintings,' I said. She nodded. 'You are just going to let him sell them? I thought you wanted them.' She shrugged.

'For my daughter. For Max's *only* daughter now,' and she began to pull on her gloves and prepare to leave. She left a One Guilder note on the table and stood up to leave. I stood too. I had been well schooled in manners by my mother.

'Wait for me to send you a message.'

'How? You don't know where I am.' She smiled like I was a naive child to be indulged and patted my cheek fondly like an aunt or a big sister.

'I know where you are staying. Don't worry. We will meet again soon and I will outline the plan to help you. But please keep your head down. Don't talk to people and don't, whatever you do, mention what you just told me. Promise?' I nodded and realised that I had lost this hand of poker and was playing in a very different game and the stakes were much higher than match sticks.

Chapter Fifty Two

Jellicoe left the cafe and walked quickly away, leaving the boy standing confused, gawping after her. She couldn't fathom his naivety. If there was a war now, God help us all if this is the brains which would have to save us. She laughed to herself at that. But this boy, like Beatrix, had been born in war but raised in peace and maybe that had softened them and she almost envied their innocence.

He had handed her a brighter bargaining token than she thought possible. Johanna, so they all believed, was Max's daughter and there was no one left to tell them otherwise and no proof that she wasn't. True she had blonde hair and blue eyes and none of Max's heavy European features; but she could argue that Johanna resembled her mother. She had lived with the doubt from the start about whether Max or Werner was Johanna's father and it suited her now, as it had then, not to question it. Johanna's birth certificate said that her father was Max Prins and official documents never lie do they? She smirked at the naivety of a softened world and especially, the post war world which bred such simple and trusting people as Tarron Ash and Beatrix 'Prins'.

Felix however was from the same world as her. He was tempered in the fire of war and his core was steel. Did he know that he was Beatrix's father? Is that why he had said that he loved the child? In which case he would also know that Beatrix could not be Max's heir, unless there was a will which she had never seen? Unlikely. Max wasn't so organised. But Felix was.

So how to proceed? She had not mentioned Beatrix's 'condition' to the boy and realised as the conversation progressed that he too didn't mention it. Beatrix had said that she left England before she could be certain, so he probably still didn't know, and Jellicoe doubted very much that Felix had mentioned it to the boy. Felix didn't offer information and had his own hand to play. Well, she was also hatching a plan and she had to phone Felix to make the next bit happen.

She found a call box and checked her purse for change. Looking out of the phone kiosk, she saw Tarron wandering aimlessly back towards his lodgings and turned away so that he wouldn't see her.

It took a moment for Felix to answer, saying little as he always did.

'I have new information,' she said. Silence. 'Can we meet?'

'Tonight. Windmill Gallery. 8.30,' and he hung up. Perhaps Felix was still living the war. Whatever happened he would not change now. That much she could be sure of in a world which was rapidly changing around her.

Chapter Fifty Three

Marianne had been planning this for weeks and found it hard to contain her excitement. It reminded her of the war years; those vivid years which lived in her now in glorious colour as opposed to the black and white era of her life in Colchester. She ran the memories through her head and hardly had time to talk to anyone as her plan unfolded, carefully, patiently and she thought, with a skill and cunning which Felix would be proud of.

'Marianne, can you hear me? Who are you talking to anyway?' It was that new nurse, what was her name? Jewel?? Jules?? No idea. Did it matter? Not much longer now.

'Hmmm,' she replied absently looking up from her newspaper, scouring the pages for more news of the sale of Max's painting. There had been something in an old copy of The Times and she had torn out the item and hidden it in her handbag.

'I said,' Nurse Jewells continued, slowly and loudly as though to an infant or an imbecile, 'I said where are all your hankies? Have they been stolen as well?' Marianne shrugged.

'No Idea,' she said feigning absence but alert in all of her senses. More alert than she had been for years; tingling and alive with anticipation. She laughed out loud and

Nurse Jules shook her head, sighed and continued to make beds and sort out patients laundry, muttering to herself.

'First it's Bessie's spectacles, then Edna's woolly hat. I'm sure they've just lost them but no – "*they've been stolen*". Marianne looked at the stupid nurse with a blank expression on her face and grinned. The nurse sighed, patted her arm and said, 'There there. I didn't mean to upset you. You read your newspaper,' and as she marched off in response to shouts from along the corridor, Marianne heard her say, 'at least she's quiet.'

This was something Marianne had realised as soon as she was able to think straight. Keep quiet. Don't ripple the pond. It was exactly what she had tried to do during the war and had been successful then. Only this time, she had to take her medication as well and soon realised that this was making her unable to think straight.

Firstly she had to stop taking her medication. That was easy. She put the pill in her mouth, watched by the nurse, and took a sip of water which she swallowed. She had grown adept at shoving the big horse pill under her tongue. It tasted like bile and cesspits but she didn't flinch. As soon as the nurse turned her back with a cursory '*good girl Marianne*,' like she was five years old and not fifty something – lost count – didn't matter anymore – as soon as the nurse turned her back, the 'good girl' spat her pill into her handkerchief and shoved it up her sleeve.

After a few days, she felt dizzy and had violent headaches, but knew from her experience with Max that this would pass and she needed to get through it. If she told them about the dizziness and headaches, they would increase her medication, or inject her, or give her liquid medicine to drink, so she put up with it, feigning one of her - '*leave me alone*' phases to stop them from questioning her too closely. Her heart pounded with the withdrawal and she thought she might die trying, but she was prepared to die to get out of here and get back to Beatrix.

After a week she was feeling good and today euphoria had set in.

The daily walk had become an essential part of her plan. She had to dispose of the medication and had found a part of the garden behind some birch trees which seemed untouched by the care of the gardeners. She simply tossed the pills into the soft earth beneath the trees and ground them in with the heel of her shoe. A discarded dustbin had lain there for a while, untouched since last winter. There were cobwebs and debris from the trees covering the lid and half concealing it from view. Inside, wrapped in a spare coat she had found in the day room, was a pair of round, tortoiseshell spectacles and a blue knitted hat.

The newspaper cutting was folded carefully into her handbag which she was allowed to keep with her but which was searched regularly by staff. She took the page from her bag, reading it again, knowing it by heart and staring into a black and white reproduction of Max's intense, sad gaze.

Verification of Old Master; picture to go on display prior to auction.

She knew of the Gallery. *The Windmill* was where Jan Van Stein had operated, before he fled as the Nazi oppression began to bite deeply into the freedoms of the Dutch people. He refused to wear a yellow star and took what he could and left for America. She stood thoughtfully staring at the piece of paper in her hand amazed that she remembered so much.

The treatment she had received recently had unlocked the door which had been bolted shut against the pain of those days. The pain was still there but she was immured to it, and the memories were fluid, running through her veins with a life force she had not felt for years.

She placed the cutting carefully inside the folds of the hat, placed the hat in the dustbin and secured the lid, disguising it as best she could. She strolled back to the main path and felt content holding her handbag close to her. They had never really searched the bag thoroughly, only looking for sharp objects or pills, or things with which patients could hurt themselves or others. She felt secure in the knowledge that the identification papers and money stitched carefully between the linings were still there; a habit from the war. One which she had kept up in peacetime and in her days of sanity in the real world. When she was well, it was the first thing she checked and she felt relief flood through her with the knowledge that it was still intact.

From the veranda, Nurse Belinda Jewells was watching Marianne saunter back through the copse of trees, smiling to herself.

'Not a care in the world,' she hissed feeling the weight of the world on her shoulders. 'It must be lovely to be so simple. I wonder what is going on in that empty head of hers,' and she shook out the table cloth from the day room and bustled back inside to tidy up the books and magazines before tea time.

Marianne would leave soon. She had written another letter this time to Beatrix and felt that she was going to deliver it herself. She couldn't trust anyone else. Soon. In time for Beatrix's birthday.

Chapter Fifty Four

The Windmill Gallery was in darkness when Jellicoe arrived but she recognised this as one of Felix's trademarks. He would hide in the shadows and watch and be in control. Well that was ok with her. She had information. In their world, that was a valuable currency, like sex. There was a time when information such as she had now had saved lives and sex was often the means of delivery.

As she approached the doorway, the door opened into the darkened Gallery. She stepped inside and he closed the door silently behind her. This was the shop front where customers would come to buy, but it was too dark to see the paintings on offer and she wasn't here as a customer.

He led the way into a hallway at the back of the shop and through an oak panelled door into another space.

She was silent as they entered the next room, which was well lit and the walls hung with paintings of her and Marianne and their past. At the end of the long gallery was a single easel and a spot light focussed on the portrait of Max Prins. *Checkmate*. It had the desired effect.

She looked as though she had seen a ghost. This was Max in his later years; Max as she last saw him: the old Max when he was sick and losing his mind. The Max whom Felix had tried so desperately to save.

Felix watched carefully as Jellicoe's face moved from shock to remorse and then quickly to neutral. She was still a professional, he thought, but not a threat. Not tonight.

She moved along the wall of paintings and saw, in sequence, their life together, and she was momentarily overwhelmed. Tarron was right. There was a story here if you knew what to look for; it was all here, the whole thing; love, betrayal, revenge, war and death. Only 'Peace' was missing and perhaps that could never be possible in their world.

Felix poured two measures of gin from a side table, added ice and handed one to her. They silently touched glasses, not taking their eyes off each other and then sat in a couple of wing back chairs beside a small table.

'I remember them all,' she said, 'especially that one.' She indicated the painting of *Checkmate*, now verified and up for sale. 'He called it his *Swan Song*. I thought it was his best by far.' Her voice was steady and betrayed none of the emotion which Felix could feel pouring from her. He simply nodded agreement.

'As things turned out, it was his final work, and possibly his best. Yes,' he said. They sat silently amongst the pictures for a while.

'I never thought I would see these again. It is a fine collection,' she said.

'Yes,' he replied. 'I have waited long enough now and these pictures deserve to be in the world. We owe it to him.'

'To all of us,' she said softly as she stood and walked along the wall again where the pictures hung. 'We all risked our lives and many didn't make it.' He walked beside her down the length of the gallery, stopping to pay tribute to each painting in turn, silently.

Twelve pictures in a row, in some sort of order; telling a story. She felt the works speak to her; a lament of love and loss; of war and chaos and broken lives. She let the tears flow and Felix was beside her and then his arms were around her and her body responded to his and he felt her warm tears on his face or maybe they were his and then their lips met, starved of love for decades; full of anger and a shared past which was over. Almost.

They broke apart, breathless and straightened their clothes. He offered her his handkerchief and tenderly wiped her eyes. He refilled their glasses. They sat and the ice had melted and the thaw was beginning.

'So, you have information. What do you want to tell me?' he said his voice softened.

'The boy. Tarron?' he nodded. 'He said...' she realised now that she was here that it was not as easy as she thought it would be. The past surrounded them and had momentarily overwhelmed them both. They had never mourned Max and for a long time there had been bad blood between them. She had thought for so long that Felix had wanted to kill her or at least to silence her. It would be good not to live in fear anymore and it seemed that the paintings could heal as much as divide.

He looked at her and she met his gaze. He moved closer and took her hand and the longing was in her again. She was back to the beginning. He led her out of the room by a door at the far end and up a flight of stairs. There was an apartment above.

'Do you remember?' he said tenderly as he removed her coat and she unpinned her hat. 'We met here once. In the war.'

She nodded. Of course she remembered. 'More than once,' she said.

'And you remember what happened?' How could she forget. His arms were around her again and unbuttoning her dress. She should hate him, this man who sold her to the Resistance. Who used her for his cause. But she used him too and she believed in the cause as well. Could she trust him now?' She tensed and he pulled back and looked at her.

'You don't trust me,' he said simply and sat on the edge of the large bed, now covered in gold satin where last time it was sprigs of lavender and embroidered flowers; she remembered the passion and the intensity of their love. Of course she remembered it all. How could she not.

'Was that why you brought me here? To seduce me?' She sat beside him.

'Believe it or not that was nowhere near my intention,' and he spoke softly and his voice cracked just enough to be convincing. He looked into her face, softer now than when she had arrived. This was not how he had planned things. He was losing his touch.

'We should go down. We have business to conclude,' but she put a hand on his arm and moved close and kissed him. She smelt of lavender and rose water and softness and the past and he needed that now. He needed reassurance that he was doing the right thing. He needed some healing time and Jellicoe could provide it.

They made love with a passion and abandon neither had experienced for a long time and afterwards lay naked on top of the covers, in silence.

More was said in their lovemaking than in all of the words they had ever exchanged.

'We are two of a kind,' he said. 'We need each other.' They talked then, a long, long talk of the past and of Max and of what happened the night Max died, and if their versions of events differed, it mattered little now.

'Except that the boy knows. He told me that he had worked out the clues from the paintings. He knows that you killed Max,' she said, sitting on the edge of the bed and beginning to reassemble her clothes.

'No proof,' he said.

'But questions could be asked. That wouldn't help would it? And Beatrix would be upset.'

'Ah, Beatrix,' he said with a sigh.

'Your daughter,' she said and felt a chill again blow through her.

'You know that as well?'

'He told me. Tarron. He said Marianne had told him.' Felix nodded. It was finally unravelling and he was in danger of losing control. He sighed deeply and got up to dress.

'He's a bloody menace that boy. A child playing a dangerous game. Where is he?'

She told him. 'Don't hurt him Felix, that's all over now.'

'He could ruin everything,' Felix said buttoning his shirt. She shrugged. She knew he was right.

'So what can we do?'

'Scare him off once and for all. Beatrix doesn't need him. She has us now. We are her parents, guardians. We will look after her best interests, and her child's.'

'And our own?' she raised a quizzical eyebrow and a smile caught the edges of her mouth where lipstick had smudged. He tugged his cuffs and the links fell out and she moved across to him, took his arm and fastened his cuffs.

'I want to help, Felix and I know that you have a 'cause' but I have a daughter and I want to make sure she is looked after....'

'She will be,' he said, 'although you know as well as I that she is not Max's daughter?' she shrugged.

'No proof,' she said. 'And we don't want to open up questions about that time do we?'

'No. It's time to move on,' he said, shrugging his jacket into place and slipping on his polished brogues.

'So what do we tell Beatrix?' she asked.

'Nothing. She believes Max is her father and Johanna is her half sister; let the past sleep now, Jellicoe. We have a new era to plan for and there is still a great deal to do. We have to win the peace. Beatrix's baby will be well taken care of. I plan to take Beatrix into a clinic in Delft before the due date. It is all arranged. She will be sedated and they will do a Caesarean. I have a good home lined up for the child.'

Jellicoe looked startled and he moved to reassure her. 'Beatrix won't miss what she has never had. She won't even see the baby. There will be no bond, and she is so young and talented. She is far too young to be a mother. A baby will get in the way.'

'As will the boy, Tarron. Get in the way I mean,' she said pragmatically.

'He doesn't know that she is pregnant,' he said, and she nodded agreement. 'So here is the plan.....' and the future was set in motion in the aftermath of their lovemaking. Felix knew that everything had changed and that a new era was dawning for all of them.

It would begin with the sale of Max's last masterpiece; then his whole collection would come to light. And finally, his talented daughter would replace the brother he had been forced to kill in the chaos of a just war so that there could be a chance of winning the peace.

Chapter Fifty Five
Boskoop, Holland February 1957

The 'driver' dropped me at the end of a road and on all sides, I could see waterways and greenhouses and fields full of plants. I couldn't tell you what they were growing but I assumed that when the weather warmed a bit, they would be flowers. Tulips probably. And there were a lot of trees. Apples I guessed, still bare, not yet in bud.

There were walkways between large trenches which were like mini versions of the canals I had seen in Amsterdam and long strips of field after field, half a mile long, each surrounded by water.

We had travelled 30 miles or so out of Amsterdam and I had a worrying time of it wondering where on earth Jellicoe's 'driver' was taking me, but he seemed alright. Didn't talk much and had a heavy accent but he told me we were going to a town where Jellicoe had a country house. Somehow I didn't see her as a farmer meself, and this definitely had more in common with farming than my idea of 'a country house.' Maybe they just did things differently out here.

When I got up this morning, there was a note waiting in reception:

'Be ready by 10.00. A car will come for you. Arturo is my driver.
J.'

That's it. That's all she said and I was hoping, praying that Beatrix was going to be here and we were going to be smuggled out together.

So he dropped me off on this road, well more of a path really, and pointed to a building at the far end of the field which was so far away I couldn't see it. I crossed the mini canal by a little bridge and saw a barge slowly moving its way along a bigger waterway to my right. And all around were empty fields and water and the low flat horizon broken only by a couple of windmills. What was Jellicoe playing at? I hefted my bag on my shoulder and my coat a bit higher up around my ears, dug my free hand into my pocket and set off at a pace which I hoped would keep me warm. I was walking into the teeth of a wind which whistled callously across the flat land. I felt exposed.

I was sure Beatrix would be here to meet me. I ran through in my mind what it would be like. What would she be like, now after all these months? Would she still want to see me? Would she want to come away with me? She would be seventeen in a day or two. I was nearly twenty one so if Felix would sign the papers then we could go to America and be married. I just needed to see her again and then she would know that we had to go away together.

My bag didn't seem so heavy when I thought of Bea, and it was that thought which kept me going forward over canals, through fields and into the icy breath of that wind.

I looked back and the driver, Arturo his name was, he was gone and so was the car. The boat glided silently through the still water and apart from occasional cries of a few optimistic birds circling the fields, there was silence. And the wind.

I came to another mini bridge and felt like I had entered Lilliput and was heading for my doom. More fields followed and I noticed that here the trees were getting thicker and taller. As I approached the end of the second field the trees were higher and screened another waterway along which there was no traffic at all and then I saw a small house, more like a hut with smoke coming from the chimney. Surely this wasn't Jellicoe's 'country house?' If it was it was some kind of joke, like a cottage in the woods in a macabre fairy tale.

I put my bag down with relief and approached the door. There was silence all around me. I pushed the door open.

'Hello, anyone there?' and jumped out of my skin as a voice I recognised, most definitely not Jellicoe or Beatrix, replied.

'Come in T'Ash. Close the door.'

Felix was standing in the corner of the room where the light didn't catch his face.

'Where's Jellicoe? And Beatrix?' I asked, looking hopelessly around and keeping the door open as a quick exit. But Arturo was behind me, blocking the light from outside, and the door slowly closed shut.

Chapter Fifty Six

Wilf sat in a bar opposite the lodging house and watched and waited. It was pretty boring work but Jellicoe had paid him well, including the debt she owed for the work he had already done in Colchester. He wanted to set up an antiques business in Holland and East Anglia. Now he could buy a van and get some stock. He was feeling very pleased with himself as he saw his 'target' shuffle out of the front door of the grimy *Red Bull* guest house near the docks and get into the waiting car.

'Arturo scrubs up well as a driver,' he thought. Poor T'Ash. He looked so dejected and Wilf hated having to do this. But it wasn't a hard job and then he could move his life on. Make something of himself and stop working for other people.

Jellicoe had called Wilf and told him to get the next boat over. He said he wasn't going to do anything until she paid him, but true to her word, she had the cash ready, in US dollars, on arrival. And now all he had to do was to plant this bag in T'Ash's room for the Police to find.

He called the receptionist from the phone on the bar where he sipped a beer, with a query he knew would take her away from the desk. It was very simple to stroll across the narrow street, lean across the counter to take the key to

T'Ash's room and be out of there again by the time she returned to the desk.

'Good luck mate,' he said to himself as he slipped the key into the letter box by the front door on his way out again. He made his way back across the road to the bar, hunched inside his coat, collar turned up against the cold and to hide his face.

Chapter Fifty Seven

'Sit down T'Ash.' I didn't move. I was going to stand my ground.

'Where is she?' I asked. He looked at me like I was a piece of dirt.

'Who?' he asked.

'You know who I mean. I set up to meet Jellicoe here, and Beatrix. We are going away together.'

'Ah, yes. Jellicoe mentioned something about that.' He sat on a stool by the fire and indicated I should take the one opposite. I stood and folded my arms. He picked up the poker and stirred the fire around a bit and a waft of wood smoke took me back to Ireland. I knew that smell. I'd been in Ireland recently. A few half hearted flames flickered and returned to glowing embers. He picked up a small lump of wood and weighed it in his hands and looked past me to Arturo.

'We may need more,' he said, and Arturo slipped out silently. I didn't turn to see him go but I felt the 'lack' of him behind me and felt a blast of cold when the door opened.

'You don't think you'll need your henchman then?' I said, sounding braver than I felt. Felix was sitting stirring the fire, and he had a poker and a lump of wood in his hands, but Arturo had left. Felix said nothing. 'If you've hurt her, either of them, you won't get away with it,' I said bravely.

'No-one is going to get hurt, T'Ash,' said Felix and threw the wood onto the fire and stood and I braced myself. He was old, fifty at least and I was in my prime, though not as fit as I could be but then I had a desk job and Felix was the fittest fifty year old I had ever seen. Maybe because he was Dutch, I reasoned and they seem to cycle everywhere.

'So where is she then? Beatrix.' I said as he unfurled his long limbs like a cat about to pounce.

'She is at home. My home. Now her new home.'

'I want her with me.'

'She is too young T'Ash. And I am her guardian.'

'You just wanted those damn paintings,' I said.

'But now I have them, and you know far too much.' That was it. It was the first warning shot across my bows. 'Please sit down T'Ash so that we can have a civilised conversation. I need to convince you of Beatrix's best interests; and yours.' The last bit was delivered with a look which meant business. I didn't move and then, like a panther, he pounced and was holding me in an arm lock around my neck. He dragged me the short distance across the small room and pushed me onto a stool.

'And no. I don't need a henchman. If anything needs to be dealt with I prefer to do it myself. Sit.' He let go of me and I stumbled but didn't stand up again. He was a powerful enemy, mentally and physically. There was silence and just the sound of the wood hissing and spitting like a viper.

He sat and then said; 'Jellicoe told me you wanted to escape with my niece.'

'Your daughter!' I shouted and tried to stand, but he simply pushed me back into my seat. 'She also told me that you 'believed' certain things to be true, which if they become common knowledge, will harm my current work.'

'Oh yes, and how did you extract this information from Jellicoe then because she was on my side and was going to help me. She promised. Did you use your famous *Resistance* tactics whatever they were?' Felix laughed out loud. I couldn't believe he was laughing.

'Oh, yes, I am afraid we did resort to that, but it wasn't so unpleasant for either of us in the end.' I couldn't believe he found any of this funny at all.

'Yes I do know stuff. I worked it out from those paintings,' I said. He made a gesture to say, *'go on then, surprise me,'* but then I realised my big mistake. I had no proof. There was no proof of who killed Max or any of it and Felix knew that.

'It doesn't matter now. But I will tell Beatrix. Somehow. One day, I will tell her that you killed her 'father', you killed Max and that you are her real father. And Marianne can back me up on that one. She told me.' He shrugged dismissively like he couldn't care less.

'Yes, of course there is very little proof of what happened in '45. The only damage I can see you inflicting is that you will open cans of worms which have been shut for a long while. You will hurt Marianne and Beatrix.'

'And you. You could go to prison for murder.'

'Unlikely without proof but it would make my life 'awkward' shall we say if too many questions are raised right now. The threat is to the future, T'Ash, not the past.'

'Oh yes. Your Auction. Well, that's another thing you see, I know that the painting you are selling was painted by Max Prins and not by 'Pieter de Hooch'. I know, you see. And I know what all the other pictures look like. So you see....' I went quiet and he looked at me like a cat looks at a mouse he is toying with, and we all know how that ends. After a pause, he said,

'Beatrix once told me of a conversation she had with you, about three levels of truth.' He waited for me to say something but I just nodded. To be honest I didn't know where this was going and I thought I had dug a big enough hole for meself already. I knew too much, I could see that now, and no-one knew I was here. My heart thudded uncomfortably in my chest and I was sweating despite the icy weather outside and the half hearted fire spluttering in the grate.

'Well you are quite right. There are many levels of truth and the secret service works on three levels; the first two being plausible cover stories based in reality but not totally true; the third level goes deeper and will only come out under serious interrogation.

'But it also depends on who's version of the truth is being told. Truth is rarely black and white, T'Ash. Right or wrong. In the case of Max's death, the first level you described, for example, was 'Death by Cheese?'

'Well only if they shot the bloody holes in the cheese and missed,' I said remembering the joke I had shared with Bea when we first uncovered the paintings. He had the grace to smile a little bit at that.

'Exactly. Yet it was a flawed memory. Max was taken ill by eating foods which he should not have combined with the MAO inhibitors I had managed to procure for him, but he didn't die that time. That was a partially true memory, but confused with later incidents.

'The second level, as I recall, was in Beatrix's traumatised memory; that her mother had killed Max and then blamed Jellicoe but that was more a notion than a memory and pieced together during a relatively unhappy and lonely childhood. But there was another, you are quite right, a third level: that Max was shot. Beatrix remembers the scene in the only way a five year old can; emotionally and in images which may not join up into a consistent time line and this traumatised her. She does not know who pulled the trigger. And perhaps no-one except Jellicoe, Marianne and me, knows *why* that trigger had to be pulled.'

'I'd love to hear your version of that one.'

'You will. But hear me out. There is a fourth level; another truth which you must understand. This knowledge, of who pulled the trigger, will hurt Beatrix very badly. As will the knowledge that her hero father, Max, is not her real father and that her mother betrayed him, with me, the only other person in the world she trusts.'

'She trusts me, but you won't let me get anywhere near her!' I yelled and stood up. This time he let me stand up and pace around. I could think better moving about. 'Did she even get my letters?' He didn't answer. 'I wrote every day. She never got them did she?'

'She needs some time to get over the trauma she has suffered. You know what can happen if mental sickness is suppressed and not dealt with. You have first hand evidence. So do I. It has become my life's work, T'Ash. There are a lot of people across Europe who are still suffering and reliving those years. I can do something to help them. People like Marianne. I want to prevent it from happening to younger people, to Beatrix and thousands of others who witnessed horrors in their young lives.

'I have set up a Foundation for mental health research with the money from the sale of these pictures and I am going to ensure that Beatrix is treated appropriately for the trauma she has suffered. No-one will get in my way.' He was standing now and I could feel the power of him. After a while I spoke, quietly.

'So what do you expect me to do? Just give her up? Walk away and say nothing about the huge forgery you are still perpetrating, now in the name of 'research' rather than war?'

'Ideally yes. That would be best for all of us, but I don't think you will somehow, so I would like you to join us. Help us to develop treatments so that Marianne and your grandmother can be well again and back in the world.'

'That's bloody blackmail that is and who's 'us' anyway? I can't believe my Bea has agreed to any of this, and Jellicoe hates your guts.' He smiled at that.

'As I said, T'Ash. The truth is rarely black and white. We have had our moments, Jellicoe and me, but now we are at peace, and the past is behind us. She sees the value of the scheme and we are looking to the future to heal the past. As for Beatrix? No. She is not involved, yet. But I have no doubt that when she realises what we can do for her mother, and thousands of others, she will understand. And if she doesn't, she will be free to go her own way when she is 21. In four years time.

'So I have to wait for her and hope she will come back to me when you have warped her mind and twisted her round your little finger? Supposing I don't agree. Supposing I walk out of here now and go to the police and just tell them that that painting on show is a forgery?'

'That would be unhelpful, T'Ash and stupid. It has been authenticated; it passes all the technical tests and the 'experts' will simply agree to disagree. Unless you have some proof?' I shrugged, desperately thinking if I had kept anything.

'A photo of Max. It is a self portrait,' I said triumphantly. He waved his hand impatiently.

'I can find you a dozen photos of old men who resemble Rembrandt. It doesn't mean they painted his self portraits. Only if you knew Max very well would you recognise him from that painting. Same with Marianne and Jellicoe. There is something about the expression of his face, his essence. A camera will never capture the soul of a man, like Max could capture it with paint.' I sat heavily and felt defeated.

Chapter Fifty Eight

Marianne lay awake that night, all night, too excited to sleep, her head buzzing with images of Amsterdam in the Spring; pictures of pre-war Holland running through her head like a film, herself as Ingrid Bergman and Felix cast in the role of Humphrey Bogart. She lay still in her bed, not wanting to attract attention; being good so that they would leave her alone. She tried hard to remember the times and dates of the ferries from Harwich. What day would they sail? How could she find out?

She found the local paper the next morning, so it must be Friday then, she thought and checked the date on the top of the paper; the sailings from the port were listed. She trembled and screwed the paper up and held it against her chest. Nurse McDonald came into the day room and noticed Marianne's excited state and frowned with concern.

'Hello pet, are you ok today?' she asked crouching beside Marianne's chair. Marianne looked at her blankly and shook her head to bring it back to the day room, Severalls. She didn't dare trust her voice and so she simply nodded and felt anxious.

The nurse rubbed her arm gently and said, 'must be nearly time for your medication but I think you have a review coming up next week as well, so they will check if the dose is right. May need to increase it for a bit if you are feeling stressed.'

'I'm fine,' Marianne blurted, more forcefully than she intended. The nurse looked alarmed.

'Course you are. Maybe a bit feverish though?' and she reached up and placed a cool hand on Marianne's forehead. Marianne closed her eyes and winced and felt the tension tighten every part of her body. She wanted to scream and run away but she knew that they would lock her up again if she did that and then her plan would fail. Soon, so soon now, tonight. 'I might have to get Doctor to take a look at you pet, and for now, best stay indoors. It's cold out there today and we don't want you taking a chill. I'll get Nurse Jewells to keep an eye on you.'

Marianne felt the life force leave her body and tears began to prick her eyes. 'Don't cry, don't cry,' she chanted to herself, and saw Nurse McDonald frown. 'Stay here pet, I'll get something to calm you down,' and she hurried away. Marianne was left devastated. She couldn't be doped again.

She sat for a while, clutching the newspaper and it was Doctor Steans who next appeared beside her, pulling up a chair with Nurse McDonald hovering behind him.

'Not feeling too good?' he asked, taking her wrist and checking the pulse rate against his watch. He felt her forehead. She sat stock still not daring to move, hardly daring to breathe. 'Is anything worrying you, Marianne?' Silence. 'I notice you are holding a newspaper again. Is there something which has upset you?' Silence. 'The news can be very upsetting sometimes.' She shook her head. 'Does it remind you of something?' She nodded. 'Do you want to tell me about it?' She shrugged. He patted her arm and stood to leave, turning to Nurse McDonald and believing he was out of ear shot. That was the thing about this place, they treated you like infants and spoke in front of you as though you weren't there. It made her sad.

'Book her in for some talking therapy with Doctor Andrews next week and we will delay the review until we have had a chance to uncover what is disturbing her. Oh, and a Beecham's Powder might help the temperature a bit. Put her back to bed and keep her indoors,' and he was off to check on other, more hopeless cases, Marianne thought. Soon. I will be out of here soon.

Marianne slept during the day and had the strange dream again, of the swooping wings and woke in a panic. It was dark outside and patients were going to bed. She was fully alert and managed to avoid taking her pills but she had no handkerchief to spit them into and so had to use her hand and then tear a piece of the newspaper when no one was looking. She stuffed it under her mattress.

It was a cloudy night which was good but she wouldn't go until morning, after the early rounds when everyone was busy; when she had been checked and she wouldn't be missed for a while. She felt pleased with herself for working all of that out.

Just after daybreak, Marianne walked out of the garden of Severalls hospital holding her handbag tightly to her and a small bundle she had retrieved from the dustbin. She wore a large navy blue overcoat, a blue woollen hat and spectacles and managed to shuffle like an old lady. She walked a long way to the bus stop, and after a long wait, took a bus to Harwich, where she bought a ferry ticket and boarded the Stena Hollandica to the Hook Of Holland, unchallenged.

She was well on her way before her absence was noticed and by the time the alarm was raised, the trail had gone cold.

Chapter Fifty Nine

'So why did you pull that trigger?' I asked. Felix sat opposite me and rubbed a hand over his face and I saw the hint of a shadow. He was permanently well groomed but right now, he looked tired and dishevelled. Was he affected by what I was saying? Had I made a bit of progress? Somehow I doubted it. He had the upper hand every which way I turned. Now he stood and started to pace about. He was like a caged panther and I could feel the intensity of his emotion pouring out of him. It was awesome and made me wary.

'Max was a complicated man. He was a great talent but could be dilettante when he didn't feel like working. He was anti Nazi but couldn't really be bothered to fight them. He was passionate about painting but never took the trouble to finish his work. He was maddening. He loved women and took mistresses and yet he truly loved Marianne. She and Beatrix were his rock and yet he hurt them time and again. He carelessly and wantonly damaged his health despite my best attempts to keep him well. We risked our lives to get him medication during the war, not so that he could paint for us – I know that's what people thought. It was because we loved him; all of us did, and I would have done anything for my big brother Max.' I was silent and I heard the fire splutter a bit and cough out some smoke, but Felix didn't seem to notice.

'The medication had side effects we didn't know about then. It made him aggressive and unpredictable and, I gather, impotent as well. There was a risk, in the end that he would betray us all – our cell – not deliberately, but out of rage or passion.

'He knew about Jellicoe's affair with a German officer. It was common knowledge and part of the Resistance plan – she played both sides with great skill and risk – but she had betrayed us and the Nazi's were on the way to arrest us.

'It was as though Max had only just realised what was happening and he thought that we had all betrayed him, then in the row which was raging, Jellicoe referred to Marianne as a 'Jewish whore', and he took his gun from a drawer and aimed at her. Marianne stepped in front of Jellicoe and he...'

He tailed off. He couldn't speak. I just stared at the man I had thought devoid of all emotion, pouring out a story of passion with such feeling that I was for a moment sympathetic. I kept silent.

'Marianne picked up Beatrix and he pointed the gun at them instead. This time, I stepped in front of them and moved slowly towards him. I thought he would shoot me but he didn't. He turned to run out of the studio saying he would tell them everything. He had nothing left to live for, and I knew that if he got out, raving as he was, we were all betrayed. The war was almost over, but Nazis still ran the city and were looking for a chance to kill as many as possible before they left. This situation was an open invitation.

'He had gone mad. I had no choice. I was faster, fitter; I wrestled him to the ground and got the gun. He went quiet then. He looked at me smiled and said, '*do it, Felix. Please...*' and so I shot him to save us all. Jellicoe had betrayed us and I was going to get revenge but Marianne wouldn't let me kill her because as you know, Jellicoe was pregnant. So I smuggled her out of the city and planned to wait until the baby was born and find a good home for it. I planned to deal with Jellicoe later, but later never came and she disappeared. And now the past is over.....'

'And you are allies?'

'As I said. The past is over. We have a new cause now.'

We sat in silence whilst Felix gathered himself back together. 'Of course, if you insist on telling the truth – your truth, I should say, you would implicate Beatrix as well. She has been making excellent copies of work in her training programme since she arrived here.'

'So that's it. She is replacing Max in your scheme? You bastard. She is a minor.... you are supposed to be guarding her, not corrupting her!' I was incandescent now and I felt totally impotent. How could I get to Beatrix, to open her eyes and get her to see what he was doing to her?

'Oh she loves it. She has the same passion about her work as her father..... as Max had. She is not going to do anything she doesn't want to.'

'But you will convince her, influence her mind, twist her views.'

'She has a perfectly good mind of her own. I am enabling her to fulfil her talent. She is truly alive when she paints. Don't give her cause to dislike you any more than she does.'

'You are turning her against me as well!' I sat heavily onto the stool and picked up the poker, and before I could think it through, I leapt at him, but Felix was too well trained and still quick. He had me in an arm lock before I could bring the poker down on his evil skull.

'Don't be a fool T'Ash. Assault or murder won't help anyone. We had a deal. I paid you in good faith to start a new life. Grow up and start thinking about others. If you really love Beatrix you will see that the life she has here is far better than you can offer her right now. She needs to be cared for, which I can do. She needs training, which she is doing. Above all, she has lost her mother and has a traumatised childhood. She needs stability and right now, that is what she has.' He crouched in front of the stool I was now slumped in. 'Go to America. Live your dreams. Build a life worthy of her, and I promise that at 21 she will choose her own path. Make a life for yourself that she will want to share.'

'Never. I am not giving up on her.' He groaned and took the stool opposite and leaned forward to speak very quietly.

'I thought you would be stubborn, so let me tell you a story. Years ago we used this place as part of our operations. As you can see, we are far from prying eyes and it was possible to hide Jews and fallen airmen out here until we could get them away. As the fields get closer to the canals at the back of the nursery, the trees get taller so that the front ones are the most recently planted and the ones furthest away, at this end near the hut, they are the mature trees, or seed trees. We could hide people amongst them when the Nazis searched the town.'

'What has this got to do with anything now? I thought the past was done.'

'To some extent, yes. It is just that amongst the tallest trees are small seed houses, boxes really, and that is where men escaping from the Nazis would hide. Now I suppose they could be used for anyone who needed to escape from the police.'

He was talking in riddles. 'What has this got to do with me or Beatrix or anything else right now?

'I think it only fair to warn you that you may find yourself in trouble before you can implicate others. Before I came here today, I alerted the police to the theft of a small painting from my collection. In itself it is not worth much but in the wrong hands, I told them, it could be sold for a lot of money as a forgery.'

'So which one was stolen?'

'Oh not one of Max's. I have other uses for those. This is a small 17th Century canvas of an uninspiring winter scene by an unimportant painter. We got it for the canvas, not the picture. At auction, in its current state, it would probably fetch a few hundred US dollars. But if papers can prove that it is by, oh, let's say Egbert Van Der Pol, or Samual Van Hoogstraten,' he sucked in a breath: 'you could add a few more noughts to that price.'

'Why are you telling me this?' He walked up close and leant over me, forcing me to lean back so that his face was not touching mine.

'Because that painting is now in your hotel room and is about to be 'found' by a chamber maid, with the false documentation which will result in a charge not only of theft, but of attempted forgery as well.' I didn't take it in at first. I couldn't work out what he was telling me...

'You set me up?'

'I would rather you had stayed in America as planned and got on with your own life and left Beatrix and me to live ours.'

'But it's not her life. Her life is with me.....'

'So we can tell the Police to add *'attempting to abduct a minor in my guardianship*' to the charge sheet? Your word against mine T'Ash. Will you co-operate and play nicely with us? Wait four years for Beatrix to grow up? Or will you spend that time in jail and ruin the opportunity for Marianne and many, many others to have the treatment they deserve? Will you risk traumatising the girl you profess to love and ruining her one big chance of happiness?'

He placed the ship token from the Monopoly set on the table. 'Arturo will take you to the port of Rotterdam,' he said and walked out into the frosty spring day.

Chapter Sixty

It was my birthday and Felix had plans for later, after the viewing of the painting. I had never felt so alone in my life.

Where was T'Ash? Why had he abandoned me? I sat on the floor of Ben's studio and let the pain rip through me and watched as a pool of water soaked through my skirt and apron and spread like a map of the world around me.

I was breathing heavily and felt another spasm grip, shake me senseless and then let go. So this was what contractions felt like and this baby was on its way into the world and I was unprepared and alone. It was too early. They had all said, Felix and the medical staff I had seen since being here, that it would be born the end of March: April 1st, All Fools Day was my due date. I laughed out loud to release the strain and tried to get up off the floor where I had slumped when the first pain gripped like the teeth of a chainsaw cutting me in half. I had continued to pant through two, or was it three contractions now? Was this baby going to be born on my birthday?

I stood, leaning heavily on the counter and seeing my hand spread the vermillion paint, which I had been mixing to add into the shadows of the painting. I picked up my brush, wiped the paint from my hand onto my apron and dabbed at the shadows of *'The Artist's Apprentice'* to warm them.

I wanted to shut out the reality of what was happening. I wanted it to be over. I wanted Jellicoe to come so that she could take the baby safely away from Felix, to be with Johanna. No that wasn't right. I wanted to keep it. This was part of me and T'Ash, but there was no way Felix would let me. Unless I got away soon. If I could stop these pains then maybe I could get away. Jellicoe said she would help me. Back to Colchester or even to America. To T'Ash. I still had a month to go so this was just a false alarm. It was too early.

I dropped the paint brush and slumped again as another contraction ripped my mind and body apart and then sat on the floor, breathing hard and wanting Mother or Jellicoe to be here.

Someone would come soon when they knew that I was missing from home and not arrived at the Gallery. Someone would come so I had to get away before they found me if I wanted to keep my baby.

Chapter Sixty One

Felix was pacing the gallery. The walls were empty now of his collection which had been taken back into safe storage ready for later release and *Checkmate* stood in splendid isolation on its easel, lit with warm light in a darkened room, like a shrine to his lost brother.

He had doubts and the pacing seemed to highlight them. Jellicoe appeared beside him as he was lost in thought.

He smiled at her wryly. 'You haven't lost your touch,' he said.

'No but you may be losing yours, although I hope not.' She stood on tiptoe and reached up to kiss his cheek. 'So, what is causing the great Meester himself to be distracted?'

'The boy, Tarron has been a complication.'

'But he is gone now. I was assured by Arturo that they are on the *'Neiuw Amsterdam'* out of Rotterdam tonight.'

'Yes. He's done that once before.'

'Not this time. Arturo will get on board with him. T'Ash will not be able to jump ship. I would worry more that he could cause trouble from America,' she said. Felix nodded thoughtfully.

'Yes, he has been more persistent than I expected,' he said. Jellicoe linked his arm and steered him to a sideboard which had drinks prepared for viewing guests.

'So, am I losing my touch or is it simply age? You and I know each other well. We understand how things work. But I hadn't factored in how uncompromising young love can be,' he said

'I don't remember us having that luxury, but maybe the ability to compromise is a sign of maturity,' she replied

'And what about Beatrix? How far will she compromise? She is still in denial about giving birth, but when this auction is over I plan to take her to Delft and book her into the clinic.'

'It's a bit early,' said Jellicoe moving slightly away from him so that she could judge his mood better.

'Two weeks early is safe enough and will make life easier all round.'

'And then you leave for the Grand Tour?' she said with a smile in her voice.

'The Trip of a Lifetime for Beatrix. She will get to see Art Galleries in all of the great European cities.'

'I think you will enjoy that too,' she said moving closer again and teasing him. He wouldn't lighten up today though. It seemed to Jellicoe that his mood was entrenched, unsettled.

'She will be distracted from her… situation…. and loss, and then, when we return in the summer, she will be inspired to paint again and we can prepare for the grand Autumn auction of the rest of this collection'.

'So where is she this morning?'

'At home, resting. With Mrs. Vries.'

'I am guessing she will be here for the viewing and the speeches?'

'Of course. And the timing has been planned around her confinement and to celebrate her birthday. Another 'distraction' for her.'

'She won't be distracted forever, Felix. She is a strong willed young woman.'

'Maybe I am losing my touch. Which is why we will be stronger together.'

The door crashed open and a very flustered Mrs. Vries bustled down the gallery, her hat askew as though she had put it on in a hurry.

'Dr. Van Gelder. I am so sorry…' He put out a hand to steady her and steered her to a chair. Jellicoe brought a glass of water.

'What's happened,' he said when she had enough breath to talk.

'I was in the kitchen preparing the pea soup for Beatrix's lunch, as you prescribed, Doctor, so I didn't hear when she left.'

'She left? Where did she go?' Mrs. Vries shrugged and gulped the water. She had clearly ran all the way here, or at least moved far more quickly than was sensible for someone of her years and girth. Felix looked over the top of her head towards Jellicoe.

'Do you think she could be at the studio with Ben?' Jellicoe shook her head and Mrs. Vries cut in quickly.

'I saw Ben out there just now. He said I couldn't come in but I ignored him.' Felix patted her arm.

'Yes well done. I'm glad you did.' He was still looking at Jellicoe.

'When I arrived Ben was helping to get the outer gallery ready for the opening at 2.00'.

'Hell. I told her to stay indoors and rest…'

Jellicoe put a hand on his arm. 'This is exactly why we are a team. You stay here and prepare for the viewing. I will go and find her. She won't have gone far and Mrs. Vries can wait at home, when she is recovered.'

Felix nodded and watched Jellicoe as she walked the length of the gallery and the unsettled feeling in his gut had not fully gone away.

Chapter Sixty Two

I am standing on the rail of SS Nieuw Amsterdam as the port of Rotterdam recedes in twilight. I feel the wind on my face, the salt spray mingles with my tears and I hold in my hand the last letter I will ever write to Beatrix. I am threatened with imprisonment if I return but they cannot imprison my soul which will fly freely if I let go of the rail now, and freefall into the foaming torrent which washes in the wake of this steel prison and wraps around my heart like a vice.

My dearest Beatrix,
My love forever, my true soul mate. I cannot let them take you from me. I will try to reach you again, but now I am in despair.
Please tell me that he hasn't turned you against me because I will jump from this ship if he has, right here in the middle of nowhere.
The tide will carry me back to you. Horizons unknown lie ahead, always a horizon, forever unreachable, and my mind, soul will keep on questioning, will not rest, will cut and smudge its love for you again and again, over and over, until it flows away and drifts into a curl of smoke. Fire creeps at the edges of my life devouring chaos, angry spikes and coils of frustration knotted too tight to burn. As sunlight blazes its triumphant exit, the ashes are confusion; baffled, unexplained. Unresolved until the end. I am falling through the centre

of our own creation, my darling Beatrix, but I swear that I will see you again and you will be there, at the centre of my life, forever.....

There is moment of total peace and I let myself fall.

Hands grab at me and I land on a solid steel deck and my head is splitting open and more hands pull at me and then I am so cold and the water washes over me and everything turns finally into the darkest part of blackness.

Chapter Sixty Three

Jellicoe started her search at the house on Keizersgracht and the maid let her in. She took her time looking, and enjoyed being alone in Felix's house until she heard the front door close and Mrs. Vries voice raised to the maid. Jellicoe hurriedly replaced the documents she was reading in Felix's study and slipped out to the staircase.

'She's not back yet,' she shouted to Mrs. Vries as she headed for the front door, 'I've checked the house and neighbourhood. I'll try the studio,' and she left before Mrs. Vries could question her further.

She headed straight for the studio feeling certain that of the few places Beatrix would frequent, this was the most likely. The building seemed silent but there were lights on in the studio upstairs, so if Ben hadn't returned, then perhaps Beatrix was here.

She heard the cries and froze on the step. It was a long drawn out cry of pain followed by gasps and then sobbing. She didn't hesitate. She took the steps two at a time and burst into the studio. Her heart was thumping and she was momentarily thrown off balance by the sight she saw.

Beatrix was crouched in a corner, her body hunched, legs drawn up to her chest panting heavily. There seemed to be blood all around her and covering her apron. Her underclothes were discarded on the floor in a pool of water.

Jellicoe's mind went into operational mode and she approached Beatrix gently, speaking quietly so as not to frighten the child.

'It's alright, Beatrix. I am here to help you. Will you let me have a look and see what's happening?' The child looked up and her eyes were faraway in a place where only pain was real.

'It's me. It's Jellicoe. I am going to help you Beatrix.' Firmer this time. There was little time to cajole as another contraction hit and Beatrix doubled up again and Jellicoe held her firmly.

'Ok, now breathe. That's it. Try not to push. I need to see what's happening.

'Nooooooo,' cried Beatrix, and the sob was heartbreaking. But Jellicoe, like Felix, had been tempered in the furnace of war and childbirth was not going to deter her. She waited for the contraction to pass. It had followed the other quite quickly so she needed to check beneath the skirts to see where all the blood was coming from. She hoped for the best.

'Can you sit up, or stand? It will be easier for you,' she said looking around for something clean onto which a baby could be safely delivered; she saw a roll of fresh canvas, unused; and some brown paper for wrapping pictures; these would have to do. And a knife. She would need to cut the cord. In a drawer she found a Swiss Army Knife and lit the small stove to sterilise the blade.

Another contraction came and Jellicoe realised, if it was still alive, this baby was coming fast. She had to look. Getting Beatrix to hold her firmly, she let the contraction pass and then moved swiftly to look under the girl's skirts, lifting the apron first and seeing the red smears down Beatrix's legs and hands. It didn't look good. The girl's slim shape was disfigured by the heaving bulge which seemed to have a life of its own, and her face distorted and damp with pain.

Jellicoe gently felt the sticky redness which covered the girls apron and had smeared her arms and legs. She felt it on her own hands now, and held her fingers to the light and sniffed it, and laughed. It was paint; so typical of an artist that they get caught short and continue to work until it is too late. She laughed from relief because there was no blood, just the healthy waters which had broken. She rolled her scarf into a pillow and gently lay Beatrix onto the canvas, compliant momentarily, resting until the next powerful pain took over her.

The baby's head was crowning and Jellicoe felt her spirits rise and offered a silent prayer that there would be no complications. She could do with a nice clean bed and some water and towels and Mrs Vries would be useful too, but there was no time to get help.

'Ok, Beatrix. When the next contraction comes, you need to push and then wait, alright?' There was a slight nod from Beatrix who took a deep breath in and let out another roar as the contraction tightened her bump and shook her for a while and the head emerged.

'Yessss! said Jellicoe triumphantly. 'Now wait. I have to check.' The cord was not caught around the baby's neck and she could see the next contraction building.

'One more push. Make it a big one. Make it count....' and a long, shuddering contraction forced the shoulders of a wet and slippery baby into Jellicoe's waiting hands. She was euphoric and for a moment couldn't move in the silent moment which followed, and then the baby let out a gutsy yell, Beatrix laughed and Jellicoe felt tears roll down her face. Holding the baby up, she handed it to its mother.

'Your daughter, Beatrix,' she said and wiped the baby's eyes, nose and mouth with her handkerchief. Reaching for the coat she had removed earlier, Jellicoe wrapped it around the wet and wriggling infant and its mother, and then turned to the business of clamping the cord and cutting it whilst Beatrix gazed in pure love and bewilderment at the small miracle she had created.

Chapter Sixty Four

I am sitting in a bed, warm, comfortable and carefully washed by Jellicoe's sensitive hands. Not my mother's, but as close as I can get for now. My mother is now an *Oma* – a Grandma - and I want to make sure that she sees baby Scarlett Marianne Ash soon, whilst she is still able. *If* she is still able.

Baby Scarlett lies on my chest and breathes slowly, content. She is warm against my skin and I want to hold her here forever. She begins to root and snuffle for food and I smile at her; her dark eyes flicker open and then close again and her mouth takes over, searching for food. Instinctively I bare my breast, swollen but not yet full of milk, and I steer her perfect rosebud mouth towards the nipple.

Jellicoe comes silently into the room and smiles at me.

'You are still awake? I will have to take her to my room so that you can rest,' she says and then she sees the look which crosses my face. She sits beside me on the bed and strokes my cheek and hair.

'I didn't mean that, Beatrix. I am not going to take your baby away, I promise you. But you will need some rest.' I nod and she helps me to get the baby latched on and I close my eyes as the sharp pain and pleasure of her firm suck shoots through me. When I open my eyes again, Jellicoe is smiling at us.

'Maternal love. There is nothing like it. Men will never understand,' she says simply. Neither of us speak for a moment, but the great 'unspoken' has to be said. I hold the baby closer and she wriggles in my arms.

'Do you trust me, Beatrix?' Jellicoe says quietly. I tear my eyes from the baby's soft downy head and look into Jellicoe's face. We have formed a bond in the studio, only hours ago, and I feel safe here in her bed, in her own rented house on Prinsengracht. I nod and she takes my hand.

'We have to face Felix at some point, but this much I know. He can only take your baby if you agree. A court of law will not let him take her without your signature.' I nod again.

'I thought he could,' I say. 'He is my guardian.'

'He can try to convince you; he can use emotional blackmail and he will try everything in his power but even Felix, however grand and well connected, is not above the law.' I stoke the baby's cheeks as she sucks half heartedly, more for comfort than food.

'A baby complicates his plans for you and Felix likes total control,' she continues.

'You make him sound like an ogre,' I say. 'He has been kind to me.' She turns away and I see the conflict cross her face.

'No, he isn't an ogre, but he is a determined man and he is passionate about his work. Your work.'

'But look at her! How can you not love her?' I say gazing at my achingly beautiful daughter. 'Is there any news from T'Ash?' I add, feeling somewhere, deep down that there won't be. He has gone, and I now have Scarlett and a new life ahead of me. I can't let his memory fade but for now, his face is replaced by the vision of our daughter. 'I thought he should know that he has a daughter,' I say and she pats my hand and then turns away from me.

'All in good time. It is early days. Let us take one step at a time...'

'Felix will be angry that I want to keep her,' I say, stroking the tufts of dark hair which stick up defiantly on Scarlett's head.

'Maybe,' she said.

'I don't want her to be sent away to stay with Johanna's family either,' I blurt and the tears spring unbidden down my face.

'No, of course you don't, and do you know what? Seeing you today and witnessing the birth... you were so brave and strong and there is so much love in you.... I realise that it was the hardest thing I have ever had to do, giving Johanna to another family to raise. I was living in fear, Beatrix, running away from ghosts, and now they are lain, and I don't want you to spend your life in fear and loss.

'Your mother saved my life once, and Johanna's, and when I met you, I wanted to hate you... or at least to dislike you.... but I couldn't.... Felix and I have finally won the peace...and now, well I see now what I have missed... my own baby so far away...' She stood and moved to the dressing table and opened a drawer to take out a clean handkerchief and wiped her eyes. 'So I have a better plan. You see, Felix needs us now. He cannot continue his 'mission' without us. So we tell him our terms.'

I am grinning stupidly from the bed as baby Scarlett's mouth falls open and her head lolls to one side in a milky stupor.

'Which are?' I ask.

'One. Miss Scarlett Ash stays right here in Amsterdam with us. Two, we need an extra pair of hands, so her 'Aunt' Johanna needs to return to her native city and help us out. Three....Oh that's about it. I can't think of anything else....'

and we both laugh, a real laugh of joy and relief and the baby snuffles contentedly against my breast.

'Is it really so simple?'

'Most things are, my dear, when we don't let the men over complicate them.'

Chapter Sixty Five

The viewing day had been a great success but there was still a sense of unease which ran through Felix like a warning shot from somewhere deep inside where instincts were fine tuned by the life he had led.

Jellicoe didn't return to the studio and Beatrix didn't show up either. He sent Ben to look for them and when Ben didn't return, he knew something was wrong. Then a note arrived from Jellicoe which simply said:

'I have taken Beatrix to my house. Mother and baby are doing well. Congratulations, *Opa*. – Grandpa.'

Ben returned beaming from one side of his face to the other.

'I guess this makes you a 'Great Uncle?' He said, shaking Felix affectionately by the hand.

'Something like that,' Felix muttered. He left Ben to conclude the day's business and took a cab to Jellicoe's house, where he was met by a slumbering Beatrix and a newborn baby girl, lying in a cradle.

He held his daughter's child and she smiled at him, all beauty and downy hair. It was the perfect smile of eternal love; and something in him stirred and he was wary of it.

Beatrix opened her eyes and saw Felix holding her baby but she didn't move. She watched him absorbed in the child, holding it so tenderly that she was sure there were tears in his eyes. He looked up and saw that Beatrix was watching him.

'She is exactly like you were as a baby,' he said and handed Scarlett back to her mother. 'This is for you. For her when she grows up. It was your mother's,' and he took the ruby ring from his finger and placed it on Beatrix's right hand.

'Come home soon, my dear. I will have the nursery prepared for her. So long as you won't swap it entirely for the studio?'

'I will at least be painting her if nothing else,' she said.

'In the style of?'

'Probably myself,' she replied, and he kissed her cheek and left the room.

Beatrix let out a long held breath which she didn't realise she was holding and the tension left her.

Felix stopped at the front door to talk to Jellicoe and he saw Ben running towards them.

'It is the Police. They are at your house, waiting in the front room. Mrs. Vries is beside herself.' Jellicoe and Felix exchanged a look.

'Will you try to get away?' she asked Felix. 'The old connections could be revived?'

'No.' He said simply. 'No. I will face them and see what they want. No more running. We agreed.' He pats her cheek and turns to Ben. 'We need to protect our remaining assets. Operation Windmill?' Ben nodded and disappeared in the direction of the studio.

'Wait, I'll get my coat,' Jellicoe said and they walked arm in arm to his house.

Mrs. Vries was in a state. 'They are in the front drawing room, Doctor. I am so sorry. I told them you were busy at the Windmill Gallery.'

'I am sure they knew where I was.' He was glad that they had come here if they were going to arrest him. Privately, not in public. These things mattered to Felix.

'Doctor Van Gelder?' The Sergeant and his Constable stood as Felix and Jellicoe enter the room. Felix braced himself. The Sergeant moved towards him and put his hand into his pocket. Felix didn't move. He waited for the words he believed would follow.

'I have a message for you, Sir; it came through on our wire at main headquarters half an hour ago.'

Jellicoe looked from the Sergeant to Felix, who was looking unruffled by all of this. She realised that she needed to compose herself or she could implicate them without reason. Felix took the brown envelope which contained a telegram, and opened it. He sat heavily in a leather armchair. Jellicoe was beside him.

'What is it Felix, what's happened?'

'It's Marianne. She was on her way here.....'

Chapter Sixty Six

Marianne feels the wind blow through the upper deck; and the sound of predatory wings swooping. Fear grips her. She cries out but knows that no-one will come. Emptiness fills her as the dark wings swoop once more and force her to reel backwards into her seat.

She wakes with a start. She has had that dream again of being abandoned and always feels desolate when she wakes. She sits bolt upright and looks around, unused to sleeping in public. She has been sleeping a lot since she has been ill. The seat rocks beneath her and she remembers where she is. Still on the boat, but no idea how far into the vast open sea they have travelled. She glances through the wet windows and sees the ocean both sides; endless sea; and the boat rocks from side to side more noticeably than before. The desolation of her dream lingers and she wraps her coat closer and looks around the deck. She notices the man sitting opposite and is sure he wasn't there when she dozed off. He is tall and thin and reading the paper – her paper. He has picked up her paper and is now finishing the crossword. He reminds her of Felix. She is struggling to remember again.

He finishes the article he is reading in *her* newspaper and looks up.

'You're awake,' he says. 'The wash from that ship which passed us just now, *The SS Niew Amsterdam*. It caused us to rock a little and you awoke.'

'I'm sorry, do I know you?' she asks, a little afraid of speaking to strangers.

'I've no idea.' He lays down the paper. He has been reading the births and deaths, a page she dislikes intensely and never reads. She snatches up the newspaper and cracks the pages open randomly. It forms a barrier like a metaphorical placard which reads 'leave me alone'. He says nothing, just looks at her calmly.

When she looks up again, he is gone and she wonders if she imagined him and stares at the endless mud grey waters and feels as though she is floating. She feels the cold wind again and shivers, and then the swooping noise and she knows that she is not sleeping this time. Fear grips her chest.

'I wanted to stay a bit longer,' she says, hopelessly to no one. 'To see how it all turns out. To see my Beatrix again.'

She feels the wind blow through the cabin and hears the wings beat rapidly and knows that finally, it is time to let go and sink into the darkness which surrounds her.

Part Three

Living Out Loud

4 years Later

Chapter Sixty Seven
January 1961

It took four long years of making the most of it. Of trying to forget. To heal the shattered bits of me, physical as well, from the fall on the boat. Broken bones heal eventually. Broken hearts never do... unless....

And this was the weird thing. A series of coincidences all rushing headlong to a collision which would make this glorious outcome. I had achieved my dream. I was in America and I was making a start at being a writer. Mum was happy. My sister and her family peopled our lives with love and noise and I was working in the hotel for money and writing pieces for the Irish Gazette. But it was never going to be enough. The dream had turned to ashes and I needed my soul-mate to make me whole again.

We Irish in America depended on the mail but we also knew that it didn't all make it through. The Gazette asked me to do a piece called *'Return to Sender'* about the lost post. I got curious whilst I was researching this piece and that was it; like a man obsessed I missed the deadline for the article but I didn't care. I was a bloodhound on the scent of my own destiny, searching for a lost word from Beatrix in haystacks of mail rooms....

I found it in a mail sorting office with foreign postage stamps all over it and *'not known at this address'* scrawled across it. I asked Kathleen and she said:

'Oh, I've moved four times in three years so the chances of it finding me were pretty remote...'

The letter Bea had written to me three years ago, and I wept with love and lost hope when I read it. Joy, disbelief, anger, confusion; you name it and the Gods chucked it all at me in that one letter.

My Dearest T'Ash,

Many months have passed and my life has changed forever. I have no idea now where you are or whether you will receive this letter, but I am compelled to write it anyway.

Felix told me that you didn't want to have anything to do with the baby but I feel sure that if we were to see each other again, you would feel differently. I am close to my time now. By the time you receive this our child may be born. Felix wants to give it away for adoption but I will never let that happen. I cannot keep the baby on my own. I need help. I am sure that Mrs. Vries won't help me and there is no one else, except Ben, my Art tutor. ....

I feel a warmth and a love for the child growing inside me when I remember that it is our child T'Ash. We loved each other once. Could you find it in your heart to love me again?

There was a baby. That's what they weren't telling me, what they didn't want me to know. That explains why they were keeping her away from me. She had a baby. *Has* a child? Our child....

I had never lost faith. I was planning to go back in March anyway, when Beatrix was of age and she could choose. Well it was January now and I didn't have long to wait. Six weeks and then I could ask her myself, as I promised I would.

But I was in agony right now. Did Felix make her give away our baby? Was it a boy or a girl? And I surely knew the difference now with all my little nieces and nephews being so raucous and demanding all around me. Has she given up on me? Has she got someone else by now? Who is the mysterious Ben?

Is she still alive?

Huge questions, too big to think about and I need answers NOW.

I wait outside the post office until it opens and send a telegram to Dr. Felix Van Gelder at his P.O box in Amsterdam. I am certain it will reach him, and then I pace in an agony of waiting.

By 11.30 the editor sends me a message. Someone has booked a long distance call from Holland for noon today our time, to speak to me.

I sit in the editors office and drum my fingers and pace up and down and I feel my heart hammer in my chest and when the phone rings I jump out of my skin and feel light headed.

He sounds a long way away and there is crackle on the line but I know it is Felix and his voice is emotional and he sounds like an old man and kinder than I remember and I don't want to kill him anymore just to know that Beatrix is alive and so is our child. He laughs as he says:

'Scarlett has won my heart. She is now the age Beatrix was when I had to let her go. Being with her has renewed my life. Even Jellicoe, for all her faults, I am fond of now, and I am enjoying witnessing Johanna growing into a fine young woman. I want to continue to be a part of their lives, and I don't want to lose them. It has taken me too long to find them.'

'So is there room for me in this great big family then, as mine's now scattered across the oceans?' I say, and he replies,

'You and I are linked by blood through Scarlett, T'Ash, whether we like it or not. You are family already, and I hope we can grow to get along.' It is my turn to laugh as he gives his blessing for me to see Beatrix again and meet my daughter.

I am anxious to see her, and Scarlett, and he tells me how it can be arranged and we agree where and when. I run out of the editor's office passed startled journalists, whooping for joy, and I take all of my savings out of the bank – the money I have made from writing pieces for the Gazette, the rest of the money Felix gave me - and I book the flight and write a letter to Bea; one Felix has assured me she will get for her 21st birthday.

Chapter Sixty Eight
January 1961

And then one day when I am reading the story of The Three Bears to Scarlett, she asks 'Where's my daddy?' Felix and I both look at each other. He *harrumphs* in an awkward way, so unusual of him, and mutters something about having work to do and leaves the room. I stare after him and raise my eyes. He can't seriously leave me to do this on my own?

'He's in America.'

'Where's that?'

'A long way away across the sea.' And then the dreaded four year old question.

'Why?'

I lift her onto my lap and find another story book to distract her but I cannot distract myself.

'Why?' Good question.

Later that night, I write a letter to T'Ash, but before I can post it, I have to talk to Felix.

Felix told me the truth after Scarlett was born and I have had four years to come to terms with the fact that he is my father; but some things were never quite resolved.

'What you did was wrong,' I said.

'Yes. I agree. Your mother and I betrayed Max, but that betrayal led to you and now Scarlett so although it was wrong, I can never be sorry....'

'But the forgeries...'

'Who do I apologise to for that? The Airmen and Jews we helped out of Holland to safety?' and I couldn't disagree.

We have laid the ghosts and the war is over for all of us but a new battle ground has opened and I want to fight it alongside Felix.

I am no longer the Art Forger's Daughter. I have become the Art Forger and the money we earn goes to *The Felix Van Gelder Foundation* to research new treatment for mental health. It is too late for my mother, but we can help countless others escape the shadow world she slipped into when I was powerless to help.

Since my father painted Old Masters in the 40's, modern techniques have become more sophisticated, making forgeries easier to detect. My early painting– *The Artist's Apprentice* by 'Gabriel Metsu', sold three years ago and was a huge success. It brought in, along with the sale of my father's catalogue from the little cellar in Stockwell Street, many millions of dollars about which Felix was scrupulous; after securing his promise to Jellicoe to support Johanna for life, it went to the Foundation as anonymous donations, and is managed by a Trust of the great and the good. Since then, I have painted modern works of the 19th and 20th century for which I have a real passion; two paintings by my hero, Vincent Van Gogh, a Cezanne and two Renoirs. They hang in famous galleries around the world and in private collections and it is enough that I know I made them. I no longer crave my name on them.

I have been busy but I still have time for Scarlett who follows me around the studio whilst I paint; ironically born in an artist's studio, onto a canvas, she dances and sings and shows little interest in the paintings or the paint, and she loves to be told stories.

One day I will tell her the story of Max and Marianne, the mother I lost the day I became a mother myself. I still miss her and I wish she could be here, but now, surrounded by my new life, there is a joy which Marianne would have wished for me, and I know that she would have loved Scarlett.

'I need to tell Scarlett something,' I say when we are driving to the Hook of Holland. I am taking the Ferry to Harwich so that I can sign the papers for ownership of my grandpa's house in Colchester. Felix is coming with me and Scarlett is having a holiday with her 'Aunt' Jellicoe and Johanna, two streets away from where we live. She is over excited about sleeping in a big bed with Johanna.

Now that I am of age of course, I can leave Felix. I can find T'Ash and we can live with Scarlett in Colchester in my grandfather's house, if he still wants me. Or we can continue the great adventure in Europe, with Felix.

There is no contest.

'I don't know where to start, to tell her about T'Ash. It will be better coming from me and if she knows now, then she will grow up without the baggage...' I tail off. He knows more than anyone about 'baggage'.

'Yes. She needs to be told. But first, I have something to confess to you. I haven't told you the whole story yet. Not quite.' I look up sharply.

'What do you mean?'

'I mean about T'Ash. I didn't tell him you were pregnant. I didn't want to give him the chance to claim you... I am sorry.' I couldn't quite take it in. The implications...the heartbreak I had suffered. The rejection.

'I was going to give you this tomorrow, on your birthday. It was going to be a pleasant surprise....' He smiled a half, lopsided smile at me and took a small package wrapped in brown paper from his jacket pocket and handed it to me. 'I didn't want to lose you quite so soon,' he added and he focused on the road, wearily, and for the first time I saw the old man he was becoming. Why didn't I hate him? Shout and scream at him? But I didn't. I stared at the package with *Beatrix Prins* written in T'Ash's neat sloping hand with postage from America and dated a week ago.

'Open it on the boat,' he said, and his voice was thick with regret.

But I couldn't wait. Four years was long enough. The Monopoly Ship token fell out of the envelope, and a twist of pear drops and the smell was evocative of T'Ash. There was also a letter, in his small, unmistakable writing telling me that he would keep his promise and come back for me and Scarlett. Felix patted my hand and focused on the road and the tears were streaming down my face as I read T'Ash's words, and we were together again with an ocean still between us.

Chapter Sixty Nine
March 1st 1961

I sit on the shingle beach outside the chalet in Wrabness, and I write....

I watch the ships to pass the time and know time flies, soaring on wings of memory, carrying us on tides of destiny toward our destination. Until all breath stills and shining hope pales into rivers of nothing, she will still be smiling at me on a silver ribbon of light. Hope soars again on wings of innocence and cries from crystal skies the news I have waited to hear: that she is here, and rising on the wings of love, hope has conquered fear. Love endures....

That's what I write, what I hope for, and then I see her at the end of the beach and think at first that my feelings have conjured her and that it isn't her and if I run towards her she will fade away but she doesn't. She walks slowly towards me. I stand up; everything is in slow motion and she stops and I hope that she doesn't evaporate or blow away with the breeze and then she drops her bag and is running towards me and I drop my notebook and I am running towards her and we melt together somewhere in the middle and she is real and crying and laughing and so am I and we dissolve into each other forever and the time and distance disappear as the tide washes in around our feet and blurs the words on my notebook, in my mind, and we are one again.

The Last Word
T'Ash

So we have agreed then, Beatrix and me, to let the past rest for the sake of Scarlett and the new life she has ahead of her in an optimistic decade.

I wrap the package in brown paper and string and place it safely in my desk. A ream of typed pages; a manuscript, entitled:

'*The Art Forger's Daughter, by Alfred T. Ash. A Novel,*' the loose pages tied together with a red ribbon.

It will be my gift to Scarlett, for posterity; her mother's story. But it can lie for now with the ghosts and wait until its tale can no longer harm the living.

Acknowledgements

I would like to thank John Belli for research into mental health and medication and for responding so positively to all of my unusual questions. His eclectic knowledge remains unparalleled as does his meticulous attention to detail.

Johanna Ellerbroek-Brown for her tales of growing up in Amsterdam during the Nazi occupation. She is an inspiration and helped with the details of life in Holland at that time. All inspiration is due to them. Any mistakes are my own.

Norma Curtis who has supported my writing journey from the start and has helped me to understand the 'business' of publishing as well as the 'art' of writing. She has been a true friend and writing inspiration for many years.

Charlie Peacock for being midwife to this book and also designing the cover: for being a prolific reader, for feedback and support, not least picking up on my anachronisms. But most importantly for being my lifelong soul-mate and understanding my need to write.

Charlotte, also a prolific reader, for reading my draft copies with insight and intelligence and helped to improve the flow of the story. She offers love and reassurance when I really need it.

Eddie, Emily and Matilda who are always just around the corner to offer love and support and listen to me going on about the latest plot related dilemma when they had a huge production of their own to plan.

About the Author

Anita Belli was born in Greater Manchester and moved to London to train at The Place and London Film School.

She has worked as a director in the arts and has a personal and active interest in dance, film and literature, winning awards as a writer and filmmaker.

Anita lives on the Essex Coast of England with her husband and dog, and their children and grandchild are never far away.

She welcomes visitors to her website www.anitabelli.com

Made in the USA
Charleston, SC
21 February 2017